About the author

Kenneth (Ken) Ansell, agriculturalist and farmer turned professional artist, started his working life in Cornwall before moving to Cambridgeshire and finally Devon. A keen horseman, he has experience in breeding and schooling young horses together with point to point racing and hunting. He now has a small farm on the edge of Dartmoor where he lives with his wife and family.

Pendogget's Mare

Kenneth Ansell

Published by
Filament Publishing Ltd
16, Croydon Road,
Beddington, Croydon
Surrey, CR0 4PA,
United Kingdom
www.filamentpublishing.com

+44(0)208 688 2598

ISBN 978-1-910819-28-9

Printed by IngramSpark.

CHAPTER 1

Byron Pendogget trudged down the narrow track towards the little stone farmhouse that sheltered behind a belt of gnarled pine trees. A January drizzle swept in wind blown gusts from the bare slopes of Bodmin Moor, churning the twisted branches and soaking all things in its path. The old man paused to wipe a mixture of sweat and rain from his brow then turned to the black and white collie that followed close at his heels. 'Come on old lady, get away on'. The bedraggled animal's tail wagged imperceptibly as she ran on ahead towards the shelter of the porch.

Byron pushed open the door and made straight for the large stove that provided heat for comfort and cooking. He opened the grill to warm his hands, rubbing them together in front of the glowing coals with an appreciative 'Ah!' Then he took off his waterproofs,rubbed his tousled grey hair on a scrap of towel and rummaged under the sink for a tin of soup, selecting one from the jumble of tins and packages. He reached for the tin opener which hung on a piece of string above the draining board and, having opened the tin, poured the contents into a chipped enamel saucepan and placed it on the stove before sinking back into the well worn arm chair.

'Why do we have to grow old Meg?' he groaned, stretching his stockinged feet towards the stove. At the sound of her name the collie got up and moved over to place her head on his knee; she pushed her nose closer to the old man's body and wriggled as he stroked the smooth black ears. 'You're an old fuss pot,' he said gently. 'Go on away with you'. He pushed her down and she returned to the stove to stretch full length and steam in the warmth.

Byron closed his eyes and the next thing he knew the soup was boiling over. He jerked awake, got up quickly to rescue most of it, found himself a plate from the dresser and set about preparing his midday meal by cutting two thick slices of bread and a hunk of cheese. As he sat down to eat, a red van pulled into the farmyard and a moment later the kitchen door was pushed open and a cheery voice called 'Morning Mr. Pendogget.' Jim Saunders had know Byron for more than ten years but for some reason it had never felt quite right to use his first name.

The old man paused, the spoon half way to his mouth. 'Hello Jim, you're late this morning. Would you like some soup?'

'No thanks Mr. Pendogget, Penny will have dinner waiting at home. I'm late because old Primrose decided to drop her calf just as I was leaving this morning so that put me all behind.' He put a brown envelope on the table.

Byron grunted. 'Another bill looks like. Everything alright? With the cow I mean.'

The postman grinned. 'Took a bit of pulling but a good heifer calf.'

'You'll make a farmer yet,' Byron chuckled as he got up to fill the kettle. 'Would you care for a cup of tea?'

Jim nodded; he enjoyed his chats at Hendra and the old man seemed to be a mine of information on all sorts of topics and on this occasion he was after some advise. He cleared his throat. 'Penny's folks are coming next weekend.'

'Oh yes, that's nice,' said Byron trying to sound interested as he pushed the blackened kettle over the hotplate and reached for the tea pot.

'She thinks we ought to take them out for a meal one evening.'

'Quite right too, where were you thinking of going?'

Jim shrugged. 'The County Hotel I suppose, it's the poshest place I know and Penny wants to make a good impression and well….' he hesitated, 'You know what up-country folk are like.'

'Indeed I do young man. Let's see, you have two lumps right?'

Jim nodded. 'She - Penny's mother that is - thinks Penny should have done better than just a country postman. Now, it would be different if I were farming full time.'

Byron shook his head wistfully. 'Don't you believe it Jim, if your mother-in-law comes from the town she won't be too keen on any small farmer either. Believe me I know.' There was a touch of bitterness in his voice, which surprised his listener.

'You've been married then Mr. Pendogget?'

The old man did not reply immediately and the postman feared he had offended him. 'Sorry it's none of my business, but when you said…'

'That's alright Jim,' Byron said slowly. 'It was all a long time ago.' He poured the tea and drank in silence; then said suddenly 'how old are you Jim?'

'Twenty nine why?'

There was another long silence, then: 'Would it surprise you to know I have a daughter not much older than you?'

The young man shook his head. 'Well, there's something, all these years I've been calling on you and I never knew you'd been married let alone got a family.'

'Well, there you are Jim, not a very happy experience for me I'm afraid but that doesn't mean you can't make a go of it, so take your in-laws out and let them see what a decent sort of chap you are.'

'It's not as easy as that Mr.Pendogget, you see I never feel right in these up-market places and I'll be expected to order the wine and things and I don't know much about that sort of thing. They tell me you could give me a few tips, could you?'

Byron smiled. 'Who are *they*? The postman looked embarrassed. To be truthful 'twas my mother who told me.' The old man thought for a moment. 'What was her name before she was married ? 'She was a Bolitho.' Byron gave a long sigh. 'Oh yes a Bolitho would know,' he said quietly

'Did you know her, Mr. Pendogget?'

'No, I knew some of the family but that was before you were born. Anyway the important thing now is to help you with your problem if it is a problem which I doubt.' The old man smiled. 'It is really quite simple as long as you don't take the whole thing too seriously. The ignorant rely on the waiter who probably doesn't know any more than they do these days, those who think they know insist on red wine with red meat and white wine with white meat - fish or poultry - but those who really know drink what they like. Is that any help?'

'Yes thanks, I'll remember that red with red and white with white, easy isn't it.' Jim grinned and gulped down the rest of his tea. 'Thanks and if there is anything I can do for you any time just let me know.' He got up and made for the door. 'Don't forget, any time. Cheerio!'

When he was gone Byron relaxed in his chair once more. 'Ah, those were the days,' he mused quietly, then looking round the untidy kitchen added: 'but who would have thought it would come to this?' He got up and cleared the table. 'Come on Meg we had better get on and check the stock.'

It had stopped raining and he put on a waxed jacket in place of the plastic coat and found a dry cap on the back of the door. They made their way to a small field where two horses were grazing. He leant over a stone wall and watched a grey mare and her four-year-old offspring cropping the short grass. 'The last of the line,' he said softly, 'a bit like me I suppose, well as good as,' he added as an afterthought. He pushed open the nearby gate and walked towards them; the younger of the two, a blue roan filly, whickered a greeting and waited to push her nose into the half open front of his work stained coat. Byron smoothed the grey-flecked hairs on the curve of her neck and spoke meaningless words, soft and soothing as though to a small child, while the filly gently nibbled his lapel.

The old mare walked over and butted him playfully, almost knocking the old man over. 'Steady on you old fool,' he said giving her a shove with his elbow, 'there's no need to be cocky just because you managed this,' he nodded towards the filly, 'when you ought to have been past that sort of thing.' He chuckled. 'Thanks to providence and a good friend the Pendogget line stays in the records and one day your daughter will show 'em.' He stepped back and made a clicking sound at which both animals tossed their heads and cantered round the field to their owners delight. Both moved as true thoroughbreds should but the roan filly was superb so that the old man gasped with sheer pleasure. 'Lor, Mist old girl, you've bred a rare one there and no mistake,' he chortled, 'and she's well named - Greystone Mystery - I'll warrant she'll be a mystery to some I could mention.' He grinned at the collie smugly. 'Come on we've got more important things to do.'

The two horses settled to graze again, lifting their heads every so often to watch the man and dog until they disappeared over the hill. The field bordered a forestry plantation on one side, the rest was bounded by a stone wall part of which butted onto the open moor. Suddenly Mist started up and swung round, ears pricked, listening to some distant sound. She snorted several times and pranced up the side of the wood with neck arched and nostrils flared. Mystery, sensing the excitement in her mother, galloped after her, lashing out with a hind leg as a white and tan hound pushed its nose through the barbed wire fence. The hound retreated but was followed almost immediately by another, then another until a dozen were running in a line through the brambles. The old mare snorted again as a russet shape darted across the corner of the field and jumped the wall onto the moor. A hound whimpered, another's yelp turned into a long howl and in moments the hillside was echoing to the clamour of a pack of foxhounds in full cry.

A red coated huntsman jumped a rail into the field, several riders followed and galloped towards the wood , then they all turned to follow the last of the pack over the wall and onto the short springy turf of the open moor. The excitement was too much for Mist, who had followed hounds many times in her younger days. She gave a grunt, pricked her ears and sailed over the wall in the wake of the disappearing riders. Mystery ran up and down in panic, frantically calling for her mother until blind desperation made her scramble over the wall to follow the rest.

The fox ran straight, past the great marsh at the head of the valley, then to a clitter of stones on the high ground where it paused for a moment before crossing the granite strewn turf beyond Rough Tor and on towards the rocky outline of Brown Willie. No matter how often he turned the tell tale scent was there for the pack to follow and where the hound went the riders were never far behind: red coats, black coats and in the rear tweed clad children on fat ponies, arms and legs flailing in the endeavour to keep up with their elders. A voice shouted 'We'll have to try and stop them, they're off the trail and onto a fox'.

Mist, with the filly close behind, soon passed the rearguard and were gaining rapidly on the front runners. Someone yelled 'Loose horses!' A man in a red coat tried to head off the riderless horses but to no avail. 'Not much we can do till we get to the boundary fence,' he called. 'In any case the pace is too hot; there's no way we're going to stop those two'.

They reached a narrow road where the pack checked before crossing just in front of a parked Land Rover. The occupant got out and jumped onto the bonnet waiving his cap in the air and shouting 'He's run towards Hagtor straight across my new grass. You'll never stop them now'.

The huntsman hesitated. 'Do you mind if we go on Mr. Tregarth?' he asked recognising the landowner. 'We'll have to try and stay with them'.

'That's alright you get on and catch the damned thing: he's already had two of my geese. There's a gate about a hundred yards along.' He pointed in the direction and watched them gallop away, barley noticing the two loose animals other than to wonder at such quality stock being out on the moor.

The huntsman reached the gate and swung it open. 'Gate please' he called back. 'And for God's sake don't let those loose horses through!' But it was too late; Mystery's superior had taken her to the front and she squeezed past before the next speed rider could close it.

They managed to stop the old mare and closed the gate. 'She'll find her way home', a woman said as Mist wheeled and galloped along the fence calling wildly as the filly disappeared with the hunt. Mystery paid no heed but laid back her ears and ran on with the ridden horses, her instinct catching the contagious sense of flight which makes all herd animals run without knowing why.

The pace slowed, then suddenly everything came to a halt. The hounds crowded round a pile of rocks while blown horses stood in a cloud of steam. The huntsman blew a long blast on his horn and called the pack away for it was a deep earth and a secure sanctuary for fox and badger. One by one the hounds gathered at his horses heels as he called them by name, and as the evening mist rose from Hagtor Mire he turned his horse towards home. 'This is going to get pretty thick before dark,' he said peering into the gloom.

'Could somebody catch that loose horse and take it to the nearest farm? I'll telephone round tonight and see if I can find out who it belongs to.'

The filly wheeled as two horsemen approached and she led them at a canter to the far side of newly reclaimed grassland. 'Get her into that corner!'

shouted one, pointing to where a low wall topped by a rusty strand of wire joined the new fence. Mystery watched them nervously as they approached and as one rider attempted to grasp her mane she kicked out and scrambled over the wall taking the wire with her. It snapped at the post but not before it had torn a deep gash across her chest.

'Oh my God! What do we do now?' asked the man who tried to catch her.

'Don't ask me,' said the other. 'The best thing we can do is get off this moor while we can see a hand in front of our faces. Let's hope somebody finds her in the morning.' They watched as the pain stricken animal kicked and bucked herself free of the wire before galloping off into the mist.

She slowed to a canter, the homing instinct taking her in a wide arc that eventually would have taken her back to Hendra, but the path she followed ended abruptly at a still dark pool and beyond that stretched the rushes and black mud of Hagtor Mire. She trotted round the pool and sank hock deep in ooze. Panic welled up inside her and she plunged forward sinking deeper with each effort until she was in the bog up to her belly. A chill numbness stiffened her limbs and a cold torpor spread through her body as the liquid mud slowly engulfed her flanks.

All was quiet, nothing moved except the silent grey mist drifting through the rushes. Night turned grey to black and still the filly lay motionless as the slime closed over her quarters. A bedraggled fox paddled between the clumps of rushes seeking an easy meal of worms and beetles. It sniffed the stricken filly and sensing there was life there gave her a wide birth and trotted away towards the dry ground. Suddenly the fox stopped, listened intently then turned to lope off in the opposite direction.

Far off in the blackness a muffled drone came nearer and stopped. There was the sound of a vehicle door clicking shut; a gruff word of command and then silence once more. Two men stepped down from the dark blue cattle lorry that had pulled off the track beside a ruined engine house that once served a mine. Each man had a black and white collie at his heels as they moved some hurdles into position to form an enclosure inside the ruins.

'They'll be lying in that old gully above the pool on a night like this Slogger,' whispered the shorter of the two men.

Slogger Dixon nodded as he placed the last hurdle to form an easily closed gate. 'Let's get to it then before this fog lifts, us don't want nosey parkers a wondering what your ol' wagon is a doing parked up here at midnight. Your missus might get the wrong idea if ever it got back to 'er.' He grinned a toothless grin as they made their way towards the pool.

In a deep cleft of the old mine workings a dozen Blackface sheep huddled against the remains of a stone wall. With a quiet hiss Slogger sent his dog round them. 'We'll push 'em down towards the pool Bert,' he whispered. 'Get your bitch down that side , we don't want 'em in that boggy place.'

At a signal Bert's collie streaked off into the murk. Both dogs were used to working in the dark and like all good collies they never barked when working sheep. It came then as a shock to Bert when he heard barking in the direction of the pool. 'What the hell is going on over there?' he growled shining his powerful torch in the direction of the sound. 'Get some rope and a halter from the lorry.'

'You'd better be quick about it.' Slogger was crouching by the filly's head. 'By the looks of it, 'tis a near gonner. 'Put that bloody light out!' yelled Slogger. 'Do you want Tregarth out here with his shotgun?'

'There's something over there,' Bert said hoarsely. 'We'd better take a look, these ewes won't shift from here until we push 'em out.'

Slogger called his dog and the two men made their way towards the barking collie. 'There's something in the bog,' Bert whispered excitedly. 'Looks like a big bullock. Were in luck if it is.' They picked their way along the muddy path to get a closer look.

'It's a bloody 'orse,' Slogger gasped, 'and it looks a good 'un at that.' he turned to his companion. 'Bert me old mucker, it looks as though we've hit the jackpot.'

Bert studied the situation, trying the ground as he splodged among the rushes. 'Tis pretty soft all round,' he said pushing the heel of his Wellington boot into the mud. 'It'll fetch more alive than dead so look sharp. I'll get some rope and a halter from the lorry.'

Bert returned with some ropes and one of the wooden hurdles which he laid on the mud beside the animal. 'There, you can crawl onto that without sinking out of sight.' He gave the ropes and halter to Slogger.

The big man hesitated. 'Why me, it was your idea?' 'Because you are supposed to be a horse man, or so you keep telling me.'

With a grunt of resignation the Slogger crawled onto the hurdle and put the halter on Mystery's head, then he tied a rope round her neck and began to pull.

'Don't break its bloody neck,' Bert called anxiously.

Slogger grunted. 'Stop wittering and catch hold of this rope, I'm going to try and get the other one round it lengthways.' There was more grunting until eventually he slithered off the hurdle with both ends of the ropes in his mud plastered hands. 'Christ! Its cold,' he said giving the ropes to Bert so that he could scrape the black ooze from his saturated coat and trousers.

Bert grinned. 'Don't you worry mate, we'll soon get warm pulling on these.' He handed over the neck rope and took a firm grip of the two ends of the rope that went round the animal. Both men braced their feet against firm rush clumps and took up the slack.

Pull when I say,' Slogger ordered. 'Right , now pull.'

Mystery felt the ropes tighten. So far she had submitted to the men's actions with barely a movement; now she gave a great shiver as the pain penetrated her deadened senses.

'It's moving!' yelled Bert.

'Shut up and keep pulling.' Slogger gritted his teeth and took another turn of the rope round his hands.

The filly lunged once then steadfastly refused to budge. 'It's no good,' Slogger said relaxing his grip. 'If the bugger won't move itself it's sure as hell we can't shift that dead weight.' He thought for a moment. 'Unless you can get your lorry close enough to pull it out. What do you reckon?'

Bert shook his head. 'No way, she would be down to her axles in a couple of yards.'

They stood silently for several minutes. Slogger spoke first. 'Trouble is the damned thing is facing the wrong way and likely to get itself in deeper if we're not careful. Have you got another bit of rope I could tie to the halter?'

Bert nodded and fetched another length from the lorry.

'Your turn,' Slogger said indicating towards the hurdle. 'Even you can tie two bits of rope together.'

Bert reluctantly did as he was told and within a few seconds was back on firm ground. It was his turn to hand over the rope and remove a layer of mud. His companion grinned with satisfaction. 'Now you know what it's like,' he chuckled.

Bert snatched back the rope. 'Well, now you've trussed it up like a chicken what do we do now?'

'Just catch hold of this rope and pull on both when I say.' Slogger gave him the neck rope then tied together the ends of the rope that went round the body. He put the loop over his head and turned round so that the knot was against his chest. 'Right, we're going to try and turn it round, so come to this side and when I say, give it all you've got.'

He waited until Bert was in position then gave the word throwing his considerable weight against the lines. Once more Mystery came to life and made an effort to move and this time the pressure of the ropes brought her head and shoulders round a few inches.

'Again!' Slogger yelled.

Bert braced himself, slipped on his backside and with a curse scrambled up to try again.

Slogger muttered obscenities as the rope bit into his chest. 'It's moving!' he shouted. 'Christ, it's moving!' Slowly the mud spattered shoulders came round, and with each struggle by the animal the men pulled harder until she was almost facing them.

'Hang on.' Slogger relaxed his grip on the ropes. 'Let's take a breather,' he gasped.

Bert needed no second bidding and found a dry patch to sit on while he rubbed the life back into his numbed hands. 'Worth a few 'undred quid I reckon,' he whispered excitedly.

The big man grunted. 'Only if we get 'un out in one piece and away before daylight; and another thing, it's in pretty bad shape so do you reckon you can cope? I mean horses aint like sheep or bullocks y'know and this one looks like quality to me and could turn out to be a load of trouble.'

'Of course I can cope,' Bert muttered. 'My old man used to be a dealer didn't he. 'Orses is in me blood.'

'Your father has been dead this past ten years and you've not been near one since, and the only thing in you blood is rough cider.'

'Aw shuddup and let's get the bloody thing out before it freezes to death.' Bert stood up and picked up his ropes.

'Okay, now then!' Slogger yelled as the filly attempted a lunge forward. The two men pulled until the veins stood out on their foreheads. She moved a few inches and one fore foot struck firm

'And again!'

The feel of something solid under her feet seemed to give Mystery fresh heart. She struck out with both front legs, her head and neck lunged forward and her quarters lifted above the surface with a loud sucking noise.

'Just once more Bert and we're there.'

They braced and pulled again. This time the hind feet found a hold and with a last desperate plunge Mystery stood quivering on solid turf.

'Don't let go of them ropes,' Slogger commanded urgently. 'We don't want to lose it now.'

Bert grimaced. 'You needn't worry, that's not going very far nor very fast, its as lame as hell,' he commented as Mystery took a hesitating step keeping one fore leg off the ground.

Slogger groaned. 'Dear God! Don't say it's broke its leg after all that sweat. If it's a knacker job we needn't have bothered.' He went over to examine the injured limb and gave a sigh of relief. 'No it's not busted but there's a fair ol' gash – looks as though its been in some wire. Let's see if we can get it into the lorry, give us your torch.' He swung the beam over the filly and scraped off some of the black mud, then he turned to Bert and said slowly: 'I reckon I know this one.' He took a piece of rag from his coat pocket and cleaned off part of the neck. 'Tis a roan, a blue roan and there's only one of that colour in these parts and that belongs to old Pendogget along o' Hendra.'

Bert picked up the ropes . 'Well I'll be damned if I'm going to take it back,' he said. 'His loss is our gain so let's get the bugger loaded before we get company.' He pulled on the halter rope while Slogger put his full weight against the filly's quarters as she painfully hobbled up the ramp. Bert tied her to a ring at the front where she stood shivering.

'Chuck that old bit of blanket on it,' shouted Slogger. 'Come on let's get this ramp up and be on our way.' They whistled the dogs and clambered into the cab. 'It's funny aint it,' he said.

Bert started the engine and ground it into gear. 'What's funny?'

'Just that we started off to nick a few ewes from John Tregarth and ended up with old Pendogget's mare.'

'So what's so funny about that?'

Slogger chuckled. 'Sorry, I forgot you're from up-country so you wouldn't know.'

The lorry lurched forward and soon only the distant grind of the gearbox could be heard by the sheep huddled in the gully by the pool.

An hour after the vehicle had disappeard into the mist a white shape loomed out of the greyness of the ruin. An old man on a grey horse peered wearily at the tell-tale marks left by the rustlers. Byron pocketed his torch and sat listening for any indications that they were still in the vicinity. He had followed the tracks of the hunt when Mist had returned home alone; now he knew that his filly had been taken. His head sank to his chest and with an agonised groan he turned the mare and headed back into the fog.

~

CHAPTER 2

It was daylight by the time the blue cattle lorry jerked to a halt in Bert's yard. He had dropped Slogger off before they left the moor and it had been another five miles of narrow side roads driven at a snails pace and without lights before he reached the isolated huddle of tin sheds and the peeling caravan that was Bert's home.

A large red faced woman stood in the doorway, her bare arms folded across an ample bosom. She took a cigarette from the corner of her mouth and flicked it across the patch of rough grass that passed for a lawn. 'What 'ave yer got this time Bert?' she called in a raucous voice.

Her husband grinned. 'Summat a bit out of the ordinary, wait till you see.' He let down the tail board as Florrie walked down the muddy path to get a closer look. 'Cor! What's to do with that then?'

'It's a horse.'

'I can see that yer damned fool. What I want to know is how do you reckon to turn it into hard cash? It's not like sheep and bullocks y'know, you can't pass it off on the quiet for someone's deepfreeze.'

Bert frowned. 'Don't you start that, you're as bad as Slogger. Don't worry, I know just the chap to take this little mare off our hands, and anyway if the worse comes to the worse she's worth a few 'undred knacker price. But it aint come to that yet and I bet Paddy will be able to get that leg right in no time, then we'll make a bomb.'

'Oh, that chap,' Florrie retorted. 'The less you have to do with the likes of him the better. He's been had up twice already so you'd better watch out.'

Bert walked up into the lorry. 'We've done alright so far and I don't see why it shouldn't go on that way. Anyway, don't just stand there, come and give us a hand to get her into Dolly's loose-box.'

Dolly was their one and only cow and the so called loose-box a large tin shed. Florrie open the door while Bert led Mystery gingerly down the ramp and into the box. He fetched a handful of oats in a bucket and put water under the filly's nose.

'Don't over feed her,' Florrie commented sarcastically.

Bert was not listening. 'We'd better clean her up after breakfast,' he said, 'and that leg don't look too good.'

Florrie made a closer inspection. 'She's cut all over her front; barbed wire I reckon.' She fetched a bucket of hot water and began cleaning the wounds.

'What about my breakfast?'

'T'hell with your breakfast. This happens to be an animal you've pinched not a sack of candlesticks and I aint going to stand by and watch it suffer while you feed your face, so if you want breakfast you know what you can do.'

Bert pulled a face and shrugged. 'All right, what do you want me to do?'

'Just hold her while I get some clean water and disinfectant if that's not too much to ask.' She went back to the caravan and returned a few moments later with the necessary items. When she had finished she began to sponge some of the caked mud from the neck and shoulders. 'It's a nice 'orse Bert, reminds me of the days when father had the van and him and your old man used to travel and do a bit of dealing.' She paused, then added wistfully, 'Ah, they were good old days'

'Good old days be damned,' exclaimed her husband. 'Wet, cold and hungry days more like it, choppin' turnips or pulling mangels. The only thing us kids got was what we could pinch. Come on I'm starving.'

Florrie stood firm. 'never mind about your stomach, that animal wants more grub than you've given it if it's to stay alive, so when it has had a proper feed you'll get yours and not before.' She folded her arms and waited until he fetched more corn and an armful of hay. Mystery made no attempt to eat either.

Florrie looked concerned. 'it don't look too lively, Bert, and it aint touched that grub.'

Bert shut the loose-box door. 'You wouldn't look very lively if you'd been stuck in a bog all night.' Nevertheless he looked worried as they walked back to the caravan.

Next morning the man called Paddy drove his battered van into the yard and called 'Anyone about?' Bert appeared from one of the tin sheds wiping his blood stained hands on the butcher's apron he was wearing. 'Just skinning an old ewe what died in the night,' he said by way of explanation.

Paddy grinned. 'Sure you have,' he said. 'And a nice and tender one no doubt; but I haven't come to look at sheep have I now.'

'It's over 'ere,' said Bert leading the way to where Mystery stood dejectedly in the far corner of the box. The Irishman looked over the door and eyed her intently. His long silence was too much for Bert. 'Well, come on Paddy, what do you think then?'

Paddy spoke without taking his eyes off the animal. 'I'll tell you what I think,' he said slowly. 'I think you've got yourself a load of trouble and the sooner you get rid of it the better.'

'What do you mean a load of trouble?'

'Well for one thing you have a lame and sick horse there and for another, Holy Mother it's a blood horse and a blue roan at that.'

'So?'

'Have you any idea how many thoroughbred horses come out that colour? I bet there's not another like it in Cornwall. Now, I can only guess how you got her but I'll tell you this any honest dealer or auctioneer would pick her out in a yard full of horse flesh if a description has been put out, and that goes for any slaughterer from Penzance to Bristol. Then there's the question of Horse Passports and it could be microchipped, so my advice is to take it back to where it came from.'

Bert shook his head. 'Not after all the trouble we've been to, I'll be buggered if I'm going to let it all go just like that.'

Paddy looked thoughtful for a moment. 'Well,' he said drawing the word out. 'I might just know someone who could help you out of this little mess, but mind, you'll not be getting much profit out of him seeing as how it's such a dodgy business.' He waited for Bert to rise to the bait; it took less than two seconds.

'How much do y'reckon then?'

'Well it's like this, I have a brother-in-law that brings a few horses over from Ireland now and again. Now it so happens that he's due to come over in a day or two and if I put in a good word for you he might just take it off your hands for say fifty pounds. Of course he would be taking a risk but he might, and I stress might, be able to pass it off in a bunch of his young horses.'

'Fifty quid!' Bert exploded. 'Only fifty bloody quid! She must be at least ten times that.'

The Irishman moved towards his vehicle. 'That's the best I can do, if you've got any better ideas go ahead, I can only tell you that I'm not interested at any price.' He got in and started the engine. 'If I were you my friend I would stick to sheep stealing,' he said with a wry smile as he began to drive away.

Bert thought for a moment. Hang on,' he shouted, running to catch up with the van. 'Alright, ask him to pick her up, she might look a bit better in a few days.'

Paddy nodded and drove out of the yard leaving Bert looking over the stable door. 'Bloody fine white elephant you turned out to be,' he growled.

Florrie was more philosophical. 'Never mind luv, fifty pounds is better than nothing and after all you and Slogger did your good deed like proper little boy scouts pulling the poor beast out of that bog.'

That night she crept out of the caravan while Bert dozed in front of the television. With a hand full of carrots and a few lumps of sugar she made her way to the loose-box, switched on the light and offered the filly a lump of sugar in the palm of her hand. Mystery touched it with her muzzle but would not eat. With a sigh Florrie put the remaining lumps into the manger with the carrots. 'I bet you're somebody's baby,' she said stroking the lowered neck, 'but there's nothing I can do about it.' She putout the light and bolted the door behind her.

*

Outside the night was clear. Far off in the distance a fox barked to be answered by a vixen's scream still further away, for it was the season of pairing. The harsh sound was heard by Byron Pendogget as he sat in front of a dying fire. It caused Meg to prick up her ears where she lay by the stove, still wet from a long day on the moor. The old man dosed fitfully while the collie snuffled and grunted as she pulled bits of dead bracken from her wet coat with her teeth. They had roamed the moor from one end to the other in the hope that Mystery had somehow evaded capture and had strayed off with one of the pony herds, or that she had been put into s field and not been noticed yet. The long day had taken its toll and it seemed to Byron that there was not a bone in his body that did not ache.

A night wind came up from the distant sea to stir the pines and rattle the old leaded panes on the window. Byron woke, shivered and poked the fir with a length of rusty angle iron. The dog came over and licked his hand. 'We've done all we can old lady,' he said while gentle pulling one of her ears. 'I suppose we had better report it tomorrow, not that they ever do anything.' He stood up and put a hand on the mantelpiece to steady himself. 'Come on let's get ourselves to bed.'

The next morning the old man could barely stand as he wrestled with his shirt and trousers. He sat down on the bed. 'Come on you damned old fool,' he told himself, 'there's animals to feed and jobs to do, no time to be groggy..... must get going.' He went downstairs and mad a cup of tea; the strong, sweet liquid made him feel better. It was still dark as he stood in the back porch willing himself to go outside into the chill which had followed the wind.

He fed Mist and the bunch of yearling bullocks that he wintered in the old milking shed. Next he fed and milked the single house cow leaving just enough for her white-faced calf which was banging the partition to be let in. This done he carried the half full bucket into the kitchen and began to take off his waterproofs. It was all such a regular routine he could have done it in his sleep; for a fleeting moment he had the strange feeling that he was still asleep, that there was no weight in his body. He moved towards the table, reaching out to steady himself but it seemed much further away than he anticipated –much further in the dimming light with the buzzing inside his head and the room swimming into ultimate blankness.

'Are you alright Mr. Pendogget?' The familiar voice sounded far away as Byron opened his eyes.

'Is that you Jim?' he asked raising himself on one elbow. 'What's happened, what am I doing down here?'

The postman helped the old man into a chair. 'I don't know Mr. Pendogget, I think you must have passed out.'

'That's a damned fool thing to do, can't think what came over me.'

'Would you like me to call the doctor?'

Byron shook his head. 'Good Lord no, but I'll tell you what you can do, there's some aspirins in that draw over there,' he pointed to the dresser, 'I've got one hell of a headache.'

Jim found the aspirins and filled a cup with water. 'Here you are but I still think I ought to call the doctor.'

'Doctors are for sick people and I'm not sick, a bit tired perhaps but I'm not ill so don't make so much fuss.'

'Sorry but…' Jim thought for a moment, 'is there anyone I can contact - I mean, someone who could come and look after you for a day or two until you feel better?'

Byron reached out and touched his arm. 'You are very kind young man and it is I who ought to be sorry, but I repeat, I am not ill and I don't need looking after.'

Jim sat down and gazed out of the window in silence. Eventually he cleared his throat and said hesitantly: 'You mentioned you had a daughter, do you think she would come for a few days?'

The old man grunted. 'She doesn't want to be bothered with the likes of me, in any case I'm not sure I can find her address. She sends me a Christmas card but it's a sort of business thing, I expect it comes out of a computer and I'm not much of a one for writing back. I haven't seen her since she was a little girl.'

'Was there an address or even just a post mark?'

'Oh I don't know, let's see… yes Wimbledon, you know, the place where they have the tennis. She lives there and judging by the Christmas card she has some sort of clothes shop in London.'

'I suppose she's married so it would be a different surname by now.'

'Not the last I heard,' Byron said irritably. 'Mind, I wouldn't put it past her not to tell me, didn't tell me her mother had died until two weeks after the funeral.'

'Oh I'm sorry.'

'Well you needn't be, I would not have been welcome there anyway and Tina wouldn't have the time to sort out an old codger like me so I should forget it.' He swallowed another pill and loosened his tie - he always wore a collar and tie, something else the postman thought unusual. 'Now, if you don't mind,' the old man continued, 'I'll just have a little nap in the chair. All this talking has made my head worse.'

Jim nodded and got up to go. 'I'll pop back this afternoon and walk round the ewes for you if you like, your bitch might like a run.'

Byron raised a hand with a quiet 'Thanks, but don't put yourself out.'

'Oh, it's nothing. See you then.' The cheery tone belied the anxiety the young man felt as he walked back to the van. ' There can't be too many Tina Pendoggets in Wimbledon,' he said to himself as he drove out of the yard.

'Let's hope she hasn't got wed and changed her name.

At four oclock he returned and parked his battered Land Rover outside the back door. 'Just time to walk round before it's dark,' he thought as he pushed open the back door. Meg squirmed through the gap and ran into the yard, then quickly came back to be made a fuss of. 'You were glad to get out old girl, come to see your old friend have you?' He ruffled her ears, then had a sudden thought. 'Bet you've been in all day.' He ran into the dark kitchen. 'Are you alright Mr. Pendogget?' he called and was relieved to see the old man stir in his chair.

'What's the time Jim?' he asked peering round. 'Good Lord it's getting dark, I must have been asleep.'

'It's four o'clock. How do you feel?'

'Not too good, still got this rotten head.'

'Right.' said Jim, 'that does it, I'm ringing for the doc.' He switched on the light and looked round for the telephone.

'In the front room,' Byron said weakly. 'The number's in the little book under Health Centre.' The fact that the old man volunteered the information confirmed in Jim's mind the urgency of the situation. He went quickly into the next room and began to dial.

It was over an hour before the doctor on call arrived. 'We'll take him in just for a check up,' he said as he put his stethoscope back into his bag. 'I'll give the hospital a ring, in the mean   time do you think you could stay until the ambulance comes? Just keep him quiet and perhaps you could pack a bag, wash kit pyjamas etc.'

The postman nodded. 'I reckon I could do that.' He turned to Byron. 'Don't worry Mr. Pendogget, I'll look after the stock and Meg can come home with me, I reckon she'll settle, we're old friends.'

'Thanks Jim, a lot of fuss over nothing, I don't need to go into hospital.'
He said in a loud voice.

'Yes you do Mr. Pendogget,' the young doctor called back as he took Jim aside and asked quietly whether there was anyone, a relative perhaps, who could come in and keep an eye on the old boy for a day or two.

Jim nodded. 'There's a daughter.'

'Do you think you could contact her? Nothing to get alarmed about you understand but I think he ought to have somebody to look after him until he's fit again. He is a good age and we don't want to take any unnecessary risks.'

Jim thought for a moment. 'I'm pretty sure I can find her address if she still has the same surname. There can't be many Pendoggets in Wimbledon, in fact I made a few enquiries this morning; I'll see what I can do.'

'Thanks, I'm up to my eyes at the moment so haven't got time to sort out that kind of stuff but if you have any problems let me know.' He nodded to Byron and made a hurried exit to his car with a cheery waive to the postman.

Jim completed the evening chores following Byron's detailed instructions and was back in the kitchen by the time the ambulance arrived. The old man offered only token resistance as they helped him into the vehicle while Jim repeated his reassurances to look after the animals. Just before they closed the doors Byron leant forward and said earnestly, 'Jim do you think you could make some enquiries about my filly, she's missing Jim and I reckon somebody has taken her. I haven't reported it yet but...'

'Don't you worry Mr. Pendogget, as I said I'll take care of things.'

The old man became agitated. 'Yes but you don't understand ...'

'Sorry but we must be going,' the ambulance driver interrupted as he reached for the door handle. 'We should have been back half an hour ago. He nodded to his companion and Jim stepped back to give them room. He could still hear Byron calling: 'Don't forget Jim, Mystery that's her name, you know, the old mare's foal...'

The ambulance started and Jim watched the red tail lights gradually disappear down the farm track. Meg whined and pushed her nose into his hand. 'There old girl , he'll be alright,' he fondled her ears. 'Now I wonder what the last bit was all about? Poor old chap getting a bit confused I shouldn't wonder.' He turned to the dog. 'Come on let's get you home.'

~

CHAPTER 3

Tina Pendogget replaced the telephone receiver and walked slowly over to the cocktail cabinet and poured herself a gin and tonic.

'Who was that darling?' The voice came from the direction of the kitchen.

'I don't know,' she replied hesitantly.

Hugh Valcourt's pale round face appeared instantly at the serving hatch. 'You look a bit put out, it wasn't one of those heavy breathing efforts you read about in the papers?' He grinned, folded his arms and leant attentively against the hatchway.

She smiled faintly. 'No, it was from somebody who knows my father.'

He looked puzzled. 'I thought your father was dead. Isn't that where all this came from?' He waived his hand towards the expensively furnished dining room.

'There's not need to be so pointed about it, and that was my stepfather; I'm talking about my real father.'

'Good Lord, I didn't know you had a real father - well you know what I mean. You've never mentioned him before.'

'Well, if you would only stop talking to me through that damned hole in the wall I might tell you about him,' she replied testily.

'Sorry,' the head disappeared. 'Anyway it's about ready.' He immerged carrying a steaming dish. 'There you are , omelette a la Velcourt, no nasty meat, fats or additives.' He put the dish on the table and stepped back in admiration.

Tina sat down at the table. 'You might have taken that silly apron off,' she said with a half smile. 'Although I must say the frilly bits rather suit you.'

He frowned and removed the offending garment. 'I've got a new shirt on and that was the only thing I could find to cover it.'

'I wonder it would go round you,' she said giving him a gentle poke in the mid-rift.

Hugh served the omelette with salad and raw grated carrot. 'Yeah, I know, I do my best but I put on weight just thinking about food. So what's with the phone call then?

'It's some unexpected news from Cornwall. I didn't think it would affect me so much after all these years.' She poured two glasses of wine and looked pensively at her companion.

Hugh took a sip. 'Okay, so you were going to tell me about this father of yours.' He suddenly looked concerned. 'He hasn't died or anything has he?'

'No, but he has been taken into hospital, so this chap said,' she paused for a moment. 'He also said he needed taking care of and could I come.'

'What, down to Cornwall?'

'It's not the end of the world you know Hugh.'

'It is at this time of year darling. Can't imagine how anyone could possibly survive down there in the middle of winter, and why this sudden urge to help a father you haven't seen for how long?'

Tina shrugged. 'Oh I don't know, over twenty years I suppose. I must have been about ten when mother married Edward. Ten-year-old little girls are not the best thing to have around on your honeymoon, so I was packed off to the farm.'

Hugh grunted. 'Well there you are then, and I bet you hated it.'

'As a matter of fact I loved it once I got used to wearing thick clothes all the time, even in bed.' She smiled. 'There were lambs I remember so it must have been Spring; he borrowed a pony to ride and taught me how to milk the cow and there was a lovely foal called Misty or Mist, something like that. Of course it had only been about five years since mother and I had left so I suppose I was still a bit of a country girl.' She sipped her wine thoughtfully. 'I wrote to him several times when I was at school but he never replied so in the end I gave up.' She gave a long sigh. 'Pity, because we got on quite well.'

'Is that why you kept your surname instead of taking Edwards?'

Tina shook her head smiling. 'Nothing so romantic I'm afraid, but I ask you, who would want to be called Jones when you already have a name like Pendogget, especially if you want it to be remembered?'

Hugh finished his omelette without speaking, then poured himself more wine and pushed his chair back. 'All I can say is it's a damned inconvenient time to go charging off anywhere let alone the back of beyond. I'm sorry for the old boy naturally but surely you could arrange for somebody to look after him down there. Even you must agree that a week before the January sales is no time to be deserting a highly profitable retail business.' But Tina was not listening, her thoughts were miles away where mists swirled off black peat bogs and cloud shadows scudded across a sea of grass towards an horizon that stretched for ever; childhood memories, blunted by time but real nevertheless. 'Did you hear what I said?' Hugh said emphatically. 'How am I going to manage while you're away?

She looked at him intently. 'You can always go back to your wife,' she said tartly.

'That's not what I meant and you know it. We are supposed to be business partners remember?'

She was smiling again. 'Calm down Hugh, I haven't said I'm going yet and in any case you know perfectly well you could cope, after all we do employer three buyers and surely to goodness you could sort things out between you for a few days.'

He began to clear away the plates. 'Well I must say I would not like to leave our nice comfortable flat to go and stay in some draughty old farm house.'

Tina bristled. 'My nice comfortable flat Hugh, and my father is in hospital so I can stay in a hotel or something.'

Hugh threw up his hands. 'Ah well, you will do what you want to do and nothing I say is ever going to stop you. That much I have learned over the years.'

They loaded the dishwasher in silence. Tina went into the lounge, turned up the gas fire and sank into an easy chair.

'Do you want the television on?' Hugh asked as he followed her.

She shook her head. 'No thanks I want to think. Put some music on if you like, a bit of Johan Sebastian would fill the bill.'

'Bach it is then.' He reached for the CD. The neat mathematical ingenuity of a Bach fugue appealed to Tina. She loved the way the apparent disorder was worked on by each separate part of the orchestra until the whole piece was resolved into perfect order - very satisfying.

'If only life were like that,' she muttered as the piece ended.

'Like what?' Hugh opened his eyes.

'Like a Bach fugue, everything falling nicely into place at the end.'

'Well it isn't, not in my experience anyway.' He got up, switched off the player and stood looking down at her. 'So what about this trip, are you going?'

'I'll tell you in the morning,' she said yawning. 'In the mean time I need some sleep.'

In bed she lay awake listening to Hugh's heavy breathing, her thoughts wandering seemingly at random over events in her life. Her childhood at boarding school, postcards from her parents mailed in exotic places: Rome, Cairo, New York - 'Wish you were here' - but she never got the chance. They usually arranged to be home for school holidays then it was a fortnight somewhere not too expensive with Edward's two older girls whom she disliked intensely. It was a sort of hell and she was always glad to get back to school. She thought about Hugh and how their business partnership seemed to have slipped so easily into what was generally termed a 'relationship.' Perhaps that had been a mistake, but anything was better than being alone and she had to admit to herself that she was no raving beauty to be able to pick and choose. Mother had always said she took after the Pendoggets. 'They must have been a plain lot' she muttered, turning over and trying to remember what her father looked like. She knew he was a lot older than her mother and even twenty years ago he seemed an old man to a child of ten, but the face? Hair greying at the temples, eyes that were twinkley and kind, watching her all the time she was there. She remembered the rough gnarled hands, the hands of a peasant, that was how her mother had often referred to him - 'That peasant, all he thinks about is the farm and his wretched horses.' She tried to remember more of the time before they left when she was four or five, playing among hay bales, seeing the first lambs; she had been present when one was born and had cried herself to sleep when the same lamb had died a few days later. She learned to accept such things, or at least forget them as other new and exciting things happened all around her. Then suddenly it had all stopped and all she could remember was looking back through the window of the taxi at the thin figure standing in the front porch watching them go. Somehow she knew it was the end of the happy times.

'It all might have been so different,' she said out loud and felt under the pillow for a handkerchief.

Hugh stirred and sat up. 'What's the matter?' he asked, switching on the bedside light. 'Good heavens, what are you crying for?'

She shook he head. 'Oh, you wouldn't understand Hugh, go back to sleep.'

Tina's day started early. She was usually up first and if the weather was fine went for a jog on the common. She decided this was one of those mornings and put on her tracksuit. Hugh caught a glimpse as she went out of the door.

'God, you're bloody energetic,' he mumbled, then turned over and went back to sleep.

She had showered and dressed by the time Hugh appeared in the kitchen. Tina poured him some coffee. 'I'm going down on Sunday,' she said casually.

He merely grunted, sipped his coffee before muttering 'Thought you would, you just can't resist a challenge can you.'

'What makes you think it's a challenge then?'

He grinned. 'Just the thought of a city girl like you down among the turnip heads in all that mud and manure. I hope you've got some wellies.'

'There is no need to be sarcastic and my father is not a turnip head thank you very much. He…he's just a kind, sick old man and I intend to take care of him.'

Hugh looked at her intently. 'It's a bit late in the day for that, I don't suppose he would recognise you after all these years.'

'Well, we'll just have to see, won't we.' Now that she had made her decision Tina felt much more relaxed and took her time finishing her make-up. Slowly and methodically she brushed her hair, counting the strokes as her mother had taught: eighteen, nineteen, twenty. 'Not too bad,' even though it was only 'mousey' as mother was so fond of saying. She sighed and put the brush down. 'A girl has to the best with what she's got, and what was the other one? Oh yes, take care of the inches and with any luck the pounds will take care of you.' Well done mother you certainly got that one right.'

She looked at her watch. 'Come on Hugh,' she called, 'you know what it's like on Saturdays, if you don't get a move on it will be quicker to walk, and it's your turn to drive.'

There was the sound of coffee cup against saucer and a muffled curse from the direction of the kitchen and Hugh immerged with a piece of toast in one hand while struggling to shove his arm into the sleeve of his jacket. Tina resisted the temptation to help. 'You should damned well get up earlier,' she told him as he stuffed the toast into his mouth and almost choked in the effort to get into the offending garment.

The journey was the usual nightmare of traffic jams and road works only to culminate in the frantic search for somewhere to park. More than once she had wished she had plumped for a nice little 'run about' instead of the gas guzzling second-hand Porsche which she had chosen with the view to enhancing their 'Corporate Image.' There was only one thing worse than travelling by car and that was the tube with its overcrowded carriages and smelly platforms. Tina had often thought how nice it would be to 'live over the shop', but a flat in Kensington was financially out of the question.

'So where are you going to stay?' Hugh asked as they pulled up in the last remaining parking space behind the boutique. They had been discussing plans for the forthcoming sales and the question came out of the blue.

Tina shrugged. 'I've no idea, but I dare say Tracey will be able to dig something out of one of the West Country Tourist Guides. The bookshop round the corner is bound to have one. Oh, and that reminds me, since you are supposed to be the financial wizard of this outfit you can think up ways and means of giving that girl a pay rise, she deserves it.'

Hugh frowned. 'It's all very well for you, all you have to do is choose a few clothes. It's me who has to balance the books.'

'Well thank you very much,' she said getting out of the car. 'Just as long as you remember that if I don't choose the right ones we're both out of a job. Come on or we'll have a queue outside the door.'

The shop was not large but catered for a clientele that was young and affluent and for whom a trip to town invariably meant spending money on themselves. Tina had built a reputation for style rather than trendiness with the result she found her customers getting older and richer: daughters were bringing their mothers. Business was booming so that now they were able to expand into commissioning their own designers and were beginning to supply other retailers.

Tracey was waiting in the small back room that served as an office. 'The new designs have arrived,' she said putting a pile of drawings and photographs on the desk.

Tina looked at them pensively. 'Not bad.' She read the covering letter. 'They work in Glasgow, good for Glasgow. Do they have a name?'

'I think they're just called Scottish designs.'

Tina shook her head. 'No that won't do - shades of tartan and hairy tweeds, we need something with a more chic ring, something trans - Common Market.' She thought for a moment, then said brightly, 'I know, what about Ecoss? The Collection d'Ecoss, that should please the Scots and the French and keep the posh mums interested.' She pushed her chair back and gazed at the ceiling. Tracey was quite used to these contemplative moments and stood quietly waiting for some sort of pronouncement. It came after a long period of pencil tapping.

'Tracey. Do we have anything in Cornwall, designers, outlets, anything at all?'

The girl shook her head. 'Not as far as I know, why?'

'Oh, no particular reason, just that I have to go down there next week and I might have killed two birds with one stone - and that reminds me, could you find a nice little pub or something not too far from Bodmin for Sunday night?'

'Okay will do, in the mean time do we go ahead with the Glasgow people?'

Tina nodded. 'Ask Hugh to do some costings and arrange a contract. In the mean time we had better get the sale items sorted out.'

It took the whole day and well into the evening before Tina was satisfied that they were ready. 'We'll eat out tonight , I reckon we've earned it,' she said as they walked back to the car. 'It might be the last decent meal I get for the next few days.'

～

CHAPTER 4

The first spots of rain spattered the windscreen as the Porsche turned of the main road into a narrow high bank lane signposted Blackaford 2 miles. Tina eased into low gear where a one-in-five sign marked the beginning of the winding climb towards the cluster of houses under the edge of the moor. It was raining harder as she accelerated to take a steep bend at the same time switching on the headlights to penetrate the evening gloom; as she did so a horse and rider suddenly appeared as if from nowhere. Instinctively she braked and sounded the horn; the car skewed into the stone faced bank with an expensive sounding crunch. The horse wheeled and reared while the rider threw his weight onto the animal's neck to keep balance. 'Woe! Steady feller! Woe!' Gradually the horse calmed as the man patted its neck and spoke in a low soothing voice. 'Steady then, that's better, good boy.' Eventually the animal stood still, head erect and nostrils flared with only the occasional snort to indicate its alarm and defiance. Even to Tina's untutored eye, this was no ordinary horse.

She grabbed her coat and got out to inspect the damage, which amounted to a buckled bumper and smashed headlight. The tall figure had dismounted and was standing at the horse's head with his back to her as she walked purposefully towards him. He wore a long rainproof coat that reached almost to the ground, below which she could just make out the boots and spurs. The collar was turned up to meet a rain sodden cap so that nothing of the man was visible at all. It gave Tina an eerie feeling and she paused, then heard the muttered words 'bloody women.' which made her bristle and she went forward and tapped him on the shoulder.

'Look what you've done to my car,' she said angrily.' The man did not move as she continued, 'how am I going to get that put right over the weekend and anyway what the hell were you doing in the middle of the road?'

Slowly he turned round and she found herself looking into a pair of dark, deep set eyes which seemed to see right through her. For once she felt unsure of herself. 'Well?' she prompted.

The eyes did not waiver. 'Madam,' he said with deliberation, 'you are a bloody idiot.' With that he turned, put his foot in the stirrup and swung into the saddle, then looking down at her added 'people like you ought not to be allowed on the road.' The horse wheeled causing Tina to step back hastily and before she could call him back horse and rider disappeared through a nearby gateway. The rhythmical thud of galloping hooves faded and Tina walked angrily back to her car, got in and slammed the door. 'Ill mannered brute,' she said out loud.

It was almost dark when she pulled into the car park of the 'Fox and Hounds' and although it was past opening time the only light came from a small upstairs window. 'Well at least there's someone at home,' she thought as she walked over to the side door where a porch offered shelter from the rain. She banged on the door. 'Come on, come on.' She was beginning to get impatient. It had not been an auspicious start to her spell of filial duty.

Eventually there was the sound of footsteps and the door was unbolted. The figure silhouetted in the doorway was female, tall but well rounded and spoke with a London accent.

'Hello dear, you must be the lady from Wimbledon, we don't get many visitors this time of year. Come in, you must be perished.' She led the way into the back kitchen where a large wood burning stove gave a welcoming glow. 'Sorry I kept you waiting but I wasn't expecting you quite so soon and we don't get many locals till gone eight on a Sunday.' She indicated a chair and took a small visitors book from the dresser shelf. 'Let's see, Miss Pendogget, isn't it? She smiled. 'That's a good old local name I know.' She handed the book to sign and began filling the kettle. 'Would you like a cup of tea, or would you prefer something stronger?'

'No thanks, tea will do fine, I'll just get my bags while you are making it.'

When she returned, the cups were on the table and the kettle was boiling. Tina watched as her hostess made the tea and cut into a large fruit cake. She judged her to be about forty, a woman who had taken care of herself and still battled against the spare inches in spite of the fruit cake. 'Can I help?' she asked.

'No thanks, you just make yourself comfy. By the way, my name is Gloria Lockey, I hope you'll call me Gloria, almost everybody else does - the regulars in the pub, I mean.' She put tray of tea things on the table and sat down opposite Tina. 'So what do I call you? I mean I can't go on calling you Miss Pendogget, can I?'

Tina smiled. 'I suppose not. It's Tina.'

'Good. So how do you like your tea?'

'Just normal but no sugar, thank you.'

'Good for you, wish I could cut down but I still have a tiny bit. Now if I was naturally slim like you, life would be a lot easier.' She laughed and brushed a peroxide curl from her forehead. 'So what are you doing in these parts at this time of year?' She poured the tea and smiled at her guest. Tina gave a brief account of the reasons for her visit. Gloria nodded. 'Well I hope it all goes well and if I can be any help, just let me know. I've heard of your father but have never met him; by what I can gather he keeps himself to himself but that's not unusual with the moor folks.' She offered Tina a biscuit and when she declined helped herself to a Digestive and began the process of dunking it in her tea cup. 'Anyway,' she continued, 'it's nice to have someone from town to have a natter with. You get a bit lonely at times, even in a pub, you know.'

'Is there a Mr. Lockey?' Tina asked hesitantly.

'Gone to higher things,' Gloria said laconically.

'Oh, I'm sorry.'

'Well you needn't be. Higher things in this case means a brunette schoolteacher in Potters Bar. He's been gone over ten years and good riddance.' She laughed and Tina found herself laughing with her.

They finished tea and Gloria was clearing away the things. 'I'll just put these in the sink and then show you to your room so that you can freshen up. As soon as the barman comes I'll cook us a nice supper. Is there anything you don't like?'

Tina cleared her throat. 'Well, er yes, you see, I don't eat meat.'

Gloria stopped at the bottom of the stairs. 'Oh dear, that is going to make life a bit complicated but I daresay we'll cope. Nothing serious, I hope?'

'Oh no, there's nothing wrong with me, it's just that I don't believe in eating dead animals.'

Gloria raised her eyebrows but said nothing.

The stairs were narrow and curved in a half spiral. It seemed that every other one creaked. Their progress along the upstairs landing was also monitored by complaining floorboards.

'There are three guest rooms. all en-suite,' Gloria said proudly, opening the first door and stepping back to allow Tina to enter. 'My sitting room and bedroom are along the end there, so if you should want anything, just knock on the door, or failing that, come down to the bar. We don't have anyone else in at the moment so you have the place to yourself. George, the barman, comes at seven and I usually get a bite to eat about eight o'clock. How about a nice omelette? I rather fancy that myself.'

Tina nodded and thought it was a good job she had decided not to give up eating eggs since it seemed to be the first thing a vegetarian was likely to be offered at the Fox and Hounds - definitely behind the times but she would educate Mrs. Lockey before the end of her stay. She closed the door and fell gratefully onto the bed without bothering to unpack. She kicked off her shoes and lay with eyes closed trying to re-orientate her thoughts, to grasp what she might be letting herself in for. It had all happened so suddenly with no time to adjust.

'Best thing,' she told herself, 'is to make sure the old man is okay, arrange for someone to look after him when he got home and then get back to town at the earliest possible moment.'

Rain spattered against the window and she got up to close the curtains, pausing to look out at the blank countryside. 'Not a habitation in sight,' she commented ruefully and was about to draw them across when a tiny point of light caught her attention. It was high on the horizon where the blackness of the moor blended into the heavy night sky. So high was it that Tina thought at first that it must be a star, then remembering the glowering sky she realised it must be the light from some isolated farmhouse. 'Who on earth could live up there?' she thought and shivered as she quickly shut out the night.

*

Eight o'clock came round and she went down to the kitchen where the smell of frying onions made her realise how hungry she was. Gloria was busy laying the table.

'Come in,' she said cheerily, pointing to a comfortable chair. 'How about fried onions, tomatoes and mushrooms on the side? I hope you don't mind eating in the kitchen but as I said we don't get many staying at this time of the year and it's a lot cosier.'

'No, that sounds fine, thank you.' Tina settled in the chair and looked around the room. It was a mixture of oak beams and modern kitchen units with one wall dominated by an old oil painting of a huntsman and his hounds. She got up to look more closely.

'Interested in hunting pictures?' Gloria asked

'I'm interested in paintings but not in hunting. In fact, I'm against it.'

Gloria shrugged. 'I couldn't care less either way, except that it's good for business what with the hunt darts matches and socials, and of course the hunt meets here once or twice a year and on every Boxing Day, has done for donkey's years and I wasn't going to change that.' She lowered her voice, 'I wouldn't say too much about it if you go into the bar, they're a very horsey lot round here and I wouldn't want you to feel…well…uncomfortable.'

Tina went back to her chair. 'Too late,' she said with a wry smile. 'I literally almost bumped into one of your horsey fraternity on the way here and a very unpleasant experience it was too.' She recounted the episode.

Gloria grinned. 'That could only be John Tregarth. He rides his stallion on Sundays when there are not too many people about. I can imagine he would not be too polite; but look on the bright side, if you had touched

31

that horse he would probably have throttled you on the spot. He thinks the world of that animal, though I can't think why; but then, the Tregarths have always been a funny lot when it comes to horses.'

'You know them then?'

'Oh yes, I know John Tregarth.'

'Good, in that case you will be able to tell me where he lives. I intend to see that Mr. Tregarth pays for the damage he has caused.'

Gloria shook her head. 'It would be like getting blood out of a stone, and it will be no good you going up to Greystone Barton tomorrow because I know for a fact that he's off to some horse sale, his housekeeper told me yesterday.'

'Okay, so I'll go the day after tomorrow or the day after that if necessary.'

Gloria began serving the meal. 'You are pretty determined then,' she said as they sat down to eat. Tina did not reply, her mind intent on the job in hand as she rapidly demolished a generous helping. 'Sorry, I was famished,' she said as she pushed her empty plate away.'

'Glad you liked it, now how about some apple pie and cream?'

Tina hesitated, then nodded. 'Well why not?' she thought.

At that moment there was a knock on the door and a man's bald head appeared round the door. 'I would be grateful for some help behind the bar m'dear,' he said in a soft Cornish accent.

'Right George, be with you in a minute,' said Gloria with a mouth full of pie. George acknowledged Tina's presence with a grin and a nod. 'Proper job', he said and she was not quite sure whether he was referring to her or Gloria's offer to help.

The latter was piling the plates in the sink. 'In case you were thinking of washing up we've a new dishwasher in the back and we'll leave it all until the bar closes,' she said with a grin, then straightened her dress, made sure her hair was how it should be and took several deep breaths. 'Well, let's get to 'em,' she said and gave Tina a knowing wink. 'You'll find it quite civilised in the bar provided you don't mind a bit of language now and again. Of course if it gets too bad I turf 'em out.' She made as though rolling up her sleeves and Tina could well imagine her doing just that in true Wild West style.

The bar of the Fox and Hounds was large and functional. Tina noticed there had been no obvious attempt to 'tart it up' for the tourists. Such oak beams as there were served a structural purpose and the granite lintel over the fireplace was probably exactly as it had been when the place was built . No horse brasses and no imitation flintlocks. Instead the walls were decorated with notices and posters announcing such unlikely events as a hog roast and wellie wanging competition by the Young Farmer's club; terrier racing, skittles and a horn blowing competition by the local hunt, and a sponsored pram race run by the football club. These were in addition to the more normal information about darts matches, sheep dog trials and the results of the Christmas draw. Tina read them with interest, thinking that, just as you could judge people by the books on their shelves, so you could judge a community by the notices on its pub walls. There was an earthiness about the events for Blackaford that she found rather disconcerting.

The dozen or so customers had polarised either to the log fire or to the bar at the other end of the room. About half, Tina reckoned, had the ruddy faces and gnarled hands attributed to outdoor work and in the main they occupied the seats by the fire. Those at the bar watched her closely as she went up to join them and she detected a sudden lull in the conversation. A middle aged man with a droopy moustache offered her a stool and asked politely if she were on holiday.

'No, family business,' she replied. The buzz of conversation resumed its previous level. Gloria offered her a drink 'on the house' and Tina accepted a gin and tonic and settled back against an upright beam where she could see most of the room.

'This lady is down from London for a few days,' Gloria said in a voice loud enough to be heard by most of the company.

'Ugh!' The expletive came from a little old man seated at the far end of the bar. He wore a sweat stained brown trilby with a corrugated brim and a bright red neckerchief tucked into a frayed collar; he had obviously not shaved for several days. 'Ugh!' he repeated.

Gloria rapped the bar top with her knuckles. 'Now then Charlie, that's enough of that.' She turned to Tina and said in a low voice 'don't mind him, he's harmless enough; he's just got it in for anyone who looks as though they come from the town: it's the hunting ban you see.'

Tina looked puzzled. 'I'm sorry, I don't understand.'

'It's just that Charlie's keen on his hunting and blames what he calls 'townies' for the ban.

'He doesn't seem the type to be tallyhoing about the countryside on horseback.'

Gloria chuckled. 'Lor bless you no, old Charlie follows on his bike, has done since he was a lad so they tell me, and he's turned eighty you know. Well as I was saying, he lives for it: out two or three times a week in all weathers, of course he was at the last big meet before the ban and apparently got knocked off his bike in a bit of a scuffle. That's why he's not particularly well disposed to strangers from the town.'

Charlie was peering again. 'I know what you're saying,' he said looking at Gloria. 'you wait 'till some chap wi' green hair knocks you over, least I think it were a chap - had earrings and tattoos. You can't tell these days...' His voice subsided into a mumble.

'Now that's enough, Charlie,' Gloria said firmly. 'Miss Pendogget doesn't want to hear all your woes.'

At the mention of her name, Tina noticed the old man suddenly crane forward to get a better look at her. 'Did you say Pendogget?' he asked in an altogether different tone of voice.

'That's right, I'm Tina Pendogget, my father has a farm not far from here.'

Charlie came towards her and, fumbling in his breast pocket, took out a pair of rimless spectacles through which he studied her closely. 'By George missus,' he said with a toothless grin, 'I could tell you some tales about the goings on up at the Barton in the old days. Oh, we 'ad some proper do's an' no mistake. 'Now take the time your.....'

'How many times do I have to tell you, Charlie?' Gloria interrupted. 'Take no notice Tina, he only wants you to buy him a drink and he's had quite enough already.' She turned to the old man. 'And I suggest you get yourself off home, Charlie, while you can still ride that bike of yours.'

Charlie looked at Tina appealingly. 'But I only....'

'No buts, Miss Pendogget is tired and doesn't want any of your silly stories so off you go.'

Grudgingly, Charlie turned to go and, shaking his head muttered, 'We rode some good 'uns him and me but nobody wants to know anymore, nobody remembers..'

Tina watched the shambling figure move towards the door and had a sudden urge to call him back, to hear more about the old days and maybe learn something about her father; but perhaps he was mistaken, perhaps he was thinking of another Pendogget. In all events the moment passed and she was left wondering.

'Sorry about that,' Gloria said.

'Oh that's alright.' Tina thought for a moment. 'He seemed to know my father, and what was all that about the Barton: I thought you said that Tregarth man lived there.'

Gloria shook her head. 'I'm afraid the poor old boy gets a bit muddled these days so I wouldn't take too much notice of him if I were you. As for the Barton, there must be half a dozen Bartons between here and Bodmin.'

'That's right, Miss,' Droopy Moustache interjected. 'It's just a name for a large important farm - such and such a Barton. The Tregarth's is Greystone

Barton, but old Charlie..well, you never know when he's spinning a yarn just to get a drink.'

'What's that about Charlie Hawkins and Tregarth? The questioner pushed his way to the bar and banged his glass to get attention.

'Nothing to do with you Slogger,' Gloria said, and turning to the barman, 'one more for Slogger and that's it.'

Slogger Dixon steadied himself with one hand while he dug into the pocket of his mud spattered overcoat with the other. He threw five pound coins onto the bar. 'My money's as good as anyone else's aint it?' The landlady did not reply. 'Well Charlie Hawkins is a silly old fart,' he continued pocketing his change, 'and as for Tregarth, we all know about him don't we.' He turned as though addressing the whole room.

Gloria bristled. 'I don't know what you mean by that,' she said polishing a glass vigorously.

'You know very well what I mean,' he continued. 'All that talk about accidents. I reckon 'e gave 'er a push.'

'You watch what you say Slogger Dixon,' Gloria said angrily. 'There are laws about saying things like that.'

Slogger grunted. 'I don't care, and I'll tell you this, if it wasn't for the Tregarths I would be farming me own place now.

Gloria stopped what she was doing and for a moment and looked as though she might lose her temper. She resumed after a second or two and said calmly 'your father lost his farm for the same reason you are out of work - dishonesty and booze; if you don't pay your rent you expect to be chucked out. In any case it was old man Tregarth that did it not John.'

'Oh, it's John now, is it? Well you can tell John Tregarth and that daft kid of his that the Dixons don't forget.' He downed his pint, banged the empty glass down on the bar top and made for the door.

'That's the beer talking Slogger Dixon,' Gloria called after him.

His mumbled reply ended in ….off as the door slammed. The atmosphere in the bar returned to normal and Gloria gave a sigh of relief. 'Sorry about that, you must think we are a funny lot,' she said smiling at Tina. 'I would hate you to think we have little dramas like that every night.'

'I'm afraid I seem to have sparked off local resentment all round what with Mr. Tregarth and now this,' Tina said with a wry smile. 'Perhaps I had better turn in before anything else happens. Seriously though, I am pretty shattered and it's likely to be a dodgy sort of day tomorrow so I'll wish you all good night.'

Once in her room, she kicked off her shoes and slumped onto the bed. 'Lord, what an odd set up,' she said out loud. 'You were right Hugh, I've never felt more like a fish out of water in my life.'

The hubbub downstairs gradually subsided to be replaced by noisy 'Good nights!' outside; then at last all was quiet. Tina prepared for bed and gratefully slipped under the duvet. She lay listening to the rain lashing against the windows while the old building ticked and gurgled her to sleep.

~

CHAPTER 5

The morning dawned wet and cold with just a hint of sleet in the air. Gloria had been up several hours by the time Tina came down to breakfast. 'I must go to the hospital this morning,' she said reaching for the cornflakes. 'Then I suppose I had better go out to the farm to see what needs to be done there, although I haven't a clue about farm animals and things.'

Gloria nodded. 'The young lady who made your booking said something about a relative being ill.'

'Yes, that's right, it's my father. I shall have to find my way to Hendra somehow, I haven't been there for years,' she omitted to say how many, 'but I think it's on the Ordinance Survey map so it shouldn't be too difficult.'

'If I were you, I wouldn't worry too much about the farm. If I know the moor folks, someone will have already taken care of the stock, although it might be just as well to check the house. I doubt they would think of turning the water off and the weather forecast is not good: there might be a freeze up.'

Tina looked surprised. 'I didn't think you had hard frosts in this part of the world.'

'Nor we don't down here but the moors are quite a bit higher up. It's always a couple of overcoats colder up there, so be warned and take plenty of warm clothes and some wellies.'

'I've brought some ski-boots and a windproof jacket so I think I'll be warm enough.' Just the same, she put on an extra jumper and stuffed a woollen bobble hat into her pocket before setting out.

The road to Bodmin wound round the edge of the moor; every so often she had a glimpse of steep slopes of browned grass swept flat by the wind. She shivered at the thought of driving up there and wondered if she would find the way to the old farmhouse she barely remembered.

She found the hospital and after explaining the situation at the reception desk, was eventually ushered along a corridor by a young nurse who indicated some double doors and hurried on. Tina paused to look through the small glass panels along the row of wards in an effort to recognise a face among the patients she could see. It would be terrible to walk past or worse still go up to the wrong man. She closed her eyes and tried to visualise his features but it was all very hazy. Suddenly she was terrified that it had all been a great mistake to come and she should turn round and go straight back to Wimbledon.

'This way.' It was the young nurse with a tray of instruments. She turned round, pushed a door open with her bottom and waited for Tina to follow. 'Fourth bed on the left,' she said indicating with her head. Tina took a deep breath and walked slowly along the row of beds. To her relief and satisfaction, she recognised him immediately. He lay with his head on the pillows, eyes closed on a peaceful doze. The face was as she remembered, a few more wrinkles but still ruddy and tanned against the white of the pillow. The hair was now white an remarkably plentiful for a man of his age; she tried to calculate how old he was, getting no nearer than at least seventy five. It was a face gentle in repose and she felt the tears of regret at not having known this man who was her father.

He stirred and opened his eyes, looked at her and closed them again. After a while he opened them again and this time stared, then sat up and peered through half closed eyes. 'Who.. How?' he groped for a pair of horn rimmed spectacles on the bedside table. She picked them up and gave them to him. 'Then I'm not dreaming,' he said putting them on. 'Is that really….. you're so like your mother…..for a moment….it is you Tina?'

She nodded, not knowing what to say

'But how did you know?'

Tina smiled. 'A friend of yours telephoned,' she paused and added 'I didn't think you would recognise me after all this time.'

He reached out and took her hand. 'My little maid,' he said giving it a squeeze.

She bent down and suddenly put her arms round him in a long hug. 'Oh Dad, that's what you used to call me: your little maid.' She felt the tears coming again and stood up to blow her nose.

Byron patted the bed. 'Sit down and tell me all about yourself.'

She gave him a potted history of her life from age ten to the present, leaving out only those bits of which she thought he would not approve. 'Why didn't you answer my letters?' she asked.

He thought for a moment. 'When your mother married again, I realised I would only be a liability to you. It was necessary for you to start a new life with a new father and therefore better to forget about this old peasant in the backwoods. No child could have two fathers, and he could give you so much more than I possibly could, so.....' His voice trailed off and the tired eyes closed.

She stroked the rough hand. 'Well I'm back now to make sure you're properly looked after when you come out of this place, but in the mean time you must tell me if there is anything you would like me to do.'

He started, as though suddenly remembering something. 'Yes..yes,' he said quickly. 'The animals, make sure they are alright. Joel Menheniot my neighbour will help and young Jim Saunders, he's the postman and...' he gripped her hand tightly 'get them to look for Mystery.'

Tina looked puzzled. 'I'm sorry?'

'Mystery, my young mare. She's been stolen. You must try and get her back - report it to the police.' His head sank into the pillows.

'You mustn't get so excited,' Tina said smoothing the sheets. 'If you give me a description, I'll see what I can do.'

Byron smiled. 'Good girl, I can see I can rely on you,' he patted her hand. 'Makes an old man proud, now if you pass me that pencil and paper, I'll write it all down and you can just hand it in to the police station.' He scribbled some notes and gave them to Tina. 'Can you read my writing?'

She nodded, folded the paper and put it into her handbag. 'I'll do it this morning before I go out to the farm,' she said reassuringly.

At that moment the ward sister came up. 'I think Mr. Pendogget ought to rest now,' she said drawing the screens curtains. 'Perhaps you would like to come back at visiting time: six thirty to eight thirty.' The tone had a finality about it that could not be argued with. Tina got up and prepared to leave. 'See you tonight then,' she said giving him a peck on the cheek.

He waived a hand and nodded. The sister was preparing a sedative. 'Well that seems to have perked him up no end,' she said putting a glass of water on the table next to him as Tina walked away.

'That was my daughter,' the old man beamed.

'That's nice, does she live round here?'

'No, she's come down from London.'

The sister smiled. 'She must think a lot of you to come all that way.'

Byron nodded. 'Yes,' he said quietly.

Outside the ward, Tina waited for the sister to come out. 'Can you tell me how he is?' she asked. 'I mean, why was he brought in?'

'Oh nothing very terrible.' The nurse was reassuring. 'I think he had just been overdoing things a bit. A few days rest to get the old blood pressure down and he will be as right as rain. Doctor Ferguson will tell you more if you like to pop in tonight when he's on duty.' She smiled. 'Don't worry, we'll take good care of your father.'

Tina walked out into the cold air, her thoughts a jumble of memories and regrets. She felt in her handbag for the car keys and found the piece of paper with the details of the missing filly; she decided to get that job done first. A passerby directed her to the police station, which was within walking distance, and she set off a brisk pace.

At the police station, the sergeant at the desk looked dubiously at the note. 'Went missing yesterday.. hmm.. probably cats' meat by now, I'm afraid,' he said laconically, then noticing the shocked look on Tina's face added, 'Sorry madam but I' m afraid that's where most of 'em go. We'll notify all the local abattoirs and auctioneers but I don't offer too much hope.'

There was a bitter wind blowing down the street as Tina looked for a respectable looking pub for some lunch. She found one, bought an Ordinance Survey map in the shop next door and settled down by a roaring fire to have a sandwich and half a pint of lager. She pinpointed Hendra on the map, folded it so that she could refer to it easily and, finishing her meal quickly, hurried back to the car as dark clouds piled on the hills above the town.

By the time she reached the open moorland, the sky to the North was banked with grey tinged with yellow. Twice she was halted by shepherds bringing their flocks across the unfenced road on the way to lower ground. Groups of ponies drifted before the wind, their long tails plastered against their quarters while black cattle sought the shelter of rocks and gullies. Had Tina lived on the native moors, she would have recognised the signs but she had been transplanted too long and drove on heedless of the occasional white flake that lodged on the windscreen.

At a bleak crossroads, she stopped to consult the map. Vague memories of a narrow lane to the right came back to her. She traced the next turning with her finger and sure enough it passed the end of the long farm track that led to Hendra. She found the turning and, after about two miles, recognised the rusty iron gate which marked the entrance to the farm.

The little sports car bumped over potholes and stones as it descended the steep gradient of the last few hundred yards. She turned a sharp bend and there it was, just as she remembered it, except now it seemed much smaller. There was a red van parked in the yard and she was surprised to see what appeared to be a postman carrying a bale of hay into one of the barns. She pulled up beside the post office vehicle and followed the man into the building where he was busily feeding some calves.

Jim Saunders was taken by surprise and swung round with a sudden exclamation. 'Oh! How d'ya do? I wasn't expecting to see anyone out here on a day like this, didn't hear your car in this wind.'

Tina smiled. 'And I didn't expect to see an afternoon delivery on a day like this.'

Jim grinned. 'You must be Miss Pendogget,' he said holding out his hand. 'Twas me that telephoned you, I hope you don't mind.'

'Oh no, it was very good of you to take the trouble,' she said grasping his hand.

'No trouble at all. Your father is a nice old gentleman and I'm glad to be able to help. Jim Saunders is my name, I live about a mile away down the lane so if you need any help you'll know where to find me. In the mean time I'd better get on and finish these; I've got my own to do when I get home.'

'No, please carry on. I'm only too grateful that there is someone to look after things, you see I'm a complete ignoramus when it comes to animals and farming. I haven't lived here since I was a child.'

'Yes I know.' Jim talked as he worked. 'Mr. Pendogget told me; we used to have quite long chats. I suppose he didn't see many people to talk to and I've got my own small farm - just part time, you know - and I'm always asking for a bit of advice about one thing or another. As for helping, there's not a lot to do except give these calves a few nuts and a bit of hay. The ewes are all up on the moor,' he looked anxiously up at the sky. 'They'll be okay unless we get a deep snow. There's one cow to milk, have you ever milked a cow?'

Tina smiled. 'Surprisingly I have, but not since I was ten years old.'

'Well she's not giving much so I'll come in and milk her once a day, that way she'll soon dry up. There's half a dozen bullocks in the straw yard, they will need hay; oh yes and there are a few old hens scratching about. Don't forget to shut them in at night or 'Old Charlie' will get them for sure.'

'Old Charlie?'

The postman grinned. 'Sorry it's a nickname for a fox. There's an old dog fox around here very partial to a plump bird: I should know, he's had two of mine in broad daylight.'

Tina was beginning to look worried. 'I'm not sure I could cope with all that.'

Jim began to walk back to his van. 'That's alright, Miss, we'll give you a hand.' He whistled and Meg came bounding from behind the buildings. 'I'm taking the old bitch home with me for the time being but you can have her back whenever you like: she would be company for you out here.'

Tina shook her head. 'I can assure you that I have no intention of staying at the farm. The Fox and Hounds in Blackaford will do me nicely until I can make arrangements to have my father taken care of, then I must get back home. I shall be glad to come to some financial agreement with you, Mr. Saunders if you could take care of things for me. I don't think it is right for you to do it for nothing; and there was a Joel somebody or other my father mentioned, perhaps I could come to some arrangement with him too.'

Jim frowned. 'There's no need for that Miss Pendogget. Us moor folk look after our own, 'tis the only way up here. As for Joel, he left less than twenty minutes ago with you father's grey mare. He said it would be easier for him to look after her at his own place and he was in a bit of a hurry to get his ewes down just in case that lot comes down,' he nodded upwards towards the bank of grey cloud. 'Could be rain but it could be snow so I shouldn't hang about too long if you intend to get back to Blackaford tonight. That hill can be a swine once it get slippery.'

'I'm very grateful to you both,' Tina said feeling duly chastened. 'Where can I get in touch with you and this Joel in case anything happens that I can't deal with?'

Jim scribbled the telephone numbers on a scrap of paper and gave it to her. 'Wish I had a bit more time,' he said getting into the van. 'I would feel easier if we had fetched the ewes down closer to the house but you can't do everything and I must get back to do my own chores. One of us will be over in the morning and bring them down into the orchard where we can keep an eye on them. We don't want to lose half the flock in a snow drift do we.' He pushed Meg into the passenger seat and started the engine. 'Cheers!' he called as the van headed out of the yard gate.

Tina watched it disappear round the bend, listening to the receding hum until it faded into the rising moan of the wind. Suddenly she felt desperately alone in an alien and hostile landscape. This was not what she remembered from her childhood days; then, it seemed, the sun always shone and she was never alone. Now she was cold, a little frightened and the nearest human being was probably over a mile away. For a brief moment she considered getting into the car and driving back to the warmth of the Fox and Hounds as fast as she could; there was a moments hesitation and something inside told her that this wild moorland place was where she belonged: this was home.

She put on her boots and windcheater and wandered round the farmyard in search of childhood memories. It seemed to her that very little had changed: the small red tractor was very like the one she had ridden on when she was quite little. She spent time looking through the old stone buildings, bemused by the jumble if rusty implements and tools, some of which must have been at least fifty years old. In the hay barn a ginger cat suddenly appeared from among the bales and rubbed itself against her legs, purring as she bent down to stroke it. The animal was sleek and obviously well fed, 'plenty of rats and mice,' Tina thought with just a slight creepy feeling. She left the barn and walked quickly to the house with the cat at her heels.

She went to the front door and suddenly realised she had no key but in any case by its appearance it had not been opened in years. The cat had gone straight to the back door and sat waiting to be let in when Tina arrived. She turned the handle and pushed; the door opened reluctantly and she found herself in the dark kitchen. She located a light switch and was relieved when it worked instantly; twenty years ago she remembered, it was necessary to start a diesel generator in the barn before anything electrical worked and if that failed they had to use paraffin lamps. She could recall their blue tinged light and the click click as they were pumped at night when she lay in bed. 'Well at least there has been some progress,' she said out loud.

Tina looked round the half familiar kitchen with its slate flagged floor and earthenware sink under the window, and of course the large, solid, fuel stove where she used to sit on cold winter evenings: that much had not changed. The additions were a small electric cooker, stained with the greasy remains of recent meals and a large dilapidated refrigerator which stood in the corner next to a pile of old blankets that was obviously the dog's bed. There was an empty bucket on the table and a dried pool of sour milk on the floor. The cat, having squeezed through the door before Tina could prevent it, moved towards the stove but as it gave off no warmth the animal curled up in the only arm chair and was soon asleep.

Two steps led up into the living room where there was the smell of wood ash which had accumulated over several months in the large granite linteled fireplace. Memories of blazing logs and watching the firelight dance on the ceiling flooded back. The old bureau in the corner by the window was littered with bills, farming magazines and an assortment of sales leaflets. A telephone perched precariously on the threadbare arm of the nearby settee; she lifted the receiver to hear the comforting burr that told her it was still connected.

The door on the far side of the room led to a small entrance hall and the stairs. Across the hall was the 'front room' which, like the front door was seldom if ever used as far as she could recall. The room had a damp smell and was even colder than the rest of the house. It contained the minimum of furniture but she noticed he still had the rosewood piano which her mother used to play. She remembered the brass candle holders and her father trying to sing, her mother laughing and a big fluffy cat that kept jumping on the keys. She tried to remember its name but could not, like so much of that childhood it was gone forever. There were several framed photographs on the top of the piano, mostly of horses and people on horses but the one that caught her eye was a gilt framed photograph of her mother and father on their wedding day. She took it down, brushed away the dust with her sleeve and studied it thoughtfully. How young her mother looked and he was so obviously stretching up to his full height to make himself taller than his young bride, so proud yet so vulnerable in a suit that was just a fraction too large for his lean frame. She put it back, lifted the piano lid and casually pressed one of the keys, the tinny sound echoed through the empty house, stirring the ghosts of what might have been. She wondered what would have happened to her if her parents had stayed together, if she had grown up at Hendra like a normal child instead of a succession of young nannies and second rate boarding schools. 'Probably be married to some young farmer, stuck miles out in the countryside with a handful of squabbling brats,' she said out loud, slamming the lid so that the piano's insides jangled.

It was getting darker outside and she switched a light on and sat down to contemplate how on earth she was going to organise her father's affairs and at the same time fulfil her business commitments two hundred and fifty miles away. She shivered and suddenly remembered what Gloria had said about turning off the water - she had better find the stopcock. It took several minutes to trace the pipes into the adjoining lavatory where she found the elusive valve and turned it off. She turned on all the taps she could find and hoped that it would be sufficient to prevent a major catastrophe. When she was satisfied that she had done all that was necessary she switched off the lights, picked up the ginger cat from the armchair and opened the back door. There was a glare of white and to her dismay Tina saw that an inch of snow had fallen while she had been engrossed in the house. The step felt slippery underfoot and she thought of Jim Saunders' warning, quickly closed the door behind her and hurried out to the car.

To her relief, it started without trouble but she felt the ominous wheelspin as she turned in the yard and long before she reached the bend in the track it became obvious that she was not going to make it. In desperation she revved the engine, the wheels spun as the back end slewed sideways until one rear wheel dropped with a sickening bump into a rain gully beside the track. Tina groaned as she got out to survey the damage and she knew that nothing short of a tractor would put the car back onto the road.

Snowflakes the size of ten pence pieces were swirling between the high hedgebanks as Tina realised with horror that she might have to spend the night at Hendra. She trudged back down the hill to the house and once more pushed open the back door. As it closed behind her she felt something brush past her legs and with a startled cry she switched on the light. The ginger cat scuttled into the kitchen and resumed its place in the chair while a relieved Tina went into the living room where she remembered seeing an electric fire. 'Don't get jumpy,' she told herself as she switched it on and after bolting the back door settled in front of it to ponder her situation.

~

CHAPTER 6

As the first flakes of snow began to fall that afternoon John Tregarth strode out of the horse sale yard and into the adjacent field where the horse lorries were parked. He turned up his coat collar and pulled the peak of his cap even further over his eyes so that the minimum area of face was exposed to the biting wind. He cursed himself for being fool enough to drive so far in January just to buy a hunter.

'There must be a dozen good horses a damned sight closer to home,' he muttered pushing his hands deeper into his overcoat pockets. Few of the horses that had passed through the sale ring had caught his fancy and those that did were knocked down at too high a price. It began to look as though he had come a long way for nothing.

He paused to watch a fat, duffle coated Irishman give a nice looking chestnut horse a final brush before going into the sale ring. The man noticed Tregarth's interest. 'And have you been suited sor?' he asked cleaning the brush against the edge of his lorry. Tregarth gave a non-committal grunt, which the dealer took to mean no. 'Now this is as nice a hoss as you'll see anywhere,' he continued pushing his battered hat to the back of his head. 'I'm about to take the feller into the ring now but if you'd care to take a look at him, sure I might be saving meself the auctioneers fee if we could do a deal and I could let you have him for little more than I gave for him in County Wexford.' He patted the chestnut's neck and pushed at its shoulder to make it stand better. 'Sure, he'll make four figures in the sale ring and you won't find a better animal this side of the water.' The lilt of the speech was seductive and the tone reassuring as though from a bosom friend. He slapped the horse's rump. 'Warranted sound, no vices, good to shoe....' He continued listing the animal's finer points ending with: 'now what do you say to a couple of thousand and a bit o' luck money?'

Tregarth studied the animal. Normally he would have ignored such entreaties but he had come a long way and found nothing that took his eye as much as the big chestnut horse. The dealer was still talking. 'Now, is that not a grand sort of hoss sor?' Tregarth had heard the patter a hundred times before and knew he would have to let it run its course.

He watched bemused as the man beckoned to a lank haired youth in a camouflage jacket who was filling a hay net at the back of the lorry. 'Jamie, just show this gentleman what kind of animal he is.' Jamie dutifully picked up each of the horse's feet in turn, pulled its tail and gave it a vigorous scrub under the belly with his knuckles. 'Quiet to shoe, box and clip,' he repeated. 'A great hunter, can lep like a stag .'

Tregarth did not reply but moved closer to the horse's shoulder while the Irishman continued to talk. 'Sixteen three if he's an inch sor.'

'Hmm.'

'Ah well, you see he's not standing on level ground. Now if you would like to take him out onto the road….?'

Teeth were examined.

'Rising eight sor, I have all his documents.'

Tregarth had to admit to himself that he liked the look of the animal but there was always some risk in buying outside the sale yard. 'Let's see him move.'

The dealer's face lit up at this first sign of real interest. 'Right you are then Jamie, slip a saddle on and show the gentleman what this feller can do. Put him round that bit 'o green there.'

The youth fetched a bridle and a well worn saddle, tightened the girth and led the horse to a nearby Land Rover where he climbed onto the front bumper and vaulted into the saddle.

'There, didn't I say he was quiet,' grinned the Irishman with delight.

Tregarth watched the youth put the horse through its paces: it moved well enough and he nodded to the dealer. 'So what are you asking for him?'

There followed a process of haggling which was a standard ritual and Tregarth eventually purchased the animal for fifteen hundred pounds and felt well satisfied; but the Irishman was not finished with him; he sidled closer and in a confidential tone said 'You look like the sort of gentleman that would be interested in a deal and I think I might have one for you and seeing as how I've let you have the chestnut for next to nothin' I was thinking you might be willing to help me out of a slight predicament concerning a little mare that's inside me box there, something I'm sure a gentleman like you would understand. Would you care to take a look?' He led the way up the ramp to the far end of the lorry all the time keeping up the mind-lulling commentary. His voice reached the maximum lilt as he switched on the small interior light.

The first thing Tregarth saw was a nice looking head with a white star but the eyes were dull; there was no movement as the two men walked up the ramp and as he took a closer look he whistled through his teeth as he saw the chest wound and hollow flanks of what was clearly a quality animal. 'Good God man, what have you been doing to her?' he demanded angrily. 'How on earth did she get into that state?' He turned to the dealer. 'If I though you had been knocking her about I'd…..'

'No sor, no' the Irishman interjected. 'Tis nothin' like that, now why would I want to hurt a pretty creature like that. No, you see we had a bit of a bad crossing and she went down and….' His voice trailed away to silence while he watched Tregarth intently.

The latter had walked up to the mare and was gently stroking one ear. 'There there little lady, what have they been doing to you?' he said quietly, then angrily turning to the dealer: 'this animal is sick, I suggest you get a vet to see it as soon as possible and if you don't I will.' He turned to go but the man caught hold of his sleeve. 'Hold hard a minute sor.'

'Well?'

'Y'see 'tis like this, I have to get off to the boat tonight so she either has to come with me or I have her put down.' There was a genuine note of regret in the dealer's voice.

'Either way she's a dead 'un,' Tregarth said pensively.

The Irishman shrugged. 'That is as it may be but it would be a terrible pity. You've seen the mare and there's quality there that's too good for pet food for sure. Now what I was going to suggest is that I could throw her in with chestnut for the round two thousand and that way you would have a bargain whatever happened. What do you say?'

Tregarth studied the filly as Mystery slowly turned her head to look at him. He shook his head. 'There's no guarantee that I could get her home in one piece and then there's going to be vets bills and I really don't want another…' He stopped as the mare took half a step towards him and one ear flicked forward; he told himself not to be a fool but heard himself saying: 'Knacker price, I'll give you knacker price, two hundred quid and that's it.'

The Irishman hesitated for barely a second. 'Done,' he said offering his hand which Tregarth grasped and the deal was done. The chestnut horse's documents were handed over and the dealer explained very unconvincingly that the roan mare's had been lost in Ireland and there had not been time to replace them. Tregarth was dubious but it had become a matter of saving the animal's life and so he put aside any qualms and signed the cheque.

The mare was carefully loaded the front of Tregarth's lorry next to the small inspection door, that way he could check her easily from time to time on the way home. He put a hay net in front of her but she showed no interest; he began to wonder if he had done the right thing in buying her, consoling himself with the thought that the chestnut was probably worth the money anyway. He decide not to tie her up but put the partition across to separate the two animals, then he led up the chestnut and tied him towards the rear. When he was satisfied both animals were comfortable he closed the ramp and thankfully started for home.

It was already getting dark as he pulled out of the sale ground and onto the main road, mindful of the fact that he needed to get the mare home as quickly as possible but that driving too fast might shake her off her feet and cause even more problems. He cursed every speeding juggernaut that passed him, rattling the ageing horsebox to its last rivet. Not until he crossed the Tamar did he relax a little, even so he watched the sky anxiously as the night closed in. The old engine began the long grind up towards the high moor; as the road wound upwards the temperature indicator on the dash board rose to the danger mark as steam seeped into the cab from the radiator. 'Damn!' Tregarth lowered the window to get a better idea of where he might be able to pull up and let the engine cool. By this time there was a line of traffic behind him as he recognised a familiar sign half a mile ahead. The Travellers Rest was a pub he had stopped at many times before on his way home from the annual horse sale. ' Looks as though we'll have to pay old Fred a call; should be near opening time.' He looked at his watch and put his foot down on the accelerator.

At a few minutes to six, he drew into the pub car park and switched off the engine. All was quiet in the back of the lorry and he took a torch from under the dash board to inspect his cargo. Satisfied that all was well he went up to the front door and banged as hard as he could with his fist. There were footsteps and mutterings from inside and Tregarth waited while someone worked on a formidable collection of locks and bolts. Eventually the door was opened by a bent old man with a blue veined face and a nose like a piece of red pumice.

He peered up at his visitor, grinned and stepped back. 'Ah, 'tis you John Tregarth,' he said in a deep gurgling voice. 'Didn' expect to see the likes o' you on a night like this. What brings you this way?'

'If you let me in Fred, I'll tell you,' Tregarth said striding past into the bar.

The landlord fumble for the light switch. 'Give us a chance to get the bar open. God knows where the boy is, he leaves it all to me till he gets back of a evening and his wife's no bloody good to anyone,' he mumbled as he removed the cloths from the beer pumps while Tregarth stood with his back to the fire warming his backside.'

'Scotch, I suppose?'

Tregarth nodded. 'Yes please, and you can fill this.' He handed over a small hip flask. 'I'll be needing a bit of inner warmth before I get home tonight.'

Fred poured the drink. 'So what brings you to the Travellers Rest?'

The whisky was downed in a single gulp. 'Jesus, I needed that,' Tregarth said wiping his mouth with the back of his hand. 'Your memory's going Fred: it's the second Monday in January.'

'Lor yes, I should have known, Five Oaks annual sale,' He poured another whisky and one for himself. 'We used to have some rare times at Five Oaks in the old days when we was young. There was yer father, Charlie Hawkins and me, oh yes and Byron before……' He paused and stared into his drink. 'That was before all the trouble of course, long before you were even thought of.' He grinned and went across to put another log on the fire. 'So what's the latest news with you? How's that boy of yours getting on? Let's see, he must be nigh on sixteen by now.'

Tregarth swirled the whisky round the glass, deep in thought. 'I don't know what to make of him and that's the truth Fred. He hardly says a word at home, at least not to me, and he does such daft things; I swear he does it just to annoy me.'

'You mustn't be too hard on him John, not many youngsters have to go through what he's been through. It's bound to have an effect.'

'I suppose so,' Tregarth sighed, 'but it has been over five years now. Of course he misses her, God knows I do. You know, sometimes he behaves as though it was all my fault. I just can't get through to him.' He shook his head and drained his glass.

Fred was drawing the curtains. 'It's snowing fit to bust out there,' he said

Tregarth walked over to see for himself. 'Damn! I was hoping to get home before that lot came.' He paid for the whisky, pocketed the flask and made for the door, buttoning his overcoat as he went. 'By the way Fred, could you let me have a bucket of water, my radiator has boiled over?'

The landlord nodded and went into the back, returning promptly with a bucket which he handed over. 'There's a tap by the back door, you can leave it there.' Tregarth gave his thanks before topping up the radiator, then leaving the bucket as requested he made a brief inspection of his charges before climbing into the cab.

Conditions were getting worse and he realised he would have to choose between the longer route round the edge of the moor which would put another hour on the journey, or go up across the moor and down the old drove road with the risk of getting stuck in a drift. He wound down the window and stuck his head out. 'Not too bad,' he thought and considering the state of the engine decided on the latter course.

The lorry ground through the gears on the long climb to the top road. Tregarth frowned as the windscreen wipers worked hard to clear the two triangles of visibility in front of him. He glanced in the mirror at the line of headlights behind, most drivers having given up the attempt to pass. 'You'll have to bloody wait,' he growled, changing down again as he felt the wheels begin to spin. He gritted his teeth and concentrated on the road ahead, cursing the fact that he had never bothered to repair the defunct cab heater. As he rubbed one hand against his thigh he vowed never to go to Five Oaks sale again. 'Keep going damn you, keep going!' He gripped the steering wheel with both hands and stared anxiously into the whiteness ahead.

The vehicle was barely moving as the spinning wheels showered a following car with slush. Gradually the brow of the hill sank below the level of the radiator cap till at last the steaming bonnet pointed skywards and with a final revving of the engine they passed the summit. 'Whew!' In spite of the cold Tregarth tipped back his cap and wiped his brow. 'Well done old girl,' he patted the dashboard affectionately. 'You'll get us there yet.' He stopped talking to concentrate on a series of hair pin bends all the while peering ahead for the turning that would lead to Blackaford and home.

The signposts were partly obscured by the drifting snow. He slowed down, unsure of the precise turning and eventually choosing one that looked vaguely familiar. After half a mile he stopped: the road was going up when it should have been a level run until a mile before the village and this one was definitely going up, not only that but just ahead looked very steep indeed. 'Oh Christ!' he groaned, 'it's the wrong bloody road.' He looked in his mirrors: there was no hope of turning. He accelerated to get a run at the hill, the back wheels slewed as the cab reached the crest; the lorry hung on the brow and for a moment he thought they were going to make it, then the forward momentum was lost and it gradually slid backwards to come to rest half way down the hill.

'Oh shit!' He switched off the engine staring vacantly at the snow piling up on the bonnet. 'What a bloody awful place to get stuck with a load of horses,' he groaned and sat for several minutes wondering what to do. Outside the cab a mass of white swirled and settled to obliterated the landscape and he knew it would not be long before the drifting snow filled the roadway to the level of the hedgebanks: nothing on wheels would get through that night. He was considering whether or not to stay put until morning when he heard the unmistakable thump of a horse's hoof striking half way up the back of the cab. At first the location of the noise did not register, then the thump came again and he realised it was much too high up to be the normal stamp of a restless animal. 'The roan mare,' he gasped and made a grab for the torch.

Quickly he leapt out of the cab and opened the side door. Mystery was laying on her side wedged against the far side of the lorry in such a position that she was unable to get her legs back under her to get up. Her struggles brought one hind foot crashing against the front partition at the level of a man's waist. He shone the torch into the compartment and cursed his luck as he saw it would be impossible to get the mare back on her feet without unloading the other horse. He scrambled to the back of the vehicle and let down the ramp. He led the chestnut out and tied him to the side of the lorry, then he took off his overcoat and put it over the animal's back. 'There you are old chap, that'll keep you a bit warmer and I'm not going to need it for a bit I can see that.' He clambered into the back where the mare lay and, carefully avoiding the thrashing legs, went to her head and took hold of the halter rope. 'Now then little lady we've got to get you up if we can before you do yourself an injury so let's get you away from that side for a start.' His voice seemed to calm the mare as he braced himself against the partition and began to pull; by the time her withers were clear he was soaked with sweat. He paused to mop his brow. 'So far so good, now for the difficult bit.' He folded the front legs into a natural lying position, grateful that she had given up thrashing about; then he moved to the other side of the animal and, bracing his feet against the side of the lorry began to push the withers in a rocking motion, at the same time talking to her softly. 'Come on little lady up you get…now then make an effort.' Then more urgently: 'That's it…. come on….hup…for Christ's sake hup.'

The forelegs were pushed out in front as the neck came up. Tregarth scrambled to the front to push the chest upwards. The mare grunted, made two attempts to brace her front legs and on the third lurched backwards and up to stand on four quivering legs. For a moment Tregarth stood with both hands under her chest hardly daring to believe that she could stand on her own. Slowly he relaxed and stepped back. 'Whoa now, steady, good girl.' He slumped against the side, felt in his jacket for the hip flask and took a long swig. 'Whew that's better. Come on let's see how you move.' He took hold of the halter rope and gently led her forward. 'Not too bad, but what the hell are we going to do with you now?'. He estimated that they were still at least ten miles from Greystone Barton: much too far for the mare to walk in her condition. He patted her neck. 'There must be a farm somewhere close where we can fix you up.' He tied her up, returned to the cab and picked up the old bridle that always hung behind the passenger seat. He adjusted it to fit the chestnut, put his overcoat back on and led the mare carefully down the ramp then, mounting the hunter, set off up the hill with Mystery plodding alongside.

It was slow going, for the chestnut's iron shod hooves were treacherous on the freezing snow. At the top of the hill the blizzard whipped the snow into a stinging white cloud so that it was difficult to see more than a few yards. They were now on the open moor and in danger of losing the road altogether when suddenly a signpost loomed out of the murk. The horizontal arms were unreadable but by the light of his torch he could just make out the words East….Cross on the upright post. 'East Moor Cross,' he muttered to himself. 'What a God forsaken place to end up in but at least we know where we are…' His reverie was interrupted by the roan mare which began plunging forward, eventually pulling the rope through his hands. 'Where the hell do you think you are off to', he yelled as she trotted off with ears pricked.

Tregarth put his heels to the chestnut and tried to follow, but the unshod hooves of the mare found a surer grip and she soon disappeared into the gloom. He steadied the hunter. 'Whoa, not so fast or we shall be arse over head.' He bent low over the horse's withers to follow the line of tracks where they turned to the right and led downhill. Tregarth cursed 'Damn the animal, seems hell bent in going somewhere, the question is where?

~

CHAPTER 7

Tina gazed at the flakes lodging against the outside of the window frames. She felt stiff and cold despite the single bar electric fire which seemed only to emphasise the chill when she moved more than three feet from it. Her eyes wandered from the window to the bureau and from there to the telephone. 'Well at least there is contact with the outside world,' she thought. 'Perhaps Gloria could get someone out: they must have tractors that could get through a few inches of snow.' She went over and lifted the receiver, listened for a moment then slammed it down: it was dead. She tried her mobile but there was no signal.

Tina fought back the panic as she walked into the kitchen to look for something to make a cup of tea. There was a blackened kettle on top of the cooker and after a good deal of rummaging in the cupboards she found some tea in a biscuit tin. There was a tiny drop of milk in the bottom of the bucket on the table but it did not look very drinkable and in any case it was certainly not pasteurised. She poured it down the sink and settled for tea with no milk as she held the kettle under the tap, then remembering the water was turned off went to find the stopcock again.

The brass tap banged and chortled as a stream of none too clear water splashed into the sink. In a few minutes the kettle was singing while the glowing cooker ring gave some warmth to the kitchen. She began to think it would not be too bad after all. Even as the thought went through her mind the light flickered and went out. She watched horrified as the red glow of the cooker slowly faded. 'Oh my God,' she groaned. 'Meter... is it on a meter?' She looked round but could see no further than the table. 'Even if it is I'll never find the damned thing in the dark.' She groped her way back to the living room where the fire was dying to a dull orange and pulling her coat close round her, curled up in the arm chair and closed her eyes.

The snow muffled all sounds from outside save the low moan of the wind in the chimney. Tina had a strange feeling that reality was slipping away, that in the dark and cold anything could happen, but what she had no idea. 'It's so damned quiet,' she thought, then repeated it out loud: 'It's so damned quiet!'

Something flopped into her lap; she screamed, only to find the ginger cat scrambling onto the arm of the chair. 'Come on, Tina Pendogget, what's the matter with you? Surely you, above all people are not going to pieces just because you are on your own. That would please the chauvinist in Hugh.' She could hear his taunts: 'And what was that about women being equal to men…when the chips are down….you can't go against nature….' Well it was all right for him, he had never been stuck on his own on Bodmin Moor in the depths of winter. The though of him in his frilly apron trying to cope cheered her momentarily. 'Wimbledon just does not prepare you for situations like this,' she told herself, kicking off her boots to pull her numbed feet up under her body.

Gradually she sank into a fitful doze, a half-dream state where Hugh stood helpless in waist high snow while she was skidding towards him in the car suddenly to be confronted by a man on a black horse. The horse reared and snorted and she woke with a start. The snort came again but this time it was real. Tina got up and peered out of the window. 'My God,' she said struggling into her boots, 'there is something out there.'

Tina stumbled closer to the window to get a better look but whatever it was it had gone on towards the farm buildings leaving a trail of footprints in the snow. As she watched a second shape materialised through the grey swirling flakes. The black silhouette of a horseman, like a phantom of some bygone age, halted outside the window. She could feel the rider's eyes peering at her through the naked glass, then silent as a shadow the shape drifted on to merge with the darkness. She stared at the tracks as the snow slowly erased them and wondered whether to rush out and shout for help. Perhaps it was merely some sort of snow mirage, an hallucination brought on by cold and hunger? Even as she watched the marks disappeared as though to confirm the uncertainty, leaving her bewildered as the confusion of dream and reality grew.

She was jerked out of her mental dilemma by a loud banging on the back door. 'Well that was real enough,' she told herself with a mixture of reassurance and apprehension. There was a moment's hesitation while the banging persisted, then it stopped and Tina heard the door knob turn and the scrape as it opened. She bent down, picked up the poker from the fireplace and waited. A man's voice called 'Is there anyone at home?'

Tina did not answer, then told herself that she was being quite silly. If this was the phantom horseman then he was obviously lost and the least she could do was allow him some shelter; nevertheless she kept hold of the poker as she replied, 'In here, who is it?' The tone was as matter-of-fact as she could make it

There was the sound of heavy footsteps and a torch beam swung across the room and onto her face. She squinted and held a hand to her eyes. 'The electricity has gone off, we are completely blacked out.' She emphasised the we and hoped it sounded convincing.

'Does your phone work?' the voice asked.

'No. Look, would you mind switching off that torch?'

'Damn! Where am I?' Tregarth asked directing the beam round the room.

'Hendra, Pendogget's farm.'

There was a long silence and Tina heard him whistle through his teeth. 'Byron Pendogget?' he asked slowly.

'That's right, I'm his daughter.'

Another long silence and the torch light rested on her face again.

'Good God! You're the woman who nearly ran me down yesterday.'

Tina relaxed a little, at least she knew who she was talking to. 'Ah, so it's Mr. Tregarth.' There was an edge to her voice but she let the poker slip to the floor.

'That's right,' he sounded uneasy. 'Where is your father?'

She hesitated. 'He's not here, I just came over to tidy things up and got stuck. My father is…..'

'Oh,' Tregarth cut in and Tina thought she detected a hint of relief. It puzzled her but before she could ask any questions he went back into the kitchen where she could hear him rummaging around. 'You should have started a fire,' he said throwing a pile of old newspapers in front of the fireplace. 'Make some paper sticks while I get some wood.'

'Make what?'

'Oh, come on, I'll show you.' He rolled a newspaper then twisted it into a knot. 'There, make three or four of those.' He threw her the torch, 'and when you've done that go and find some matches, there must be some about somewhere.'

Tina bit her lip but found herself doing as she was told, telling herself that a man with so few social graces was just not worth picking an argument with. When the sticks were made she went into the kitchen and found a box of matches next to a stub of candle on the windowsill. By the time Tregarth returned with an armful of wood, she had lit the candle and stuck it into the brick fender with its own melted wax. He made no comment but laid the fire and put a match to it.

As the flames grew, Tina had the first opportunity to study the man. He stood leaning against the fireplace, the light flickering across his face as he looked into the blaze. He was tall, the long shapeless overcoat hung on a lean frame and as he took off his cap she noticed that the unruly mop of dark hair was greying at the temples. It was not a handsome face but there was strength and determination about it which was accentuated by the occasional clenching of the face muscles as though biting on something. She judged him to be about forty.

'Lucky I found the candle,' she said trying to make some sort of conversation. 'I expect the electricity often fails out here.'

Tregarth either did not hear or did not wish to reply, instead he squatted to move a piece of wood into the flames, remaining on his haunches until it crackled. The overcoat steamed, smelling of horses 'and heaven knows what else' Tina thought. He straightened up and looked at her. 'You say old Byron's not here,' he said quietly.

'Yes, he's had to go into hospital for a few days. Why, do you know him?'

He turned his gaze back to the fire. 'I suppose he's never told you.'

She pulled the armchair closer and sat down. 'Told me what?'

'Oh nothing. Better come from him, it was all a long time ago anyway.' He moved an ember with his boot and watched the sparks drift up the chimney

Tina tried hard to dislike this man but found it difficult; he was boorish, ill mannered and had been the cause of her damaging an expensive car: she ought to hate his guts. 'Do you know you nearly wrecked my car?' she said. 'I hope you are insured otherwise I've a mind to sue you for damages.'

'You can try,' he retorted dryly.

Before she could think of a reply, he picked up the torch and went through into the hall. 'I need to borrow some blankets,' he called back. 'Mind if I get some from upstairs?'

'Help yourself,' she told him and added quietly, 'as if anything I might say would stop you.'

She heard his footsteps ascend the stairs and he returned a few minutes later with an armful of blankets. 'I'm sure old Byron won't mind, it's all in a good cause.' He selected four of the best and instead of offering at least one to her he rolled them all under his arm and reached for the torch. 'Don't let the fire out,' he grunted as he pulled on his cap and made for the back door.

Tina heard the now familiar scrape as the door opened and with a puzzled shake of the head picked up one of the rejected blankets, wrapped it round her and settled back into the chair. 'Well, at least it's warmer,' she thought, 'but lord knows where old sore head has gone.' The warmth was relaxing, her eyes closed and a wisp of hair fell across her face.

The sound of the back door opening jerked her into consciousness. She looked at the fire: it had reduced to a tiny orange glow. 'Oh my God, I've let it out,' she muttered as she got up to throw a log on the embers. Melting snow hissed as a cloud of steam and smoke billowed into the room. She was acutely aware the Tregarth was watching her; she waited for the tirade and was surprised when he merely walked past to kneel on the hearth and blow on the dying embers until they flickered into life. Without a word, he fed the flame with small pieces of half charred wood until once more the room danced in firelight.

She thought of apologising but decided it would be too demeaning; there was no reason why she should have to feel guilty, after all this was her father's house. Tregarth stood up and took off his wet overcoat , hung it on the back of a chair in front of the fire and loosened his neck scarf; then he snuffed out the candle with a curt 'we may need that,' before sitting down on a straight backed chair at the other side of the fireplace. Tina could not see whether his eyes were closed or not; he did not speak, neither did he move for what seemed an eternity. Eventually she could stand it no longer.

'You haven't told me how you come to be here,' she said tucking the blanket tightly round her legs.

He explained the events of the afternoon in a very few words.

'And the blankets?'

He grunted. 'That old barn is damned draughty and one horse has a thin coat and the little blue roan mare is not too bright. I want to get her looked at by a vet a soon as possible but in any case   both of 'em could do with a bit of extra warmth.'

Tina looked up. 'Did you say blue roan?'

'Yes that's right, why?'

'Oh nothing, it's just that my father was worried about a blue roan filly or something.'

Tregarth grunted again but said nothing as he bent down to pull off his boots and she noticed that he had a hole in his sock. 'Won't your wife be worried?' she asked

'What makes you think I have a wife?' His voice sounded strangely soft.

'I know you have a son.'

He nodded and fell silent once more. Tina was about to ask how old the boy was when he suddenly said, 'She's dead'.

It was such an abrupt statement that Tina was taken aback. 'Oh, I'm sorry,' she said.

'That's alright.'

She waited for some sort of elaboration but it did not come. The fire blazed momentarily. 'I remember it like this when I was a little girl,' she said in an effort to make conversation.

Tregarth did not respond immediately but leant forward to poke the fire with the poker which he had found on the floor by his chair. He watched the sparks and then said 'I don't remember you around, I always thought the old boy lived alone.'

'My mother and I left when I was five and I've only been back once. I'm afraid I lost touch after that, you know how it is.'

He poked the fire more vigorously. 'No, I don't know how it is. Seems to me poor old Byron drew a duff hand all round.'

Tina bristled and was about to ask what it had to do with him when a sudden gust of wind blew down the chimney, scattering a cloud of grey ash across the threadbare carpet. Tregarth looked out of the window. 'Wind's getting worse,' he said. 'Pity anyone with sheep out on the moor, there will be a lot buried in drifts by morning.' He shook his head. 'Haven't seen anything like this since the winter of ninety five.'

Tina thought for a moment. 'I'm sure my father's are still up there, I recall the postman mentioning it. I'm afraid everyone was too busy to worry about their own animals to see to ours.'

The hours slipped out almost unwittingly and she liked the sound of it.

Tregarth got up and walked over to the window. 'How many are there?'

'I don't know.'

'Well, how big is the farm?'

'About a hundred acres I think.'

He thought for a moment. 'With moorland grazing, there could be over a hundred up there. We ought to be able to find most of 'em. Chances are he's been feeding them and weather like this they tend to gather near the moor gates.'

Tina looked up in astonishment. 'You don't mean to say you are going out there in weather like this just for a lot of sheep.'

He gave a grunt of disgust. 'They may be just sheep to you, Miss Pendogget, but they are your father's livelihood and losing any of them and the lambs they carry could spell heartbreak and ruin. Any flockmaster would do the same and that includes your father if the situation were reversed. In any case after all these years you owe him something, perhaps we both do, so are you coming or not?' He was already pulling on his boots and she reluctantly did the same and prepared to follow him out.

He handed her a yellow plastic So'wester he found hanging in the porch. 'Here, put this on, it'll keep your head dry.' There was a collection of crooks in one corner, one of which he selected for himself and another for Tina. 'Stop you going arse over head down the slopes,' he said prodding his into the snow to test the depth. 'Hmm, a level nine inches, that means there could be drifts up to three feet by now, so follow close behind me.'

Before leaving the shelter of the buildings, he turned to her and asked if she knew the layout of the farm. She shook her head. He muttered something about her being a bloody lot of use and set off up the track beyond the building. She tugged at his arm. 'I remember this leads to the moor,' she shouted.

He nodded. 'Come on then, and look out for tractor ruts, use your crook to test the ground.' Before she could follow his advice, her foot slipped from under her and as the wind threw her off balance, she grabbed at the overcoat in front of her. Tregarth spun round to catch her by the arm; the strength of his grip made her wince. 'Sorry,' he said relaxing his hold, then added softly, 'take care and follow close.' He held her arm for a moment longer before turning to set off up the track. It ran between two drystone walls where the snow was already up to the top of Tina's boots. Tregarth strode on while she did her best to follow in his footsteps.

'In his master's steps he trod where the snow lay dinted,' she croaked grimly as the effort of putting one foot in front of the other became increasingly painful. By the time they reached the moor gate, she was exhausted. Tregarth was leaning over it peering into the darkness, swinging the beam of his torch backwards and forwards across the snow.

'Can't see a damned thing,' he yelled above the sound of the wind as Tina arrived breathless. He gave her the torch. 'Here, take this and go that way along the wall and I'll go the other way. If you see them, flash it. By the way, do you know if your father works a dog, I didn't see one at the farm?'

Tina pushed back the flaps of the So'wester. 'Sorry, I couldn't hear that.' He repeated his words and she nodded. 'Okay, yes he does have a collie but it's not here now so why do you ask?'

'Can you whistle, you know, loud enough to get a taxi in London?'

She shrugged. 'I think so. Why?'

'Well it's like this,' he shouted opening the gate. 'Sheep that are used to being moved with a dog will usually respond to the sound of a whistle. Any sort of whistle will make them bunch up. That way, we ought to spot them even in this.' He put two fingers to his mouth and blew a shrill note that could just be heard above the storm; almost immediately several humps of snow came to life, shook themselves and began moving towards the gate. 'See what I mean? We'll try and get round them,' he said as he moved off into the darkness.

Tina stayed until she could no longer hear the occasional whistle, then began her circuit along the wall. She tried to whistle: the effort was puny compared with Tregarth's, nevertheless it succeeded in animating a snowy mound a few feet away. The torchlight was reflected in two startled eyes as the animal gave a bleat of alarm and made off towards the gate followed by several more of the flock. Tina felt a glow of satisfaction as one by one she saw the animals come to life, shake themselves and struggle off towards safety and the prospect of food. When she judged she had gone far enough, she turned at right angles to the wall and began a wide arc back towards the gate, flashing the torch as she went. Almost immediately she stepped into a snow filled gully up to her armpits. The shock left her gasping and it was several seconds before she could muster a cry for help but the sound was lost in the wind. She turned round and tried to clamber out but the sides were sheer and the was nothing to grip and pull herself up. The more she struggled, the deeper she sank into the snow and what was worse she had dropped the torch. 'Oh God! How the hell do I get out of this?' The utterance was almost a prayer.

She stopped struggling and began to assess the situation more calmly. 'Don't worry,' she told herself, 'he's bound to come looking for you. Try and find the torch….must find the torch.' Desperately she felt round the edge of the gully, then took off one glove and tried again. She felt something hard and retrieved the crook then used it to sweep an arc around the hole until she felt it touch something hard. Carefully she drew the object towards her, pressing her face against the freezing snow to reach out further until her hand closed over a cold smooth barrel of metal. 'Thank God,' she muttered pulling it to her to check that it was still working.

For what seemed an eternit,y she waived the beam backwards and forwards, shouting until she was hoarse and her teeth chattered so much that the sound was stifled. 'Surely he can't have gone away without me,' she thought in a sudden wave of panic. 'No one, even Tregarth, would do that.'

'What the hell are you doing down there?' The voice was calm and reassuring as Tina looked up at the figure standing by the gully.

'I thought I would see what it was like to be up to my neck in freezing snow, so I jumped into the nearest hole,' she replied wiping the snow from her face.

'Well now you know, we had better see about getting you out, unless of course you would like to stay there and watch the dawn come up as well.' He reached down and gripped her forearm. Tina handed him the torch and held on with both hands as he slowly pulled her out. Together they brushed the snow from her coat and jeans as she stood shivering by the hole her body had made in the drift. Tregarth took her by the elbow. 'Come on we had better get you back to the house.' They started to trudge towards the gate. 'You did a good job there,' he said; Tina got the impression he was laughing at her.

'What do you mean?' she asked indignantly.

'All that shouting and hollering and waiving the torch. I counted at least sixty old ewes coming from your direction, all scared out of their wits and going hell for leather through the gate towards the farm. I reckon we've got somewhere between seventy and eighty which is not bad considering the conditions and most of it is due to your antics in that gully.'

'It's not funny,' she retorted. 'I might have died of exposure in there.'

'True, but you didn't. We'll leave the gate open and any stragglers will catch up.'

They walked the rest of the way in silence, following the last of the sheep down the track. By the time they reached the yard, it was full of bleating snow-caked animals. 'Right!' Tregarth yelled above the din, 'let's get them some grub.' He pushed through them to the stone steps that led up to the hay loft and a few moments later was throwing down hay bales. 'Come on, keep moving or you'll freeze to death standing around there. Help me spread these round the yard.'

Tina did as she was told, dragging the heavy bales while Tregarth cut the strings and scattered the fodder. By the time the job was finished even her feet began to feel warm as she followed him into the barn below the loft. The beam of the torch showed two horses tethered at the far end where a layer of straw had been put down on the concrete floor. The blankets had been thrown over their backs and tied round with baling string.

'A bit makeshift, I'm afraid,' Tregarth commented, 'but at least they are warm and dry.' Tina noticed that only one animal appeared to be eating the hay he had put in front of them, while the other stood dejectedly in the corner hardly moving. When she remarked on the fact, he grunted apprehensively. 'She's got chilled, I suspect. I'm afraid she wasn't in very good shape to start with, poor devil. Here, hold this.' He handed her the torch and began to readjust the filly's blankets, all the while talking softly in a half audible whisper as his large hands caressed the drooping neck with a gentleness that surprised Tina. He selected a handful of hay and offered it to the animal without success. 'They will have to do until morning,' he said sadly as they went out and closed the doors.

Inside the house, it was warm compared with the temperature outside inspite of the fact that the fire was nearly out and once more Tregarth had to get down on his hands and knees to blow it into life. When it was well ablaze, he turned to her. 'Right, get your clothes off,' he said unbuttoning his overcoat.

'I beg your pardon?' Tina backed away with a puzzled look of alarm.

He frowned, then with the ghost of a smile said, 'No, not that, you daft woman. You are soaking wet so get 'em off and put 'em by the fire before you catch your death. Wrap the blanket round yourself till they get dry.' She hesitated and he picked up the poker and gave it to her. 'Here, keep this by you if you like but I've got things to do outside so you'll be quite safe.' He grinned as he went through the door to the kitchen and she heard him mutter, 'No, certainly not that.'

She jerked off her sopping coat and threw it angrily on the floor conscious of her soggy look and bedraggled hair. 'No, certainly not that,' she mimicked. 'Who the hell does he think he is?'

By the time he returned, she was hunched in the arm chair, wrapped in the blanket with just her knickers and bra on and feeling like some dowdy Indian squaw. The rest of her clothes were draped round the fire on any convenient piece of furniture. He passed them without a glance to drop an armful of logs into the fireplace. 'You've abandoned the poker then,' he said picking up the implement from the floor and putting it back in the hearth. Tina did not reply but snuggled deeper into the chair with a tight grip on the blanket. He grinned and went out again.

When he returned, he was carrying a bucket half full of fresh milk which he placed by the fire. 'There was a cow that needed milking,' he said tersely. 'Would you like some?'

Tina looked at the steaming liquid with obvious distaste. 'I don't think we should drink raw milk,' she said as he fetched two cups from the kitchen.

Treagrth gave an explosive 'Ah!' poured a cupful and gulped it down. 'Don't tell me you believe those idiots who tell you that practically everything you eat or drink is bad for you.' He poured a second cup, pulled out the whisky flask and added a generous measure of the liquor. 'Here, drink this,' he said, 'the booze will kill off most of the bugs and make you sleep into the bargain,' He held out the cup and she eyed it for several seconds before taking it. The rich, warm liquid still tasted of cow in spite of the whisky and brought back memories of a skinny girl of ten watching her father milk and being given a half-pint measure brimming with warm froth. How horrified her mother had been when she learned that her daughter had been give raw milk.

'Are you hungry?' Tregarth's voice cut through her thoughts. He had taken off his overcoat and jacket and was hanging them among her clothes by the fire. Suddenly she realised how hungry she was and nodded. He picked up the torch and went out into the kitchen to return a few minutes later with a tin of luncheon meat and some biscuits. Tina eyed the meat but said nothing about being a vegetarian if only because it seemed quite ludicrous in the circumstances. He opened the tin and gave her half its contents and half the biscuits.

Tregarth ate his standing and she became acutely aware that he was watching her intently. The blanket had slipped from her shoulder exposing the soft roundness of her breast. She pulled the blanket closer without looking at him and continued her meal. He shifted his gaze to the fire. 'You had better get dressed,' he said quietly. 'It will get cold in the night. I'm going to have a last look round.'

Grudgingly, Tina did as she was told. Her jeans and the rest of her clothes were still slightly damp but at least they were warm and by the time Tregarth returned she had settled into the chair and was once more dozing comfortably. Twice in the night she opened her eyes to see him in the same place gazing into the fire as a fresh log blazed. Once she heard the back door scrape and looked at her watch: half past three and she wondered what he could be doing at that hour. She did not hear him return but sensed him moving about the room and went back to sleep.

When daylight came, she woke stiff and cold. The fire was nearly out and she looked round expecting to see Tregarth but he was not there; instead there was a note written in pencil on the back of an envelope and placed on the seat of the chair opposite, it read simply: 'Will send help.' She went to the window and saw a fresh line of tracks leading from the barn to the farm road and on up the hill. 'Well I'll be....' she said out loud as she pulled on her boots, 'he might have said something.' She yawned and stretched: it seemed that every muscle in her body ached. The bathroom was much the same as she remembered as she douched the ice cold water over her face, then feeling reasonably refreshed she prepared to leave.

Outside the morning was bright and clear. The wind had dropped and there was a sparkle about everything as she stepped out into the snow nearly to the top of her boots. The sheep called to each other as they stood in little groups round the scattered wads of hay which had been put out quite recently. She carefully picked her way through them and the other animals. It was obvious Tregarth had fed them before he left. The barn where the horses had been was empty and the blankets neatly folded and left on a bale. She picked them up and wondered what Gloria and the customers of the Fox and Hounds would think if they learned that she had spent the night with John Tregarth. She shrugged. 'So what, anyway I don't suppose our paths will cross again,' she told herself.

The sun rose over a white wilderness, touching the farm roofs with pink and setting the eaves to drip. Shadows were crisp and blue on the softened contours of the moor and all was silent save for the plaintive mew of a buzzard as it soared in the blue sky. Tina looked at her watched and thought of the hordes of pale-faced commuters who, at about this time, disappeared into London's underground system to re-emerge eight hours later dull eyed and weary. By now Wimbledon would be a sea of slush, a maelstrom of skidding lorries and traffic jams, while well dressed wives picked their way along carefully cleared pathways to avoid wetting their expensive suede boots. 'I wonder what Hugh is doing?' she thought as she walked back to the house.

The ginger cat appeared from nowhere as Tina pushed open the back door. It followed her round as she tidied the room and put out the used blankets to be cleaned. It rubbed against her boots, purring with pleasure at the presence of a human being. She gave it some milk, poured the rest down the sink and washed the bucket, then she turned off the water, put the cat outside and went to inspect her car.

It took several minutes to brush the snow from the windscreen and get the door open; eventually she was able to get into the driver's seat and after the minimum of trouble started the engine. She sat for a while as it ticked over and the heater's warmth permeated her aching limbs. She was just wondering how she was going to get the vehicle out when she heard the unmistakable sound of a tractor coming down the road. A few minutes later a large red machine with four enormous wheels appeared round the bend stern first and stopped a few feet away from the front of the Porsche. A large middle aged man clambered down, walked over and introduced himself as Joel Menheniot.

'John Tregarth called me out at crack o' dawn this morning to pull his lorry up the hill. He said you would be needing a hand to get up the track.'

'Yes, that's very kind of you.'

'Think nothing of it,' he said as he attached a tow rope.

'Many's the time your father has helped me out of a hole so it's the least I could do.' He had fixed the other end of the rope to the tow bar of the tractor and was standing smiling at her. 'You don't remember me, I suppose?'

Tina shook her head. 'No, I'm afraid, you see….'

'Oh I know, you needn't explain. You were only a little girl when I lent Byron a pony for you to ride.'

She thought for a moment. 'Rusty, that was his name. Yes, I do remember, and Mrs. Menheniot brought over a cake with cherries on it.' She laughed and took his hand to shake it. 'It's lovely to see you again.'

He was obviously pleased and gripped her hand between both of his. 'And how is your father?' he asked anxiously.

'Quite comfortable, I think. Of course, he worries about the farm but I tried to reassure him as best I could but you know what he's like.'

Joel patted her hand. 'Don't you worry about a thing, m'dear. We'll take care of all that and I'll get in to see him as soon as this lot is over. In the meantime, we'd better get you on your way.' He grinned and climbed into the tractor cab. 'They've got the snow plough as far as the lower Blackaford so I'll tow you as far as there, okay?'

Tina nodded and gripped the wheel with both hands as he eased the big machine forwards. There was a sudden jerk and a scraping sound as they began to move. Joel opened the throttle and the diesel engine roared as the car lurched out of the gully and onto the track then they started the slow grinding journey to the junction with the Blackaford road. It took half an hour to reach the cleared part; Joel unhooked the tow rope and backed his machine onto the verge so that Tina could get past. She got out of the car and walked over to him. 'Can I pay you for the fuel or something?'

He frowned 'That's not necessary, young lady. As I said, your father would have done the same for me.' He put the tractor into gear and moved off.

Tina shrugged and got back into the car. 'Oh dear, I hope I haven't offended him,' she said to herself as the car slowly made progress over the candled snow. By the time she had covered the ten miles to Blackaford, she was physically and mentally exhausted. Explanations to Gloria were brief and left the landlady plenty to ponder over while Tina had a hot bath and went to bed.

～

CHAPTER 8

John Tregarth arrived at Greystone weary and disgruntled, to be greeted in the stable yard by Thomas Bolitho who was sweeping snow from the front of a range of loose-boxes. 'And what sort of hour do you call this to be getting back?' the stud groom demanded.

'Never mind about that Thomas, I'll tell you later.' He strode over to the boxes and began to walk down them. 'Have we got a couple empty? I've bought two and one will need looking at.'

Thomas nodded. 'The one down the end and I can shift the bay mare out of the one next to the tack room.'

'Good, come and give me a hand to unload.'

They walked to where Tregarth had parked the lorry and Thomas let down the tailboard. 'Well, let's see what we've got then,' he said stepping up into the back. He studied the purchases with a critical eye. 'Chestnut looks useful but what on earth possessed you to buy the mare. You'll be lucky if she lasts long enough to get a vet out to her.' He shook his head dolefully. 'In the ten years I've been your stud groom, aye and twenty years before that for your father, I've never seen anything like that come home from a sale. Best get her into the warm and call Mr. Beresford a bit sharp.'

Tregarth began to lead the chestnut down the ramp. 'Oh come on Thomas she's not as bad as all that. Bring her down and I'll get on the phone as soon as I get in.'

The stud groom muttered something inaudible, gently led his charge into the vacant box and went to fetch corn and hay for both animals while his employer walked to the house, his long overcoat trailing in the deep untrodden snow and his hands deep in his pockets. As soon as he turned the corner a slight dark haired youth emerged from the tack room, went over to Mystery's box and looked over the door. Thomas came behind with a bucket of oats. 'Now don't you be getting in my way young Nocholas, I can't be doing with hindrances when there's work to be done, so off you go now.' The youth opened the door and watched as the feed was put into the manger. 'That one doesn't look very well.' he said as Thomas came out.

The stud groom snorted. 'Well it doesn't take a genius to see that,' he said brushing past. 'And if you've got nothing better to do you can go and fetch some hot water and we'll make her a hot bran mash.'

Nicholas hesitated a moment then walked off in the direction of the house; he knew better than to cross Thomas when he was in that sort of mood. Being referred to as Nicholas instead of the usual Nick was a sure sign that he had to tread carefully. When he returned with the water Thomas was putting a warm rug on the mare and was just buckling up the straps. 'There, that's better m'dear,' he said soothingly. 'Right Nick let's get that bran mash.' They went over to the feed store and Thomas measured a bowl of bran, mixed it with the hot water and gave it to Nick. 'Here, make yourself useful and put that in her manger.'

Thomas was fetching hay when Nick came over to him. 'I think you had better come,' he said leading the way back to the box. Mystery lay stretched out on the floor, her flanks heaving and giving a low grunt at each breath. 'Damn!' Thomas said quietly and went over to examine her more closely.

Nick leant over the door. 'What do you reckon is the matter with her?'

The stud groom knelt down to listen to the breathing. 'Pneumonia I shouldn't wonder. The sooner Beresford gets here the better, in the mean time straighten up that rug while I fetch a bale of straw.'

Nick did as he was asked but would have preferred to leave the situation to others. Getting involved could mean pain and grief and he had experienced all that too many times before. 'You'll probably die,' he said shaking his head. 'They'll pump you full of drugs and stuff but still you'll probably die.' He had an overwhelming urge to quit then but Thomas returned with the straw before he could escape. The bale was placed next to the mare's withers. 'Now boy, when I lift her shoulders you shove the bale behind 'em understand? Right now, one two three push!'

Together they managed to wedge her in a semi upright position and Thomas stepped back approvingly. 'There, that's better, don't do for 'em to be stretched out too long; next thing is to get some nourishment in her and that's going to be tricky if we drench her, d'yer know why?'

The youth nodded. 'In case it goes into the lungs.'

'That's right, well done, we'll make something of you yet. So it means a little and often and I haven't got time just now and neither has your father, so that leaves you. I know you can do it because I watched your mother show you with that grey pony of yours.'

'You mean the one that died?'

Thomas frowned. 'Now if you start with that attitude you might just as well give up now and put her out of her misery with a bullet. So which is it?'

Nick looked at the mare as she lay with her nose resting on the straw bedding. He was trapped and knew he would have to battle against the old enemy win or lose. He nodded and slowly moved towards Mystery.

Thomas grinned. 'Proper job, I'll mix up some of my special jollop and we'll see how you get on.'

Nick sat on the bale and watched as the dull eyes closed and the fine pointed ears drooped back in an attitude of utter dejection. He listened to the laboured breathing and knew that the battle was already half lost. Now he was committed to join the struggle on the side of life and realised it was going to be a hard one. 'Don't you dare die,' he said between clenched teeth. 'Don't you dare.' He slipped onto his knees and gently massaged some warmth into the damp, cold ears as he had often seen his father do when horses came in cold from hunting. The mare responded by lifting her head to rest her nose on his thigh with a long appreciative grunt. He looked up to see Thomas' face over the stable door. The old groom had been watching quietly and nodded his approval. 'That's right boy, a little comforting, that's what she's needing. Now let's try and get something in her.'

'Give it to me, I'll do it,' Nick said with a firmness that caused Thomas to raise one eyebrow. He went in and handed over the drenching bottle without a word, then stepped back into the corner while Nick lifted the mare's head with one hand and gently forced the neck of the bottle between the jaws with the other. His mother's words came back to him: '…behind the front teeth and in front of the grinders…pour slowly and give time to swallow… feed it not drown it…' It took all of twenty minutes to get the pint of liquid down the animal's gullet; despite his care a large proportion of it spilled down his arm to soak his shirt, sweater and jacket in warm sticky fluid. When he looked up Thomas had gone.

Nick felt a glow of satisfaction. Deep down he valued the stud groom's esteem and Thomas for his part did his best to understand the sensitive youngster who sometimes behaved like a rebellious colt and at other times showed wisdom and understanding far beyond his years. The glow was short lived as he heard his father's voice across the yard. 'Vet's on the way Thomas, how is she?'

'Not too good John, but she's in good hands.'

'What do you mean, in good hands?'

'Young Nick has taken it on, he's in with her now.'

'Good Lord, wonders will never cease. Don't tell me he's actually being useful for once. This I've got to see.'

Nick heard the crunch of approaching footsteps and looked up to see his father's silhouette in the doorway.

'Are you coping alright, Nick?'

The youth nodded and continued with the task of cleaning himself with a wisp of straw.

There was an awkward silence before Tregarth said, 'I'm going to check the ewes if you need me.' Another nod and almost imperceptibly a return nod from his father as he turned away.

Nick stood up and went out into the yard where Thomas was mucking out one of the boxes. He straightened up and leant on the fork. 'Well?'

The youth shrugged. 'I got it down her without choking.'

'Good, and what did your father say?'

'Nothing much.'

Thomas looked him up and down. 'You know boy, you'd get on better if you got a decent hair cut instead of going round looking like a bloody Nancy. Still, it's nothing to do with me.'

'You're too right it's not,' Nick retorted and immediately regretted saying it.

Thomas closed the box door, choosing to ignore the remark. 'I'm off now to give your father a hand, so you had better stay and look out for Mr. Beresford. No mooning about now and no sloping off, right?'

Nick frowned. 'Okay okay, I'll stick around but don't expect wonders, remember I'm the useless one of the outfit as dad keeps telling me.'

'That's silly talk,' Thomas said irritably. 'Sometimes I lose patience with you young Nicholas, now take these back to the tack room and do as I say.' He handed Nick the broom and muck fork and set off to follow Tregarth.

When he had put the tools away Nick returned to where his charge lay motionless save for the heaving flanks. He watched over the door for several minutes trying to detect some sign of an improvement but there was none. He turned and kicked at a pile of snow angrily; he made snowballs and threw them at the tack room door, then he stuffed his hands into his pockets and walked towards the house.

When he reappeared he was carrying a small sketch pad and a handful of coloured crayons.

He took them into the loose-box, sat down cross legged on the corner and became so engrossed in his drawing that he failed to hear the arrival of a vehicle in the yard.

Tom Beresford was a stocky, bustling man, ruddy complexioned with dark tired eyes that seemed to ponder everybody and everything as though searching for some deep hidden flaw. Already that morning he had wrestled with a difficult calving until his back ached and his legs felt like jelly. The calf was dead and the undersized heifer not far from it; he was less than pleased with his morning's work. Now he had driven five miles in appalling conditions and had only just made it up the drive. It was times like these that he longed for a cosy little town practice looking after old ladies' lap dogs and budgies.

He looked round the empty yard. 'As usual,' he thought, 'nobody about, they must think I'm a bloody clairvoyant.' He began to look in each of the loose-boxes until he reached the one containing the roan mare. For almost a full minute he watched the animal before going inside to set about taking temperature and pulse. It was only then that he noticed Nick who had remained silently sketching in the corner. 'Ah, there is somebody about then. Are you in charge, young man?'

Nick shrugged. 'I suppose so.'

'Well I don't need to tell you that we've got a sick horse on our hands and she's going to take quite a bit of nursing to pull through. Do you think you're man enough for the job?'

Nick stood up. 'I'll try,' he said quietly.

'Good I'll just fetch some stuff from the car, then I'll tell you what has to be done.'

He returned with some small bottles and a large packet which he placed on the straw bale, then he gave the mare two injections and turned to Nick. 'Here's what you do,' he picked up the packet, 'make up some of this and give it to her every four hours, you'll find the instructions inside. Can you do that? It means getting up through the night.'

The youth nodded and put down his sketch pad to take the packet.

'What have we here?' the vet asked picking up the drawing which depicted the recumbent horse. 'Hmm, not bad, you ought to take it up.'

Nick shook his head. 'Not a chance,' he said ruefully. 'Dad would do his nut if I even mentioned it.'

Beresford smiled. 'Yes, I can imagine,' he said putting the used syringes in a plastic bag and stuffing the antibiotic bottles into his mackintosh pocket. 'As far as the mare is concerned that's all we can do for now. If she gets any worse give me a ring, but in any case I'll be out first thing tomorrow. Nice looking animal it would be a pity to lose her.' He went out of the door bolting it behind him. 'See you in the morning then,' he called as he walked back to his car.

John Tregarth came up just as he was getting into the driving seat. 'Morning Tom.'

The vet grunted. 'Could be better.'

'You've seen the mare then, what do you think?'

Beresford thought for a moment. 'To tell you the truth John I'm not too optimistic. It's not so much the infection, the trouble is she's just got very weak, her resistance must be pretty low. You should have called me sooner old chap then I might have been able to do more. As it is it's the old T.L.C that's going to pull her through more than anything I've done.'

Tregarth was puzzled for a moment. 'Oh yes, Tender Loving Care.'

'That's right and that means it's down to that lad of yours if he is prepared to nurse her. Otherwise I don't give her more than a fifty fifty chance.' He started the engine and shifted into gear. 'Let's hope he's got the same touch as his mother eh?' He let out the clutch and carefully eased his way down the drive.

Tregarth watched the car until it disappeared round the curve of the drive. 'I don't think there's much chance of that,' he said quietly to himself. He turned and walked back to where Nick was putting the finishing touched to his drawing. As the sound of his father's footsteps came closer he quickly stuffed the pad inside his anorak and began adjusting the mare's rug.

'Tom Beresford says it's up to you,' his father said sharply. 'You know what to do?'

The youth nodded without looking up. There was a long silence before Tregarth added, 'let know if you want any help.'

Another nod.

'Good.'

Nick finished what he was doing and turned to speak but his father had gone. A few minutes later Thomas appeared. 'Better come and get some food Nick, we don't want Mabel on at us for letting it get cold.'

The midday meal at Greystone was taken in the large kitchen. It was a communal affair; Mabel Bolitho had made it quite clear that she could not cook and keep house and at the same time look after her husband in a separate establishment. 'Can't be in two places at once,' she had insisted, and so John Tregarth had long ago abandoned the master and servant relationship. It was the main meal of the day, evening dinner having degenerated into high tea augmented by a late cold supper. 'That's how it was in you grandfather's day and that's how it will be now,' Mabel had decreed, ignoring the fact that she was barely fourteen when he died and could hardly remember what he looked like let alone the household routine.

Nick ate in silence while his father and Thomas discussed the afternoon's work. Mabel presided over all, her sharp blue eyes darting from one to the other like a little grey bantam hen coddling her chicks. 'Now I want to see a clean plate from you Nicholas….More potatoes, Thomas?….What about you, John?'

Nick finished his meal and before Mabel could offer second helpings, was off into the kitchen to prepare the next drench for his patient. He quickly put on his outdoor clothes and hurried out to the stables. The mare had not moved, neither did she look up when he entered. Talking quietly all the time he gently forced the neck of the bottle between her jaws and let the warm sticky liquid trickle into her mouth. By the time it was gone he was stiff and cold but he stayed for nearly an hour coaxing the animal to eat the choicest bit of hay, a few oats or a horse nut. He even went outside for a handful of grass from under the snow but it was mostly in vain: the appetite had gone and she merely moved the offerings with her sensitive upper lip then let them fall through his fingers. It was a fruitless exercise but it made him feel he was at least doing something and he kept at it until it was nearly dark.

'Nick!' It was his father's voice from the kitchen door that roused him from a torpid doze. He got up stiffly, made a last adjustment to the horse rug and returned to the warmth of the house. The expected admonishment did not occur and he was surprised when all that was said was: 'Make sure you wrap up warm and remember, once you've done your job out there don't stay too long. Now come and have your tea and get warm.'

Nick took off his anorak and rubbed his numbed hands in front of the fire. 'I'm due to go out again around seven o'clock,' he said with a hint of authority.

His father smiled. 'Yes, I know son. I've been through it all many times.' He put a hand on the boy's shoulder. 'Don't be too cut up if it doesn't turn out the way you hope. It won't be your fault.'

Nick shrugged off the gesture. 'Okay, I know,' he said irritably.

John Tregarth watched him for a moment as he walked away to sit down at the table, then with a barely audible sigh he followed and sat opposite. Thomas came in and washed his hands at the sink. 'How many mares have been booked to Titan so far?' he asked as he pulled up a chair.

'Not enough,' Tregarth replied dolefully.

The stud groom stirred his tea, deep in thought. 'Trouble is we've had no winners from him yet and we can't expect breeders to fall over themselves to pay stud fees for an unknown quantity. If some of his progeny could just win a point-to-point or two it would be a start.'

'Well give him a chance, his stock have only been racing a couple of seasons and you can't expect miracles. Mind, we could do with one but we're not getting the quality mares yet; it's the old story: get one good dam to breed a winner and others will follow.'

Thomas nodded towards a faded photograph that hung on the wall next to the fireplace. 'We need another one like that, your father once told me that mare won more races in one season than most of 'em do in a lifetime.' He smiled wryly, 'and you know who's got the last of that line.'

His employer nodded. 'That reminds me, did I mention that the old boy is in hospital?'

'No, you only said about spending the night with his daughter,' Thomas said with a wide grin. 'And she's the last of the line.'

Tregarth was about to reply when Mabel pushed a large plate of bread and butter between the two men. 'That's quite enough of that talk Thomas,' she said sharply. 'You ought to know better and you are as bad John. What happened that night I suggest you keep to yourselves. I for one don't want to know and I certainly don't think you should talk about it at the meal table. Anyway, how is Byron Pendogget, nothing serious I hope?'

Tregarth was grinning. 'No Mabel as far as I know.'

'Is that the Mr. Pendogget grandad was always on about?' Nick asked.

His father nodded. 'The very same, and you'll be following him into hospital if you don't get some food down you, come on you've got a long night ahead.'

The youth poked at his plate of scramble eggs. 'I'm not hungry,' he said pushing his plate away.

'Oh come on Nick,' his father said angrily. 'How on earth do you expect to keep going if you don't eat?'

Nick flushed. 'I'll do it, just don't keep on about it.' He stood up. 'I'll be up in my room if anybody wants me.'

'Nick!' Tregarth spun round and made as though to follow him.

'Leave him be John,' Mabel said putting a hand on his arm. 'He's upset about something, best let him alone.'

Tregarth grunted. 'What did I do for God's sake, why go off in a huff like that? I only told him to eat his food. It's for the boy's own good and you should know that and not take his part every time.'

'Well he's only a boy John and…..'

'Only a boy nothing. When I was his age, I had to show a bit of respect.'

'When you were his age,' Thomas said quietly, 'you were away at boarding school.'

'That's right,' Tregarth said angrily 'and that's where he would be if they hadn't chucked him out.'

'They only suggested he would do better at home,' Mabel said calmly. 'nobody said anything about being chucked out as you put it.'

'Well it amounts to the same thing,' Tregarth growled.

'I reckon that mare is a thoroughbred or near enough,' said Thomas changing the subject quickly. 'Were there any papers?'

Tregarth shook his head. 'The chap said they had been lost and was too anxious to get rid of her to worry about that side of it; to tell you the truth all I wanted was to get the poor beast attended to as soon as possible. She looked too nice a mare to be put down just like that.'

Thomas grinned. 'I remember when you were not much older than young Nick you bid for a Dartmoor foal at the Ashburton sales, just because you thought it would go for cats meat. Your father always said you were a bit soft where horses were concerned.'

Tregarth frowned. 'There's no place for sentimentality nowadays Thomas, buying that animal was a gamble I admit but one that might just pay off.'

'If you say so John,' Thomas said and winked at Mabel.

They finished the rest of the meal in silence and while Mabel cleared the table the two men got up to make their way to the study. Tregarth picked up two glasses and pushed his chair back as a large black and tan hound brushed past Mabel its tail thrashing the table leg.

'And you can take that tike with you,' she said pointing to the dog. 'He does nothing but get in my way.'

Her employer grinned. 'Come on Talisman time to seek sanctuary.'

At nine o'clock Nick came down to the kitchen to mix the prescription, pausing on the way out to listen to the muffled conversation coming from behind the study door. He could make out his father's strident voice and Thomas' softer tone but what they were so earnestly discussing he could not make out except he could detect the two men were worried about something. 'But then they never tell me anything,' he muttered to himself as he went out the back door.

When he switched on the light in the loose-box he could see the mare had not moved since he left. He gave her the drench as before and to his horror as soon as he had finished she gave a shudder and slid from the supporting bale to lie full length as though dead. It took several agonising seconds for Nick to realise that the flanks were still faintly moving, the animal was still breathing. Quickly he folded the front legs under her as Thomas had shown him, then bracing his legs against the wall he tried to push the bale under her withers but after struggling for several minutes he realised he would need help.

His father was still in the study pouring over what looked like accounts. He looked up enquiringly.

'She's flat out and I can't get her up,' Nick explained, then added with a shrug, 'I reckon she'll be dead by the morning.'

Tregarth closed his eyes for a second then looked up at his son. 'Don't give up yet Nick,' he said intently. 'Never give up until it happens. Come on I'll give you a hand.'

Together they returned to the stables. 'Sometimes they'll stretch out like that to rest,' Tregarth said unconvincingly, 'but we had better prop her up again otherwise you won't be able to get Tom Beresford's magic mixture in her.' He grinned. 'Now, I'll get the withers up and you push the bale under her.'

Together they succeeded in returning the mare to her original position. 'Well done boy,' Tregarth said mopping his brow. 'It just takes a bit of team work. Come on, better get your head down for a few hours.'

As they walked back to the house Nick felt an unaccustomed glow; for once he had done something right it seemed. He ruffled Talisman's ears as he went up to his bedroom. He set the alarm for two o'clock, took off his sweater and trousers and got into bed. It seemed that his head hardly touched the pillow before the jangle woke him and he was fumbling for his clothes.

The night air was cold and he shivered until his body acclimatised to its bite. Snow crunched underfoot and the sound of a bullock's husky cough came from the cattle yards. Far up on the moor a fox barked. The familiar sounds were enhanced in the still, clear night: a Christmas card night where a frosted moon conjured up pale shadows, a night when anything might happen. He looked up at the stars. 'Just one small miracle,' he said softly, 'that's all we need, just one small miracle.' It was the nearest thing he had come to praying for a very long time.

Mystery was exactly as they had left her. One ear flicked slightly as he entered the box but otherwise she did not move. He took the warm drenching bottle from inside his coat and began the task of persuading her to take its contents. By the time he had finished he was cramped and cold. For a while he sat on the bale, then reluctant to leave his charge he fetched a blanket from the tack room, piled some straw in the corner and sat down to wait.

The rhythmical grunts of the mare's breathing had a hypnotic effect and gradually he dozed. Once he woke suddenly when the grunting stopped and waited anxiously until it began again, fearful that it was the end and the battle was lost. When at length it resumed he drifted into sleep and troubled dreams. Once more he was in the dimness of the old barn where he used to play; he could hear his mother moving about outside and the scrape of the big wooden door opening. She came towards him, bending as though to kiss his cheek; he could feel the warm breath and the gentle caress against his face. So real was it that he put his hand out and touched a velvet softness that pushed against him -pushed and pushed until he opened his eyes and found himself looking into the deep curved nostrils of the roan mare. It took several seconds to realise what had happened and when he did it made him sit bolt upright causing the mare to start backwards snorting. No, he was not still dreaming she was really on her feet.

Slowly he got up and walked towards her. She stood perfectly still while he adjusted the rug, then on trembling legs she took a step forward and began to nibble tentatively at the hay net. Nick put his arms round the thin neck. 'Oh you beauty,' he whispered. 'You made it, this time you made it.' He wiped hot tears from his cheeks as he ran back into the house, remembering another winter's night and the numbing realisation of what his father was trying to tell him. That night the old enemy had won. He paused at the door and looked up at the stars. 'Well', he croaked, 'at least this time you got it right.'

He hurried indoors to tell the good news and after some hesitation banged on the door of his father's room and went in.

'What the hell....?' Tregarth sat up and looked at the clock by his bed. 'What's up Nick? Don't tell me she's gone.'

'No dad, no, she's up. Honest, she's up and feeding.' Nick blurted out.

Tregarth swung his legs out of bed and began to pull on his trousers and sweater over his pyjamas. 'I don't believe it,' he said excitedly. 'Come on let's have a look.'

He followed Nick back to the loose-box and looked over the door. Mystery was quietly pulling at the hay net to select the choicest bits of leaf. Tregarth gave a satisfied grunt. 'You've done it boy, my God you've done it,' He grasped Nick's shoulder and gave it a squeeze.

'I didn't do much,' the youth replied in a slightly embarrassed tone.

'Rubbish, I told you what Tom Beresford said: tender loving care, without that she'd be dead. We'll make her a fresh bran mash then you can get some sleep.'

They walked back to the house together, neither spoke, there was nothing more to be said.

~

CHAPTER 9

Soon after dawn the next morning the sky softened to a dove grey and the first signs of a thaw sent a trickle of water down the gutters. Over the next two days the snow gradually receded until the last narrow fingers of white finally relinquished their hold on the North facing walls and deep gullies of the high moor. The black peaty soil soaked up the water like a sponge and sent the excess cascading in brown torrents to fill the streams and rivers of the lower land. After snow came flood, it was always so and the people who lived by the river watched the swirling levels anxiously while making their preparation for what was to come.

In Blackaford sandbags appeared at every doorway at the lower end of the village and as though by magic a dozen strong men appeared at the door of the Fox and Hounds the moment the river reached the flood mark on Fore Street bridge. Carefully, almost reverently they moved the barrels up from the cellar and placed them on the floor of the bar. There was an air of purposeful calm and as she watched it Tina realised that it had happened so many times before that it had become a well tried routine. When it was done Gloria 'chalked up' the pints the men would have on the house come opening time.

By ten o'clock that night the spate was over the bridge and lower Fore Street was under a foot of water. Villagers stood anxiously by their sandbagged front doors, every now and then reinforcing the defences as trickles of brown liquid seeped through. Television and radio warned of more floods for the next few days and although it had been Tina's intention to return to London she decided to stay in Blackaford while her car was repaired and the dangerous conditions had subsided.

Hugh was predictably irritated when she telephoned him the next morning and she had to calm his protestations with promises that she would be back as soon as her car was repaired, in the mean time her side of the business could be run with the aid of her laptop. She discussed her plans with Gloria who was doubtful whether the local garage could replace the headlamp within a week.

'Yours isn't the sort of car we get around here much, so they will have to send away for the parts, they can sort any dents out but…' She raised her hands and shrugged in a gesture that implied Tina would not be travelling home for some time.

'Ah well, I suppose I'm due a few more days off, God knows I've earned it after the Christmas rush and in any case it will give me more time with my father. I would like to get to know the countryside around here so perhaps I shall do a bit of walking. Is there a bus to get me to the hospital, I think I might enjoy not driving for a bit?'

Gloria nodded. 'One a day except market days when there are two. Catch it at the bridge at a quarter past eight and you'll get a return from Bodmin just after five.'

There was a pause before Tina said 'I thought I might have gone to see Mr. Tregarth. I hope he's going to cough up something towards the repairs to my car. I wonder if you could give me some directions?'

Gloria raised one eyebrow. 'Well, if he didn't offer the other night he'll not do it now,' she replied tartly, 'but if you want know, Greystone Barton is up there.' She pointed out of the window to a tiny cluster of lights high up on the moor. 'It's a good five miles by road but there are a few short cuts across the moor. The Barton is a big house, you can't miss it, it's the only farm for miles. I can show you on the map if you like.'

The next morning Tina visited the local garage to discover that Gloria had been quite correct in her surmise about the length of time needed to repair the Porsche. 'Basher' Harris –so called on account of his stock car racing exploits – studied the vehicle with a series of discouraging grunts and the occasional intake of breath. 'O' course I'll need to send away fer the new headlamp,' he said after contemplating the problem for several minutes, 'but the body work looks a bit too complicated for us to tackle, you might be better to get a few quotes from one o' the Bodmin garages if you've a mind but I don't suppose they'll have the parts neither. We don't get many of these expensive foreign jobs round yer.'

Tina shrugged and said it would be of little consequence where the car was repaired and it might as well be Blackaford as anywhere else this side of Wimbledon. 'Just get the lamp fixed and I'll get the rest done later, in any case it should come out of the other party's insurance, after all it was Mr. Tregarth who caused the accident.'

Harris grunted. 'You'll be lucky,' he muttered making a note of the year and model. 'Leave it with me madam and if you'll just give me a phone number I'll let you know when it's ready.'

She gave him the number of the Fox and Hounds and her mobile phone before threading her way between the cars on the forecourt and walking back to the pub.

The trip to Bodmin was something of an adventure for Tina. She had not ridden on a country bus since she was a small child and quite enjoyed the fact that the journey was going to take three times as long as it would have done had she gone by car. There was the added bonus of being able to see over the tops of the high banks that flanked the narrow lanes as the little bus cruised from village to village picking up the occasional passenger, often waiting several minutes for a regular who happened to be late. Her fellow travellers were mainly female: young wives with children in pushchairs or middle aged women with large shopping bags and clothes that were ten years out of fashion, if indeed they had ever been in at all. There were never more than half a dozen on the bus at any one time and Tina wondered how long the bus company could continue to run the service.

They picked up two teenage youths dressed in the current uniform of cropped hair, baggy trousers and camouflage tops. She overheard their plans for the day which included, apart from the pub, a trip to the job centre, an activity that had become a weekly routine.

Tina remarked on the slowness of the journey to a large woman who had taken the seat next to her. 'I know my dear,' the woman replied. 'Tis a proper nuisance but there, we haven't got a village shop no more so tis either the bus or go without. 'Course there's Mr. Trevelyan's van comes round but he's terrible expensive.' She shook her head and for the rest of the journey extolled the virtues of living in town, finishing with a fervent wish for a council house in Bodmin and a change of job from farm work for her husband. 'Where he can start at half past eight instead of six o'clock in the morning and finish at five instead of coming home at God knows what hour at night.'

Tina recalled her mother's reason for leaving Hendra: 'It wasn't so much your father as that dreadful place,' she used to explain, and for the first time Tina realised the problems of adjustment that her mother had faced. She had been a city girl, taken with Cornwall in summer but unused to the rigours of a moorland farm in February. It had always puzzled Tina how her parents came to marry, they were such poles apart.

The walk from the bus stop to the hospital gave her chance to buy some fruit and a couple of magazines she thought her father would like. He greeted her with a smile and seemed in good spirits. She told him that Jim Saunders and Mr. Menheniot were looking after the farm and he nodded in approval. 'I got stranded there on Monday night,' she continued. 'A chap called Tregarth landed up there with two horses - got stuck on the road so he said - most peculiar he....'

'Who?' Byron interjected.

'Tregarth, John Tregarth, he seemed to know you.'

The old man snorted. 'He might know me and I know the Tregarths and I would be best pleased if you kept away from the likes of him.'

'Now just calm down,' Tina said as his face reddened. 'I don't understand what you are getting all worked up about but it won't do your blood pressure any good.' She offered him a grape. 'As a matter of fact he was a great help in getting your sheep in when it snowed.'

Byron grunted but said nothing.

They sat in silence until Tina said, 'one of the horses was the same colour as the one you've lost. What was it, blue roan?'

The old man sat up, his eyes wide. 'That's it,' he said excitedly. 'The Tregarths have got her, damned thieving hounds, it's just like them, George Tregarth would take the shirt off your back and like father like son. We'll have to get her back you know, she's the last of the line and the Tregarths would give their eye teeth to get hold of her.' He threw back the bed clothes. 'I must get out of here.'

Tina caught hold of his arm. 'Don't be silly dad,' she said firmly. 'I don't know what you've got against the Tregarth family but whatever it is there's no point in risking your health just for a horse so get back into bed and stay quiet.'

'Well that's just where you're wrong,' he said angrily. ' I suppose being brought up in the town it will be difficult for you to understand but that young mare means a lot to me, she's like one of the family and that's more than you've...' he stopped abruptly and grasped her hand. 'No I didn't mean that, I'm sorry.' He got back into bed and sat in silence once more.

Tina spoke first. 'Tell me about the Tregarths.'

Byron shook his head sadly. 'It was all a very long time ago, too long to be of any consequence now. It just riles me to think of the Tregarths at Greystone that's all, and if they've got Mystery...'

'Now you're getting worked up again,' Tina cut in anxiously. 'Look, if it will put your mind at rest I'll go and see him tomorrow, how about that.'

Byron smiled and patted her hand. 'You're a good girl,' he said wearily. 'I can't tell you how nice it is to have you around. When they let me home I'll show you the moor and I'll tell you about the Pendoggets, that is if your mother hasn't already told you.'

She shook her head. 'I think you had better get some rest. I've got some shopping to do and then I've got to catch the bus back.' She briefly explained about the car. 'It means I shall be here for a few more days so we'll have plenty of time to talk. In the mean time don't you worry about a thing and just concentrate on getting better.' She leant over to straighten his pillows and kissed him on the forehead. 'See you tomorrow,' she said cheerfully.

A light lunch at a nearby pub, a visit to the shopping centre and it was time to catch the bus home. She was the first on and the driver gave her a friendly nod as he recognised her from the morning run. One by one familiar faces appeared through the door with just the occasional stranger who, like an outsider at a works outing, sat apart from the return fare passengers who greeted each other with familiar smiles and nods. Tina could not help wondering why anyone should be travelling out of town who had not made the trip in on the only bus of the day. While she was musing on the possible reasons for one way tickets to the back of beyond the large woman, shopping bags bulging, greeted her like a long lost friend and eased her considerable bulk into the space next to her. She began talking almost before her bottom touched the seat, complaining how everything had gone up and describing the bargains she had found. 'And what about you my dear, how have you got on?'

Tina confessed she had done very little shopping and that the purpose of her journey was to visit her father in hospital. The woman nodded approvingly. ''Tis nice to know daughters care these days. Mind, I do look after my own mother, you would never guess it but she's turned ninety and her mind as clear as a bell.' She clutched the seat in front as the bus lurched forward. 'I hate these little buses, don't give you half enough room.' She smiled at Tina, 'I expect you got a car.'

Tina nodded.

'Didn't think I'd seen you on this bus before. Do you live here abouts?'

'No I'm from Lon… up country, it's just my father who lives locally.'

The conversation lapsed until the woman said, 'and what would be your father's name if you don't mind me asking?'

'Pendogget, he farms at Hendra.'

'Pendogget,' the woman said thoughtfully. 'Ah yes, I've heard mother talk about the Pendoggets.'

'You have?' Tina suddenly became very interested. 'Please tell me more, you see I left home when I was very young so I know very little about my family and my father doesn't seem to want to talk about it.'

The woman shrugged. 'Can't say I know much. I remember mother saying something about old Mr. Pendogget but that would be your grandfather. She used to work at the big house when she was a girl, now what was it called - Grey something or other.'

'Greystone Barton?'

'Yes, that's it - Greysone Barton.'

Tina nodded thoughtfully. 'That ties in, I expect grandfather worked there at some time.' She smile at the woman. 'Thank you Mrs......?'

'Judd m'dear, but I was a Tremlet and mother was a Bolitho. We live in Trewarda village so if you're passing any time I'm sure mother would love a chat and she's a mine of information concerning the moor folk, she's bound to know your father.'

'Thank very much that's very kind. Tina wanted to explain more why she knew so little about her family but they had arrived at Mrs. Judd's stop and she was already easing her bulk towards the door. 'Cheerio my dear,' she called as she heaved her shopping bags down the steps. 'Don't forget, any time you are passing....' The bus started and Tina could only repeat her thanks as Mrs. Judd disappeared behind a cloud of diesel smoke.

It gave Tina a strange feeling to have met a complete stranger to whom the name Pendogget meant something. It was the same feeling she had experienced at Hendra: the notion that she had come home, that she belonged. The thought was very gratifying and she resolved to find out more about this family of hers . What was the connection with the Tregarths and why was her father so reluctant to discuss it? Then there was the conversation with Charlie Hawkins about riding horses - some good 'uns he had said. She wondered whether he father had been a groom or something, and yet somehow it didn't fit. She resolved to visit Greystone Barton in the morning.

∼

CHAPTER 10

The next morning was fine and Tina announced her intention to walk to Greystone as she and Gloria sat down to breakfast. As they ate Gloria gave her the standard advice she gave to all walkers on the moor: 'Get an Ordinance Survey map, stick to the footpaths where possible, take sensible clothing and footwear, shut all the gates.' Tina nodded. 'There's a chance my car might be ready this afternoon so I'll get back in time to go to the hospital.'

'Then don't leave it too late,' Gloria said firmly. 'It can be treacherous up there at this time of year so if the mist comes down turn back the way you came otherwise you'll be in trouble.'

Tina smiled. 'Don't worry, I've walked in most of the mountains in Europe so I don't visualise any difficulties with a five mile hike.'

Gloria packed a sandwich lunch and gave her directions for the first mile or so, after which her knowledge of the cross country route was very sketchy and Tina knew she would have to use the map. Greystone Barton was clearly marked as a place of historical interest, a fact which served to heighten her curiosity so it was with a brisk step that she set off up a narrow highbanked lane towards the rugged outline of the moor.

As the last house was left behind she savoured the freshness of the open country. Rooks cawed and squabbled in the bare branches of oaks, moulded and bent by the prevailing Westerly winds so that the whole copse leant towards the granite slopes in front of her. She paused to watch the birds as they poked at last year's nests with their beaks then launched themselves into the air to circle in two's and three's round the small wood before returning to shuffle and posture with outstretched necks and ruffled feathers. The preliminaries to pairing and nest building were obvious even to a town dweller and roused in her the eternal optimism of winter's demise.

The road ended at a small white painted cottage which looked empty and forsaken except for the fact that the paint was new and an extension had been added. 'Holiday cottage,' she thought. 'Ought to be lived in all the time not just at week ends,' then smiled to herself for it was just the sort of hideaway she had often planned for herself. 'But that was before....'

Beyond the cottage the road became a track flanked by drystone walls and half a mile further on it ended at a gate to the open moor. Tina sat on large rock to consult the map. Blackaford was behind her in the valley, a patchwork of small fields stretched down to where the square church tower presided over the little sprawl of slate roofs, then more fields gradually fading to a misty haze where she knew the sea would be pounding jagged cliffs. The wind from the sea had an edge and the air a clarity that not been apparent down in the valley. Tina breathed in the heady scent of peat while far away the plaintive call of a curlew stirred a longing which she found difficult to explain.

According to the map the route went through a large forestry plantation; once through that she reckoned it would be possible to save at least a couple of miles by striking off across the moor. The sun felt warm on her back as she shouldered the little pack Gloria had lent her and set off towards the dark line of trees.

Inside the wood the air was still, the spicy smell of conifers sifted through the ranks of trees. She thought of Hugh, an ardent conservationist who was vehement in his condemnation of 'the regimented lines of unnatural green'. 'Of course Hugh never gets out of his car,' she said to herself as she watched a jay flit through the shafts of slanting sunlight.

By the time the open moor was in sight again she was ready for lunch and chose a freshly cut pile of logs against which to rest her back while she sat and ate her sandwiches. Somewhere over to the left the far off buzz of a chainsaw told her that a forester was at work. The noise stopped and the thought that somewhere in the wood another person was probably sitting down to eat was vaguely comforting.

She ate the sandwiches, opened a can of fizzy lemonade and settled back to enjoy the fresh air. The logs were surprisingly comfortable, the sun was warm on her face and there was a quiet stillness such as she had only experienced in great cathedrals. There was a satisfaction in the quiet solitude, in knowing that only she and the distant forester were experiencing the grandeur of those column-like trees. She thought how rare and precious solitude and privacy were in a modern world and how pleasant it was to be alone in the wood. Gradually her mind absorbed the silence as she drifted into oblivion.

She woke with a start, stiff and cold. The chainsaw was going again and her watch told her that she had been asleep for over a hour. A thin layer of cloud veiled the sun and a chillness in the air reminded her that it was still winter. She quickly gathered the lunch wrappings, stuffed them into the pack and set out for the edge of the wood.

She climbed over a gate with a warning notice against fire and was once more in open country. Another glance at the map showed that if she followed the edge of the wood to the first corner, then turned left across the moor, she would hit a minor road about half a mile from Greystone Barton. The sun was momentarily lost but she knew that she had to keep it on her right hand side when it came to crossing the open moor.

The way along the wood's perimeter was strewn with boulders and crisscrossed with deep gullies half hidden in dead bracken. Several times the ground gave way under her feet and she longed for a stout stick to test the ground as Tregarth had done in the snow but she had no knife with which to cut one. Once she fell flat on her face and the jolt resulted in an ankle that hurt whenever she put too much weight on it. The journey to the corner took longer than anticipated and once there she stopped to rest her bruised and aching legs.

Her course lay towards a distant pile of rocks which she lined up on the map, then with the sun on her right shoulder she started off across the moor. Soon the bracken and gorse gave way to short springy turf and the going became easier. Blackface sheep darted away as she approached, while a troop of unconcerned ponies cropped the sparse grass round the edge of a patch which grew lush and green. She wondered why they were not tempted by the obviously better grazing, until one of the ponies took a step into the patch and immediately sank into its knees in black ooze. It pulled itself back with an ominous sucking noise and Tina made a mental note to avoid bright green patches.

The sun had disappeared behind a bank of grey cloud but the rock pile was clearly visible and she could even see a tractor in the distance travelling along what must be a minor road. The terrain ahead looked flat and easy to cross as she picked her way between tussocks of coarse grass. She found a sheep path and followed it through clumps of green rushes and around areas of black peat mud. The path ended at a large pool, its still, dark waters reflecting the deepening grey of the sky.

Tina hesitated and scanned the ground beyond the pool; it looked easy enough and as long as she could avoid the bright green areas she was confident of getting across it. It was either that or turn back and she was not going to do that; she decided to push on round the pool and look for a path on the other side. Progress was slow and several times the mud came over the tops of her walking boots so that she took to stepping from tussock to tussock in order to keep dry. The procedure caused considerable pain in her injured ankle and she could feel it beginning to swell.

When she judged she was diametrically opposite her starting point on the far side of the pool she paused to check her bearings with the rock pile but the horizon had become a soft grey line which seemed to be getting closer. She turned round, the thought of retracing her steps to the wood came to her mind but that too had disappeared into an enveloping greyness. Tina realised with horror that whole landscape was being swallowed by a thick blanket of mist.

The first fluttering of panic set her pulse racing. 'Come on Tina Pendogget,' she told herself. 'Don't get all worked up, this is your ancestral stamping ground, Pendoggets just don't get lost on the moor.' The bravado was short lived as the realisation dawned that she was indeed lost.

The question was whether to go forward or try to retrace her tracks to the wood. She had just decided to turn back when she noticed another sheep track heading off in the direction she wanted to go. The temptation to follow it was too much for Tina who never liked turning back once she had set her mind on something. 'Right then, its onward,' she said in as confident a voice as she could muster. She was not sure what a sheep weighed but it looked as though ponies had been along it and she was confident that where they could go she could tread safely.

It was not easy following the course of the track which meandered to and fro between stagnant pools and areas of yellow moss that quivered like jelly whenever her foot inadvertently left the path. It was like walking a tight rope and it took all the will power she could muster to keep panic at bay as she kept her eyes fixed on the black muddy line that marked the only safe way.

Her ankle was aching badly, forcing her to stop every now and then to rest. By now it was impossible to see more that a few steps ahead and she was beginning to feel very cold. The dampness seemed to penetrate every item of clothing while her legs from the knees down were soaked. A large clump of rushes looked familiar, was it possible she had passed that way earlier? Tales of lost travellers walking round in circles for hours now seemed less far fetched. She remembered her father's stories about the piskies that led unwary wanderers into the bogs. As a child they gave her nightmares which she had never forgotten.

She limped on, the dread growing that perhaps she would not find her way out before dark and would become just another statistic that succumbed to exposure in this desolate place. Suddenly the path ended in an expanse of lush green vegetation. So abrupt was the path's disappearance that one more step and she would have been in the bog. For several minutes she stared at the innocent looking death trap, remembering the hideous sucking noises that had accompanied the pony's release a little while earlier. She was tired and wanted to sit down but there were no dry places so she stood, resting her injured foot as best she could. As she stood there a faint high pitched sound drifted down through the mist: like wind whistling through rocks but there was no wind. 'Oh God', she thought, 'I'm going potty, I could swear I heard....' She listened intently but the sound had gone. 'Come on Tina Pendogget,' she said firmly, fighting back the tears of fatigue and hopelessness, 'there must be a way out of this so stop imagining things or you'll be seeing piskies next.'

She was about to try a likely track to the left when she stopped suddenly and stood very still. There it was again off to the right; she held her breath as a sound like the thin, plaintive cadences of distant panpipes drifted across the mire. She had heard how the mists played tricks with the imagination but these sad, vibrant notes were surely real. The hair on the nape of her neck prickled. 'Pull yourself together,' she told herself. 'If there is something or somebody out there then whatever it is must be real.' She was about to call out when the music wavered then faded and all was silence once more. She told herself it must have been her imagination - just a trick of the wind but it came again and she turned to move towards the sound, trying to decide what it was. She had walked several steps before she realised that the ground felt firmer. 'Oh God, let me be out of it, please let me be out of it.' She stumbled onto dry turf as the sound got louder; it was quite close now and she stopped to listen. It was a flute, she was certain it was a flute. 'Is anybody there?' she called.

For what seemed a long time there was silence again, then from somewhere high up in the mist a youthful voice asked 'are you lost?'

Tina gasped with relief and peered upwards but could see nothing. 'Where are you?'

'I'm up here,' came the reply

'Where is here?'

'Just follow the music.' There was a mischievous tone to the voice which made her feel uneasy, nevertheless she limped towards the sound of the flute as the notes swelled to a crescendo. The way was uphill and suddenly a dark shape loomed out of the gloom. It was a large rock and perched on top was the player sitting cross legged in the swirling mist. He was slightly built with dark hair to his shoulders and a thin elfin like face. Tina stared with disbelief, she felt her legs begin to buckle and put out a hand to rest against the granite, questioning her senses and hardly daring to look up.

The music stopped and she risked a glance upwards but the apparition had gone.

'I thought you might be lost.' The voice came from behind her and she turned to face a youth holding a small instrument case.

'So you are real,' she said with a grin of relief.

The boy chuckled and repeated his question.

'Tina sat down and rubbed her ankle. 'Yes I am lost so where are we?'

'Where would you like to be?'

'I was trying to get to Greystone Barton, do you know it?'

He grinned. 'If that is where you want to be then Hey Presto! That is where you shall go, just follow me.' He waived the case like a conjurers wand and set off into the mist.

Tina hesitated.

'Don't worry,' the mischievous tone was there again. 'I won't lead you into a mire, only the bad piskies to that and I'm one of the other sort.'

Tired as she was, Tina could not help smiling. 'And what sort of pisky is that?'

'Why, the sort that leads travellers safely to their destination of course. Where did you start from?'

She described as best she could her route from Blackaford.

His dark eyes became serious. 'Have you really crossed Hagtor Mire in this?' he indicated a wide arc with the instrument.

'If you mean that dreadful marshy place out there, then I suppose I have,' she said getting stiffly to her feet.

The boy whistled through his teeth. 'Whew, you really must have a friendly pisky on your side. Not many people could find their way across that bog, they say it can swallow a bullock in less time than it takes to tell.'

Tina was not sure how much to believe, she guessed that many of the stories about bogs were exaggerated, nevertheless the sight and sound of the pony scrambling out of the green mire was enough to convince her that the moor was no place to be in a thick fog. 'How is it you know Greystone Barton?' she asked following him down the slope.

'I live there,' he said without looking back. 'I'm Nick Tregarth.'

'Oh,' Tina paused to catch her breath. 'Then John Tregarth will be your father?'

'That's right, do you know him then?'

She hesitated. 'Not really, my name is Tina Pendogget, I've only met him once, well twice I suppose.' She thought she saw the youth grin and changed the subject quickly. 'I'm curious to know what you were doing playing the flute in the middle of Bodmin Moor?'

They reached a gate with a notice PRIVATE LAND on it. He unlatched it and held it open while she went through. 'Well, it's like this,' he said as he fastened the gate behind them. 'Our housekeeper Mrs. Bolitho is a sort of witch who can't stand the sound of decent music and if I play my flute in the house she will probably turn me into a frog, so I have to come outdoors. I like it best when the mist comes down, it does things for the sound. The locals think I'm nuts of course.'

'And what does your father say?'

He shrugged. 'I don't think he cares much.'

They walked slowly across several grass fields and with each few yards downhill the mist became less dense until at last they were below the cloud. Fields and woods were clearly visible across a wide valley in the bottom of which the slate roofs of Greystone Barton showed through a screen of tall oaks.

'Well there it is,' Nick said pointing with the flute. 'Once we cross the stream at the bottom of this field we shall be on level ground and you will find the going a bit easier.'

They approached the house from the front, crossing the stream by a rickety wooden footbridge onto what had once been terraced lawns. Now they were grazed by a score of half wild sheep which scattered in all directions as the two walkers climbed the first set of stone steps. Tina sat down on a plinth that could once have supported some sort of statue; she looked at the imposing façade of the Barton, not sure what she had expected. The woman on the bus had called it 'the big house' and Tina had visualised a large farmhouse but this was much more impressive. It was built of granite and roofed with the local grey-blue slates which also covered the upper third of the walls giving extra protection against the moorland weather. There were six large windows downstairs, three either side of a porticoed doorway and seven matching them upstairs plus four little gabled windows in the roof: 'for the servants no doubt,' she thought and wondered if her father had slept in one.

Nick waited until she was ready to move. 'You had better come in and get your ankle seen to. I've no doubt Mrs.B will have some ghastly potion that will cure it.' He led the way to the back of the house through a stone archway, across a cobbled yard to a large iron studded oak door. As he pushed it open Talisman nearly knocked Tina over in his eagerness to get out. Nick called the dog back and the animal came obediently to his side. 'He's a bit put out because I left him at home this time but we only do our Cornish version of the Hound of the Baskervilles in the summer when the emmets are around.' He grinned and held the dog by its scuff to let her pass.

'What on earth are emmets?'

'You have to be one to ask the question. Emmets are the tourists, it's the old Cornish word for ants, you know, swarming all over the place.'

'Then I'm only half an emmet for I was born not far from here,' she said with more than a hint of pride.

They were in a large room with a stone flagged floor and beamed ceiling from which hung a brace of pheasants and several rabbits. The latter were freshly killed for tiny drops of blood hung from each nostril and dripped onto the floor. Nick noticed she was looking at them. 'Father shot them this morning,' he said. 'There will be rabbit pie tomorrow with any luck.'

Tina shuddered. 'I don't know how you could eat the poor little creatures,' she commented.

'Better not let father hear you say that, rabbits have eaten off nearly an acre of turnips down by Broadoak wood.' He pulled off his wellingtons. We leave our wet things here.'

Tina removed her jacket and boots to follow the youth up some steps into a dark passage. Her socks left wet footprints on the flags and she was very conscious of the fact that she looked as though she had just been pulled out of a bog.

'Is that you Nicholas?' The voice was high pitched and strident as Mabel Bolitho's grey head peered round the door. 'Put a light on boy and who's that with you, can't see a thing in that gloom.' Nick switched on the light and the housekeeper's eyes focused on Tina's bedraggled figure. 'Who ever you are you look soaked, best come in and get warm.' She pushed open the door and led them into the kitchen and began to stir a large saucepan on the cooker.

'Bubble bubble toil and trouble,' Nick whispered as they entered, then loud enough for Mabel to hear: 'this is Tina Pendogget, she was coming to see father and got lost on the moor.'

The stirring stopped and for a moment Mabel stood still, spoon in hand, her eyes on the contents of the saucepan. The stirring began again while Tina stood in the middle of the room not knowing what to say or do. Eventually the housekeeper turned and in a quiet voice said, 'You had better get those wet things off. If you'll just wait a minute I'll find some dry clothes for you.'

Tina looked down at the muddy water oozing out of the bottom of her jeans and trickling across the kitchen floor. She felt miserable and cold and was closer to tears than she cared to admit; at that moment the door opened and John Tregarth stood there with a horse blanket over one arm. He took one look and said 'Good Lord, it's you again.'

It was too much. She turned away to hide the tears as Mabel came over and took her gently by the elbow. 'Have you no manners John?' she demanded as she led Tina upstairs. He looked uncomfortably at Nick. 'What did I do for God's sake and what goes with the Pendogget woman?'

'Believe it or not she's come to see you and it seems she's walked across Hagtor Mire in this fog.'

'Jesus,' was all Tregarth said as he threw the blanket over the back of a chair.

Upstairs Mabel was showing Tina the bathroom when a door banged below. The housekeeper shook her head. 'That'll be the study door,' she muttered. 'Bin like a bear with a sore head all day. Something's riled him and that's for sure so I expect that will be the last we shall see of him tonight.' She handed Tina a clean towel. 'But there, you mustn't think too badly of him, he don't mean to be so rough, it's just that…well…you know…'

Tina did not know, but was too anxious to get into a hot bath to prolong the conversation and was grateful when Mabel turned on the taps. While the bath ran she glanced at herself in the full length mirror. The sight produced a groan of dismay. 'Why is it that whenever I meet that man I look like this?' She pulled the wet strands of hair through her fingers with a despairing shake of the head.

A hot bath and dry clothes went a little way to restoring her confidence but the nearest fit were jeans, shirt and sweater that belonged to Nick and they were at least a size too big as were the leather slippers that Mabel had produced from the bottom of the airing cupboard. 'Nought out of ten for glamour,' she told herself dismally as she slopped along the landing clutching the jeans to stop them falling down. The lighting was dim and the impression distinctly Victorian with dark grained doors along a red carpeted corridor. 'The Station Hotel, Netherwallop,' she grinned to herself, 'sooner be there than here. Ah well, look on the bright side Tina Pendogget, you might have been at the bottom of a bog.' She could see through the windows that the fog had thickened so that the winter dusk had come early and already it was dark.

The kitchen was bright and warm as Mabel bustled round still muttering to herself. Thomas came in with an armful of logs, nodded and carried on in the direction of the study. Nick lounged in a tattered armchair, his stockinged feet resting on a low table with one ear pressed to a small radio. Tina sat down in the nearest chair and watched Mabel prepare the evening meal, wondering if she should offer to help as it seemed to be assumed she would stay for supper. She decided against it as the wiry little woman gave the appearance of someone who would not tolerate another female in her kitchen.

Mabel walked over to the window to draw the curtains. 'Tis murky out there that's for sure,' she said rubbing the steam from the glass a peering out. 'I can't see nobody taking you back tonight m'dear so I reckon tis the guest room for you.'

'Oh no I couldn't possibly….' Tina's protests were cut short by an imperious waive and an emphatic 'nothing else for it, I'll make up a bed.' Mabel wiped her hands on her apron and went towards the door. Tina felt something akin to panic. 'Hang on a minute,' she said in desperation. 'Surely I can get someone out from Blackaford, and what about Mr. Tregarth what will he say?'

Mabel gave her a brief glance and with a derisory 'Ugh!' carried on towards the stairs.

Nick looked up. 'She's right you know. You're stuck whether you like it or not 'cos there is no way of getting the Lord and Master out of his lair and Thomas isn't safe driving at night when the weather is fine let alone when you can't see across the yard and as for getting a taxi in this - forget it.'

Tina frowned. 'Okay if you say so but I'll have to let them know at the Fox and hounds or they will be sending out a search party.'

Nick got out of his chair. 'In that case we had better get it over and done with before the L and M gets too far down the whisky bottle. Come on we've got to brave the study.' He led the way into a large dimly lit hall, oak panelled and hung with gilt framed oil paintings of horses and hunting scenes. The door to the study had the stuffed head of a snarling fox mounted over the lintel. Tina looked at it and shuddered while Nick took a deep breath and turned the brass door knob.

The only light in the room came from the log fire in the big open fireplace. John Tregarth sat in a leather armchair, his legs stretched out towards the blaze and the heels of his black riding boots resting on the wrought iron hearth rail. Talisman lay at his feet, his head beneath a small table on which stood a half empty bottle. Only the hound moved as the door opened.

There was an uncomfortable silence until Nick said 'we've come to use the phone. Miss Pendogget is staying the night and she wants to ring Mrs. Lockey.'

The only response was a grunt and a vague nod. Nick indicated towards a large mahogany desk where a telephone perched on top of several directories amidst a litter of bills and papers. Tina found herself tiptoeing across the room to pick up the receiver. She hesitated and looked round for Nick only to find he had beaten a hasty retreat to the kitchen. 'I….I can't remember the number,' she said and wondered why she should be so apologetic about it. 'You don't happen to…..'

He rattled off the number before she could complete the sentence.

'Thank you,' she said as she tapped in the numbers, noticing for the first time the large portrait of a dark haired girl in a blue evening dress which hung over the fireplace. Her speculation as to who it might be was interrupted by Gloria's voice. Tina explained the situation, there was a long pause before Gloria replied 'thank you for letting me know' and rang off abruptly.

Tina replaced the phone slowly. It wasn't like Gloria to be so curt, she thought, but concluded that the pub was probably busy and the call had come at an inopportune time. She murmured a thank you to the silent figure in the chair and left the room.

Nick was standing in the hall looking at a painting of a grey horse. 'This might interest you,' he said. 'Her official name was Greystone Lady but Thomas always refers to her as the Pendogget mare, I don't know why. Could be some connection with your family.'

Tina shook her head. 'I shouldn't think so, small farmers don't have much in common with racehorses I would have thought. She must have been very special, that is quite an imposing picture.'

The youth nodded. 'It's a Lionel Edwards. She's what they call a foundation mare, all the Greystone line are descended from her. They say she was the best 'chaser there was in her day. Mind, that was a long time ago, in fact she belonged to my grandmother.'

'Well, I'm afraid I know nothing about horses,' Tina confessed, 'but now you mention it that's the second time I've heard my name connected to this house. I suppose you don't happen to know whether a Byron Pendogget ever worked here?'

Nick shrugged. 'Could be, though I don't recall father saying anything about it,' he thought for a moment, 'I remember grandfather talking about a Pendogget but I don't think he worked here. Thomas would know but he's always cagey about the family history, too many skeletons in the cupboard if you ask me.' He grinned self-consciously and added quickly, 'supper will be ready, better get in.'

By the time they got back into the kitchen Mabel had started to serve portions of meat pie while Thomas poured cider from a large earthenware jug. Tina hesitated, considered her vegetarian status, shrugged and began to eat; only then did she realise it was rabbit. She recalled the blood stained bodies hanging in the boot room and paused, glancing at Mabel. The returned look made any hesitation momentary: this was not the time to discuss Animal Rights.

'You must take us as you find us,' Mabel said as she cut thick slices from a large home made loaf. 'It may not be what city folks is used to but it does here a bouts.'

Tina chewed on a piece of rabbit: it tasted very good. 'It's fine, really and I'm most grateful for your hospitality.'

The housekeeper grunted and picked at her own meal with little enthusiasm, unlike her husband who was into his second helping before Tina had finished her first. They ate in silence until the plates were ready to clear away then Thomas pushed back his chair, pulled out a short stemmed pipe and began to fill it with tobacco from a battered tin.

Mabel glowered. 'You can smoke that outside,' she said with a nod towards Tina. 'We'll have a cup o' tea.' She smiled and touched her lightly on the shoulder. 'In the mean time young Nicholas you can take your father a helping of this pie, he's going to need something in his belly before the night's out.'

The youth frowned. 'Not me, not while he's in that sort of mood. I'm sure to get the rough end of it.'

Thomas picked up the plate. 'I'll take it,' and turning to Nick, 'just you be a bit more respectful young man. If I was your dad I'd tan your ar…..hide as old as you are an' it'll do no harm to remember there's a visitor present.' He went out and did not return until the others had finished their tea.

'And I suppose you had to sample the bottle,' Mabel said disapprovingly.

Her husband sat down in the armchair. 'We had one or two together and I could have a few puffs at me pipe at the same time. Just chatted over a few things, nothing wrong with that.' He tapped the pipe out into the fireplace. 'So you're Byron Pendogget's daughter,' he said turning to look at Tina. 'I expect your father has told you about Greysone.

'Well no,' she replied with a puzzled frown. 'As a matter of fact he has never mentioned it.'

'Hmm,' Thomas looked thoughtful. 'Better to come from him,' he said stuffing the pipe into his jacket pocket. 'They tell me he's poorly, I'm sorry to hear that. Tell him Thomas Bolitho asked after him.'

'Yes I will, thank you.' She was about to question the stud groom further when Mabel interrupted with a curt 'Thomas you can stir yourself and help me with the washing up and you can clear the table Nicholas.'

'Can I help?' Tina asked as the two males dutifully set about their tasks.

'No, young lady, thank you, 'tidn't your place to do kitchen work in this household.' Mabel's tone was matter-of-fact and final and although Tina thought it was a strange way of putting it she made no comment but picked up one of the farming magazines and began to flip through it.

Nick finished his task and left the room while Mabel and Thomas talked quietly at the sink. Tina could catch only bits of the conversation but heard her father's name mentioned at least once and Mabel saying firmly '…Maybe but it's not our place to…' There was a quick glance at Tina which made her feel uncomfortable. The subject changed and the conversation became more audible. '….There's another half a dozen ewes missing…they can't all have got stuck in a bog, that's more than twenty in the last six weeks. Someone's having 'em for certain, if you ask me….' Thomas lowered his voice so that Tina did not hear the end of the sentence.

Nick came into the room and with a grin handed her a small faded photograph of two small boys and a donkey taken on the lawns in front of the house. 'Turn it over,' he said.

On the back in pencil was written 'Byron and George.'

'When you said your father's name was Byron, I suddenly remembered this old photo in the back of one of the albums. I had always wondered who Byron was it's such an unusual name. Thought you might be interested.'

'I am,' she murmured studying the children's faces. 'Well, the one leading the donkey is definitely not my father, the hair is much too dark and curly.'

The youth nodded. 'You're right, that's my grandfather.'

Tina moved nearer the light. 'I suppose the fair haired boy on the donkey could be my father. Would you mind if I borrowed this for a while?'

'I don't see why not, nobody ever looks at those albums these days. Quite exciting isn't it?'

'What is quite exciting?' Mabel interjected.

Nick pulled a face behind her back and muttered 'Riding on a broomstick.'

'I heard that Nicholas Tregarth and any more cheek like that from you and you will feel the back of my hand, big as you are. Thomas tell that boy off.' But Thomas' thoughts were elsewhere.

The subject of the Pendogget connection with Greystone Barton was not broached again, in fact Tina had the distinct impression that it was being studiously avoided. Thomas and Mabel talked about trivial domestic matters and Nick curled himself on the dog-worn sofa to watch television so at nine o'clock Tina asked to be shown her bedroom.

In spite of the cold, damp feel to the sheets she soon dropped off to a sleep broken by fitful dreams of Tregarth and Nick, both silently watching as she sank deeper into Hagtor Mire while the shadowy figure of her father hovered somewhere in the background.

She woke suddenly to the barking of a dog and the sound of Tregarth's voice under her window. By her watch it was half past midnight and she turned over to try and get back to sleep but there was a shout of 'Who's that! See him off Talisman,' then a growl and a yell, 'Dixon if that's you it'll be a shotgun next time.' Finally the sound of the dog being called off and a door slamming.

Tina pulled the bedclothes closer and thought of her warm Wimbledon flat. She resolved to get back to it as soon as possible.

CHAPTER 11

The fog had been replaced by a fine drizzle when Tina looked out of the window the next morning. She had heard movement in the house hours before but it had seemed like the middle of the night so she had quickly gone back to sleep again until a tap on the door and Mabel Bolitho's voice announced that breakfast was ready.

The bedroom was cold and the bathroom even colder. Tina dressed quickly and went downstairs. The house had resumed a damp clamminess which had been only briefly dispelled by the previous evening's fires; only the kitchen felt truly warm. The smell of frying bacon was disconcertingly appetising and it took a considerable act of will to confine herself to cereals and toast.

'You'd best start,' Mabel advised. 'The men will be a while and young Nicholas is not up yet.' She placed a large teapot on the table.

Tina nodded. 'Thanks, I'll just have cornflakes, a piece of toast and coffee please.'

'I'm sorry, tea is what we drink here in the mornings,' Mabel said firmly and poured the strong brown liquid into a large cup and pushed it towards her.

Nick came in and was duly chided for his lateness. He ignored the comments and sat down at the table. 'I'll show you round the farm after breakfast,' he said with his mouth full of cornflakes. 'Would you like to see the horses?'

'Yes, thank you very much but I can't stay long as I have to get back to see about my car and then visit the hospital.'

'That's okay. I expect the Lord and Master will be taking you back when he's finished with the sheep. Talk of the devil,' he whispered as the back door banged and the two men came in shaking the moisture from their coats.

'Wet through,' Tregarth commented without looking at Tina. 'This weather gets right through to your bones.'

They washed their hands at the sink and as Tregarth dried his he turned to look scathingly at Nick. 'Just got up I suppose and I bet you have'nt fed that mare yet.'

The youth shook his head sheepishly.

His father grunted, 'I though not. How many times do I have to tell you? Feed the animals first, then you have yours. Now just get out there and do it. You can finish your breakfast when you get back.'

Nick got up and left the table red faced while his father helped himself to bacon and fried bred. 'Did y' sleep well then?' he asked Tina gruffly.

'Thank you, yes. Like a log eventually.'

'Good,' he sat down and poured a large mug of tea. ' So the old Squire's ghost didn't disturb you?' he asked with a smile as he stirred sugar into his tea.

'No, should it have done?' She sipped her own without looking at him.

Tregarth studied her for a few moments. 'You really don't know do you,' he said slowly.

Tina looked puzzled. 'Don't know what?'

He was about to reply when Mabel cut in. ' Now then John, if nothing has been said then it's not your place to interfere.' She turned to Tina. 'Best to ask your father my dear, he'll tell you all about it.' She smiled and for the first time since arriving Tina began to feel at ease.

Nick returned and finished his breakfast without speaking, his eyes fixed on a point somewhere in the middle of the table. He pushed his empty plate away and stood up abruptly. 'I'm going to show Miss Pendogget round. I suppose that's alright?'

His father looked up from his plate of eggs and bacon. 'If you like, but don't go in with those visiting mares particularly the two that came in yesterday. We don't know what they are like yet and don't go messing about with Titan, you know how he is when there are mares in season.'

As they walked through the boot room Nick muttered, 'yes sir, yes sir three bags full sir,' and gave a military style salute. Tina wanted to tell him that it was only for his own good but thought better of it and instead asked what a visiting mare was.

'Well it's like this,' the youth explained, 'the stud season starts shortly and racing breeders like to send mares here early to be covered by Titan so that the foals are born as soon after the first of January as possible, that gives them an advantage over later foals if they start racing as two-year-olds on the flat. But we don't get many high class mares yet and I don't suppose we will unless some of Titan's progeny start winning races. Most of the business comes from hunters later in the season and they're not as profitable.'

They approached the stable yard through a high stone archway on top of which was a rusty weather vane depicting two hounds in pursuit of a tailless fox. The vane creaked in the shifting wind. The yard itself was cobbled with loose-boxes on either side, while the far end was taken up with a large building that must have once been a coach house. The stable clock with peeling gilt numerals was fixed high above the central archway, its hand set permanently at a quarter to three. Above the clock a coat of arms depicting a boat and some sort of animal was carved in stone; Tina tried to read the inscription but was interrupted by a tug on her sleeve. 'Come on, I'll show you the mare I'm looking after,' Nick said with an air of pride.

She followed to one of the loose-boxes and watched as he went inside to pat the animal's neck. 'I call her Roany on account of her colour. You can come in she won't hurt you.'

Tina opened the door apprehensively and stood by the youth as he ran his hand along the mare's flank. 'You don't see many this colour, usually they start like this but go much greyer by the time they're four or five. Dad reckons this one will stay blue roan.' He ran his hand over the soft muzzle. 'It was my mother's favourite colour in horses,' There was along pause before he looked up and asked, 'Do you believe in reincarnation, you know, coming back as something else?'

The question took her by surprise. 'I'm not sure but I don't think so, why?'

'Oh nothing,' he murmured.

Tina was studying the animal thoughtfully. 'So that is a blue roan', she said slowly.

'Yes, father only bought her a week ago. She was very ill and we didn't think she was going to live but we managed to pull her through,' he said with an air of satisfaction.

A niggling thought began to insinuate itself in Tina's mind: a thought she would rather not have. 'You call her a mare, but what is the difference between a mare and a filly?'

Nick shrugged. 'Just a matter of age. Usually when they get to about four we call them mares. Father reckons that's how old this one is.'

There was a sinking feeling in the pit of Tina's stomach as she recalled her father's instructions about a blue roan filly. Could this possibly the one, if so….? She dismissed the thought and followed Nick out.

There were a number of horses heads looking over the tops of their doors and Tina looked at them pensively, hoping her companion would not probe her almost total ignorance of the horse world. He led her to an adjoining area where a black head with wild defiant eyes and flared nostrils suddenly appeared over a reinforced stable door. 'That's the stallion,' Nick informed her. 'he's called Titan, well The Titan to be precise, watch he doesn't give you a nip.' They stood watching the animal in silence as it arched its neck and snorted, prancing round the box with its long black tail extended and eyes wild and bright. Power and grace were in every movement and Tina thought she had never seen anything so beautiful and yet so frightening. Nick watched the horse with an expressionless face. 'Dad bought him in

Ireland when he and mum went over to stay with grandad and grandma Pridmore. They moved to New Zealand when mum died and have asked me if I would like to go down there but…..'

'You're father won't let you?'

'No, it's not that, it's just - well….' His voice trailed off again.

'You couldn't leave your father on his own, is that it? I would have thought he could well look after himself.'

The youth shook his head. 'He wasn't always like this, you know, bad tempered and stuff.' They moved on to the next loose-box. 'This is one of Titan's sons,' he said patting the neck of a big bay horse. 'We hope to win a few point-to-points with him next season, then who knows, he might be good enough for National Hunt racing. If he is any good it means we can increase Titan's stud fees, we also get better mares coming which are more likely to breed winners and so on.'

'Oh I see,' Tina said in a voice that did not sound very convincing. 'It all sounds very complicated but I wish you luck.'

'Better tell that to father, he needs it.'

At that moment John Tregarth entered the yard with Thomas close behind. They went over to where the chestnut hunter looked over the door. 'I'll take him to the meet at Blackaford crossroads tomorrow,' he said. 'It will give me the opportunity to see how he goes. Oh, and about the roan mare, I think we should keep her in for a few more days until I decide what to do with her.'

Thomas frowned. 'I was going to rug her up and turn her out in the orchard for an hour or two if the weather was right; a bit of grass would do her the world of good. In any case don't you think you ought to have a word with Nick? You left her in his charge remember.'

'All right I'll have a word with him, in the mean time she stays where she is. Okay?

Thomas muttered something inaudible as his employer turned to walk over to where Tina was having the intricacies of bridles and saddles explained to her.

'I suppose you would like a lift back to Blackaford?' he asked casually

She shook her head. 'No thank you Mr.Tregarth. I walked here and I'll walk back.'

He shrugged. 'Well please yourself, only this time stick to the road.' He turned and disappeared in the direction of the house.

'Don't mind him,' Nick said apologetically. 'I expect he's got a fair old hangover this morning.'

'I'm afraid your father doesn't hold me in very high regard Nick.'

'Oh, don't worry, he's the same with most people these days. I expect something has screwed him up so the best thing is to keep out of his way until he straightens out.'

Tina thought she had better change the subject. 'I ought to be getting back, I'll pick up my things from the house; don't bother to come I'm sure you have plenty to do. Just point me in the right direction.'

'You don't have to rush off. What about your dodgy ankle?'

'It's fine, I'll manage - I must get to the hospital this afternoon.'

'In that case turn left at the end of the drive and just keep down that road. Shouldn't take much more than an hour or so.'

She turned and with a slight waive of the hand thanked him for his help, then as an afterthought called back 'and thank your father for me.'

Mabel was in the kitchen when Tina collected her belongings. 'I'll be off now,' she said offering her hand. 'Many thanks for your hospitality.' The hand was grasped with unexpected enthusiasm and the housekeeper gave her a rare smile.' A Pendogget is always welcome while I'm housekeeper here. Give my regards to your father and say that Thomas will be over to see him as soon as he gets out of hospital.'

Tina looked surprised. 'I didn't realise you knew him that well.'

Mabel shook her head. 'There seems to be a lot you don't know my dear. You had better get your father to do some explaining before you put your foot in it with you know who.' She nodded towards the study door.

'I ought to say my thanks in there,' Tina said

'I wouldn't bother my dear, not just now. I've put your things in the hall with a few biscuits in case you get peckish on the way home.'

Tina gave her thanks again and with a number of unanswered questions going through her mind, started off on the road to Blackaford.

It was lunch time when she reached the Fox and Hounds. Gloria was occupied with customers at the bar so Tina went straight to her room to put on some fresh clothes. There was a note on the dressing table to say that the car was driveable and she could pick it up as soon as she liked. 'Well at least I can escape back to civilisation and comfort,' she told herself with a sigh of relief. She carefully put the Tregarth photograph in her handbag before making her way downstairs and, leaving a note for Gloria, went out by the back door. 'She can think what she likes,' she said to herself as she set out for Basher Harris' garage.

It felt good to be behind the wheel of the Porsche again and in no time she was bumping down the farm road to Hendra. She pushed open the unlocked back door and made straight for the front room and the mahogany sideboard: the most likely place to find old photographs. There were three drawers down the centre with compartments for glasses and china on either side. It was not until she got to the bottom drawer that she found what she was looking for: a faded green album. She remembered it vaguely from her brief childhood visit when her father showed it to her but to her young mind it had been a blur of figures in old fashioned clothes, innumerable horses and cows with rosettes and silver cups. It had all been very boring for a ten-year-old, now she wished she had paid more attention.

There was nothing that interested her among the snaps fixed on the pages but as she moved towards the window to get more light two small photographs slipped from the back of the album onto the floor. Hastily she picked them up as she recognised the outlines of Greystone Barton. One was of two young boys in front of the house with their arms round each other's shoulders and grinning inanely at whoever was holding the camera. There was no doubt they were the same two boys that were in the Tregarth photograph. The other was of a young woman dressed in the fashion of the nineteen forties looking very pretty and chic; who she was Tina could not guess. She put them both in her hand bag and went out into the yard.

It came as a shock to see a large scruffy looking man standing beside her car. 'Can I help you?' she asked putting on her no-nonsense tone of voice.

The man half raised his sweat stained trilby. 'I were looking fer Mr. Pendogget,' he said looking towards the house.

Tina got into the car, locked the doors and opened a window. 'Well I'm afraid he's not here just now.' She thought uneasily of the unlocked back door, 'but Mr. Menheniot will be here in a few minutes, he is looking after things,' she added quickly. 'If you have something to say to my father I'll pass it on Mr…..?'

'Dixon, he'll know, Slogger Dixon. Just tell 'im ol' Slogger knows where his 'orse can be found.'

'Well?'

The man hesitated. 'Ah well, yer see I thought as 'ow it might be worth a bob or two to the old boy, in gratitude as yer might say.'

Tina rummaged in her hand bag and brought out a ten pound note. Slogger looked at it blankly so she added another. 'Tregarth's got 'un,' he said, abruptly taking the notes and making off up the track towards the moor.

Tina sat for several minutes, a jumble of thoughts going through her mind. She started the engine and drove slowly down the farm track, her mind focused on the events of the past twenty-four hours and in particular the horse that Nick had shown her.

When she got to the hospital Byron was sitting up in bed reading a newspaper. 'You didn't come yesterday,' he said without looking up.

'I went up to Greystone Barton,' she said and waited to see what response he would make. He looked up quickly. 'What on earth were you doing there girl?'

'Never mind what I was doing,' she replied, taking the newspaper and folding it neatly.

'Were you looking for my filly…you know… you said you would…?'

'No as a matter of fact,' she hesitated, 'but I think she might be there. A man called Slogger something or other told me Tregarth had her and I did see a horse that answered her description there.'

'I knew it, I knew it,' The old man jerked up and down in bed excitedly. 'When you said Tregarth had a roan I knew it would be her, I just knew. History does repeat itself and there's proof of it.' He started to get out of bed and Tina had to push him back forcibly. 'What on earth are you talking about? Just calm down and if it's true I'll see what I can do to sort things out.'

'Bah! You can't do much, you'll be off back to London before long and in any case dealing with Tregarth is a man's job.' He lay back on his pillow with his eyes closed.

'Are you feeling alright?' Tina asked anxiously.

'Just thinking.'

There was a long silence until he sat up again and said chirpily, 'I reckon I'll be home in a couple of days.'

'Not if you don't calm down a bit.'

'How can I calm down when Tregarth has got my filly-damned horse thief, I told you they were no good. My bet is he found her wandering on the moor and it would be typical of him to tuck her away and keep his mouth shut.'

'I'm sure it's not like that,' Tina said without conviction. 'At least Thomas Bolitho doesn't seem the type to condone that sort of thing.'

Byron nodded. 'Thomas and Mabel are the only good apples in that barrel but they are only servants to a master.'

'Well I wouldn't put it quite like that,' she said with a wry smile. 'Anyway Tregarth says he bought her in a sale and I must say I'm inclined to believe him.'

'Tregarth says, Tregarth says, what do you know about the Tregarths? I'll tell you this, I bet John Tregarth can't produce a receipt nor a cheque stub to prove it. You ask him if you like, and as for believing what he says well….I would prefer it if you would have nothing to do with John Trgarth.'

Tina was faintly amused. 'I must say it's a bit late in the day to come the heavy handed father and since you are so against that family perhaps you can explain these.' She reached in her handbag and took out the photographs.

'Isn't that you with John Tregarth's father? You seemed to be getting along well enough then.' She put them on the sheet in front of him and sat back to hear what he would say. To her surprise and dismay he picked them up and handed them back with only a cursory glance.

'I don't know where you got them from,' he said quietly, 'but it's a part of my life that is best forgotten, no good to think of what might have been, best to let old ghosts rest.' He reached for a handkerchief and blew his nose loudly.

Tina was not sure what to say. She returned the photographs to her handbag and waited until her father seemed more relaxed. 'I'm sorry, I didn't want to upset you but I wish someone would tell me what it is between you…us… and the Tregarths.'

Byron shook his head. 'It's along story and this is no place to tell it. When we get home, that will be the time, things you ought have known years ago if….'

'If I had been a proper daughter?'

'I wasn't going to say that. You had to live your life and you have done very much better than if you had lived with this old peasant.' He took her hand and patted it gently. 'I suppose you will be getting off back to London and that shop of yours and I can get back to where I left off.' He frowned and looked agitatedly round the ward. 'They've put my clothes somewhere and I'm damned if I know where. Could you just see if you can find them?'

Tina shook her head. 'You will be given your clothes when you are fit enough to leave and not before, so settle down and get some rest. The doctor says you'll need at least another couple of days and they want to keep you in until the results of the tests come through.'

'Bah! There's nothing wrong with me that fresh air won't cure.'

'And another thing, I want to make some arrangements for a home help. I think you need someone to look after you.'

'Don't you start bossing me about young lady, it was bad enough with your mother. You get off back to London and find some poor blighter of a husband to make miserable and leave your old father to sort his own problems.'

Tina smoothed the pillow. 'You are a stubborn old devil, mother always said that, but you'll get nowhere trying to start an argument with me. I've made up my mind and that's that.'

He looked up with grin. 'My God, I can see the Pendogget in you, my girl.'

The conversation was interrupted by a young nurse. 'Medicine time Mr. Pendogget,' she said brightly, shaking a thermometer before putting it under his tongue. She took his pulse. 'Hmm, what have you been up to while my back is turned?'

Byron pulled out the thermometer. 'Young woman I am old enough to be your grandfather and I don't like being treated like a child so kindly get on with what you have to do without comment please.'

The nurse grinned at Tina and placed two pills on the bedside table. 'Make sure he takes these,' she said quietly. 'They'll make him a bit drowsy so don't worry if he doses off.'

'Bah!' Byron said as soon as she had gone. 'Why is it as soon as you get into hospital they treat you as though you were daft or already dead?'

Tina poured a glass of water and watched as he swallowed the pills. 'That's better. Now, as I said before I'll sort a few things out ready for when you go home so don't worry.'

'The only thing that worries me is what has happened to that filly,' he retorted.

'I promise I will do all I can as soon as possible,'

'And when is that likely to be?'

Tina hesitated. 'Well, I have to get back to Wimbledon so it will probably be the next time I come down in about a fortnight's time.'

'A fortnight!' The old man exploded. 'Good God woman, in a fortnight she could be in John o Groats or worse, no we've got to do something before then. I'll sort it out, a few telephone calls from that mobile contraption they bring round should set the ball rolling.'

Tina gave a little groan. 'Now don't you go accusing people, until you know the true facts, you'll only land yourself in a lot of trouble. Just leave it to me.'

Byron said nothing but settled back into his pillows and closed his eyes. 'Off you go.'

She kissed him on the forehead. 'I'll telephone you on that mobile contraption.'

He nodded. She went to the door and looked back; his face looked younger in repose, it was as she remembered it all those years ago, years that could have been so different for both of them. She vowed to make amends in the future.

As she drove back to Blackaford, Tina's thoughts turned back to their conversation about the Trgarths and Greystone and she realised there were parts of her family background that were a complete blank. The family photograph album contained nothing prior to her parent's wedding apart from the two snaps she had found in the back. Nothing of her father as a young man, no grandparents, none of the usual family groups you would expect to find. It came as something of a shock to realise that she had no idea who her grandparents were, what they looked like and where they lived. All she had were three photographs tying the Pandoggets to the Tregarths, but why and how? And who was the young woman in the nineteen forties outfit whose face seemed vaguely familiar?

She swung into the Fox and Hounds car park and went straight up to her room. She took the photos out of her hand bag and studied the face of the woman carefully, then it came to her, it was the face of the girl in the portrait that hung in Tregarth's study.

~

CHAPTER 12

The next morning Byron made a long telephone call. He spent the day either rummaging in his locker or peering surreptitiously into all the cupboards in the ward. After lunch a nurse brought him two more yellow pills which he palmed, made a great show of swallowing then flushed them down the toilet at the first opportunity.

Just before seven o'clock the evening visitors began to arrive. There were several patients wandering the corridors in dressing gowns so no one took much notice of the old man with a small bundle under his arm making his way towards the main entrance. Byron arrived just as the first influx of friends and relatives surged through the glass doors. They gave little more than a cursory glance at the hunched figure going in the opposite direction.

Joel Menheniot's Land Rover was parked in the ambulance bay and Byron lost no time in clambering beside his friend.

'Thank God you're on time,' he said rubbing his cold hands. 'Did you bring all I asked for?'

Joel nodded. 'It's all in the back. You had better get dressed before you freeze to death. I don't know who's the daftest, you for getting off your sick bed or me for helping you.'

Byron grunted as he struggled into his trousers. 'I told you it was important and I meant it. There, that's better.' He climbed back into the front seat to put on his coat and wellington boots. 'Couldn't find my damned clothes anywhere in there, must keep 'em under lock and key down in the cellar or something. Come on, let's get out of here before they twig and send out a search party.'

Joel muttered something inaudible, started the engine and headed out towards the road. They travelled in silence until the town was well behind them. Byron spoke first. 'How are things at Hendra, Joel? I got worried when I saw that snow. If I'd known that was coming I would never have let them cart me off.'

His companion grinned. 'By all accounts you weren't in any position to have any say in the matter and if you want my opinion…'

'Well I don't, thank you very much.'

'Now don't you get on you're high horse wi' me Byron Pendogget, I've known you too long for that. I'll speak my mind and say you're a bloody fool to go to all this trouble for a damned horse. It's not worth risking yer health, that's all I've got to say.' He stared ahead and set the windscreen wipers going. 'As for the sheep I expect you know that maid o' yours and John Tregarth got 'em down.'

'Tregarth,' Byron muttered, 'why did it have to be him?'

Joel turned his head and looked at him. 'Fate,' he said with a grin.

'You keep your eyes on the road.' Byron folded his arms and settled back into his seat. 'Come on let's get to Hendra, I'm dead beat. Must be old age.'

'Missus says you're to bide wi us tonight. Hendra's too cold and damp she says.'

Byron grunted but said nothing, his thoughts were elsewhere.

Mrs. Menheniot produced a beef casserole with mashed potatoes which made Byron realise how hungry he was and how dull hospital food had been. When he had cleared his plate and finished the treacle tart that followed he gladly accepted the offer of a hot water bottle and Mrs. Menheniot showed him to his room. 'I reckon you should call the hospital,' she told her husband when she came down.

Joel Shrugged. 'They can't keep folks in hospital against there will and if Byron feels well enough to leave then that's that.'

'Just the same they ought to know,' she insisted. 'As long as they know he's alright there won't be any trouble. You can say he's comfortably tucked up in bed ad we'll persuade him to go back in the morning.'

Joel reluctantly made the call before settling down in front of the television for the rest of the evening.

Next morning it was blowing a gale. Byron got up early, impatient to get home; Joel was equally intent on delaying his departure until after morning milking. 'Then I can give you a lift,' he explained. It also gave him more time to persuade Byron to return to hospital. He broached the subject over breakfast but as he feared his old friend was adamant. 'Just give me until tomorrow morning,' he pleaded. 'Then I promise to go back, you have my word on it.'

Joel gave a long sigh. 'Why don't you let me sort this out with John Tregarth. I'm sure 'tis just a mix up somewhere and can be cleared up in a few minutes.'

Byron shook his head. 'You don't know the Tregarths like I do,' he said vehemently. 'They would take the shirt off your back if they thought they could get anything for it. You know what they did to me, good God your memory can't be that short.'

'That was a long time ago Byron, and in any case 'twas this one's father as crossed you.'

'Hmm! Like father like son,' the old man retorted. 'No, this is Pendogget business thanks just the same.'

Joel made one more attempt to dissuade Byron before they got out of the Land Rover in Hendra farm yard but with no success, in fact his words were scarcely heard.

'Would you mind hanging on until I get my van started? The battery's bound to be a bit flat by now so we may need some jump leads.'

Joel indicated that he would and rummaged on the back to immerge with the relevant equipment. It took very little time to connect the batteries and get the old Ford van to spark into life. 'Where are you going in that?' Joel asked.

'I'm going to have a look round the Barton.' He let in the clutch before Joel could say a word

Half an hour later, the van was parked by the iron gates of Greystone Barton and Byron was walking slowly along the field hedge towards the stable buildings. He looked at his watch, it was barely eight o'clock and he was banking that everyone would be at breakfast. He paused at the stone arch to listen: there were no human sounds only the familiar noise of horses pulling at their hay nets and the occasional scrape of a hoof on concrete. He stepped back quickly as a strong wind sent a plastic bucket skittering across the yard. Somewhere a door creaked rhythmically for several seconds until with a final bang it jammed shut. No voices, no footsteps: the yard was deserted.

Byron turned up his coat collar and quickly walked along the row of loose-boxes peering into each one. At last he stopped and with a satisfied 'Ah!' he unbolted the door and walked in. 'So there you are my beauty, but dear lor, what have they done to you?' He shook his head in dismay at the sight of her hollow flanks and sunken neck. The mare turned at the sound of the familiar voice and pushed her muzzle into the old man's chest. He smiled. 'So you have'nt forgotten your old pal then,' he whispered, patting the lean neck. 'Don't you worry, we'll soon have you home again and John Tregarth will be sorry he ever laid a hand on you.' He went out into the stable yard bolted the door behind him and walked determinedly towards the house.

It was raining hard as he made his way to the back door and banged it as hard as he could with his fist. 'Tregarth!' he yelled at the top of his voice, 'I want a word with you!' He went on banging until his fist hurt; eventually the door opened and he was confronted by a harassed Mabel.

'What on earth is going on?' she demanded peering at the figure in the doorway. 'Good Lord 'tis you Byron. What are you doing hear making all that racket at the back door. If you want to see someone you should come round to the front door as is proper.'

Byron shook his head. 'I'm not a front door visitor any more and in any case what I have to say is more fitting for the tradesman's entrance, so I would be grateful if you would tell John Tregarth that I'm here.'

'Won't you come in, 'tis terrible out there?'

'No.' He thrust his hands in his coat pockets and turned his back on her. 'I'll not come into the Barton while there is a Tregarth in it, you know that Mabel Bolitho,' he said over his shoulder.

Mabel grunted. 'You don't change,' she muttered as she made her way back to the kitchen.

Byron looked around the small courtyard as though conjuring up some half-forgotten memories. The rain trickled from his flattened grey hair down every line in his face and into the buttoned up collar of his coat. The sound of his name startled him and he turned to see John Tregarth standing in the doorway. For several seconds the two men looked at each other without speaking before Tregarth said 'My God, man, you look like a drowned rat, for heaven's sake, come in.'

The old man ignored the invitation and came straight to the point. 'You've got my filly and I want her back,' he said angrily.

Tregarth shook his head. 'What on earth are you talking about.'

'Oh yes you have. Come out here and I'll prove it'

'Now look, I don't know what you're on about but I do know you will catch your death of cold if you stand out in that rain much longer so either you come into the house or go home; I'm not prepared to have a row with you on the doorstep.'

Byron gritted his teeth. 'I might have known, you're just like your father. Well you won't get away with it this time, this is one piece of Pendogget property the Tregarths won't filch.' He turned abruptly to walk purposefully towards the gate.

John Tregarth watched him go. 'Silly old bugger, I wonder what's got into him,' he murmured as he walked back to the kitchen. Nevertheless he looked thoughtful as he sat down at the table.

'What did Byron want?' Thomas asked pouring himself a second cup of tea. 'I thought he was suppose to be poorly in hospital.'

'Oh I don't know. He's got it into his head that we've got a filly of his. You've not found any strays on the moor?'

Thomas shook his head.

'Then I don't know what the hell he's on about. He wouldn't come in to explain.'

'I don't suppose he would,' Thomas said thoughtfully. He sipped his tea slowly. 'You don't think there is any connection with that roan filly you bought?'

'What on earth makes you think that?'

Thomas shrugged. 'Well, just think a minute. You buy a quality animal, admittedly in poor condition, for next to nothing from someone who by your own account was pretty shady to say the least. How do you know she wasn't lifted from one of old Byron's fields one dark night?' There's been a hell of a lot of rustling on the moor as we know only too well.'

Tregarth shook his head. 'No, couldn't be, we would have heard about it.'

'But suppose the old boy was taken ill before he could contact the police? You know what they say - if it's been gone more than two days, forget it. Remember when we lost those bullocks?'

Nick, who had remained silent during the conversation, suddenly got up and left the room. His father watched him go. 'Well, there's one who is obviously convinced that I'm a receiver of stolen property.'

'That's a bloody shame,' said Thomas emphatically. 'It's the only thing on the farm he's shown any interest in since.....I can't remember when.'

'Damn,' Tregarth said quietly. 'I suppose I had better go and see the old boy tomorrow just to make sure. She looks to be well bred, do you think he'll have registration papers? That might clear up a few points.'

Thomas suddenly got up and put on his coat. 'It's time I checked the ewes,' he said.

'Don't be daft, you've got bags of time and you haven't answered my question. Does she look the sort to be in the book?' The stud groom shrugged. 'Could be,' he murmured without looking at his employer.

'Thomas, do you know something I don't?'

Thomas paused at the door. 'All I know is Byron's old mare foaled a few years back. She's in the stud book as we all know, that being the case I expect he used a decent stallion.' He turned the door knob and went out letting the door bang shut behind him.

Tregarth turned to Mabel. 'What's got into him? It was a simple enough question.'

The housekeeper stopped her washing up and gazed out of the window after her departing husband. 'He's known Byron a long time remember,' she said quietly.

'So Byron's mare had a foal,' Tregarth said slowly, 'I hope he used a good stallion, she would be well worth it.'

Mabel had a sudden fit of coughing and left the room.

'All right I'll go and see him tomorrow,' he called after her and added quietly, 'perhaps it's time to make a few amends. If it is his filly then I'm the loser but he can pay the bloody vet's bill.'

By the time Byron reached his van he was soaked to the skin. He shivered violently as he pulled onto the road and headed towards Hendra. At Joel Menheniot's he suddenly braked and swung into the yard, skidding to halt just as Joel came out of the back door.

'You're in a devil of a hurry,' he called. ''Tis a wonder you didn't run me down. What's got into you?'

'Can I borrow your livestock trailer and Land Rover?'

Joel hesitated. 'Well of course,' he said slowly. 'But what do you want it for if that's not too much to ask?'

Byron eased himself out of the van with a groan. 'I'll tell you when I get back.'

'Are you alright? You look to me as though you ought to be back in that hospital bed, not moving stock about on a day like this. Look, whatever it is why don't you let me do it for you?'

'I'm alright, just the old chest playing up again, and thanks but I've got to do this myself.'

Joel frowned. 'I don't know what you're up to and I don't suppose there's a cat in hell's chance of me stopping you, just take an old friend's advice and don't do anything silly, not in your state of health.'

'Are you going to lend it to me or not?'

With a look of resignation, Joel went back into the house and returned with the keys. He tossed them over with a curt, 'behind the tractor shed.'

'You're a real friend' the old man said with a grin.

'I'm not sure I wouldn't be a better one if I said no.' He looked hard at the bedraggled figure leaning against the van door. 'Why don't you come inside, get yourself dry and have a bite to eat before you go charging off? Missus 'l fix you up.'

Byron hesitated and looked at his watch; there would be plenty of time before it got dark. 'Thanks,' he said. 'Be alright if I leave my van in the barn?'

Joel nodded, waited for him to park then led the way to the kitchen. Within half an hour there was hot soup followed by a pasty and strong tea. Mrs. Menheniot took his wet clothes to dry by the kitchen stove while he sat in his long johns with a towel round his waist.

It was mid afternoon before he finally left the Menheniot farm and headed the Land Rover and trailer towards Hendra. He parked in the yard and busied himself checking the stock until dark, then he went indoors, lit the fire and slumped into the armchair. Within a few minutes he was asleep.

It was cold when Byron finally stirred. He got up stiffly and switched on the light, the electric clock on the wall showed a quarter to eleven. 'Just about right,' he muttered as he buttoned up his coat. 'Now, where's that big torch?' It took less than five minutes to find all he needed: the torch, a halter, some horse cubes and an old towel which he cut into four squares. 'That should do it' he said. 'Plenty of baling string, and we're off.'

It was nearly midnight when he parked the Land Rover and trailer in a lay-by a few yards from the gate to Greystone Barton. The rain had stopped and the moon glinted between black, scudding clouds as Byron walked briskly up the drive towards the stable buildings carrying a small bag. He waited until the moon had disappeared behind a cloud, then slipped into the yard and went quickly to where Mystery stood with her head over the door. He spoke to her quietly and she whickered softly at the sound of the familiar voice. He entered the loose-box and slipped the halter on the lowered head. He gave her a few horse nuts in the palm of his hand, then taking the pieces of towel from the bag he wrapped each hoof and tied them round the fetlock. 'There my beauty,' he whispered, 'you'll be as quiet as the grave.' He looked towards the house: there was only one light on and he knew it came from the study. 'We'll have to go very steady,' he told the mare, 'Mr. John Tregarth looks to be still awake.'

The observation was only partially true for Tregarth was in fact asleep in his armchair, a half empty bottle of whisky on the table in front of him. Talisman lay at his feet grunting contentedly with every expulsion of breath. One ear twitched and suddenly the hound jerked up as a low growl rolled up from deep in his throat.

Tregarth woke with a start. 'What's the matter old chap?' he whispered. The dog's hackles rose as it stalked towards the window giving a low bark as it went. Tregarth pulled the curtains and peered out. 'Can't see a damned thing,' he muttered, then as the moon briefly lit the yard he said louder, 'By God! I think there's somebody poking about out there. Right, come on boy, I'll lay even money that we've got another visit from our friend Slogger Dixon and this time he'll get what's coming to him.' He pulled on his boots, selected a heavy stick from the collection in the corner of the kitchen and went out.

Talisman's growl became louder and Tregarth slipped a length of baler cord through his collar and held him close. He led the dog round the back of the stables and through the hay barn, pausing to scan the yard before moving across to the tack room: the most likely target for a thief. A movement along the line of stables caught his eye. 'Dear God! He's taking a horse,' he growled in disbelief. Tregarth stepped out of the shadows and yelled, 'Stop where you are Dixon or I'll set the dog on you.' The man said something which Tregarth could not hear and began to run tugging at the halter rope as the mare pulled away in panic and galloped through the gate.

'All right you've asked for it this time,' Tregarth bellowed. 'Get him boy.' He let the baler cord slip through his fingers as the hound lurched forward and raced towards his quarry. The figure that had been leading the horse spun round and fell to the ground with a muffled cry as the big dog reached him. Talisman caught hold of his coat and hung on until his master ran up and pulled him off. 'All right you can get up now.'

The figure did not move.

'Come on man, the dog hasn't touched you. The game's up.' He poked a leg with his stick but still the man did not move. With growing apprehension Tregarth knelt down to get a closer look. 'Come on man you're not hurt.' He took hold of the arm that was shielding the head and began to pull the man to his feet. As he did so a fleeting shaft of moonlight lit the face. Tregarth stared in disbelief. 'Oh my God,' he said hoarsely, 'Byron Pendogget you damned old fool.'

He picked up the limp body and carried it into the house, yelling for Mabel as he entered the back door. The fire was still glowing in the study so he took him in there and laid him on the settee. By the time Mabel appeared in her dressing gown Tregarth had loosened Byron's collar and was dialling for an ambulance. The housekeeper stared in disbelief. 'What on earth… what has happened?'

Her employer was busy giving address and postcode details to the emergency service. He covered the mouthpiece, 'I'll explain later, just prop his head up and get him comfortable.' He turned his attention to the girl at the other end of the phone. 'It's a farm, tell them I'll have a light at the end of the drive so that they can't miss us.' He looked up at Thomas who had stood behind Mabel in his pyjamas. 'The old fool tried to take the mare,' he shook his head, 'if only he had come in this morning we might have sorted it out, now look what we've got.'

~

CHAPTER 13

Tina woke with a start and groped for the telephone beside her bed. 'Who the devil can be ringing at seven o'clock in the morning?' she muttered peering at her digital alarm. The woman's voice at the other end was quiet and matter-of-fact. 'Is that Tina Pendogget?'

There was a slight West Country accent and Tina knew it was the hospital. 'Yes,' she answered apprehensively.

The voice continued as though reading from a script. 'I'm sorry to call you so early. This is Bodmin hospital, I'm afraid Mr. Pendogget was re-admitted at one o'clock this morning. His condition is giving us cause for concern and we felt you ought to know.'

'Yes, thank you' was all Tina could think of saying. She put the phone down and leant back on the pillow with her eyes closed then sat up with a sudden jerk. 'What did she mean by re-admitted, how could he be re-admitted when he's never been home?'

'Eh, what?' Hugh stirred. 'What are you talking about and who was that on the phone at this hour?'

'Go back to sleep,' Tina said wearily. 'You'll need all you can get. I'm going down to Cornwall this morning so you are in charge for the next few days.'

Hugh sat up. 'But you've only just come back. What do you want to go gallivanting off down there for again?'

'That was the hospital, they are concerned about my father, I need to go.'

Hugh flung back the bedclothes. 'Well I' sorry for the old boy and all that,' he said angrily, 'but there you are, don't clap eyes on him for nigh on twenty years then all of a sudden he's the beloved parent and you have to be at his bedside. I find it a bit hard to swallow.' He got up and started to dress.

Tina sat on the bed. 'You don't understand.

'So you keep telling me.'

She watched him put on his track suit. 'So it's a spot of jogging then?'

'That's right, got to keep in trim, ease the old tension you keep putting on me.'

'You need it, you're putting on weight.' She slid back into bed and closed her eyes again.

Hugh crossed the room and flung back the curtains. 'I would just like to know where I figure in all this?' he asked turning to face her. 'It's alright for you going off like this but what about the business? You seem to have forgotten that we are equal partners and I can't go on doing your job as well as mine.'

Tina sighed. 'I realise that Hugh, just bear with me until I get things sorted out, then we'll get back to normal. It shouldn't take more than a day or two.'

He looked at her intently. 'You've changed Tina. I know it's your long lost father and all that but this whole thing seems to have dragged out a long time and I can tell something is bothering you. I'm not sure that getting back to normal will be that easy.' He paused. 'You have'nt met someone else. I mean another man?'

'For heaven's sake Hugh get off on your jog and let me get organised. There's a lot to do and not much time to do it in.' She gave him a slap on the backside as he went out of the door.

Hugh came back for breakfast pink and glowing and in a much better mood. 'I think we ought to get extra help,' he said with a mouthful of toast.

Tina shrugged. 'If you think we can afford it.'

'We'll damned well have to. I'm not going to do two peoples work indefinitely.'

'Please yourself.'

Hugh bristled. 'Well you might sound a bit more interested, after all it's as much your business as mine.'

'Let's talk about it when I get back shall we. In the mean time I'm going to pack some things and get on my way.' She got up from the breakfast table and walked past him into the bedroom.

It was a dreary journey under glowering skies and with rain most of the way. There was no elation as she crossed the Tamar bridge and passed the Cornwall boundary sign. Tina's thoughts centred on the frail old man in a hospital bed: the one tenuous link with her half forgotten childhood.

She drove straight to the hospital and was immediately ushered into the intensive care unit. Byron was asleep or perhaps unconscious and breathing through an oxygen mask; one arm was attached to a drip and there were more connections which Tina did not understand. She wanted to ask the young nurse who was busily checking the readings on a machine next to the bed but in the end settled for simply asking how he was.

The nurse smiled her professional smile. 'Quite comfortable and stable at the moment,' she said as she noted down the figures on a clip board.

'How did it happen? He seemed to be getting on so well.'

The nurse looked at her watch. 'You will have to ask Doctor Ferguson about the details, he'll be doing his rounds any time now and I'm sure he will be able to explain everything.'

Doctor Ferguson was young, plump with thinning blond hair, he smiled sympathetically when Tina introduced herself. She was led into a small office, indicated for her to sit down and tapped up the details on a computer screen. He studied it for several minutes before turning to face her. 'I'm sorry all this has happened. It appears your father discharged himself two days ago, unfortunately we did not discover it until he was well off the premises and by that time we could do nothing about it. Of course we cannot keep anyone here against there will but....'

'Yes I understand that,' Tina interjected, 'but he could not have simply walked out.'

'That's right. He had no access to his outdoor clothes so he either went home in his pyjamas and dressing gown or somebody came and fetched him. Almost certainly the latter: quite irresponsible.' He paused to study the screen again. 'Apparently he was re-admitted at one thirty this morning in a state of collapse. A Mr. J Tregarth accompanied him in the ambulance. Would he be a relative?'

Tina looked puzzled. 'Did you say Tregarth?' she asked, convinced she must have misheard.

'Yes that's right. When I was called he seemed very concerned, said something about an accident so I referred him to administration in case the police had to be informed. Things can get very complicated these days what with Health and Safety and all that.'

'Do you know what sort of accident – I mean, was it a car accident or what?'

'Mr. Tregarth was very vague about the circumstances but apparently he had a fall, the bruising bares that out, but any more than that I can't say.'

Tina shook her head. 'Heaven knows how that came about but the important thing is how is he and why in intensive care?'

Doctor Ferguson leant back in his chair and paused as he considered his words. 'It's not the fall we're worried about but he has been through some sort of trauma, shock call it what you will. We know he has a heart condition and of course he is a considerable age, on top of that we suspect a bronchial infection which, to say the least, does not help matters. I don't want to alarm you unnecessarily but I feel you should be fully aware of the situation.'

'Yes, thank you, I quite understand.'

'You can rest assured we will do all we can. I assume you will be staying in the district for a few days?'

Tina nodded.

'Good, then if you could let me have a contact number we can keep you in the picture as it were.'

She gave him the number of the Fox and Hounds and her mobile. He turned back to the computer, tapped in the information and looked at her with a reassuring smile. 'You can come and see him any time, don't worry about visiting hours.'

Tina walked out into a cold, dark evening. It was drizzling again as she crossed the car park and got into the car. She sat watching the visitors coming and going, her thoughts ranging over the recent turn of events until the cold made her shiver and she quickly turned the ignition key.

As she drove towards Blackaford the puzzle of Tregarth's involvement was uppermost in her mind. Some sort of accident they had said; she promised herself that if Tregarth were involved she would find out how and why and if necessary look into the legal aspects: John Tregarth would have to pay, one way or another. The lights of the Fox and Hounds loomed out of the dark.

Gloria met her at the door. 'Got your phone message,' she said. 'Sorry to hear about your father. How is he?"

'Not so good, I'm afraid.'

'Oh dear. Anyway, come in and get something warm inside you. Oh, and by the way you've got a visitor.' She gave Tina an odd look and added: ' Don't worry he's in the bar so he can wait until you've had a bite to eat.'

Tina was curious but too tired to worry about the mysterious caller just at that moment. She wanted a cup of tea, a hot meal and a gin and tonic, not necessarily in that order. Without taking off her coat she slumped into the armchair by the kitchen stove and closed her eyes.

Gloria made the tea and handed her a cup. 'Don't worry, I'm sure he'll be alright. Tough as old boots, so Charlie says.'

Tina sipped her tea pensively. 'They don't fetch you all this way unless it's pretty serious,' she paused, 'who is it wants to see me?

Gloria raised one eyebrow. 'Well as a matter of fact...' She was interrupted by a call for help from the bar. 'Sorry, must go, duty calls. I'm afraid I haven't had time to put up a vegetarian meal for you but there's a hot bacon and egg pie in the oven and the veg. is under the grill.' She made for the door calling back over her shoulder. 'If you think you can face it help yourself.'

Tina finished her tea, hung her damp coat in the hall and thought about the bacon and egg pie. She was hungry - no, she was famished, and it smelled very good. 'Oh to hell with it,' she said out loud and opened the oven door, cut herself a generous slice, added the peas and mashed potatoes and set about it with a will. She was finding her vegetarian diet very difficult to keep up in a small isolated community like Blackaford and it was rapidly becoming a case of 'When in Rome...' Her next thoughts turned to the gin and tonic and her surprise visitor.

There were about a dozen people in the bar when Tina ordered her drink; most she recognised as regulars and there were a few who gave her a friendly nod as she sat down at one of the tables. She looked round for her likely visitor and picked out the tall man with his back to her talking earnestly to Gloria. It was the well cut blue pin-striped suit which set him apart from the rest. A bit old fashioned she thought, not the sort of thing you expect to see in a village pub. She watched him for several minutes, there was something vaguely familiar about the back of that tanned neck and the dark greying hair. She was about to get up and walk over when Gloria looked past him and nodded to her. The man straightened up and turned round: it was John Tregarth.

Her surprise must have been obvious. He looked down self-consciously at his well pressed trousers and brightly polished shoes. 'Just had a session at the bank,' he said by way of explanation. 'Thought I had better call in and tell you before you hear it from anyone else.'

'Hear what from anyone else? It seems you have some explaining to do Mr. Tregarth and if it's about my father I most certainly do want to hear about it.' Her voice had an edge.

He sat down opposite her and there was an awkward silence during which he revolved his glass between his thumb and forefinger, then without looking at her he recounted the events of the previous day. Not until he had finished did he look up and in the dim light Tina could sense the dark eyes watching her intently. She began to feel uncomfortable.

'What do you expect me to say Mr. Tregarth?' she asked angrily. 'From what you have told me you are directly responsible for my father's condition and that being so my reaction is to go to the police and see what they have to say.'

'I've already done that,' he said quietly. 'I have found from bitter experience that it is better to get things cleared up as soon as possible.' He shook his head. 'If only the old foo...sorry...if only your father had done what I asked we could have discussed the whole damned business and none of this would have happened.'

For once Tina did not know what to say. There was another prolonged silence during which he got up from the table and stood gripping the back of the chair so that his knuckles showed white through the skin. When she said nothing he turned with a muttered 'sorry,' and walked towards the door.

'Mr. Tregarth,' Tina's voice was strident. 'I hope you have a good solicitor.'

He stopped but did not look round, only a faint nod of the head indicated that he had heard and understood what she was saying, then he strode out without looking back. The door banged and Tina realised that all eyes in the hushed bar room were on her. She turned defiantly and stared back. Gloria clinked a glass. 'Another G and T coming up,' she called, someone laughed and as suddenly as it had stopped the normal hubbub resumed.

'I thought you might need this.' Gloria put the drink on the table and sat down. 'You can tell me it's none of my business but I haven't seen John as worked up as that for a very long time so I'm curious to know what that was all about.'

Tina muttered her thanks for the drink and took a sip. 'Whew that's strong.'

'It's a double, but you haven't answered my question,' she grinned, 'and anything that stops my customers in mid slurp demands an explanation,' she paused. 'Of course if it's personal....'

'No, not really and anyway I expect it will all come out sooner or later.' She recounted what John Tregarth had told her.

Gloria shook her head. 'So you reckon poor old John is responsible for putting your father in hospital?'

Tina flushed with anger 'What do you mean 'poor old John'? That man apparently receives stolen goods in the shape of my father's horse and then assaults an old man when he comes to collect his property. I call that criminal and I told him as much. He's just the sort to literally ride rough shod over people to get what he wants and I'm not going to be intimidated by some huntin', shootin' bad mannered peasant like him. If anything happens to my father I'll hold him to account and that's certain.'

'You must do what you think is right,' Gloria's voice was calm, 'but I've known John Tregarth a lot longer than you. It's true he doesn't have many social graces but I don't think he would knowingly do what you describe but…? She held up her hands. 'It's for you to decide but make sure you get all the facts first, that's all I have to say,' she paused, 'I must get back to the bar.'

Tina sat for a while sipping her drink and mulling over the events of the day. She felt alone, isolated and to cap it all the one friend she thought she could rely on had made attempts to defend the man. Was it a case of closing ranks she wondered? After all she was an outsider and a 'towny' at that so perhaps it was only to be expected. She looked up to study the occupants of the bar. 'There they are,' she thought, 'red faces, hairy sweaters and welly boots and not a civilised thought between them.' The glass was empty and she felt slightly light headed. She wanted to tell them that her father was a moorland farmer and she had been born on the moor and she was not to be treated as an outsider; instead she glared at the young man sitting on a nearby bench, got up and walked over to the bar. 'I think I'll have an early night,' she told Gloria. 'If the phone should ring…'

'Don't worry I'll give you a call. I hope you sleep well.'

Tina nodded and went to her room. She kicked off her shoes and lay back on the bed listening to the splatter of rain against the leaded windows. 'It's just too bloody awful,' she said out loud as the tears came. It had been a rollercoaster ride from her first arrival at Hendra to the present and she wondered whether the next move would be up or even further down: something she did not want to think about. Then there was the business of her father's hospitalisation and John Tregarth's part in that. Visions of the confrontation between the two men formed in her mind and with them fresh feelings of anger towards the man whom she was convinced had assaulted her father knowing full well the old man was in the right. There would be headlines: LANDOWNER ASSAULTS PENSIONER. She could see it now and the thought gave her some satisfaction.

She unpacked and prepared for bed. The room was cold, the bed was cold, she felt miserable and longed yet again for the warmth of her Wimbledon flat. Eventually tiredness overcame any discomfort and she drifted into an uneasy sleep.

The sound of voices outside on the landing woke her with a start. A loud 'Shhh,' and the creak of a floorboard outside her door caused her to sit up and listen intently. She made out a man's voice, then a giggle that was unmistakably Gloria's. The sound of the man's voice again, this time giving a muffled curse: Tina sat up wide awake. She quickly got out of bed, tip-toed to the door and opened it an inch just in time to see Gloria in a black negligee returning to her room but it was the figure at the top of the stairs that held her attention: a tall dark haired man wearing a blue pin-striped suit.

CHAPTER 14

A cold grey dawn drew wraiths of mist through the bare branches of the hospital oaks; the hall porter's breath hung in the air as he pushed open the glass doors and stepped outside to allow Tina to pass. Byron had been put into a private ward. He looked small and shrivelled so that her heart missed a beat with the thought that she might be too late. She sat down not daring to touch him; his eyelid's flickered and he turned to look at her.

'I suppose you think I'm a silly old fool,' he said in a hoarse whisper.

She shook her head and squeezed his hand. 'No I don't think that, stubborn perhaps.'

She smiled, 'But then that makes two of us.'

'Pride,' he said suddenly. 'Pride and stubbornness, don't let it ruin your life too.'

'Sorry?' Tina looked puzzled and was about to ask a question when a nurse came in and said quietly 'Doctor Ferguson would like a word before you go. In the meantime, it would be a good idea not to tire him too much.'

'I'm not dead yet, young woman.' The old man's voice was surprisingly strident. 'So don't talk above my head as though I were.'

The nurse looked at him and smiled, then she turned and with a nod to Tina and left the Room. Byron tried to sit up. 'There are things you ought to know,' he said collapsing back on the pillow.

'Now you heard what the nurse said' Tina said soothingly. 'I'm sure they will keep until next time.'

The grey head nodded imperceptibly and when the tired eyes closed she got up quietly and tip-toed out.

Doctor Ferguson told her nothing she had not already guessed and she for her part told him as little as possible about the reasons for his self discharge from the hospital. They shook hands and Tina wandered down the corridor in a half daze until she reached the main doors. She stood for a moment, then with an audible, 'Damn,' she pushed them open and walked briskly to where her car was parked, got in and slammed the door hard. The tyres squealed as she turned out of the hospital gates and headed towards Blackaford.

*

The telephone message came at eight o'clock in the morning. Tina knew as soon as she heard the ring, and the look on Gloria's face confirmed her forebodings. Tina accepted the news with a mixture of resignation and anger. 'The story of my life,' she told herself. 'Just when things are panning out well, someone always drops a bombshell to wreck it all.' But it was the feeling that she had been cheated out of the one relationship that might have mattered that caused her most hurt and anger. It was the thought of what might have beenrather than the grief that caused her to sit in her room and weep quietly.

'All those years' she said to Gloria when she ventually came down for some coffee. 'All those years and I never gave him a thought, just a name on my Christmas card list: just a name like any of the dozens of customers and companies we send to. He might as well have been dead, so what have I got to grieve over now?' Nevertheless there were tears in her eyes.

Gloria patted her hand. 'You mustn't blame yourself. I don't suppose he thought about you much. These things happen when families break up.'

Tina shook her head. 'He remembered everything about me, I'm sure he did. All those years on his own with no one to turn to, and now I can't make it up to him.' She burst into tears.

'That's good,' Gloria said as she cleared the table. 'Get it out of your system luv, there's nothing like a good cry, and when you are ready I'll give you a hand with the arrangements.'

'Yes thanks, I had forgotten about all that. I don't know where he should be buried;I don't even know if he went to church....' Tina dabbed her eyes with her napkin.

'I don't think you need to worry too much about that,' Gloria said over her shoulder.

'It will almost certain to be at St. Petroc's: funny little church in the middle of a field not far from the Tregarth's place. Our local vicar looks after it but they only hold about a dozen services a year plus the odd funeral and wedding. I've only been once and that was to a funeral - one of our old regulars. All I remember was that it was damned cold, and that was in May! Tell you what, I'll give the Reverent Dorothy a ring, she'll know.'

It was an hour later when Gloria found Tina sitting in a corner of the lounge reading the local newspaper. 'I've spoken to the vicar and,' she paused, 'It appears that the Pendoggets are always buried at St. Petroc's and have been since the year dot. She says her predecessor told her that in the old days as soon as a Pendogget was born a place would be set aside in the vault for their eventual demise. That's what I call forward planning. There's probably a place for you there if the truth were known.'

Tina grinned. 'I doubt it. I don't suppose they would count me as a paid up member but in any case I'm sure that can't be true, it must be another family with the same name.'

It was only when Mr. Coombes senior called later in the day to offer his condolences and confirm that Coombes and Son would undertake their usual services as they had always done for the family and that Mr. Pendogget would be placed to rest with his forbears; it was then that Tina suddenly realised that there was no mistake. She could only nod as they shook hands

'I knew your father,' he said quietly. 'Not well, of course, but,' he hesitated for a moment 'I always considered him a fine gentleman.'

She wanted to ask him about her father but he was through the door and gone before she could get the words out. 'Another time' she thought.

That evening she cornered Charlie Hawkins in the bar. 'You knew my father, Mr. Hawkins.' The old man nodded without looking at her. His glass was empty and she fetched him another pint with her own gin and tonic. 'As I was saying, you knew my father and from what I heard you say, you knew him a long time.' Again he nodded, took a long pull at the beer and said thoughtfully: 'We was boys together, I was a few years older, father was groom and we was boys together.'

'Sorry, whose father was a groom?'

The old man looked surprised. 'Why, mine o'course.'

Tina leant forward. 'I know so little about him, I don't even know if there is any family I ought to inform. I thought perhaps you might…..?

He shook his head. 'You've come to the wrong man, Miss. True we knocked about together but I were just the groom's son, didn't know nothin' about the family except what the housemaid or cook let out.' He paused to take a long drink. 'And I didn't take sides neither when all that who-ah were goin' on.'

'What who-ah was that?'

'You know, all that business with George Tregarth. Oh never mind, 'twas all a long time ago. You don't want to trouble your head with all that ol' stuff'. He drained his glass. 'You can be sure any relatives will get to know soon enough especially if there's a will, and it was rumoured that old Byron had a little bit stashed away. Bad news carries fast and when you get to my age you reads the hobituary columns just to make sure you're not in 'em . He shook his head. 'Poor ol' Byron, the last of the Greystone Pendoggets 'cept of course you miss. Times change and 'tidn't always for the better.' He stood up and buttoned up his coat. 'Now I'd better be off, sorry I can't be of much help. See you there.' He picked up his stick and made for the door leaving Tina more bewildered than ever.

*

On the day of the funeral, it rained heavily. 'Typical.' Tina remarked as she and Gloria got into the ancient black Daimler behind Mr. Coombes. She was glad of the company And since there were apparently no other relatives (she had put a notice in the obituary column of the local paper) she had cajoled a reluctant Gloria to ride with her. 'I just don't know what to expect.' Tina confided. 'All this business of a family vault and special church. He was only a small farmer…'

She turned to look at her companion with tears in her eyes. 'I don't really know what he was, who he was, who I am for that matter.' The sobs were genuine.

She was surprised, almost shocked to find that the tiny church was full. A pale young man in a dark grey suit ushered her into the only empty pew at the front reserved for relatives. She sat there alone, conscious of the eyes peering and the necks stretching to catch a glimpse of the only Pendogget. She pondered the idea of moving back to sit with Gloria but decided against it. Never had she felt so alone and isolated.

The service was mercifully short. As she followed the coffin out into the church yard she caught a fleeting glance of a tall figure slipping out of a side door and knew it was John Tregarth. The rest of the congregation filed past with averted eyes and respectful nods until only four were left to see the coffin taken to the newly dug grave : Joel Menheniot, Gloria and a frail old lady clinging to the arm of a large woman. Tina tried to remember where she had seen the large woman before. Suddenly it came to her: the travelling companion on the bus to Bodmin and she gave a little nod of recognition.

The vicar intoned the half-familiar words, her blond hair blowing across her face. When the ceremony was over the pall bearers shuffled away, heads down in professional reverence. The Reverent Dorothy (call me Dot.) gave her a comforting smile and followed, her vestments billowing in the freshening breeze.

Tina shook Joel's hand and thanked him for coming then she gripped Gloria's arm. 'And thank you for all that you have done.' She looked skyward 'At last it has stopped raining so tell Mr. Coombes I'll walk home, it's not very far and I want to have a look round,' then in a lower voice 'I want to have a word.' She indicated towards the two other women who were making their way slowly down the path. She caught up with them and touched the younger woman on the shoulder. 'It was very good of you to come Mrs.. er?.'

'Judd. We met on the bus if you remember.'

'That's right. I didn't realise you knew my father that well.'

'Oh no, I didn't, 'twas mother, she insisted on coming, isn't that right mother.' She addressed her mother in a louder voice, then added quietly 'She's ninety four you know and stubborn as a mule.'

The old lady nodded. 'I knowed your family from a long time m'dear,' she said in a thin cracked voice. 'But I never though I would live to see Master Byron buried.' She turned to her daughter. 'I've lived too long that's the trouble - too long.' She dabbed her eyes with a small lace handkerchief.

Tina was intrigued. 'How well did you know my father then?'

The old lady shook her head 'Did he never mention Molly Bolitho?' She asked sadly.

Tina thought for a moment. 'I've heard the name Bolitho but that was up at Greystone Barton. I never heard father mention a Molly, but then I haven't been in touch for a very long time.'

Mrs. Bolitho applied the lace handkerchief again. 'Fancy him not telling you about me. Why child, I used to look after him when he were a little 'un. Mind, I were only a chit of a girl meself.' She gave a long sigh. 'Yes I looked after master Byron, him and young George both. We had good times at the Barton in those days, before the war and before...' She stopped abruptly as her daughter took her arm and said, 'Come on mother, don't start on allthose old stories. You'll catch your death of cold if we don't get you home soon.' She smiled at Tina. 'Can't be too careful at her age.'

Tina nodded and asked hesitantly, 'Do you think I might talk to your mother sometime? It's just that she seems to know so much more about my family than I do.'

The old lady turned sharply. ' I'm not deaf nor daft young lady but you'll be welcome for a chat any time. I don't go nowhere much these days. Just ask in the village anyone will tell you where Molly Bolitho lives.'

'Yes, thank you. Take care.' Tina watched them walk slowly towards a waiting car parked just by the churchyard gate. As she did so she recalled the faded photograph of two small boys, Byron and George; but who was George? She wracked her memoryfor any hint that her father had a brother. Perhaps he died young , but no one had ever mentioned an uncle, alive or dead. Molly Bolitho was the key and she made up her mind to visit her at the earliest opportunity.

Tina walked slowly round the churchyard, reluctant to return to Blackaford until she had studied the inscriptions on the headstones in the Pendogget plot: and there they all were, her family. The most recent read 'William George Pendogget died 1976 and Mary Elizabeth died 1980, could they have been her grandparents? She had no memories from early childhood and they would have been dead before her short stay at Hendra twenty years ago. The oldest headstone was by far the grandest with a square plinth which made it stand out above the others. It was inscribed: Admiral Sir Henry Pendogget died 1823 and above his name was carved a coat of arms, she made out a ship and a sea horse: the coat of arms she had seen carved into the stable wall at Greystone Barton.

The walk back to the Fox and Hounds gave Tina plenty of time to ponder the events of the past days. She had been named the sole beneficiary in her father's will. The solicitor told her that it had not been changed in twenty years. That fact touched her deeply. 'All those years he though of me' she thought. 'And from me? A card at Christmas if he was lucky'. The hot tears were more of remorse than grief.

By the time she reached Blackaford several things had begun to resolve themselves in her mind. She would sell the farm and then look for a nice weekend cottage not too far away. She would find out more about her family and as soon as possible visit Mrs.Judd and her mother, then perhaps she would also look up Charlie Hawkins who she saw briefly in the church. There was wretched horse to see about; that was a problem she did not feel competent to deal with. It would mean going to Greystone and facing John Tregarth again, something she did not relish, then she remembered how pleased the boy Nick was when he showed her what he considered to be his mare, and now he was going to find out that it she isn't, She was pretty certain that she could prove the animal was her father's and unless Tregarth could produce receipts and papers to the contrary she was going to claim it as her property. It would be only right to go and talk to Nick, explain the situation and try not to upset the lad; he seemed much too vulnerable. She decided to pay him a visit the next day.

That evening Tina pressed Gloria for more information about the Tregarths and their connection with her family, but without success. 'All long before my time, you had better ask some of the old 'uns out there,' she said indicating towards the bar. 'They would be your best bet.'

'Do you know a Mrs. Judd? The big woman I spoke to with the old lady in tow.'

'Can't say I do, why?'

'I would like to go and visit them before I go on to Greystone and I wondered if you knew where she lives.'

'No, but I bet old Charlie does. He knows just about all the locals within miles of Blackaford. He'll be in about nine o'clock, I'll ask him for you.'

Just after closing time Gloria tapped o Tina's bedroom door and handed her a crumpled Slip of paper with the address written on it. She copied it into her diary before returning to bed where she lay listening to the wind thrashing the trees outside her window, as she had done so many times since coming to Blackaford.

The next morning she telephoned Hugh to say she would be staying on until the weekend. He did not sound at all pleased but she was used to his moods and as far as she was concerned he could either like it or lump it. Next on her list was a visit to Mrs. Judd and her mother, then it was Greystone Barton, something she was not looking farward to.

The gale had blown itself out in the night. It had rained heavily and everywhere glistened and steamed in the pale sunlight as Tina drove up the narrow winding lane to Trewarda village. She felt excited, like a child anticipating a trip to the movies, wondering how the story would turn out.

It was not difficult to find the row of stone cottages just off the main street. She parked the car, walked briskly up the path of number eight and knocked on the door. A dog barked but no one came. She knocked again and this time heard a voice; the dog was quietened, there was the sound of shuffling slippers and Molly Bolitho's face peered round the door. She looked at Tina for several seconds. 'I didn' know who 'twas,' she said opening the door wider. 'But now I can see 'tis you Miss Pendogget, come in, come in.' She led the way into the front room which had the same unused damp smell as the living room at Hendra. 'I'm sorry but my daughter's out to the vicarage this morning, she cleans you know, but if you want to talk to her I'm sure the vicar won't mind.'

'Oh no Mrs. Bolitho it's you I would like to speak to if you could spare a moment.'

The old lady's face lit up. 'Me? Well that's nice. I don't get many folks dropping in for a chat and 'tis specially nice to have poor Byron's daughter. Now, I'll go and make us a cup of tea, so you make yourself comfortable.'

Tina sat in one of the two arm chairs, a black and white Jack Russell terrier having taken over the other. She could hear the rattle of tea cups and in a short while the old lady re-appeared.

'Would you mind carrying the tray for me,' she asked. 'I can manage most things but I have to watch my feet. I'm turned ninety you know.'

Tina made appropriate noises of disbelief as she followed through to the kitchen and carried the tray back.

Molly indicated to a small table. 'If you'll just put it down there and pull up that high backed chair for me we can make ourselves cosy.'

Tina did as she was asked and the old lady sat down with a grunt. 'I prefer to sit up,' she said. 'It makes it easier to get up and down. Now, you pour and tell me what you want to talk about.'

Tina had been warned about Cornish tea: it came out of the pot the colour of oak varnish. 'It was very good of you to take the trouble to come to father's funeral on such an awful day,' she said pouring into fine willow pattern cups.

Molly reached over and patted Tina's knee. ''Twas the least I could do.'

Tina gave her a cup. 'I was interested in what you said about looking after my father and I'm intrigued to know how that came about. Why did he need looking after, was he ill, were you a nurse? You see he never spoke of his life before he met my mother and I suppose I never bothered to ask.' She paused for a moment before continuing: 'Mrs. Bolitho, I want you to tell me all you can about my family and in particular the connection with Greystone Barton and the Tregarths. I know my father stayed there as a boy and must have been friends with John Treagrth's family, then something must have happened to change all that. I would like to know what.'

Molly Bolitho looked at her incredulously. 'What's that you said? Your father stayed there and was a friend of George Tregarths?' She emphasised the words, shaking her head as she continued: 'Lor but haven't no one ever told you that your grandfather owned the estate? Aye and a good many generations of Pendoggets before that. As for George Tregarth and Master Byron, why, they were brothers.'

For Tina the last statement came as a body blow. 'Brothers?' The question blurted out. You mean that John Tregarth and I are...?' She did not finish the sentence but stared down into he tea cup.

Molly gave a wisp of a smile. 'Don't you worry my dear, you're no blood kin to the Tregarths. No, they was adopted brothers, leastways George was and I suppose that was the crux of it all.' She drained her cup, placed it on the table and folded her hands in her lap.

Closing her eyes she repeated: 'Yes' the more I think about it the more I reckon that was the crux of it.' She opened them again. 'I'll have another cup of tea if you don't mind.' She took two sips, replace the cup and saucer on the table and resumed: 'Now where was I? Oh yes, young George. Hmm, where to begin? She thought for a moment. 'You know, I can remember it as if it were only yesterday even though it must be over seventy years ago. I was a young girl helping in the house and the dairy. 'Twas terrible hard work in those days: five o'clock till breakfast in the shippon milking cows, then housework 'till four and again back to the farm for second milking 'till six, not to mention churning butter and scrubbing churns. But you don't want to her about all that except to say that we were worked off our feet so the missus, your grandmother, decided we needed more help in the house so she advertised for a house maid. 'Twas a winter's afternoon when the girl arrived at the front door looking wet and bedraggled. When she said she had come for the housemaid's job I told her to go round to the back door, well, servants didn't use front doors in those days and it made me wonder whether she had ever been in service before. I reckoned her to be in her early twenties, very well spoken quite pretty with dark hair tied up in a bun. I took her coat, which was better than anything I ever had, and put her little canvas bag in the kitchen before taking her through to see the missus.

On the way she told me she was called Kathryn Tregarth and had come on the bus from Wadebridge to Blackaford and had walked from there. Anyway she were taken on and I must say she worked hard, although I had to teach her how to milk and most other things that had to be done. It made us all wonder, your grandmother included, what she had done before.

Whatever it was it couldn't have been hard work, not by the look of her hands.' The old lady leant back in her chair and closed her eyes.

'I don't want to tire you too much Mrs. Bolitho.' Tina sounded concerned. 'I can always come back another day.'

'No that's alright dear; just need to rest my eyes now and again. So where was I. Ah yes, well, it was clear that she was a cut above the rest of the servants, and of course we all began to wonder what she was doing stuck out in a place like Greystone,' she paused and sighed. 'Well of course, you can guess: she were pregnant. Of course in them days 'twasn't like today; then it was a big disgrace if you wasn't wed and I suppose the poor maid had been left in the lurch by some man and kicked out by her family. We never did find out whether Tregarth were her real name. Luckily for her your grandparents were good Christian folk and, since they had no children of their own, they took care of her; then, before she were due to have the child she disappeared, packed her bag and was gone before morning without so much as a 'by your leave'. Your grandfather, hoped she had gone back to her family, and perhaps she had. We thought that would be the end of it, but it wasn't.' There was a long pause.

'Would you like another cup of tea?' Tina asked

Molly shook her head. 'No I'm alright thank you: just getting my thoughts together.'

She moved uncomfortably in her chair. ''Twas winter time and I remember the wind had brought a tree down across the drive and the men were out sawing it up. It had been raining for days and everything was damp and cold.' She shuddered. 'I can still feel it in my bones; lor' how I hate winter. Anyway, it was just getting dark when your grandfather rode into the yard and, leaving his horse in the pouring rain, rushed inside shouting out to come quick as Kathryn was in one of the stalls and needed help urgently.

Well, we did no more but slung our coats across our shoulders, the Missus and all, and ran out after him. Master got a torch and went straight to where the poor girl was laying on the straw. In those days all the horses were tied up in a long line with wooden partitions between them and she was in the one that Master's horse should have been in. We lit a lantern and could see that she was in a bad way and it was obvious that the baby was coming. Your grandfather carried her indoors and tried to telephoned the doctor but the line had been brought down by the fallen tree so he had to drive into Blackaford to fetch him. I remember the your grandmother getting worked up because they took so long; I suppose because of the trees down and the floods and all. By the time Doctor Graham arrived it was getting late. We explained how she must have collapsed in the stables on her way to the house and he said he wasn't surprised if she had walked from Blackaford in that condition.

'Next thing we knew the baby was born but poor Kathryn passed away before they could get an ambulance out.' Molly paused to wipe her nose. 'Sorry, but I can still see her face as she held her baby for that short while: a dark haired little thing but with a rare pair of lungs.' She smiled . 'So that's how George came to us. Of course they advertised in the papers for any relatives or next of kin but when nothing came up your grandparents decided, since they had no children of there own they would take care of the little mite. Kathryn was buried in a corner of the Pendogget plot and the child was duly Christened George William Tregarth, and a funny little thing he was too, dark eyed with black curly hair, I used to call him my little gypsy.'

'So where does my father come in to all this?'

'Well, as I said, he hadn't been born then. He came along a year later; some said 'twas heaven's reward for saving the orphan, for they had been married a good many years without having a child.' Molly closed her eyes and they sat in silence while Tina waited patiently, not wanting to tire the old lady. Eventually she asked: 'Could you give me some idea of what happened later on? What caused all the trouble between them?'

Molly thought for a while before answering. 'Of course I was married and left the Barton before all the trouble. My nephew Thomas could tell you more about that, he was groom there from leaving school and I daresay was party to some of the goings on for all I know, but of course the story was the talk of Blackaford but I can't remember the details, you'll have to ask him.'

'Yes, thank you very much Mrs. Bolitho I will.' Tina got up and began to gather the tea things. 'That was a very nice cup of tea, now can I help you with the washing up?'

Molly eased herself out of the chair. 'No that's all right my dear, just take the tray to the kitchen and I can cope. I may be old but I'm not yet helpless.' She followed Tina to the sink and took hold of her hand. 'I can't tell you how pleased I am to meet Byron's daughter, and you are so like him.' She gave the hand a pat. 'I only saw you once when you were very little and he brought you to a meet of the hounds here in the village. There you were in the back of hits ramshackle old car wrapped up like a little Eskimo.' She chuckled to herself, 'I don't suppose you would remember whether your mother was with you?'

Tina shook her head. 'Mother would never have approved, she considered hunting to be barbaric.'

The old lady shrugged. ''Tis part of everyday life down here, but she would be entitled to her opinion.'

'I'm afraid I agree with her.'

Molly tut tutted. 'Your grandfather would turn over in his grave if he heard you say that. He was Master of the hounds for over twenty years and my husband Ben whipped in to him.' She paused for a moment. 'Strange to think that if things had turned out different, your father might have followed on and you might have been a real horsey little maid. Instead George Tregarth stepped in and wore the red coat.' She began to make her way to the front room. 'I'll just have a sit down for five minutes if you don't mind my dear. I have enjoyed our chat but I'm not so young as I used to be.'

Tina took her arm and guided her back to her chair. 'I'm sorry to have kept you talking so long. You have been most helpful. Don't worry I can find my own way out.' She squeezed the old lady's hand and made her way to the front door.

'So Tina Pendogget' she said to herself as she drove out of the village in the direction of Greystone Barton. 'You belong to a family of foxhunting squires, twenty-first century dinosaurs who ought to have become extinct a hundred years ago.'

The thought should have displeased her but for some reason it did not. 'And now to visit another member of that breed,' she muttered. She began to understand some of the reasons why her mother had left after less than four years living the farm.

She stopped the car on the gravel drive of Greystone and went straight to the stable yard hoping to find Nick without having to go to the house, but it was deserted. She walked round peering over loose-box doors, most of which were empty. The few horses that were there turned to look enquiringly as they pulled at their hay nets. She recognised the roan mare, her roan mare she reminded herself. Even to her untutored eye the animal seemed to be in much better condition than when she last saw it. The mare came to the door and nuzzled her sleeve 'What on earth am I going to do with you?' she said patting the outstretched neck. As far as animals were concerned the most she had ever owned was a cat and her mother objected to that.

On the other side of the yard the box that had housed the black stallion was empty, the door open with a folded rug over it, She walked across to see if there was anyone inside; as she did there was the sound of hooves on gravel and John Tregarth rode through the archway. On seeing her he reined in and sat looking at her while the stallion chinked at its bit, neck arched and every muscle rippling as it fidgeted against the restraint. She felt the age old antipathy of the person on foot towards anyone astride a horse: well, she was not going to do any forelock tugging.

'I thought I had better come and have a look at my property,' she said forcefully.

He shrugged and dismounted. 'You seem certain she is your property,' he said as he loosened the saddle girth.'

'Don't you?'

'I gave good money for her.'

'You stole her.'

He stopped what he was doing and turned round slowly. 'There are many things I might do Miss Pendogget but stealing from old Byron is not one of them.' He led the stallion into the loose-box and began unsaddling. 'I'm very sorry for what happened to your father and if it's any consolation I've thought about it ever since and reluctantly I've come to the conclusion that the mare could have belonged to your father. It was obvious he had no doubt that night and....' He began to lead the horse towards the loose-box where he removed the saddle and bridle.

Tina followed a few steps behind. 'And?' she asked as he came out with the saddle on the crook of his arm and began to walk towards the tack room.

'And it is possible I was sold a pup.'

'I'm not sure what that means but I assume you are telling me the animal belonged to my father.'

Tregarth put the saddle onto the saddle rack and hung up the bridle without looking at her. 'I'll sign the necessary forms but on one condition: that is that she stays here.'

'So that I have to pay you its keep I suppose,' Tina said tartly.

He turned to face her. 'That is one consideration since I'm out of pocket to the tune of several hundred quid, but no, the main reason is that my boy Nick as shown a real interest in the mare and to tell you the truth it's the first time he's shown any interest in anything that goes on in the stables or the farm for a long time.'

Tina thought for a moment. 'Yes, okay. I had noticed that he seemed keen to take care of her, so it's a deal. What has Nick said about it?'

'Not a lot, but then he never says much, not to me anyway.'

Tina smiled. 'So I had better go and have a word with him then if that's okay.'

Tregarth nodded. 'Last time I saw him he was heading for the moor and I expect he's taken his flute so it shouldn't be too difficult to find him.'

She walked back to the car to put on her boots and coat, then she set out along the path, over the stream and up to the moor. It was the way Nick had led her from the nightmare of Hagtor Mire; how long ago that now seemed. It was a steep climb and she paused at the top to look down at Greystone where the winter sun shone on the grey lichen covered roofs and a thin pall of smoke drifted up from one of the tall chimneys. Further down the clouded waters of a lake were stippled by a passing shower and all around was the sound of the wind. It was a wild and beautiful place which stirred something in Tina which she found difficult to describe. A moment of yearning for things that might have been; sadness over a lost childhood and a father who was a stranger. The moment was fleeting and she quickly turned to resume her walk.

Nick was sitting crosslegged at the foot of the big rock, his flute in his lap and his eyes fixed on some spot on the far side of Hagtor Mire. He had not heard Tina's approaching footsteps and was startled when she spoke.

'Your father said you were up here,' she said quietly.

He nodded and indicated to her to sit down. 'It's quite dry,' he said reassuringly. 'The overhang shelters it just here.'

She did as he bid and leant back against the rock: it felt warm. 'Quite a sun trap you've found.'

He ignored the remark and returned his gaze to the mire. 'I suppose you will be selling the mare if you can prove she really is yours,' he said, selecting a long stalk of grass to put between his teeth.

'That has all been settled,' Tina replied. 'She is going to stay where she is, at least for the time being,' An idea was beginning to form in her mind. She thought for a moment.

'Look, I don't know much about horses but she seems to have meant a great deal to my father so I don't want to part with her. On the other hand you have obviously grown very attached to the animal. Her name is Mystery, by the way. So what I suggest is this: she can stay at Greystone if you promise to look after her.'

The youth's face lit up. 'That would be great Miss Pendogget. Thomas would give me a hand to back her in the Spring. Father says she's got a lot of quality; I bet she's fast. We......'

'Now just hold on a minute,' Tina interrupted. 'Just remember she still belongs to me. She's a Pendogget mare not a Tregarth.' She grinned and stood up. ' I want to be involved in what goes on.' She brushed the dead grass from her coat. 'And if we are going to be partners young man we should be on first name terms so Nick, it's Tina from now on. Now, I'll have to be off; there's a great deal I have to do.' She tried to sound like a maiden aunt but was not sure she had succeeded.

Nick stood up. 'I'll walk down with you if that's okay.'

Tina smiled. 'Of course.'

He paused for a moment. 'My mother used to bring me up here,' he said in a matter-of-fact tone.

'Oh yes?' The inflexion in her voice was meant to encourage him to go on. She dearly wanted to know more about the late Mrs. Tregarth.

Nick hesitated 'She was killed in a riding accident you know.' He turned quickly and began to walk down the hill. 'They found her in the old quarry on the other side of the mire.' The matter-of-fact tone was beginning to crack and he looked away

Tina put a hand on his arm. 'I am sorry,' she said, then regretted the action when she saw it caused him obvious embarrassment. His step quickened and he continued the rest of the way in silence until they reached the car. As she was getting in he said quite suddenly 'She was always afraid of the moor, I realise that now; and yet she still took me up there in all weathers.'

Tina looked at him. 'I suppose mothers tend to do whatever pleases their children. She sound like a very nice person.' She hesitated for a moment. 'Would that be her portrait In your father's study?' He shook his head and with a faint grin replied that it was his grandmother when she was a young woman. 'Father won't have any photographs or paintings of my mother put up in the house,' he added bitterly.

Tina started the engine. 'We must have another chat sometime,' she said. 'I would like to know what you want to do when you leave school and the sort of things you are interested in?'

Nick shrugged. 'The only things at school I was any good at were art and perhaps music; but what good are they when your father wants you to be a farmer? And anyway I've left school now so there's no chance of doing any of that.' He took a step back and looked admiringly at the red sports car. 'That's a smashing bit of kit, really cool. How fast will it go?'

Tina smiled 'I honestly don't know.' She let in the clutch and called back: 'Let me know if I can help,' as the wheels spun on the gravel and she accelerated down the avenue of swaying beeches.

Her next port of call was the Bodmin police station where, after waiting for nearly half an hour in the draughty reception area, she eventually spoke to the young sergeant who had taken John Tregarth's statement concerning her father. He shook his head when she asked if they were going to charge him with assault. 'There was no evidence that any blow was struck madam, that was the first thing we checked with the hospital. Just a slight graze on the temple consistent with a fall, and they confirmed that the old gentleman suffered a heart attack.'

But what about the dog? Wasn't there something about setting a dog on him? Surely that counts as an assault?'

Again the sergeant shook his head. 'No teeth marks or anything like that, not even torn clothing; we checked,' he paused for a moment, 'and of course there is the question of trespass and the right to protect property etc. It was very late at night and….'

'All right you needn't go on sergeant, you have made your position perfectly clear.'

'Not my position madam, but it is the opinion of my superiors that there is no evidence on which to base charges. Of course if you wish to try a civil action, but…..' He shrugged and left the sentence unfinished.

Tina thanked him and walked out into the darkening street. Lights in the shop windows reminded her that she had a business to run and could spare no more time or money in pursuing a vendetta against John Tregarth. As she walked back towards the car park she saw Thomas Bolitho coming towards her carrying two large plastic bags. He grinned sheepishly. 'Weekly shop, Mabel doesn't like coming in.' He paused. 'Nice service yesterday,' he said quietly. 'A good turnout.' Tina nodded with a faint smile

'Saw you talking to Aunt Molly, she goes back a long way. He was real gentleman your father and was a great help to Mabel and me particularly.' There was a long pause. 'There is something I would be grateful if you could do for me, it concerns the roan mare.'

~

CHAPTER 15

On Sunday Tina returned to London having made arrangements for Joel Menheniot to take care of the farm until such time as it was sold. The estate agent had warned her that it might be difficult to sell at that time of year and advised holding off any serious advertising until the summer with a view to an Autumn sale. Since she did not need the money desperately she had agreed, and in any case it gave her an excuse to visit Cornwall more often. A point she could use when Hugh brought up his inevitable objections.

The long drive gave her time to think. Her relationship with Hugh was getting more an more difficult. Whatever there had been between them was being stifled by petty arguments about the business, her absences, his family; they even argued about food and she was sick to death with his fads. To hell with it; she would eat anything she liked, meat if she felt like it, so what. 'If only,' she thought, 'if only we could have a good flaming row and finish it.' The more she thought about it the more appealing the idea seemed.

Then there was young Nick Tregarth, out of step with all around him and with a father who seemed to care more about his horses than his son. She would like to help the boy, set him on the right road. Yes, that would give her great satisfaction and one in the eye for John Tregarth. Which brought her to the third train of thought: if she could not prosecute him for assault through lack of evidence as the police had informed her, then she would make him pay some other way; she had no idea how but she was sure she would think of something.

*

The next few weeks were a mad rush purchasing stock for the Spring and summer fashions, arranging advertising, displays and all the ballyhoo that went with selling the latest styles. It was hard work and even Hugh was too tired to quarrel when they eventually got home in the evening. Tina was pleased to be totally immersed in her career once more with the distractions of Cornwall pushed firmly into the background

It was well into April before the subject cropped up again in the shape of a letter addressed in neat handwriting and postmarked Bodmin. She left it to be opened in the evening when she would have more time. Hugh had also noticed the postmark when he picked up the mail from the doormat

That was another thing that annoyed her: the way he always inspected her personal letters before handing them to her. 'I suppose this will mean another trip to Cornwall,' he said with a hint of sarcasm in his voice.

Tina was tempted to say that it was none of his business but that would have caused an argument and they hadn't got time for that now, not with a new consignment of dresses arriving first thing that morning. She pushed the letter into her handbag, snapped it shut with an air of finality and led the way down the stairs without replying. Hugh followed muttering, 'I don't know why you don't just clear off and live down there permanently.'

She spun round. 'I might just do that. Now let's get on or we'll never get finished.'

It was a long day and they decided to eat out in the evening. As usual Hugh suggested a restaurant which catered exclusively for vegetarian diets and Tina was too exhausted to offer any alternative ideas. It was a meal eaten in almost complete silence. Not until the coffee was served did Hugh look up with an enquiring 'Well?'

'Well what?'

'When are you off to the back of beyond?' He asked irritably.

Tina shrugged. 'I don't know. I haven't read my letter yet.'

'Then don't you think you should… dear?' The last word was added with emphasis. 'It might be from your farmer chap and the sooner we know your plans the sooner muggins here can make arrangements to keep the business going.'

'I don't want to read it here thank you,' she said tartly. 'And he's not my farmer, far from it thank goodness.'

Hugh frowned. 'Well, I just want to know where I stand. It is from that Tregarth chap isn't It.'

The ghost of a smile flitted across Tina's lips. 'Probably,' she said taking the envelope out of her handbag and opening it. She looked quickly at the signature: it was from Nick. 'Yes,' she said with deliberation. 'It is from Mr. Tregarth and I would prefer to read it in the privacy of my own home.' She folded it carefully and replaced it in the handbag.

Hugh called for the bill. 'You are deliberately trying to annoy me,' he said in a hoarse whisper.

She picked up her coat without replying and made for the door. He caught her up in the car park. 'What the hell do you mean by sweeping out like some bloody Prima Donna. What's going on?' He held out his hand for the car keys adding: 'I'll drive.'

Tina shook her head. 'It's my car and I'll drive it. Get in.'

Hugh slumped into the seat and folded his arms. 'I don't know what's come over you lately,' he said without looking at her. 'You've changed since you started to go down to this place - where is it, Blackford or some such name.'

'Blakaford actually.' She said as she started the car and backed out of the parking space. 'In what way have I changed?'

'You've gone off me for a start, so I suppose there is someone else.'

'Not necessarily' She wished she had said yes and be done with it, but she had never had to resort to lying and did not intend to start now.

'And there is this silly business about owning a horse,' he continued. 'It just isn't us Tina.'

She pulled out onto the wet glistening road, the fine rain reminding her of her first drive to Blackaford. 'It may not be you,' she said, 'but I run my own life and as far as I'm concerned I like the idea. I might even start to ride again.'

Hugh grunted. 'Don't be so daft, you left all that behind before you were ten years old, you admitted as much only the other day.' She did not reply and there was a long silence be fore he continued. 'It's not just that. I get the feeling that the business is to take second place in your scheme of things and that jut won't do.'

They stopped at traffic lights and she turned to look at him. 'Are you suggesting I'm not pulling my weight?'

'Well, if you like to put it that way, yes.' There was an edge to his voice. 'It's me who has to carry the can while you go gallivanting off to this...... Cornish backwoodsman.'

The lights turned to green and Tina gave her attention to the road. 'He's far from being a backwoodsman as you put it,' she said casually.

'Ah! So you admit there is someone else.'

She made no reply. If he wanted to think that, well he could. They drove the rest of the way in silence while Tina sorted out the best way to explain that she wanted to finish their relationship. How to do it without hurting him too much and without putting the business partnership in jeopardy. 'So much for mixing business with pleasure,' she thought as she turned into her parking space behind the block of flats.

They took the stairs to the third floor: part of their keep fit routine. Tina could sense that he was brooding and she judged that it was going to be now or never. As soon as they were inside the flat she broached the subject. 'I want to talk about us Hugh,' she said. His face assumed a pained expression and she wished he would stop looking like a whipped spaniel.

'I thought you might,' he said walking over to the drinks cabinet. He poured two gin and tonics and handed her one. 'As I said earlier you have changed. I don't know why or how but it has been coming through loud and clear for some time now and tonight you have confirmed what I have suspected all along.' He sat down on the sofa and gazed into his glass.

Tina was beginning to feel sorry for him and she knew from past experience that this was just what he wanted; this time she was determined not to be sidetracked. 'It isn't just to do with Cornwall,' she said firmly. 'I'm sorry Hugh but there just seems to be no future in our relationship, you either can't or won't get a divorce and I can't go on as we are. Has it never occurred to you that I might want a family of my own instead of having to listen to you groaning on about yours?'

He looked up in surprise. 'I've never thought of you as the marrying type. Where has the Women's Lib. and self sufficient career woman gone?' There was a note of sarcasm in his voice which did nothing to cool his partners rising anger. 'And you know very well that we agreed right from the start that we were both adult human beings and there was no need to break up my marriage until the children were old enough to understand. In fact it was you who was adamant about not getting married.'

She ignored his last remark. The trouble with you is you want your cake and eat it and if you think so much of you precious family I suggest you go back to them.'

He stood up slowly. 'Oh, come on now darling,' he said in his best wheedling tone. 'We've had a long day, let me fix you another drink and we'll talk about it in the morning.'

Tina bristled. 'Now isn't that just typical of you - never do to day what you can put off until tomorrow - no, Hugh, it won't wash. I mean what I say.'

'You mean you're chucking me out?'

'If you want to put it that way I suppose I am.'

'What, now, tonight?'

Tina pursed her lips. 'You can stay till morning if you like but it means sleeping in here.'

It was his turn to get angry. 'No thank you, I would sooner find a hotel room.'

'You can always go home - you've got one you know.'

He did not reply but set about packing a suitcase. 'I'll come back for the rest in the morning,' he said as he snapped it shut.

'You can take the Porsche,' she said holding out the keys.

He shook his head. 'There are plenty of taxis around thank you.'

Tina walked to the door and opened it, the gesture had an air of finality about it that was not lost on Hugh. He shrugged, picket up his case and walked past her without a word. She waited until she heard the lift come, then closed the door quietly. It was then the realisation dawned and she panicked. 'Oh my God what have I done?' She almost shouted the words as she ran out onto the landing, the thought that he might also leave the business uppermost in her mind. The lift was just closing as she yelled: 'Hugh, wait!' but it was already on its way down. She quickly shook off her high heels and ran down the three flights of stairs, reaching the bottom just as Hugh emerged. 'Hugh I'm sorry,' she gasped 'I should not have said those things and you were right, it would be better to talk it over in the morning, so come back up and we'll have a nightcap.' She stretched up and gave him a peck on the cheek. He pulled her back into the lift, pressed the 'up' button and took her into his arms. 'The trouble is,' he said quietly' 'A lot of what you said is true.'

*

At breakfast the next morning neither said much and the atmosphere was subdued. It was Tina who broke the silence.

'I'm sorry about last night Hugh, it's just that…. well…we seem to be reaching a dead end and I think it would be better for both of us if we ended our relationship on good terms. We need each other to run a successful business, let's not muck it up with a relationship that's going nowhere; I want you as a friend.'

'And not as a lover.'

She reached out and touched his hand. 'Sorry, but all good things must come to an end and that is where we are now.'

'In that case,' he said with a sigh, 'one of us ought to get off our backside and get some work done.' He got up from the table and reached for his jacket.

Tina smiled. 'Thanks Hugh. I need a bit of time to sort a few things out so if you don't mind I'll stay on here and come in later. You can take the car if you like.'

He shook his head. 'Quicker by tube, but thanks just the same.'

It was several minutes before she moved after Hugh had left. Eventually she settled herself on the sofa and took out Nick's letter. It was a surprisingly neat hand for a boy she thought,but typically short:

Dear Tina,

I thought I had better let you know how things are. Thomas and I are working on Mystery. She has been lunged and bitted and we shall start long-reining her next week if the weather holds. Thomas says she should be ready to back in another week or two.

We are in the middle of lambing so life is pretty hectic. Father is mad about me leaving school but so far hasn't done anything about it. I think he is too busy chasing up rustlers, we lost a lot of sheep last winter and now they have starting taking bullocks. I think the Lord and Master is pretty worried. Something is up, he has been off in his best suit quite a bit lately.

Can I email or text you about getting a job near where you are sometime?

Nick

Tina smiled. 'Well apart from not understanding any of the horse talk, that was a very good letter Master Nicholas. They must have taught you something at school, but as for coming to London I somehow don't think so.' She folded the letter and put it in the bureau drawer. 'I think it may be time for another visit to Blackaford,' she told herself. 'It's about time I chivvied the estate agents about selling the farm, and it would give Hugh time to cool off a bit.' She kicked off her shoes and settled back to relax. She had forgotten what it would be like to have the flat to herself; she savoured the feeling of independence and made herself another cup of coffee.

~

CHAPTER 16

That same morning John Tregarth and Thomas were discussing their future plans. They walked off towards the stable yard together and stopped beside the loose-box door where the roan mare quietly pulled at her hay net. John watched her intently. 'So what are we going to do about the Pendogget mare Thomas. I suppose we have to call her that now but in any case we'll have to sort a few things out with the lady'.

The stud groom coughed nervously. 'Well she seems to have put young Nick in charge by all accounts.'

'Oh, she has has she'. There was the hint of a smile on John's lips. 'She's a good looker'.

Thomas grinned. 'Aye, and so is her mare'

'That's not what I meant and you know it. One big drawback is we don't know anything about her except she's out of a top class mare. I don't suppose old Byron Pendogget had anything in the way of records showing the stallion, we could ask Miss Pendoggetto have a look, What do you think Thomas?' They were standing in the middle of the yard and Thomas walked over to the far end where Titan's head showed over the loose-box door. He patted the sleek bay neck , gently pulled one ear and said very quietly ' You know don't you old fellow'. Then he turned to face his employer. ' Well I suppose you'll have to know eventually' he said pulling his pipe out of his pocket.

'What do you mean. What will I have to know?

Thomas slowly filled the pipe which yard rules prevented him from lighting, he nevertheless put it into his mouth gave a couple of sucks before putting it back to face his employer. 'Titan', he said. 'Titan? What are you talking about, what has Titan to do with it?'

There was a long pause before Thomas continued.   'John, you know I wouldn't do anything against you and I don't enjoy abusing my responsibilities but'. There was a long pause before he continued. 'Well, you know that Byron was always good to Molly and me when we were first wed.' He stopped and studied the bowl of his pipe . 'That was a difficult time if you remember, so I owed him a favour. He rang me up one evening to say he was hoping to breed from his mare and could I put him in the way of a decent horse that didn't cost too much, Well, knowing the breeding of the mare and its blood lines I realised that this wasn't the job for some crap stallion, it required something special, something like Titan but I also knewthat Byron could never afford him so I told him I would work something out and ring him back. It was a couple of weeks later he telephoned to say the mare was coming into season and had I found him a suitable horse. I have to say I thought long and hard about this at the time particularly as we were only just getting over Elizabeth's funeral'.

He looked at John, 'And you were in a pretty poor way to say the least and as fate would have it just at that time you decided to take yourself and young Nick off to Badminton Horse Trials for a couple of days. So, to cut a long story short I loaded up Titan and took him over to Hendra'. There was a long silence before he continued ' That mare's the last of the line John and to tell you the truth I was as keen to see her go to our stallion as he was. I know it was wrong and I'm sorry but I took no fee from him, it was just a favour for old time's sake'.

His empoyer frowned 'Why didn't you tell me all this before Thomas?'

'Oh, I don't know , I thought you might have blown your top and given me the sack or something, and in any case I didn't think it would ever come to light and I certainly didn't reckon on the offspring turning up here'.

'Well you devious old bugger I reckon you owe me three hundred quid then. What would you say if I took it out of your wages?'

Thomas shrugged 'I suppose you've every right to'.

Then to the old man's surprise John burst out laughing. 'Well, if that doesn't take the biscuit, first I pay good money for an animal only to find it's stolen goods and so doesn't belong to me anyway, then I'm informed it's got by my own horse without a stud fee. If that ever gets out I'll never live it down. Does Miss Pendogget know all this?'

'What about papers?'

'All there, I signed the Service Certificate and Miss Pendogget found the rest'.

'So the lady has a genuine registered thoroughbred by my stallion for free'.

'I suppose so, not only that, it's entered using the Greystone prefix, she's called Greystone Mystery'.

John grinned ' Well you've got to give it to the old boy he certainly had a nerve, but you know what this means? It means we have a five hundred pound stake in that little mare so let's see what madam has to say about that'.

Thomas gave a sigh of relief. 'Thanks for taking it so well'.

His employer smiled. 'You know damned well I couldn't run this place without you so let's forget the whole thing, and anyway we're going to get a good livery fee out of it, not to mention the fact that it has given Nick something to think about, so it's not all bad. Which reminds me; where is the boy?'

'He's taken the mare into the sand school. I reckon she's about ready to back so are you going to get on her first?' John pursed his lips and though for a moment. 'You carry on, I'll be down in a while.'

Nick studied the roan mare as she trotted round him on the lunging rein which he held lightly in his left hand, while with his right he flicked a long driving whip just behind her heels. Weeks of care and good feeding had transformed her into a strong, healthy animal once more. There was a sheen in her winter coat as she arched her back and played with the bit in her mouth. 'Canter.' He gave the command in a firm voice, at the same time giving a little flick to the whip as Mystery broke into a steady canter round the circle. 'Whoa.' She slid to a halt and stood, ears pricked waiting for the tit bit she knew would be forthcoming. Nick offered the cube of sugar on the palm of his hand and gently pulled one ear. 'Well done girl,' he said quietly and turned to Thomas who was leaning over the gate looking on approvingly.

'I reckon she's about ready,' Nick called. Thomas frowned and shook his head. 'That may be young 'un but I still reckon your father should get up first.'

Nick tightened the girth another hole. 'I don't see why,' he said. 'I've done all the work so far.' He dearly wanted to be the first person to ride the mare, not only to impress Tina but also there were other reasons closer to home. He looked up and was dismayed to see his father standing next to Thomas. 'Why can't he leave me alone to get on with it,' he whispered to the mare as he let down the stirrups. 'I'm not a kid any more.'

John pulled a stem of grass and put it between his teeth. 'Does the boy want to get up first?' he asked quietly, and when the old man nodded he continued: 'I've been keeping an eye on them, the mare's as ready as she'll ever be and he has certainly worked hard at it, so let him do it but.....' He touched Thomas' arm. 'I don't want any rodeos and broken bones you understand.'

The groom gave another nod and walked to where Nick stood with his back to him holding the mare's head. 'He says to get up,' he said taking hold of the bit. Nick glanced towards the gate and was disappointed to see that his father had gone, but at least he was going to be allowed to finish the job himself and that was something.

Thomas led Mystery to a nearby straw bale. 'Now, just you step up on this bale and lean across the saddle and remember what I told you: no sudden moves and talk to her.' Nick quelled the butterflies in his stomach and did as the old man said. As he put his weight onto the saddle one ear flicked back; he spoke to her and it pricked forward again.

Thomas nodded encouragingly. 'Well she didn't mind that too much so this time throw your leg across and sit still.' He emphasised the last two words. The butterflies were going mad as Nick put his foot in the stirrup and eased himself into the saddle.

'Steady little lady, Whoa now.' He felt the mare quiver beneath him as her muscles tensed, once more the ears flicked back and then forward, he could almost feel the uncertainty in the animal's mind. This he knew was the pay off moment for those weeks of schooling and gentling that had gone before. If they had got it wrong half a ton of bucking horse could explode underneath him.

'Don't move until you feel her relax,' Thomas said quietly stroking her neck.

Seconds passed that seemed like hours but gradually the tension in both horse and rider eased until eventually Nick slowly dismounted.

Thomas was grinning. 'Good, now do it again but this time move your legs backwards and forwards and get her used to your weight moving in the saddle, then we'll try walking on.'

The operation of mounting was repeated several times until Thomas was satisfied, then he coaxed Mystery to walk forward. There was a moment of hesitation as the unaccustomed burden moved with the first step, then a quiet word from the rider and she walked confidently round the school. 'I'll lead you round a couple of times and then you'reon your own,' Thomas said.

The moment came when he unclipped the leading rein and stepped aside. At last Nick was riding the mare on his own: he had done it. The feeling of elation welled up inside and it was a feeling that was quickly transmitted to the animal. Suddenly she put her head down, the back muscles arched and Nick was jolted by all four feet hitting the ground at once. Instinctivey he yelled 'Whoa!' and heaved on the reins to prevent her from getting her head between her knees in an uncontrollable buck. The effort pulled him forward, he braced his feet in the stirrups but the second buck did not come. 'Whoa,' he commanded again and this time Mystery's head came up and she stood with her ears pricked, while her rider sat perfectly still talking to her gently, then he nudged her forward and they walked quietly round the sand school.

Thomas nodded his approval. In the adjacent field John Tregarth smiled and resumed his hedge laying.

That afternoon Nick composed a letter to Tina. It began with the sentence: 'Today I rode Mystery.' He re-read that sentence several times before going on to give an account of the proceedings which led up to that momentous occasion, quite unaware that some of the terms used would mean little to the intended reader. He addressed the envelope and made his way to the study to find a stamp. As he approached the half open door he heard his father's voice on the telephone.

'I'm sorry Mr. Dobson, I know it's late but you did promise delivery this morning.'

Nick began to retreat, only too well aware of his father's dislike of being interrupted in the middle of a telephone conversation; but the next remark caused him to stop and listen.

'I know it's overdue….yes……well I promise to put a cheque in the post first thing tomorrow……what do you mean I said that last time……look, if you could just this once I would be grateful, we do need it urgently……..' There was a moment's silence before the receiver was slammed down.

Nick peered round the door to see his father sitting, elbows on the desk, his face buried in his hands. The sight gave the youth an acute feeling of embarrassment and shock.

He coughed and rattled the door handle.

'What the blazes do you want, Nick?'

'Just a stamp.'

'Oh.'

For a moment the two looked at each other, Nick hoping for some explanation while his father searched for the words. 'Nick…' The telephone bell cut him short. 'Damn!' He picked up the receiver. 'There's a second class in the little draw…..Hello, Greystone Barton.'

Nick found his stamp and tip-toed out.

In the kitchen Mabel was laying the supper table while Thomas, spectacles perched on the end of his nose, read the local paper. 'I see Hendra is advertised again,' he commented.

'Shouldn't be surprised if some towney don't buy it to play at farming.'

Mabel shook her head. 'Wouldn't have thought the house good enough for that. 'Tis pretty run down by all accounts and in any case there's too much land.'

'Soon sell a bit off.'

Mabel grunted. 'Well one thing's for sure, it won't be a Tregarth that will be buying any.' She looked up as Nick came it.

Thomas turned a page. 'Hold your tongue woman,' he said irritably.

She put out the plates without another word, then turned to push down the top of her husband's paper with one finger. 'Tis only right the boy should know.'

Nick sat down. 'What should I know?'

Thomas shifted uncomfortably. 'Best speak to you father about it,' he said, quickly turning to the sports page and the racing results.

John Tregarth came into the room and the look on his face told Nick that now was not the time to ask difficult questions. They all sat down to the meal in silence and the youth sensed an undercurrent of foreboding as the others gave inordinate attention to the cold meat and potatoes. Even Mabel seemed too preoccupied to scold him for his usual meal time transgressions. Eventually Thomas pushed his plate away, folded his arms and asked: 'Well John?'

His employer looked up frowning. 'Well what?'

'Have you decided what you're going to do?'

There was a paused while John toyed with his half eaten meal, then he said slowly 'Nick, go and give the horses their late feed.'

Thomas' fist came down hard on the table. 'No John.' The tone had a vehemence so untypical that Nick stopped eating, his fork halfway to his mouth. The stud groom continued more quietly, 'No, Nick should stay, he's shown he's not a child and it affects him as much as any of us.'

The youth looked at his father who shrugged agreement as he pushed his chair back to stretch his legs towards the stove. 'Well Nick,' he said without looking at him, 'It looks as though I've made a complete cock-up of the whole business. Not to beat about the bush, we're just about broke.' He swung round to study the effect of the statement on his son.

Nick placed his knife and fork carefully on his plate, and without taking his eyes off them leant back in his chair. 'So?' The question was half whispered, his face showing no emotion save a slight raising of the eyebrows.

'Good God boy is that all you can say.'

The youth shrugged. 'It's only money.'

His father shook his head. 'I don't think you understand Nick: it means selling this place.' He turned to the old couple. 'I'm sorry but it really looks that way. I'll do my best to get you a council house or something in Blackaford, I can still pull a few strings.'

Mabel got up quickly and went to the sink. Nick could hear her sniffing as she rattled the dishes. Thomas stood up slowly and walked over to where his jacket hung on the door. He rummaged for his pipe and tobacco and equally slowly returned to his seat and began to push the rough-cut into the pipe bowl with a gnarled finger, then with a glance towards Mabel, struck a match. Soon his head was wreathed in pale blue smoke and the dottle began to crackle. He took the pipe from his mouth and wiped the stem on his jersey. 'Never thought I'd see the day,' he said. 'But I guessed it were coming, you can't go on losing stock like we've been doing.'

'Oh it's not just that,' John sighed. 'The truth is things have been going downhill for sometime now: the rotten lamb prices, beef stores fetching rock bottom money, and then there were the TB reactors last year. No, the rustling has just been the last straw that breaks the camel's back.'

'So what about you and Nick?'

'Don't you worry about me,' Nick chipped in. I can take care of myself.'

His father grunted. 'Now you're being daft boy. How on earth do you think you would be able to cope. You wasted your time at school, left against all advice and without anything worthwhile in the way of qualifications, so how are you going to take care of yourself?'

'I could get a job.'

'Ah! That'll be the day. No skills, no transport; I'm afraid you're stuck with me old chap, at least for the foreseeable future.'

Nick stood up. 'So I'm a failure, well that makes two of us then.' He picked up his jacket and made for the door. 'I'm going to give the horses their late feed. Not much point my hanging round here, nobody's going to take any notice of what I say. It'll all be the same in the end, you will decide and we'll all have to toe the line as usual; the fact is I don't care all that much. They heard the back door slam. John looked at Thomas in exasperation.

'What can you do with a boy like that?' he demanded.

The old man shook his head. 'Someone had to say it John; the boy's right. When was the last time you two had a sensible conversation, eh? Now we are talking about all our futures 'tis proper that you should let him have his say.'

'Alright, alright, you've made your point. I'll have a chat with him as soon as he comes back in. In the mean time I could do with a drink; how about you? '

Mabel gave a disparaging grunt when Thomas replied that he would. Two glasses were duly produced and a stiff measure of whisky poured into each. Both men drank it with the minimum of water. 'Single Malt?' Thomas asked. John nodded. The old man savoured it appreciatively. 'That's really good.'

'I'm surprised you can still afford the stuff.' Mabel growled under her breath.

No more was said until Nick returned. 'I'll feed Talisman,' he said turning to go. John called him back. 'Sit down Nick and I'll tell you how I see it, you can chip in if you want to, and that goes for you two,' he nodded towards Thomas and Mabel. Does that suit everyone?'

He scowled at Thomas who was relighting his pipe much to Mabel's dismay. The old man grinned and nodded. Nick returned to his chair and Mabel continued with her work at the sink without looking round.

John leant forward with his elbows on the table. 'I've had an offer from the clay company for the house and fifty acres of the bottom land provided they get the mineral rights over a further hundred and fifty acres.' He looked at the others. The old man and Nick sat impassively; Mabel sniffed. There was a long pause before he went on: 'We've known for a long time that there is china clay under the lake and most of the land around it.'

Thomas shook his head. 'They knew that in the old Squire's day but nothing would make him sell the place to be ripped apart, your father neither. Aye, and I can remember you saying the same thing John Tregarth.'

'Times change Thomas,' John said quietly. 'God only knows I don't want to see the old place pulled down, but who else would buy a rambling old house.'

'What about the rest of the property?' Thomas asked.

'Ah well, the money we get from the clay company should put the rest of the farm straight, so I intend to keep the farm and the buildings and carry on farming.'

Thomas grunted. 'With a damned great clay pit on your doorstep?'

'Yes if necessary.'

'And where will you and Nick be living may I ask?' It was Mabel's question.

'I've thought of that. There's the old grooms place in what used to be the coach house. We should be able extend that to make a decent flat for the two of us.' He waited for a response but non was forthcoming so he continued: 'With any luck in a year or two we can get planning permission for a new bungalow or something.'

'In the mean time you'll pig it in that draughty old hovel,' Mabel said indignantly

'That is no way to live John and I don't mind telling you. You'll never be eating properly and before you know it you'll both be ill, and then where will you be?'

'It won't be for long Mabel,' he replied irritably. 'And we can always go down to the Fox and Hounds for a meal; I'm sure Gloria will be able to fix us up.'

'Oh, you can be certain of that,' Mabel snorted.

Ignoring the remark John turned to Nick. 'You've said nothing yet Nick, so come on now's your chance.'

Nick's mind had not been idle while his father was talking; perhaps this was just the opportunity he was looking for. He gripped the edge of his chair with both hands. 'Why can't I leave and try for a job somewhere? I don't mind what as long as...'

'As long as you get away from here. Is that it boy?' his father interrupted. I've already told you, you're in no position to fend for yourself. When you've shown me that you are then we'll talk about it. Until then I am responsible for you and I'm not having a son of mine wandering loose in the back streets of some town.'

'It needn't be like that,' Nick pleaded. 'Miss Pen….Tina would help me, she said so.'

'Oh she did did she, and what does Miss Pendogget think you might do, work in her dress shop or whatever it is?' In any case you are supposed to be looking after her mare and you can't do that in London.'

Nick stood up and walked to the door. 'I'll tell you this much,' he said angrily. 'If it wasn't for that mare I'd be off like a bat out of hell whatever you say.' He went out and slammed the door.

John moved as though to get up but Thomas leant across to put a restraining hand on his arm. 'let it bide John,' he said quietly. 'The boy's upset, just let it bide.'

The three sat in silence until John said. 'I'm sorry, but I just can't seem to get through to him.'

Thomas began to refill his pipe. When it was well alight he stood up and confronted his employer. 'John Tregarth it's about time you were honest with the young 'un and yourself for that matter. You know damned well you couldn't run this acreage single handed; the fact is you need the boy if me and Mabel are going to be shoved off to Blackaford or somewhere. Now, why don't you just tell him that and be done with it?'

John shifted uneasily. 'I can cope on my own if I have to, and I'm not going to be beholden to the boy for staying. When he can show me he is capable of more than just idling around the I'll help him to get on. Until then he stays here and you can tell him that from me.'

He pushed back his chair, got up and went out towards the study.

Thomas looked at his wife. 'Now don't you go getting all worked up m'dear. We're more than ready to be put out to grass anyway and it'll be better for you to be nearer the shops and things.'

Mabel dabbed her eyes. 'Tisn't that Thomas 'tis just that I hate to think of the old place being pulled apart. We've lived here all our married life and you was born here, and despite of all the troubles we've had a good life, and now it's all coming to an end. Oh dear.' She began to cry again.

'Now that's enough,' Thomas said gently. 'It hasn't happened yet and who knows? Something different might turn up. Come on ol' dear, let's get to our bed; it'll not seem so bad after a good night's rest.'

～

CHAPTER 17

I want to buy it.' Tina handed a sheaf of papers to the bespectacled man behind the desk. He studied them while she eagerly waited to say more. At last he put them down, took off his glasses and said: 'Well?' in a tone calculated to dampen her obvious enthusiasm.

'Well you see Mr. Roberts it's my old family home and I want to buy it back. I only heard it was on the market a few days ago and I understand that there is already an offer under consideration, so I want to get the financial details buttoned up as soon as possible. You see.....'

'Now just a minute, Miss Pendogget; I am a mere banker, not a miracle worker and my advice to you is to think carefully before plunging into this type of investment.' He replaced his spectacles and with a faint smile he picked up the estate agent's description and began to examine it in more detail. When he was satisfied he placed it carefully back on his desk and looked at Tina over the top of his horn rims. 'Brass tacks, Miss Pendogget, brass tacks; let's get down to them. You are quite certain about this I suppose? I hope you don't mind if I question the advisability of saddling yourself with this type of property which, in my estimation, can only lead to further expense - upkeep, repairs ect.?'

'Yes, yes I'm fully aware of the implications,' Tina said impatiently. 'Nevertheless I am going to have it if it is at all possible.'

'Because it is your..hmm...ancestral home?' His smile broadened.

'Then this is an emotional rather than a rational decision.'

'If you put it that way, yes.'

The bank manager removed his spectacles and polished them vigorously. 'In that case there is very little more I can say. I know you to be a determined young lady from past experience; you are also a successful business woman, but...'

'But this is not a purely business decision? I take your point.' She knew him well enough to humour his 'let me advise you young woman' tack. Roberts sat back in his chair and looked at her intently. I suppose you have some plans for this er....' He glanced at the details, 'this eight bedroomed house, with staff accommodation and twenty-five acres of land including a lake?'

Tina hesitated. 'A guest house come private hotel,' she said quickly. 'You know, Summer visitors, Olde Worlde charm, walks on the moors, that sort of thing.'

'Not exactly the sort of thing you are used to. I hope you have done your homework.'

'Of course.' It was a lie, but only a little one she thought.

'Well in that case we had better look into the financial details. Now let me see.' He he turned to his computer screen, tapped in her details and studied it. 'Well your business appears to be doing well enough, and you say you have an agricultural property left to you by your father?'

'Yes, and the agent informs me that we have a firm offer for it.' Tina began to relax: now they were beginning to talk money and for her that was familiar ground.

'And have you got the asking price?'

'Well..er..no not quite.' Another fib: it was well below.

'So there is likely to be a considerable short fall?'

She nodded. 'No problem, I have decided to sell my flat.'

Once more the banker's eyes peered over the horn rims. 'Isn't that a bit rash, I mean how will you run your business without somewhere to live in town? Forgive me for asking but.....'

Tina smiled. 'They do have Broadband in Cornwall you know. I can easily do most of it from there, and in any case I have a very competent business partner who can run things from this end.'

There was a long, drawn out 'Oh,' from Mr. Roberts. 'It would appear that you really are serious about this; personally I would advise against it but......' He shrugged.

Tina sensed her goal was in sight, she said quickly: 'I'm sure that I can provide sufficient collateral for the transaction and of course I would need a bridging loan,' she added demurely as she passed him details of how much she thought she would need. He sighed, as he always did before lending her money then, while re-affirming that it was against his better judgement, he finally agreed. The formalities over, they shook hands and Tina left with the knowledge she could put in her bid. Her first reaction was one of exhilaration, yes, she had done it; then it gradually dawned on her just what she had done. There was no going back now: suddenly she felt scared, taking on a place like that would be a real challenge and what about the Bolithos would they stay, she would need them she was sure, then there were the Tregarths, Nick was easy but John Tregarth? That was a different kettle of fish, and anyway why should she worry about him, he would be a neighbour that was all and he would have to get used to it. Now all she had to do was to make sure her offer was accepted. She decided to instruct her solicitor to carry out the transaction without revealing her identity. It would be interesting to see John Tregarth's face if she were successful.

*

Two weeks later she received a letter from the solicitor to say that, much to his surprise, the vendor had readily accepted their offer and once contracts were signed she could take possession at the end of September. She put the letter down with a sigh of satisfaction tempered with excitement. It was only then she began to realise the enormity of the step she had taken; the realisation turned to near panic. She poured herself a strong gin and tonic and sat back to contemplate her impending change of lifestyle. 'Ah well,' she thought, 'there are almost five months to get things sorted out.' She looked at her diary and began to plan the months ahead.

Three days later a letter from Nick informed her, among other things, that the house had been sold and that he and his father were preparing to move into the stables. He did not know what was going to happen to Thomas and Mabel nor where they were going to live. It would not make any difference to Mystery: he would still look after her. As usual the letter was brief and Tina considered giving him her e-mail address now that things were settled and she did not have to worry so much about keeping anything from Hugh's prying eyes. She would go down as soon as the contract was signed. She would ask the old couple to remain where they were and offer employment to both of them. The thought made her feel good.

Mollifying Hugh was not so easy, although he had known of Tina's plans for some time he had convinced himself that nothing would come of them and life could perhaps settle back to what they had been before this dreadful business cropped up. She did her best to assure him that it would be 'business as usual' as far as she was concerned, albeit mainly through the internet, and she would give him plenty of time to sort out this living plans before the flat went on the market. As usual he took a lot of convincing but eventually accepted the situation with reasonable grace so that Tina was able to set off for Cornwall with a fairly easy mind.

It took a little over three hours to reach the narrow high banked lane that led to Blackaford. She recalled the stormy evening she had first made that journey and the equally stormy first meeting with John Tregarth and his black stallion. 'A man of many parts methinks' she said to herself as she pulled into the car park of the Fox and Hounds. She took a deep breath as she got out of the car.

It was a fine Spring evening and the warm moist scents of awakening growth wafted from the surrounding hedgerows. Rooks squabbled in the still leafless oaks as they poked new sticks into last year's nests. A pair of buzzards mewed and soared in a rising thermal until they disappeared into the dusk, and with them went Tina's last doubts.

As usual Gloria was a fund of local gossip and was therefore full of the news about the sale of Greystone Barton. 'They say some London business man has bought it,' she confided to Tina. 'Pots of money by all accounts. Of course John is keeping the land and the farm buildings.'

Tina smiled. 'Oh, John is, is he.' She emphasised the name.

Gloria flushed very slightly. 'Yes, so he told me anyway,' she added with a hint of smugness. 'So I suppose the Barton will be a private house, that will be nice don't you think? Much better than that clay company pulling it down.'

'Oh, I didn't know about that.'

'Yes, well you can imagine, when this offer came through he jumped at it. I mean, no one wants the old place bulldozed, least of all John Tregarth.'

Tina shrugged. 'I'm surprised a man like that would care much about mere bricks and mortar, or stone and slate as in this case.'

Gloria wagged a finger. 'Ah well, that's where you would be mistaken. If you knew John as well as I do you……' she stopped as her listener raised an eyebrow.

'And did he tell you what young Nicholas is going to do?'

'The last I heard was that he was going to live with John in the old groom's flat in the stables. Mind you it's the old couple I feel sorry for; it will come hard to them to move into a council house, even if they can get one in Blackaford, which is unlikely, after all there are only about a dozen all told. No, more likely they will have to go to Bodmin and they won't like that one bit.'

'I'm sure something will turn up.' Tina confided with a grin. 'Just you wait and see.' She tapped Gloria on the shoulder and went up to her room to sort out some papers for her appointment with the agents in the morning, to be followed by the anticipated meeting with John Tregarth in the afternoon, something she was looking forward to.

There were things that had to be sorted out: the proposed new boundary lines, agreement for access, rights of way plus a host of detail about which hedge belonged to who and most important of all which party would own the mineral rights. Thanks to Gloria's little snippets of information she was determined to secure the latter; there would be no clay mining outside her backdoor, but in any case there was no point in sitting on a gold mine if the gold did not belong to you. The news that Hendra had been sold gave a good start to the morning as did the final signing of the contract for Greystone Barton. Now it was hers and she savoured the though of breaking the news to John Tregarth.

As she pulled up at the side of the house he was walking across from the stable yard towards the back door. For a moment she thought he was going to walk straight past her but at the last moment, almost as an afterthought he stopped and spoke: 'If you want Nick he's in the yard,' he said casually.

Tina put on her best smile. 'No, it's you I have come to see.'

He frowned. 'Sorry but I've got an important appointment in five minutes.' He started to walk on.

'Yes I know.'

He paused and looked at her enquiringly.

Tina was determined not to be intimidated by those dark penetrating eyes. 'Your appointment is with me,' she said with an air of defiance. 'I am the new owner of Greystone Barton.' She watched his face for some sign of surprise or anger and was disappointed to see none. He said simply: 'In that case you had better come in,' and led the way through to the study.

'Would you like a drink? I expect this will be something to celebrate for you,' he said in a toneless voice.

'No thanks, too early for me but you have one by all means.'

He shook his head. 'There's nothing for me to celebrate,' he glanced round the room. 'The fact is I shall miss this old place but…..,' he left the sentence unfinished. 'Sorry, sit down.' He indicated towards a chair.

'No thanks I prefer to stand.'

'Well Miss Pendogget, what prompted you to take on this ramshackle outfit?' He propped himself on the edge of the desk.

'I would have thought that was obvious.'

John grinned. 'So you've been looking up your family history then?'

'I know Greystone belonged to them, that's all.'

And so you are the mysterious businessman from London; I suppose I should have guessed something fishy was going on.'

Tina was beginning to get annoyed. 'You sound as though you don't approve.'

He shrugged. 'I don't approve of undercover deals, but it was either that or the clay pit, and a well heeled city gent was the lesser of two evils.'

'Well I'm a city person,' she emphasised the last word, 'so what have you got against me?'

He folded his arms and looked at her intently. 'Miss Pendogget,' he said wearily, 'I have nothing against you personally, but if you must know I would have preferred to sell the Barton to somebody a little more attuned to country life.'

'You mean you don't want a neighbour who might be against blood sports and factory farming, is that it?'

He stood up and turned to gaze out of the window. 'Well, you have made your views on that fairly well known,' he said quietly. 'The trouble with people like you is they want to get away from the stink and noise which they have created in towns and as soon as they get out into the countryside they want to change it all to fit in with what they want, regardless of those who have lived and worked on the land for generations.'

Tina moved towards the door. 'I can see that it is highly unlikely that we shall ever see eye to eye on that Mr. Tregarth so I see little point in pursuing this conversation. The fact is I have every intention of making a success of my plans for Greystone and my life here.'

He turned again to face her. 'I'm sure you will do your best but I doubt you will find living up here as easy as you think, and if you are going to keep livestock it's not for the squeamish either. You'll find there are some harsh lessons to be learned and not many town women can take it, I know that only too well; but if you don't learn those lessons you'll not last long here, take my word for it'

'Thank you for the lecture Mr. Tregarth, I'll bear that all in mind,' she said tartly. 'Now I would like to discuss the possibility of employing Mr. and Mrs. Bolitho, unless you have plans to employ them yourself?'

He shook his head. 'I've nowhere to house them and I would be more than happy if they could remain where they are, even if I have to lose Thomas. They have been part of the family for a very long time and I know it would devastate them to move, so go ahead and I wish them well.'

'Thank you.' Tina was relieved and not a little surprised at the unexpected warmth the man showed towards the old couple. 'Then if you don't mind I would like to go and have a word with them and then perhaps have another look round the house.'

'Do as you please, it's yours now and I'm sure Mabel will be pleased to show you round. 'Now if you will excuse me I'll get back to work M'am.' He tugged his forelock and made a slight bow.

Tina did her best not to smile as she made her way to the kitchen where Mabel was beginning preparations for the evening meal. The old lady looked up in surprise and nodded to her. 'Miss Pendogget, didn't know you were here.' There was a pause while Mabel stopped what she was doing and wiped her hands. 'What brings you to Greystone?'

Tina was having a good look round the spacious room and gave Mabel one of her special smiles. 'How are you Mrs. Bolitho, or may I call you Mabel? Is your husband around I'd like to have a word with you both if that is possible?'

Mabel resumed her work. 'He don't spend his time about the house Miss, he'll be out with the stock where a man should be, and in any case we're expecting the new owner any minute so I reckon he will have made himself scarce up in the stable yard.'

'That's just what I wanted to talk to you about, you see.….' Tina stopped as the door opened and a breathless Thomas walked in. 'John said you were here and wanted a word. He mentioned something about the new owner but I didn't quite catch what he said, he seemed in too much of a hurry to go somewhere.'

'Could we all sit down?' Tina asked pulling up a chair to the kitchen table. 'I've something important to tell you.' The old couple looked at each other and sat down in their accustomed places. Thomas rummaged nervously in his pocket to find his pipe but was stopped by a restraining hand from Mabel; both were beginning to look anxious.

'I just wanted to tell you that I have bought Greystone.' Tina did her best to sound reassuring, 'and I wondered if you would both like to stay on here and work for me?'

Again the old couple looked at each other and, finding affirmation in his wife's eyes, 'Thomas turned and with a nod asked what he and Mabel would be required to do.

'Mabel will do exactly what she does now, cook and keep house. As for you Thomas, there will be plenty of work around the house and grounds to keep you busy.'

The old man frowned. 'I'm a skilled stockman Miss, not an odd job man. I don't know as I could take to pottering round the garden and the like. Course, if you were to have a few sheep on the bottom meadows and a house cow, rear a few calves and that, well that would be different. You see Miss, John, Mr. Tregarth, was going to give me work in the stables if we could find somewhere close to live.'

Tina smiled. 'Yes, well that's the point, if you both work for me you will continue to live here of course. As for sheep and things, I don't see why not. We could become self-sufficient for food, produce our own eggs and vegetables,' she began to warm to the idea.

'Yes, I promise you we shall have some sheep. How would that suit you?'

'Proper job Miss,' the old man grinned.

'And how about you Mabel?'

The housekeeper got up and returned to her pastry. ' If Thomas says yes then I'll bide by it. Mind, we couldn't work for less money than we're getting now.' She said pointedly.

Tina stood up with a satisfied sigh. 'That's settled then, your present wage and perhaps a bit more on top, provided….' She paused and looked at Thomas, 'provided you work for me and me alone. I won't have any 'moonlighting' for John Tregarth understand?'

The old man shifted uneasily in his chair. 'You've got to help a neighbour,' he said exchanging glances with Mabel who quickly gave the assurance that her husband would 'toe the line': she would see to it. With that, Tina shook hands and told them she looked forward to a long and happy time together.

When she had gone Thomas shook his head and reached for his pipe. 'I don't know old girl,' he said wearily, 'I can't help thinking that perhaps I'm not cut out to be a general 'dog's body' for someone that's used to city ways, though she seems a nice enough maid I just wonder how it's going to work out.'

Mabel grunted. 'Don't be daft man, beggars can't be choosers so you had better get used to the idea and make the best of it.'

The stable yard was cluttered with pieces of timber, concrete blocks and various lengths of copper piping. A concrete mixer churned away in the corner where a man in blue overalls was busy shovelling sand and cement. Tina picked her way to where she could see Nick wheeling a barrow full of horse manure. He put it down as he saw her coming and began to wipe his hands on the seat of his jeans. 'Father told me the news,' he said excitedly 'I'm glad.'

'I don't think your father is,' she said quietly.

Nick shrugged. 'Can't tell what he thinks, not that he would tell me anyway.'

'Do I detect a note of rebellion?' Tina asked with a smile.

The youth gave an exasperated 'Well.'

'Well what?'

'Miss Pen…..Tina do you think I'm capable of taking care of myself?'

'I should think so Nick, I had to when I was not much older than you.'

'Then why won't my father let me get away from here?' he asked plaintively. Tina thought for a moment. 'Perhaps it's because you are all he's got,' she said.

He gave a short laugh. 'I doubt that, more like he needs a bit of cheap labour. Sorry, It's not your problem, come on I'll show you how Mystery is getting on.' He led the way over to the loose-box where the roan mare looked out at the activity in the yard. 'In case you are wondering what this is all about,' he waived a hand towards the piles of sand and cement, 'we're making the old stable flat habitable. We may even have an inside loo if they can dig a deep enough hole for a sceptic tank,' he added with a hint of sarcasm. He fetched a head collar and led Mystery out so that Tina could get a better look. 'Don't you think she's improved?' he asked eagerly.

There was no doubt in Tina's mind that the mare looked plumper. 'Very nice,' she said, not quite knowing what one was supposed to say.

'Would you like to see her ridden?'

'If you like, but I don't want to put you to any trouble.'

'Oh, it's no trouble,' he said enthusiastically, 'she's due for some exercise. Hang on I'll get my gear and tack her up.' He led Mystery back into the box and hurried off towards the tack room, returning a few minutes later with his hard hat and the saddle and bridle.

'We've been schooling her over some jumps,' he said tightening the girth. 'Thomas reckons she'll make a jumper, and she's got a fair turn of speed.' He led her out into the yard once more. 'Shouldn't be surprised if we had a future point to pointer here.' He patted the arched neck as he led her past the concrete mixer and out of the yard towards the sand school

Tina watched them walk, trot and canter, first one way then the other, horse and rider In seemingly effortless motion. Eventually they pulled up beside her and she tentatively stroked the dark, velvet nostrils. 'You make it look very easy,' she said.

He grinned. 'So it is, you should try it sometime.'

Tina shook her head. 'It has been a very long time since I did anything remotely like that. I suspect I'm a bit too long in the tooth to start again.'

He looked down at her, and for a moment Tina saw the same air of confident superiority she had seen in John Tregarth, it was almost as though he had become a different person. The illusion was fleeting and it was the shy, diffident young man who was talking to her now. 'It's never too late,' he said.

There was a pause and he continued: 'my mother learned to ride when I was five, I suppose she didn't want to feel out of it.'

Tina wanted to know more but was reluctant to press Nick further. 'It sounds as though she was a very sensible lady,' she said, hoping it might open the conversation a little, but the youth merely said 'yes', in an almost inaudible whisper and dug his heels into the mare's flanks.

As they trotted away Tina tried to conjure a mental picture of the late Mrs. Tregarth and saw a dark, petite girl, no doubt very beautiful, evidently very sensible. 'Not a bit like you Tina Pendogget,' she told herself. Suddenly she realised she did not know her first name, in fact nobody seemed to mention it or talk about her. 'Well they wouldn't would they,' she told herself. 'Not in front of strangers.'

She followed the horse and rider back to the stable yard and watched as Nick fed Mystery and gave her a rub down. Then she wandered back to the house to walk through the dilapidated gardens, picturing in her mind what they could look like with a little imagination and a lot of hard work. The idea of producing their own food appealed to her: it could be quite a selling point when she advertised the guest house, in fact it could be the main attraction. She thought of all her friends in town who were committed to 'health foods': free range eggs, organic vegetables. Well, they could come to Greystone, indulge themselves to their heart's content and pay for the privilege handsomely. Of course, with the house to renovate as well, it was going to take all the spare cash she could find. Certainly the Porsche would have to go and be replaced by a four wheel drive: a second hand Land Rover most probably, but she would need a lot more than the few thousand pounds that would raise. It looked like yet another call on the bank. 'Ah well' she thought, 'in for a penny, in for a pound.'

It was with a feeling of satisfaction that she drove back to the Fox and Hounds. At last things seemed to be falling into place and it would not be long before she could move down permanently and get to grips with her new project and her new life. Her excitement must have been evident for Gloria chirped 'You look as though you've lost sixpence and found a shilling,' as she passed her on the stairs. 'Tell you about it over a gin and tonic,' Tina called back over her shoulder.

Half an hour later Gloria was in full possession of the facts and could only respond with : 'Well fancy that,' in a tone that left Tina wondering what she really felt and disappointed that she did not share her enthusiasm. Instead the landlady changed the subject to the latest fashions, asking Tina's advice about material for an evening dress suitable for the summer hunt ball. 'Best do of the year,' she added with a mischievous smile.

'But I don't suppose such things are going to interest you.' Tina was not sure whether that was a statement or a question, either way she chose to ignore it for she had a shrewd suspicion Gloria was itching to tell her that John Tregarth was taking her. The situation was retrieved by the arrival of the first customer of the evening and Tina was able to excuse herself and retreat to her room and a book.

*

The next two days were taken up with the affairs of her father's estate. She was surprised to find that the agent was quite effusive about the sale of the farm. 'I think we have a better price than we originally thought,' he said with a broad smile. 'Pity to split it up of course but that is usually the way these days.' He paused to give Tina chance to comment before continuing: 'So, the house, buildings and ten acres have been purchased by a local solicitor, his family are pony mad you know. Ah, God bless all the horsey folk, they are such a boon when there is a house and a few acres on the market.

Confidentially we got nearly as much for that as we expected to get for the whole farm.' He did not exactly rub his hands together but Tina thought he might at any minute.

'And the rest?' she asked.

The smile got even broader. 'Mr. Menheniot has purchased the fields nearest to his farm and a Mr. Saunders, I think you met him, the postman I think, well, he has the rest'.

'I'm glad of that,' Tina said. 'They have both been most helpful, which reminds me, what do we do about compensation for taking care of the stock etc?'

'Don't worry about that Miss Pendogget we are quite used to such arrangements. Mr. Menheniot will have half your lamb crop for doing the shepherding but he will accept nothing else for looking after the cattle and your horse.'

'Oh yes, I had forgotten about my father's old mare.' She paused for a moment, 'I shall be keeping her so she'll be coming with me to Greystone as soon as I can arrange it, so if you wouldn't mind telling Mr. Menheniot I would be grateful.'

The agent nodded. 'I'm sure that can be arranged; and about the rest of your livestock and any implements, we shall put them into a sale in early September, by which time your lambs will be weaned and things will be much easier to sell.' Tina found it strange to hear him refer to her lambs, as though she were an established farmer and knew what he was talking about

'Good, that's settled then,' she said, trying to sound confident. They shook hands and Tina left the office feeling that she had taken the second important step towards her goal and it now only remained to finalise the sale of the flat lease, tie up a few loose ends at the boutique and the next time she came to Cornwall it would be for good.

~

CHAPTER 18

A yellow September sun cast long shadows across the lake as Tina walked by its edge in the cooling evening. It had been a long day but at last her furniture had arrived and had been installed; Mabel had provided an ample meal and now she could relax and savour her first day as mistress of Greystone Barton. Thomas had selected twenty ewes from her father's flock and now they grazed, together with the grey mare Mist, in one of the small fields that edged the moor. It was the sort of scene she had always visualised in her daydreams of Cornwall.

That night she lay awake listening to the creaks and rattles as wind bustled through the ivy and sought every loose shutter. Suddenly she felt very alone and afraid, not of the house for she was surely no intruder to disturb the ghosts and memories of her own ancestors, but of the enormity of the step she had taken. She thought of what John Tregarth had said and gritted her teeth. 'Well, there's no going back now,' she said out loud Something small scuttled from under the bed and across the bare boards beyond the carpet. Tina pulled the duvet up to her ears and closed her eyes

It was a troubled sleep, full of unconnected images of people and animals; where she, Nick and her father drifted across a snow landscape looking for lost sheep while John Tregarth on his black horse watched and waited for them to be engulfed in the soft whiteness. She awoke with a gasp and pushed the duvet from her face to lay dozing in the half light of dawn. There was a clatter of hooves on cobbles, she glanced at her watch and pulled back the curtains to see John Tregarth emerge from the stable yard riding one horse and leading another, a moment later Nick followed on Mystery. Tina yawned and got back to bed. 'Six o'clock,' she said snuggling into the warmth, 'they must get up in the middle of the night.'

Her resumed sleep was short lived. At half past six somebody, she presumed Thomas, crunched noisily across the gravel drive seemingly dragging a heavy object behind him, for there was much grunting before the field gate banged shut and there was silence once more; then Mabel knocked on the door. 'Breakfast in ten minutes,' she called. 'I've done bacon and eggs.'

Tina sat up. 'Not for me, thank you. I don't eat breakfast, just coffee and toast, please.'

There was an audible grunt of disdain from the other side of the door as the old woman shuffled away muttering to herself.

The kitchen was warm, in fact it was the only warm room in the house; it served to remind Tina to telephone the central heating company who were supposed to have begun stalling that week. 'I'm expecting the builders in on Wednesday,' she informed Mabel as he sat down at the table.'

'If they're local and they say they'll be in on Wednesday 'tis wise to ask 'em which Wednesday. Don't bank on it being this week,' The old lady commented. 'And we've got no coffee.'

'Then I'll get some today,' Tina smiled, 'and I would like it every morning with toast at half past eight please and no butter, I'll get something to spread as well.'

Mabel shrugged. 'Just as you say Miss. I expect it will take us a little while to settle into your ways so you must say when things are not as you want 'em; but I hope you don't mind if I get Thomas his breakfast at seven, you see he will have been up since before six.'

'So I have noticed,' Tina said wryly. 'As was our neighbour.'

Mabel poured the dark brown tea. ''Tis no good starting work half way through the day on a farm or you'll get nothing done,' she said turning a sizzling rasher of bacon in the pan. Tina steeled herself against the mouth watering smell and was relieved that she would be breakfasting alone in the future.

On the stroke of seven Thomas came in, took off his Wellingtons and sat down in his stockinged feet. His wife placed a large plate of eggs, bacon and fried bread in front of him as he nodded self-consciously to Tina and, as an afterthought got up and washed his hands. 'I put the tup in this morning,' he said from the sink.

She looked up. 'Tup?'

He smiled. 'The ram. You remember I told you your father had a good young Suffolk ram worth keeping, well I put him in with the ewes this morning, so we'll be lambing early March. Is that all right?'

She was tempted to say don't ask me but decided on a brief 'yes.'

He resumed his seat and continued his breakfast. 'I see that litter of cubs is still about,' he said between mouthfuls. 'Saw three of them by the edge of the lake this morning.'

'Cubs?' Tina asked.

'That's right Miss, fox cubs, 'course they're nearly full grown now but I expect the old vixen is still around somewhere.'

'I would love to see them,' Tina said excitedly.

He finished his meal and pushed his empty plate away. 'You can see 'em most mornings if you get up early enough. Mind, they'll be some trouble come lambing unless they're thinned out a bit.'

'Oh no, you mustn't kill them,' she exclaimed. 'That would be barbaric, surely you could leave them alone.'

He shook his head. 'One fox about we can live with, but more than that means trouble; I know, I've been looking after sheep for more than fifty years and it'll cost lambs and chickens, you wait and see.'

'I don't care if it does, I don't want them shot or anything,' she said emphatically.

'Please yourself,' he said taking his pipe out of his pocket. 'You're the boss.' He reached for a box of matches but, catching the look on Mabel's face quickly stuffed everything back into his pocket.

Tina smiled. 'Oh come on now, I don't want us to fall out over not killing some poor defenceless animal, there is much too much to do.' She thought for a moment. 'I would like to start riding again. I haven't been on a horse since I was a little girl and I would love to explore the moor on horseback, so do you think you could give me the benefit of your experience and help me start again?'

Thomas looked pleased. 'I don't see why not m'dear, your father's old mare seems quiet enough and we've got all the tack. When would you like to start?'

'Well, I've got a chap coming this morning to advise me on the plans for this place, so what about this afternoon?'

The old man nodded. 'Fine, I'll get the mare in and give her a brush.'

Tina got up. 'Oh, by the way,' she said as she put her breakfast things into the sink, 'I'm sure there is a mouse in my room, have we got any traps?'

Thomas grinned. 'Yes I think so, haven't we Mabel?'

She nodded as Tina continued: 'I think we had better start turning out some of the junk the Tregarths left. We'll begin with that old lobby place, boot room or whatever you call it. I've never seen so many cobwebs and I wouldn't be surprised if it wasn't infested with rats with all the dead things they used to hang in there; better get some rat bait. I'll be down in ten minutes,' she added as she went out of the door.

'She's a proper madam,' Mabel said as the footsteps receded up the stairs.

Thomas chuckled. 'Maybe, but I can see her grandfather in her and if Byron had shown as much go as this maid, things might have been very different.'

'Or the same,' Mabel said.

'How do you mean?'

She poured them both another cup of tea. 'Why, haven't things come full circle again? There was always Pendoggets at Greystone and now there is again.'

Thomas stirred his tea thoughtfully. 'I suppose so, but times change.' He shook his head. 'I just don't understand why we can kill mice and rats but mustn't shoot a fox, it doesn't make sense to me, but then I don't reckon to know how folks think nowadays, especially townies.'

He pushed back his chair and stretched. 'Well, it's no good me sitting here talking; I'd best get on with that bit of hedging down by the stream or we'll have the ewes all over the moor before the tup can do his job.'

Tina and Mabel started on the boot room as soon as the washing up was done. 'Of course, in your grandfather's day this was the gun room,' Mabel said as she brushed out the glass fronted cupboard that once held the weapons.

'You knew my grandfather well?'

The old woman talked as she brushed. 'I were working here ten years before he died. He was a fine gentleman your grandfather, one of the old school: tough as nails but always fair. Not many would have taken a stranger's child and raised it as his own like he did, but I suppose you know about that.'

Tina nodded. 'Yes, I heard it from Mrs .Bolitho, some relation of yours I think.'

Mabel nodded. 'That would be Thomas' aunt. My, but she must be getting on, for she were the nanny there when I started.'

'My father never mentioned Greystone as far as I remember, in fact I still don't know what actually happened between him and John Tregarth's father. I wondered if you could throw some light on that?'

Mabel stopped what she was doing and looked at her. 'If you really want to know, it's a long story so perhaps a cup o' tea would be in order while I collect me thoughts.' They moved back into the kitchen and Tina sat anxiously while the tea was made and the two mugs placed on the table.

'Now, let me see, yes,' she took a sip from her mug and settled back in her chair. 'I were not much more than a child, fourteen or fifteen, when Miss Diana Pascoe first came to visit. I remember she was driving her own car and that was unusual about here back in the fifty's. I don't know how she got to know the boys, Young Farmers Club or what. Anyway it turns out her folk farmed in a big way the other side of Wadebridge. She were pretty, right enough and smart and you can guess both Byron and George were taken with her proper, off they'd go the three of them, picnics and rides on the moor, hunting and dances in the winter. Of course for the dances they found a forth partner but I don't think they ever paired off if you see what I mean, not until your grandfather had his stroke. Then it seemed to change, 'twas pretty obvious to us all that the old man was determined that Miss Diana must marry Byron, and that meant George was more and more pushed out of it. Course we all guessed why: the estate had been going down hill, we knew that, and then came your grandfather's illness, well they needed the Pascoe money didn't they.' Mabel paused to take another sip from her mug.

'Do you think my father was in love with Diana?' Tina asked.

'I can't say Miss but I'm sure that George was and it soon showed. It was at the engagement party. Everybody was having a good time, I know because I was waiting at table you see, anyway, as soon as dinner were over your grandfather says he has an important announcement. They wheeled him into the centre of the room and we were all fetched from the kitchen and given a glass of Champagne to toast the happy couple. Then he told us that he had decided to give his future daughter-in-law a special gift as a wedding present. Then there was a banging at the front door and we all went outside to see Thomas leading a horse up to the front door. I remember it was a lovely summer evening and we all gathered round while your grandfather told Thomas to give the lead rope to Diana; it was then that George suddenly pushed forward yelling that it wasn't fair and that the mare should belong to him.

'And did it belong to him?'

'Well no, not really. Thomas told me later that George had reared her on the bottle when the mother died, fed her every four hours day and night for three months or more. apparently it used to follow him about like a dog, I remember it coming right up to the kitchen door for tit-bits. Yes he had a rare way with horses did George, ar and women too.' She paused to finish her tea. 'So I was told,' she added quickly.'

Tina grinned. 'So what happened then –I mean after George Tregarth made his outburst?'

'Oh yes, well your grandfather tried to calm things down telling him not to be so silly and he could have any other horse he fancied but this one was going to Diana and Byron whether he liked it or not. That really put the cat among the pigeons and George points at your father and shouts that he wouldn't get both of them and off he stomps in a real huff. After that the party was a damp squib. I think Diana's parents were shocked and as for your father, he was, well gobsmacked as they say nowadays. But that wasn't the end of it; the next thing we know Diana has taken the mare home and George has packed his bags and gone no one knows where.'

Tina got up from the table and began washing the mugs. 'So what happened to break up the family?'

Mabel thought for a while before answering. 'We all thought it was a queer thing George going off just like that, him being earmarked for Best Man at the wedding which was set for September after harvest. First thing we knew was that the rehearsal was put off because Diana was unwell and of course the Best Man was nowhere to be seen; then the wedding was going to be postponed and everyone seemed to be in a right tiswas especially poor Byron. Finally it all came out: George and Diana had run off together and we heard later that they were married in a Registry Office in Truro. So that was that. Well of course it were a terrible blow to your father as you can imagine, and the old couple, I'm sure it's what finished old Mr.Pendogget for he only lasted a few months after that.'

'So that was it,' Tina said thoughtfully.

'That wasn't the half of it,' retorted Mabel. 'Things seemed to go from bad to worse. With due respect Miss Pendogget I don't think your father could cope with it on his own particularly when your grandmother took to her bed and had to be looked after. I didn't understand the ins and outs of it at the time but I do remember that bits of the estate had to be sold off . Next thing we knew Greystone was on the market. Well, you can imagine how we all felt, not knowing how much longer we were going to have our jobs; then we heard it was sold and of course there were all sorts of rumours going about as to who had bought it, but none of us expected George Tregarth and his new wife to walk through the door as the new owners.'

'I assume that was when my father moved to Hendra but what about grandmother?'

Mabel smiled. 'Thomas told me later what happened, apparently the one good thing George Tregarth did was to pay for her to be looked after properly in a home, the other good thing was that most of us kept our jobs.'

'Did that include Thomas?'

Mabel shook her head. 'He went into hunt service for a while, I don't think he liked how things had turned out at Greystone and wanted to get away for a bit. Of course he came back again after we were wed....'

At that point the conversation was halted by the arrival of a well dressed young man from the Tourist Board and Mabel was left to get on with her work and her memories while her employer wrestled with the problems of catering standards, health and safety laws and the the numerous other regulations to be dealt with before the opening of the proposed guest house.

Lunch for Tina consisted of fruit juice, an apple and a special biscuit that looked and tasted like cardboard. She sat self-consciously at one end of the table while Thomas consumed what Mabel described as a proper dinner: meat, potatoes and two veg. at the other.Mabel herself compromised with a very small portion of the beef and vegetables. For Tina it was an indication that there would have to be a change in their eating habits if they were going to eat together - just one more problem. There was apple pie to follow after which Thomas reached for his pipe as Tina helped Mabel clear the plates.

She paused and without looking at him said: 'I'm sorry Thomas but I would be grateful if you did not smoke in the house if you don't mind.' Then it was Mabel's turn to nudge him and whisper: 'I told you so.' The old man shrugged and with an audible sigh replaced the offending article.

There was an uncomfortable silence for several minutes until Thomas stood up and asked her if she had a hard hat.

'You mean a riding hat, I'm afraid not.'

The old man grunted. 'Never mind I expect we can borrow an old one from across the way. Sure to be one that'll fit you.'

Tina looked at him. 'I would prefer not to be beholden to John Trgarth if that's alright.'

Thomas chuckled. 'Don't worry m'dear nothing he has will suit you. It'll be from young Nick you will most likely be borrowing. Ill slip over now,' he said putting on his jacket.

The faded black riding hat he brought back was at least a size too big, so on Thomas' advice she began to fold newspaper into the lining. It was then that she notice the initials E P T stencilled on the cloth. 'Who is E P T ?' she asked as they walked to the newly cleared out loose-box in the little cobbled yard.

The old man frowned. 'That one must have belonged to Elizabeth Tregarth. Sorry but it was the first one hanging in the tack room that seemed your size. I'll take it back if you like and look for another.'

She shook her head and after a pause asked: 'What does the E P stand for?'

'Elizabeth Pridmore Tregarth.' There was a hint of sadness in Thomas' voice.

'That's a very unusual name, Pridmore. I've never heard that used as a first name before.'

The old man smiled. 'Ah well, that was her maiden name you see. That's how she used to sign her paintings: Elizabeth Pridmore, so she kept it, sort of double barrelled I suppose. She played the piano too, used to give concerts and all that.'

'She seems to have been very talented.' Tina tried not to sound disappointed.

The old groom thought for a moment. 'I shouldn't say this but she was, well, like a fish out of water if you see what I mean. I'm just sorry it all turned out as it did, but there, it was none of my business. Now, let me show you how to put on the saddle and bridle.'

They had reached the stable door and it was obvious that, much to Tina's disappointment Thomas would be drawn no further on the subject of Elizabeth Tregarth so she turned her attention to things equine. It was surprising how quickly the few basic facts learned in early childhood returned, and within a short while she had mastered the difficulties of getting the bit between the horse's teeth, the saddle in the correct position and the stirrup leathers the right length. Then it was out into the paddock and her first riding lesson.

~

CHAPTER 19

By the end of October Tina felt confident enough to ride out on her own. It gave her a marvellous feeling to be alone where the only sounds were the mew of a buzzard and the wind hustling through the tussock grass. At first it had been startling, almost frightening, that lack of man made noise; but now it was something she relished, even when the rain swept across Hagtor Mire to preempt a hasty and wet return to Greystone. In all these rides across the moor only one thing bothered her. It seemed that no matter what time of day she chose to go out, within a very short time she would catch a glimpse of a horseman, often as much as a mile away but always riding in the same direction as herself. It was annoying, for even at that distance there was no mistaking the proud bearing of John Tregarth's stallion.

'What is he doing following me about the moor?' she asked Thomas irritably. 'Tell him I don't like being stalked, even from a mile away.'

The old man shook his head. 'I wouldn't say he's following you Miss. Horses have got to be ridden every day and we've all got to use this bit of the moor. Tis just a coincidence I reckon.'

Tina grunted. 'Well you would say that of course. I ought to know by now that in your eyes John Tregarth can do no wrong.' She handed him the reins and walked, tight lipped, back to the house

It was a week later when Nick walked diffidently across the small cobbled yard and knocked on the back door.

'Come in and wipe your feet.'

He smiled at the familiar command. 'Right Mrs. B,' he called cheerily as he went in. 'I just wondered if Tina was about?'

'Miss Pendogget to you young man.' Mabel nodded in the direction of the study. 'She's in there on her computer so I don't suppose she'll want to be interrupted by the likes of you.' She turned back to the sink and a half peeled potato.

'It won't take a minute, honest, I just want to tell her something.'

Mabel wagged the potato peeler at him. 'Well all right then, be it on your own head but don't blame me if you get thrown out on your ear, and you can take those boots off before you go any further.'

The youth did as he was bid and walked to the study in stockinged feet , painfully aware of the large hole in one heel. He knocked on the door hesitantly.

'Come in.' Tina looked up from her computer screen and smiled. 'Good, I was just thinking of a coffee break, so what can I do for you Nick?' She stood up and called through the open door for two cups of coffee. 'And some biscuits please Mabel,' she added as an afterthought. She indicated a chair and sat down opposite him. 'Well? she prompted.

Nick cleared his throat. 'It's about Mystery.'

'Nothing wrong I hope.'

'No no, just the opposite. We, that is Thomas and I, think she's good enough to run in a point to point next Spring and we wondered if you would agree.'

Tina though for a moment. 'Well I don't know, I hadn't really contemplated getting that involved, and as you are probably aware I haven't a clue about such things.'

'Oh that's alright,' Nick said enthusiastically. 'Thomas and I can see to the paper work and of course the training. We've been schooling her over some practice fences and Thomas thinks she's very promising.'

Tina's raised her eyebrows. 'Is that so?' She thought for a moment. 'It isn't dangerous is it? I don't want her to get hurt or anything.'

Nick shrugged. 'There's always some risk.....' he paused, 'but if I could ride her I could make sure she came to no harm. Thomas says I'm good enough and it would be great if we could do the Member's Race at the Moorland point to point. That's the one that my father won three times and if I could......'

'If you could do the same it would prove a point, is that it Nick?'

He scratched at a speck of mud on his jeans. 'Of course, if you would prefer someone with more experience.....' The sentence tailed off as Mabel brought in the coffee

Tina gazed into her cup thoughtfully. 'No,' she said slowly. 'I think you should ride her. Let's just show him what we can do shall we.'

Nick's eyes gleamed. 'Great, that's really great. I won't let you down Miss..er..Tina.' He paused. 'I'd prefer it if we didn't say anything to you know who until things are a bit more organised.'

'Mums the word. You let me know what I have to do, I suppose there are entry fees and so on?'

He frowned. 'Oh yes, I forgot about that.'

'Don't look so worried, I'm sure we can find the necessary cash.'

The frown intensified. 'No, it's not that. You see this is a member's race - you have to be a member of the hunt.' He removed a piece of straw from one of his socks and studied it for a moment before continuing: 'And I'm not sure you would want to do that seeing how you feel about hunting.'

'But they have to follow a trail or something now don't they? In which case I don't see any problem.'

Nick was going to say something but merely nodded instead.

'Good, so tell me exactly what is involved.'

'Oh, you don't have to do anything,' Nick said brightly. 'Just pay the subscription and we'll do the rest.'

'And what does that consist of?'

The youth shrugged. 'I just have to hunt her a few times.'

Tina wanted to know why they had to go through all that 'palaver' just to enter a race and Nick had to explain that it was the rules because all point to points were run by hunts and are supposed to be only for hunters. They would have to get a certificate from the Master to prove Mystery had been 'fairly hunted'. 'I'll only need to go out a few times and we won't have to do much,' he added.

Tina smiled. 'That's all right then, as long as it doesn't involve chasing foxes to death I'll go along with it. Now, young man I must get on and I'm sure you have work to do.' She got up and opened the door. 'I can understand what winning that race means to you,' she said quietly. 'In your place I would want to beat him at his own game too.' Nick grinned, hooked his thumbs into the pockets of his jeans and walked towards the kitchen door.

After lunch Tina saddled Mist and set off for her afternoon ride. The moor was taking on its Autumn colours as the bracken fronds browned at the edges and the tussocks round the marsh turned ochre in the pale sunlight. Curlew and pewit called and the ever present buzzard soared, mewing its lament at the passing of summer. It was the sort of day to inspire painters and poets Tina thought as the grey mare picked her way along the rough track that skirted the mire. She enjoyed these rides alone; they gave her time to think, something she found very satisfying after the merciless pace of the city. There were several important problems to be sorted out such as the alterations to the house, purchases for the boutique and how to keep Hugh happy in the new situation. In spite of this her thoughts revolved around the morning's conversation with Nick. She realised she was being sucked into a way of life of which she did not altogether approve.

Perhaps the urban woman and the rural life style were irreconcilable after all, certainly it was not easy selecting the bits she liked and leaving out those she didn't.

She thought about John Tregarth's comment about wanting to change things, it was certainly a great temptation to try and get the best of both worlds and no doubt many would be country dwellers had tried. It struck her that very few were likely to succeed if the inhabitants of Blackaford and the inmates of Greystone Barton were anything to go by. She kicked the mare into a canter and swung off the track onto the open moor. 'Oh, what the hell!' she told the mare. 'Sometimes you have to join 'em to beat 'em.'

It was a familiar ride, keeping the mire on her left - she had learned that lesson – then to the old mine workings and in a wide arc back to the track again. Almost instinctively she looked round for signs of unwanted company in the shape of John Tregarth, but the stallion and its rider were nowhere to be seen. Pleased that she had this time given him the slip they slowed to a trot and Tina let her thoughts range over the more pleasurable topic of the redecoration and furnishing of Greystone Barton.

The mare dropped back to a walk as the rider's preoccupied thoughts allowed the reins to slacken. Suddenly the animal stopped, ears pricked looking in the direction of the old mine workings. Tina was jerked forward in the saddle almost losing her balance. 'What did you do that for? ' she muttered angrily. 'You nearly had me off you old fool.' She peered ahead to look for the cause of the alarm, at the same time suddenly aware of the curling finger of mist that drifted from the mire to touch then smother the familiar landmarks. Beyond the mine was the boulder strew rim of a disused quarry, she had looked over the hundred foot drop many times; but now she was startled to see an unfamiliar shape looming out of the mist on the very edge of the rim. The black stallion stood motionless its reins seemingly tied to a rounded boulder. Her first thought was that there had been an accident, then the boulder moved and she realised she had been looking at the hunched figure of John Tregarth. He sat motionless gazing downwards, neither did he move when the stallion raised its head and gave a low whicker, nor when Talisman materialised from behind some rubble to nudge his arm for attention. Whatever his strange vigil, Tina sensed she was an intruder. Quietly she turned the mare and skirted the mine, looking back only once at the still figure. It began to drizzle and she wished she had put on her waterproofs as the moisture seeped into the nape of her neck. Tina shivered and looked around; it seemed that every few yards the fog became more dense until they were totally enveloped. She began to get the same claustrophobic sensation she had experienced on Hagtor Mire and urging the mare into a trot she turned right handed in a direction she was sure would bring her onto the track once more. As they progressed Tina sensed her mount getting more fractious until eventually Mist swung round with a suddenness that caught her rider unawares. Tina clutched at the mane to no avail, her grip loosened and she pitched out of the saddle to land on her shoulder against a clitter of stones while the mare cantered off into the mist.

'Damn!' She was not sure which hurt the most, the humiliation of falling off or the increasing pain in her left shoulder. Damn!' she repeated. 'Now what?' She stood up but the pain made her head swim so she sat down on a large rock and tried to think. 'No good stumbling about in this,' she told herself as she felt in her pocket for her mobile phone and began to dial. 'Oh bugger, bloody typical - no signal.' She took a deep breath and yelled 'Mist!' at the top of her voice in the hope that the animal would return. The effort increased the pain in her shoulder but after listening for a moment or two she tried again. Four more times she called with all the strength she could muster and when there was no response she sank onto the ground with her back against the rock, stemming the tears with her coat sleeve. She looked at her watch, it had been half an hour since they had left the old mine.

'God knows where we are now,' she muttered. 'If only this fog would lift.'

She cradled her left arm against her chest and rummaged for something to make a sling, regretting that she had not put on a scarf that morning. Then remembered that her jodhpurs had a small leather belt which she managed to loop round her neck to support her left wrist. It gave some relief to the shoulder but the pain was still severe enough to make her reluctant to move. She sat listening and was sure she could hear the sound of hooves which prompted her to call out again: 'Mist! Mist! Good girl, come on.' Tina struggled to her feet. 'God, I don't know how I'll get on you old girl,' she murmured as the hoof beats came closer.

The animal immerged from the fog, but it was black not white, black as John Tregarth's stallion with the man himself looking down at her. 'What the hell has happened to you this time?' he asked, but there was concern on his face as he dismounted. Tina slumped back against the rock. 'Oh it's you. I fell off,' she said dejectedly.

'Where does it hurt?' he asked, gently feeling the arm.

'Shoulder.'

'Collar bone, I suspect. Done it twice myself, hurts like hell. I think we had better try and strap it up better than that before we see about getting you home.'

To her surprise he took off his coat and shirt, then folding the latter to form a sling he tied it round her neck by the sleeves and used her belt to strap the arm close to her body.

'How does it feel?' he asked as he put his coat back on.

'Not too bad.' She winced as she tried to stand up.

He gripped her good elbow and helped her up. 'Can you walk?'

'I think so.'

'Good, I reckon the best thing is to get you back to the old mine ruin where there's a bit of shelter and I'll go and fetch the Land Rover. Do you think you could manage it?'

Tina nodded. 'What about Mist?'

'Oh I shouldn't worry about her, she'll find her own way home you can be sure of that. Next time you get lost in a fog chuck the reins on her neck and let her do the rest.' He took hold of Titan's bridle and they walked slowly back towards the mine ruins. Tina felt too sick to say anything and John Tregarth was his usual reticent self so that the occasional snort of the horse was the only thing to break the silence. He led her to what was once the engine house. It had no roof but the thick stone walls still stood over a man's height giving some protection from the fine drizzle. She shivered as he helped her sit down.

'Hang on a minute.' He loosened the saddle girth and pulled out the folded blanket underneath. 'Here, put this round you.' It smelt of horse sweat and was covered in black hairs, but it was warm and Tina did not hesitate to attempt to put it round her shoulders.

John Tregarth watched until she gave a snort of frustration, then he knelt down, unfolded the the blanket and placed it round her shoulders with a gentleness that surprised her. 'The sooner we get you seen to the better,' he said straightening up, then calling the hound which had appeared from nowhere out of the mist, he swung into the saddle. 'I'll be back with the Land Rover as soon as I can. Don't run off,' he added with a wry smile.

Tina grunted disconsolately as she listened to the fading hoof beats. 'Why is it he's always on a horse and I'm always on the ground?' she muttered and winced as she pulled the blanket tighter round her shoulders. 'He was following me again,' she continued. 'Funny that, fancy sitting on the edge of that quarry gazing into space like that. Not the bird watching type that's for sure and no view to speak of, so what on earth? God! I must stop talking to myself.'

She tried to doze but by the time the pain had eased her right foot had gone to sleep. It was a very long hour before she heard the low drone of an oncoming vehicle.

John Tregarth was silhouetted in the door arch of the Land Rover. He carried blankets and a thermos flask which he handed to her with some tablets. 'There you are, hot sweet tea and something to help the pain.'

She swallowed three tablets while he poured the tea. 'Thanks, I needed that,' she said as she put the plastic cup to her lips. He grinned. 'Sorry there's no brandy but old Mabel is a stickler for the no booze with pills rule.'

The Land Rover seemed to find every bump and pothole in the track to the little lane that led off the moor. Once there the going was smoother but even so, by the time they reached the hospital Tina was white faced and drawn with the continual pain; it had taken every ounce of self control not to yell out every time the vehicle lurched.

At the reception desk Tina was ushered to a waiting area while her companion retreated back to the Land Rover saying that he never felt comfortable in hospital waiting rooms. He waited for nearly an hour and when Tina eventually emerged through the glass doors he got out quickly and hurried up the slope to meet her. 'Thought they must be keeping you in,' he said with just a hint of concern in his voice. She shook her head and eased herself into the passenger seat.

'There was along queue at the out-patients,' she said with a grimace, supporting the sling with her other hand as she swung her legs in. He closed the door and returned to the driving seat. 'Nothing broken then,' he commented turning the ignition.

'No, dislocated shoulder.'

'That's what I thought.'

The vehicle began to move and Tina felt much too uncomfortable to point out that his original diagnosis had been a broken collar bone. Neither spoke during the journey, she because of the pain, while he appeared to be pre-occupied with his own thoughts. That jaw was clenching and unclenching again she noticed; an irritating habit and she wondered what he was thinking about. The vision of the hunched figure at the quarries edge came into her mind and the question of what he was doing there. The Land Rover gave a lurch and she let out an involuntary 'Ouw!'

'Sorry,' he muttered dropping the speed as they turned into the drive. 'Not far now.'

Mabel met them at the front door and quickly ushered Tina inside. John watched from The open door, hesitated then was gone before Tina could express her thanks. 'I ought to have asked him in ,' she murmured sinking into an arm chair.

'Shouldn't think he'd come,' the old woman retorted.

Tina sighed and clutched her shoulder, then suddenly recalling the accident asked: 'Would you ask Thomas to look for Mist?'

Mabel smiled. 'Don't you fret Miss, that old mare's been home this two hours or more.'

'He said she would,' Tina said quietly. 'At least he was right about that.' She looked up at Mabel. 'I suppose that sounds ungrateful.'

The old woman grunted. 'I don't know what you mean by that Miss. Best thing now would be for me to fetch you a nice cup of tea,'

When she returned Tina stood up to look out of the window while Mabel poured. 'I think it's getting thicker,' she said. 'Tell me,' she continued without turning round, 'is John Tregarth an ornithologist?'

'A what?'

'Is he keen on birdwatching?'

Mabel handed her a cup. 'Not that I know of,' she said. 'I've known him sit out and watch fox cubs and the like, but I've never noticed his being particularly interested in birds.

Why?'

Tina shrugged. 'It's just that when I saw him this afternoon he was sitting on the edge of the quarry by the old mine as though he was watching something very intently. Perhaps it was fox cubs.'

Mabel shook her head almost imperceptibly. 'Perhaps,' she said quietly.

The next morning was sunny and warm so Tina sat in one of the garden chairs on the front lawn while she sorted through a pile of bills to be paid. She heard a familiar voice call: 'Talisman, to heel damn you!' and looked up to see John Tregarth striding across the grass while the hound bounded in front to push its wet nose in her face.

He pulled the dog away. 'Sorry, he seems to have taken a liking to you. I hope he didn't touch that shoulder.'

'No, that's alright,' she said gathering up the papers. 'I've finished anyway.'

He stood looking down at her and she noticed his hair seemed to show more grey at the temples and the lines at the corners of the dark eyes which showed white against the tanned skin when the face relaxed.

'How's it going?' he asked

'You mean these?' she indicated the pile of bills, 'or the shoulder?'

He smiled broadly and Tina realised she was witnessing a rare phenomenon. She considered the effect to be a definite improvement. 'It feels much better thank you.'

He nodded , hesitated for a moment then turned to go.

'It was kind of you to ask,' Tina said hastily. 'And by the way your shirt is in the kitchen, I'm afraid we haven't had time to get it washed yet.'

'That's alright I'll do it.' He paused and looked at her for several seconds. 'I suppose I feel a bit responsible,' he said quietly.

She looked surprised. 'Good heavens why?'

He shrugged. 'We ought to have kept a better eye open for you. Dangerous place the moor, especially for inexperienced riders, anything can happen.'

'Is that why you've been following me when I go for a ride?' she asked edgily.

He did not answer. 'As long as you are okay, I'll be getting back to work.' He called the dog and walked briskly towards the back door.

Tina watched him go. Why is it all our conversations seem to end in one of us getting in a huff?' she thought. 'Still, he did come and ask.'

John retrieved his shirt and in the privacy of his office put it to his face and took a deep breath; it had been a very long time since he last experienced the fragrance of expensive perfume.

≈

CHAPTER 20

The beech trees along the drive were bare, their leafy remnants strewn in a brown and yellow carpet which was tossed by little whirlwinds that played between the grey trunks. Tina stood at the drawing room window and watched the dark clouds gather over the moor. Her shoulder still hurt although she had long since discarded the sling. From somewhere upstairs came the sound of hammering as workmen began the necessary alterations. She knew that for the nextfew weeks the place would be a shambles and for the first time since her arrival she longed forthe comfort and order of her flat in Wimbledon. Soon it would be Christmas, she closed her eyes and visualised the lights and dazzle of the Bond Street shops, carols on street corners and enough Father Christmases to bewilder any small child. 'Not going to be much going on round here,' she said to herself and for a moment seriously contemplated telephoning Hugh and spending the holiday in town. 'Well you know what John Tregarth would say to that, I told you so, that's what he would say.' She gave a defiant grunt and went through to the kitchen where Mabel was preparing lunch.

'Christmas,' Tina said loudly. 'What are we going to do for Christmas.

The old lady shrugged. 'I does a fowl, usually goose, John always liked a goose. Then of course when Nick were a little boy we used to have a party on Christmas day, there was always the stock to feed and in the afternoon they would be getting horses and tack ready for the Boxing Day meet at the Fox and Hounds. 'There's always something to do round here at Christmas.' She stopped what she was doing and gazed out of the window with a rare smile. 'I remember we had some good times in your grandfather's day, always a house full of quests and young folks playing games: Ludo, Snakes and Ladders, hiding in cupboards. None of your sitting about watching television in those days. Of course we all went to church: Midnight Mass or eleven o'clock Christmas morning.'

Tina beamed. 'Why don't we have an old fashioned Christmas again? You know, a proper dinner party, I could invite some friends from London and….' she hesitated, 'perhaps we could have the Tregarths over, well, Nick at least. I guess it's not going to be much of a festive season for him.'

'I'll bet you his father won't come,' Mabel retorted, 'and I don't know how I'm supposed to cope with a lot of up-country folk.'

Tina smiled. 'Oh you needn't worry about them, there won't be more than two or three.'

In fact, off hand she could only think of Hugh and she suspected that he would only come if his impending divorce was settled. 'We'll invite Gloria,' she said brightly. 'I know she closes on Christmas Day.'

'Hmm.' Mabel was not impressed.

'That's settled then, we had better start making a few plans.' Tina felt thoroughly cheered up by the prospect.

That afternoon she took Thomas to look at a second hand Land Rover, not that the old man knew anything about motor vehicles but she felt that his presence might give her an edge over any car dealer. She had done her homework, knew the list price for the age of the vehicle in question and had decided what sort of a deal she could make for cash. She had also decided they would park the Porche out of sight and walk to the garage.

The salesman was confident of an easy transaction and was not at all prepared for a female who poked about underneath the chassis with a screwdriver. After twenty minutes of haggling and a test drive a bargain was reached which left the young man wondering if he had done the right thing. Thomas was impressed. 'I didn't know as you were so clued up about such things,' he said admiringly. Tina grinned. 'I'm not, all it needs is a bit of research and plenty of nerve; make a good deal but never try to get something for nothing, that's how I do business.'

'I'm sure you do miss, I'm sure you do,' Thomas said quietly as they got into the car.

'That's a good job done,' she said with an air of satisfaction. 'I'll sort out the insurance and you can pick it up in a couple of days.'

There was no reply from the old man as they turned onto the A30 and the speedometer began to hover round the eighty miles an hour mark. He closed his eyes and sat tight lipped until they skidded to a halt by the front door. Thomas was out of the car before Tina had switched off the ignition.

'I'll take you for the Land Rover as soon as it's all legal and you can pick up the ducklings on the way home,' she called. He stopped half way to the back door. 'No that's alright, I'm sure you've got better things to do,' he said shakily. 'I can get a lift in the milk lorry to Blackaford, and I'll catch the bus from there, it passes the garage on the way to Bodmin.'

'Fine,' Tina said and wondered why he looked relieved.

*

The ducklings were part of the plan to turn the lake into a pleasure area where guests could fish or just watch ornamental water fowl lazily swimming on its sun dappled surface.

At least, that was the mental picture of idyllic rural charm she had conveyed to the publishers of glossy holiday brochures. Thomas had made some pens close to the house where he could keep an eye out for marauding foxes not to mention buzzards, crows, magpies, ravens and above all mink the most recent addition to what seemed to Tina a formidable list of creatures ready to pounce on any unsuspecting duckling.

When she returned to the house she found Nick waiting for her in the study. He took a crumpled piece of paper from his back pocket and placed it on the desk. 'I would like to start qualifying Mystery so I've brought you the address of the hunt secretary and the amount due, is that all right?'

Tina looked at it and shook her head. 'I have to say Nick that I don't like the idea of subscribing to a hunt, but if that is what has to be done I suppose I'll have to go along with it.'

She sat down at the desk, wrote a cheque and handed it to Nick. 'Here, you send it,' she said with a smile. When the youth had gone Tina sat back in her chair, closed her eyes and considered the state of play so far. Predictably, the renovation work was behind schedule and would not be completed before the holiday. Mabel and Thomas were settling into her routine reasonably well but Mabel was going to need more help at some stage. Thomas on the other hand was probably under employed and had a tendency to wander over to the stable yard rather too often. Young Nick seemed to be much more enthusiastic about life in general and had even had his hair cut, then there was John Tregarth and his strange behaviour at the quarry and the subsequent care and consideration he had shown when she needed help, and she hadn't been able to thank him properly. Perhaps he would come to her Christmas dinner, but then on the other hand perhaps not. John Tregarth was not a man you could approach easily; she wondered why it bothered her. That brought her to the question of Christmas: she would have to phone Hugh before he made other plans.

The female voice at the other end of the line responded with a cheery: 'Forward Fashions how can I help you?'

'Hello Jenny it's Tina. Is Hugh around?' There was a long pause before eventually Hugh's voice came over. 'Good Lord, thought you were still crocked up.'

'You got my email then, sorry it put me out of action for a bit and it means I won't be fit enough to come up for the Christmas rush,' It wasn't true but it gave her a good excuse.

'So I wondered if you would like a break and come down here for the holiday?'

'I haven't got time for holidays,' he replied tersely. 'We still have a business to run you know.'

'Oh come on Hugh, just for old times sake. You could manage Christmas Day, bring somebody with you if you like, there's plenty of room.'

There was a long silence at the other end. 'So there's no chance of us getting together again?'

'Sorry Hugh, I told you, I don't think it would work but in any case I've too much going on here……'

'You mean your farmer friend.' He interrupted.

'No I don't mean my farmer friend as you put it. He's just a neighbour, so come on down and see how the peasantry live. It will do you good after the Christmas chaos and it will make amends for me not being there.'

There was another long pause. 'Well I must admit I'm intrigued to find out what you really are doing down there, so okay I'll try and get down on Christmas morning in time for lunch.'

'Great, I'll look forward to it – Oh and by the way there's a long email on the way about those separates and accessories. Let me know what you think. Cheers.'

At that point Mabel came in with her morning coffee. Tina sipped it gratefully. 'Ooh, I needed that,' she said eying her housekeeper over the top of the cup. 'There will be at least one house guest for Christmas.'

The old woman's face remained expressionless. 'Does that mean staying the night?'

Tina nodded.

'He or she?'

'He, my business partner.'

'Hmm, what you do is your affair, just as long as I don't have to do a lot of fancy cooking for a lot o' folks as don't appreciate good wholesome food.'

Tina was unsure what was going through Mabel's mind but she smiled and said soothingly: 'I quite understand, but don't worry, the whole point of the thing is to have a proper old fashioned Christmas like they did…' she hesitated, 'like they did in grandfather's day. Oh, come on, don't look so glum, we've got nearly three weeks to get things organised.'

Mabel shook her head. 'Twas all very well in those days,' she said curtly. 'There was a house full o' servants to cope with the extra work. I can't be expected to run round like a young 'un any more.'

Tina gave her a beguiling smile. 'You won't have to, we'll get in an outside caterer.'

'No need for that.' Mabel said firmly. 'That would cost a lot and I don't like to see money wasted when me and Thomas could cope well enough, that is providing you don't expect anything fancy.'

Tina's smile broadened. 'That's fine then, we'll all muck in and get things prepared well in advance so that there is only the cooking to do on the day. I'll let you know how many will be coming as soon as I've made a few phone calls.'

Mabel crossed the hall to the kitchen still muttering under her breath. 'Starts out with one and before you know it we'll be having to cater for half a dozen or more.'

'What's that you're on about?' Thomas asked.

'Why, it's madam out there. Now she wants to have a lot of up country folk for Christmas. She thinks John will come but bet he won't.'

A smile flickered across Thomas' lips. 'How do you know he won't?'

'Because I do. It's not as though they got on and I can't see him coming across to see her playing Lady of the Manor in what used to be his family home while he has to pig it in the old groom's place. He's a Tregarth and they don't knuckle under easily.' She nodded knowingly and began to wash the coffee cups. 'And what might you be doing indoors this time o' day. Haven't you got anything better to do than sit around my kitchen?'

Thomas got up folded his newspaper and tossed it onto the table. 'Oh shut your clack woman,' he said irritably. 'If you must know I'm waiting to show 'madam' the new ducklings I just brought back, and let's hope they fare better than those bantams that young Nick had.'

Mabel grunted. 'Well that was his fault wasn't it. If you don't shut them up at night tis only inviting 'Charlie', in.'

'Charlie?' Tina had entered the room unnoticed. 'Who is Charlie?'

Thomas gave a wry smile. 'That's what we call Mr. Fox. Nick had twelve bantams and one night a fox got in and killed all but two. Blood and feathers everywhere, I'd never seen the boy so upset.'

'So the moral is make sure you always shut them in at night.' Tina said pointedly.

'That's true, but I've seen foxes take chickens in broad daylight so better to make sure there are not too many of 'em about.'

Tina reached for her waterproofs on the back of the kitchen door. 'We won't go into that if you don't mind.'

The duck house was sited close to the water's edge. 'It would have been better if we had an island,' Thomas commented. 'Charlie doesn't like to get his feet wet, but this is the best we can do for now.'

Tina watched them delightedly. 'They look pretty all ready especially the Mandarins.' She felt like a child with a brand new toy.

Thomas nodded. 'Aye, they're near full feather, half a dozen of each: Mandarins, Mallards and Muscovys.'

'All the M's,' she grinned.

'That's right.' He was pouring water into a large shallow bowl. 'The Mallards and Muscovys ought to take care of themselves, good fliers they are. It's the others we'll have towatch.'

They began to walk back to the house. Before they reached the orchard gate Tina stopped. 'Thomas,' she said pensively, 'You are about the only person I could ask this,' she hesitated for a moment, 'Tell me about Nick's mother. What was she like and why is it no one willing to talk about her death, just something vague about an accident? I would like to know…. it's….well, I don't want to put my foot in it and upset anybody if we are all together at Christmas. I realise it will be a difficult time for both Nick and his father, especially being in their old home.' She stopped to look back towards the stables. 'I can see why they might not want to come.'

The old man nodded and said quietly, 'I reckoned that sooner or later you would want to know.' He moved a few paces forward to lean on the gate. She joined him and waited while he rummaged under his waterproofs for his pipe. When it was eventually lit he took a long drag, blew the smoke out through his nose and turned to look at her. 'So you want to know what Elizabeth Tregarth was like? Well I can tell you Miss Tina Pendogget, she was as different from you as chalk from cheese.'

Tina hoped the sinking feeling in her stomach was not reflected in her face. 'Oh,' she said and wished her voice had not sounded quite so disappointed. The old man turned away to look intently at the house. Tina could not see his face but she had a distinct impression that he was smiling. 'And about her death?' she asked, her voice faltering slightly.

There was a long pause before Thomas continued. ''Twas late afternoon,' he said slowly. 'I was just going to give the horses their feed when she comes rushing out of the house in a right old stew. 'Thomas', she calls 'saddle my horse, I'm taking him out.'

Well I didn't know what to say but she insisted so I tacks him up slowly like because I could see she were pretty worked up about something and I hoped that John would come and calm her down a bit. You see she wasn't that good a rider and she only rode on the moor when he was there.

Anyway she mounts up and off she goes. Sometime later out comes John and asks me where she is and when I told him he saddles up his hunter and goes after her. 'T would be about half an hour later he gallops back into the yard, leading her horse and yelling that there had been an accident and he needed an ambulance and a doctor. Young Nick had run out and he turned as white as a sheet. He was only ten, poor little blighter.' Thomas paused to knock out his pipe.

'It must have been terrible for the boy,' Tina murmured. 'So what was it all about, do you know?'

The old man shook his head. 'You would have to ask John about that, all I know is she seemed very upset about something, but then, she were a very up and down sort of person.

Don't get me wrong, a nicer woman you couldn't wish to meet, but one minute she would be all over you, bright as a button and the next you couldn't get the time o' day out of her. I put it down to her being artistic and that, if you know what I mean. I sometimes wonder if that's why John is so set against Nick doing that sort of thing.' He paused to refill his pipe and continued without lighting it: 'She were at the foot of the quarry, no one knows for sure what actually happened but the fog had come down and my guess is the horse stopped suddenly and tipped her off, then somehow or other she stumble over the edge. That's the only thing I could think happened. She died before they could get her to the hospital.'

'Oh I see,' Tina said slowly as the significance of the quarry dawned.

'So there it is. John were like a madman for weeks after, and the boy, well, he just went very quiet, lost interest I suppose, didn't want to talk to anyone for a long time.' He lit the pipe and said nothing for several seconds then added, 'It were a bad time for us all.'

They began to walk back towards the house when there was the sound of hooves on the drive. 'That will be Nick back,' Thomas said looking at his watch. 'Hmm, he hasn't stayed out long.'

Tina saw the black coated rider bobbing along the line of the hedge. 'Where has he been all dressed up?' she asked.

'Why, qualifying your mare of course. I thought Nick had explained that she had to be hunted to qualify for the point to point.'

She frowned. 'Yes, I had forgotten that, not that I approve mind.'

'Old Byron would have.'

'Yes I'm well aware of that and perhaps if I had known him better I might have been a very different person.'

Thomas smiled. 'I'm not sure that would necessarily been a good thing Miss Tina Pendogget.' He opened the garden gate and gently ushered her through with one hand on her elbow.

*

The week before Christmas the rain started. Greystone was enveloped in a drifting cloud that saturated normal clothing, outside work meant sweating under a layer of waxed cotton or plastic waterproofs. Tina had put off going out to do her self imposed chore of feeding the ducklings. Instead she stood with her back to the hot kitchen stove laying plans for the impending festivities while Mabel cleared away the remains of breakfast. 'I think we should all eat together, at Christmas I mean. That's how it would have been in grandfather's day isn't it?'

Mabel nodded. 'That's right. Course, I only remember what it were like after the war. There were two of us in the house: Mrs. Bolitho - that was Thomas' aunt - and me. Thomas' uncle had been killed in the war so at first there were just the two of us joining the family but when me and Thomas got engaged he was asked too. Twelve o'clock sharp, we'd be cooking all morning and then your grandmother would bang a big gong outside the back door to

181

fetch the men folk in.' She smiled at the thought. 'It's still about somewhere. Then on Boxing Day when they came back from hunting after they had seen to the horses and got themselves cleaned up we used to have a stand-up supper - I suppose you'd call it a buffet nowadays - and the farm workers and their families would come in and there would be lemonade and plenty of beer, mind, your grandfather kept an eye on things to make sure nobody got tiddly.' She sighed. 'Yes, we had some good times in those days.'

The back door opened and Thomas appeared, dripping wet and carrying a bucket which looked as though it contained soaked feathers. He reached in and pulled out the remains of one of the ducklings. 'You had better come,' he said as Tina gazed in horror. 'There are three more in here,' he said tapping the bucket, 'and as far as I can tell another missing.'

'Oh no!' Tina gasped. 'How did it happen?'

'I didn't stop to find out. I came straight in to get the gun, though whatever did it is probably long gone by now.' He unlocked the cupboard near the door and took out a single barrelled shot gun.

'You won't need that,' Tina said firmly. 'There must be a better way to deal with the situation.'

He hesitated then returned the gun to its rack. 'If you say so,' he muttered, 'but for certain whatever it is will be back for the rest unless we do something about it, it's up to you.

'I don't want any shooting,' she said putting on her coat. 'Let's go and see, then we can decide what has to be done.'

They arrived at the duck pen to find the remaining occupants huddled in one corner of the wire netting enclosure. There were feathers everywhere. Thomas was examining the outside of the sleeping quarters. 'This'll be where the bugger - sorry - this is where it got in for sure.' He poked a piece of wood into a hole about six inches across.

'But a fox could never get in there.' Tina exclaimed.

Thomas studied the ground closely. 'Nor he did,' he pointed to small pad marks leading down to the edge of the lake. He made a hissing noise through his teeth. 'Mink,' he said. 'Damn, I didn't think we'd got any in this neck o' the woods.'

Tina was staring at the carnage dumbfounded. 'Mink? I didn't realise they could do so much damage.'

The old man grunted. 'We've got the Animal Rights lot to thank for that. When they let out a whole lot from mink farms up country I've no doubt they thought they were doing something good, but this is the result.' He moved the feathers with his boot. 'Worse than a fox is mink, can creep through a space not much bigger than a rat hole and cause as much havoc as a hungry vixen and they can swim like an otter so even keeping them on an island won't help.'

'So what do we do?' Tina was on the point of tears.

Thomas shrugged. 'Well, until a few years ago we could have called in the mink hunt and the hounds would have had a good chance of finding it and doing the job.'

'You mean kill it.'

'As far as the ducklings are concerned it's a case of kill or be killed. I'll strengthen the duck house as much as possible but apart from that there's not much more we can do.'

'What about traps, couldn't we trap it?'

'Then what? Turn it out somewhere else to kill some other poor bugger's ducklings?'

He was getting angry. 'We'll move the lot closer to the house and hope that does the trick.'

'All right,' Tina said quietly, 'you've made your point so do whatever you think is necessary. I'm going in.'

It was not just that she was disappointed, she felt somehow nature had turned against her, had let her down and the snake had appeared in her Garden of Eden just as John Tregarth had said it would. The bucket of corpses was still outside the back door; she looked at it with feelings of anger and nausea.

The door banged behind her as she kicked off her boots and searched for her indoor shoes. 'Did you find that list Mabel?' she called. The old woman wiped her hands and held a crumpled piece of paper at arms length. 'Can't see without my specs,' she muttered, handing it to Tina who placed it back on the table with an air of patient resignation. 'It's some ideas for the dinner on Christmas Day,' she said, 'now don't pretend you didn't know.'

Mabel pursed her lips. 'All I know is there'll be four visitors, five if John comes, which I doubt, and we'll be eating goose with all the trimmings.'

'That's right, I remember you told me that grandfather liked goose so......'

'So you want to put the clock back.' Mabel grinned.

'Yes, well no. Oh come on Mabel all I want is for us to have a proper old fashioned Christmas instead of just the three of us sitting round gazing at the television for half the day.'

The old woman risked a smile. 'You're right o'course. A young woman like yourself shouldn't have to be stuck with a couple of old fogies like Thomas and me on Christmas Day.'

'That's not what I mean Mabel and you know it. I think it will do us all good to have some company, so we'll all eat together in the dining room and have a party. How about that?'

Mabel shook her head. 'I don't know as Thomas and me would feel comfortable with smart London folk. Perhaps us two should eat in the kitchen.'

'Nonsense,' Tina said firmly. 'You'll get on like house on fire and you know the Tregarths and Gloria better than I do anyway, so I don't see any problem do you?'

'If you say so.' Mabel did not sound convinced.

'Now, about the London guests.' Tina paused to consider the fact that Hugh had asked to bring Marion Wood, a woman who would like to be thought of as a girl and whom Tina had met several times at fashion shows. She was an ex-model with a reputation that gave rise to the office joke that Marion would. 'Hugh can go into the main guest room and his lady friend into number four along the landing.'

Mabel nodded approvingly, making it abundantly clear from the expression on her face that there would be no London 'hanky-panky' in her household.

'Oh, and there's a chance that the gentleman will opt for vegetables only, so we'd better have some eggs handy in case he wants an omelette.' Tina smiled to herself and wondered how he would react to the fact that she had abandoned the vegetarian path.

'Sounds a bit fiddly to me, but if that's what is wanted I suppose I'll have to cope somehow,' Mabel grumbled, 'but we'll put on a good spread and at least they'll get good wholesome food and none o' that supermarket rubbish.'

Tina visibly brightened. 'That's right,' she said enthusiastically, picturing in her mind's eye the laden table, a roaring log fire and her guests replete and affable while she, looking her best of course, played the perfect hostess. She hoped that John Tregarth would come.

'Talking about Christmas, Gloria Lockey has sent up a parcel for you.' Mable's voice cut through Tina's reverie.

'Eh? Oh yes, thank you. Where is it?'

'I put it in the hall up against the hat stand.'

It was a large rectangular package wrapped in coloured paper with a white envelope stuck on with sticky tape. It was addressed to Tina with the words Merry Xmas across the top. Filled with curiosity she tore open the envelope and took out the enclosed card: 'I think you will find this interesting,' she read, 'It should go well over the fireplace in your dining room where it rightly belongs. Ask John about it - Merry Xmas, Gloria.'

'Obviously a picture of some sort,' she murmured thoughtfully and looked round to see if Mabel could throw any light on the subject but the old woman had gone. Torn between waiting for Christmas Day and satisfying her curiosity immediately she plumped for the latter and quickly removed the wrappings to reveal the scene of a hunt meet outside the Fox and Hounds. This was a surprise for she distinctly remembered telling Gloria that she did not care for hunting pictures and wondered why she had sent this one. 'Ah well,' she sighed. 'I expect we can find somewhere to put it, at least for Christmas Day.' She carefully re-wrapped it, finishing just as there was a knock on the back door and Nick walked in dragging a large Christmas tree.

'Dad asked me to bring this over, said he didn't think you had got one yet,' he paused awkwardly. 'It's a Sitka Spruce, dad says it won't shed its needles as much as the Norway Spruce and looks nicer. We've got a small plantation of them he planted a few years back up by the old mine workings and they're just about ready to cut this year.'

'That's very kind of him Nick, thank you very much it looks lovely, we'll prop it in the hall until we can set it up and start putting on the decorations.' She paused as the youth turned to go. ' Hang on a minute Nick, tell me, are you and your father doing anything special for Christmas? If not would you both like to come here for a meal on Christmas evening? I've got some friends coming down I think you might find interesting, one is a fashion designer and the other is…..well you'll see.'

Nick thought for a moment. 'Yeah, okay thanks,' he said, without the enthusiasm Tina had hoped for. 'We never have anybody to stay now. Christmas is usually pretty boring so yeah I'll come.'

'Good, I guarantee you won't be bored.' She hesitated. 'What about your father?'

He shrugged. 'I'll tell him but you'd best ask him yourself, he's not into parties and such anymore so don't expect too much.'

'Tell him Gloria Lockey is coming,' she said with a grin.

CHAPTER 21

It was going to be a real old fashioned Christmas, all planned out in Tina's mind was the roaring log fire, a huge Christmas tree and a table laden with enough food to feed a regiment while she presided over the ancestral hearth looking her best and distributing largess and goodwill in equal quantities. That was how she visualised the forthcoming festivities and fervently hoped her guests would all turn up, particularly John Tregarth, she wanted to see how he would react, or was that too cruel. Suddenly she felt some sympathy for the man, he had seen his home sold to a stranger while he had to battle on running the farm with just young Nick for help and by all accounts living in squalor. At least, she thought, the boy would come, it would do him good to meet a few people not connected with farming. Still, she hoped Tregarth would come.

In the kitchen Mabel was busy with the Christmas pudding. 'She wants to play lady of the manor'. A disgruntled Mabel told her husband .

'And why shouldn't she', he asked.

Mabel grunted. ' John won't come'.

'I don't know about that, he might come if Nick does. It would do him the world of good, it's been years since he went out anywhere except market or farmers meetings'. He fell silent for a moment. 'And to think that he and Elizabeth were the life and soul of any party at one time'.

'Yes, and that time's gone, more is the pity'. She tied the pudding cloth and filled a saucepan with water. 'There's a chap from London coming'.

Thomas nodded.

'And so is Mrs. Lockey', she added disapprovingly .

He grinned. 'I don't know why you've got such a down on her, she's a good sort, would do anyone a good turn'.

'Yes I know, that's half the trouble'. She shook her head. 'There's been goings on.'

'What do you mean 'goings on'?'

'You know well what I mean, between her and John'.

'Maybe that's why she's been invited. Maybe our Tina wants to see which way the wind blows.'

'You talk daft Thomas Bolitho and it's about time you were about your business so that I can get on with mine.'

John Tregarth paused from his task of trimming a ewe's feet and straightened his back with a slight groan. He stood and watched Nick as the youth attempted to catch an elderly matron that needed clipping round the tail. 'It's no good chasing her round and round like that, get your crook round her neck, push her into a corner. Come on Nick I've shown you enough times, here let me do it', The youth stood aside and with a resigned expression watched his father catch the ewe, sit it up and start to pare a foot. 'There you go, not too difficult is it, you ought to be able to do it by now, you can finish off its back end if you like'..

'I suppose so dad',

Tregarth shook his head. ' Head in the clouds that's your trouble Nick, take after your mother, thoughts always a million miles away from the job in hand'. He finished the trimming and let the sheep go.

'It's looking black outside, reckon the forecast was right and we're in for a right old storm. When we've finished here you had better fetch the cows and calves up from the bottom meadows and push them up onto higher ground, we could be in for some flooding'.

The youth nodded but his thoughts were else were, milling over in his mind the Invitation to spend Christmas day at Greystone. Well, he was going even if his father turned it down, life was dull enough as it was without spending Christmas day cooped up with father, and perhaps he might get a chance to discuss his future and the plans for the Point to Point steeplechase. He finished the ewe and let the flock out into the home meadow.

As he closed the gate he saw Thomas running up the drive towards him. 'Can you Give me a hand ', he gasped. 'I'm stuck with the Land Rover in that soft bit by the lake while I was moving the duck pens. It'll need the tractor I reckon'.

Nick grinned. ' Trust you to get stuck, I'll see you down there'.

As he started the tractor it began to rain heavily and it took nearly an hour of slithering and sliding before the vehicles were on firm ground. By that time it was dark and Nick, tired and drenched returned to the Spartan accomodation he called home while Thomas installed the duck pen on the lawn. When he had finished he trudged wearily to the kitchen door and pushed it open.

'Don't you come in here with those wet things on, leave 'em outside in the porch please'. Mabel's voice was distinctly edgy . ' I've got quite enough to do getting everything ready for tomorrow without having to clean up after you'.

Her husband knew better than to disobey when she was in that sort of mood and went back outside as she continued. 'Did you hear her say the London chap is bringing a woman with him'. She snorted indignantly. ' I don't care how they carry on in London but if they're not wed it's separate rooms as far as I'm concerned, and there's some stuff to collect from

Blackaford, she'll tell you'. She indicated with her head towards the hall. 'Did you hear that?'

'I heard' Thomas said wearily as he entered the room in his stockinged feet. 'It's raining stair rods out there, It'll have to wait until tomorrow now and I want to slip over to the yard before it gets too dark'.

'Tomorrow is Christmas Eve and we'll have plenty enough to do and anyway what business have you got in those stables, I thought you had agreed that you wouldn't do any work for John'.

'That's right and I don't, what I do is for my own pleasure and I don't take any wages from him'. He slumped into the only arm chair in the kitchen and gave a long sigh. 'I'm no gardener handyman and you know it'.

'I know that you've been creeping off at crack of dawn most mornings and I don't need a crystal ball to tell me where you were off to.'

Thomas shook his head. 'I'm a horseman Mabel, horses are in my blood and I could no more live without them than fly to the moon, and anyway I've been helping youngNicholas with Miss Pendogget's mare, it seems she's put the boy in charge of her and I've.got to say he's making a pretty good job of it. You know, he's been a different lad since it arrived'.

'Well I'm glad they've sorted out who owns what after all that business with poor old Byron. I'm glad John has seen sense'.

Thomas smiled. ' Well at least he'll have a bit of money coming in for the mare's keep and who knows perhaps they'll work out a better arrangement'. 'In what way?' He shrugged. ' Perhaps John will take a share in her'.

*

Christmas Eve dawned with a blustery South West wind rattling anything that was loose. It was barely light at eight o'clock when Tina sat down at the kitchen table for breakfast. She had established that they would all eat together in the kitchen except when they had guests, which had not actually happened yet. Thomas had already had his and had gone out an hour before, but Mabel joined her with the toast and coffee.

'How are things going?' Tina asked. ' Let me know if there are any problems or you need some help.'

'No' t'is going alright except,' she paused and dabbed at a drop of spilt coffee with her apron, 'except Thomas and me don't think we would be comfortable having Christmas dinner with all them London folks, it's not something were used to'.

Tina gave her a big smile the sort she reserved for a favourite customer, 'That really is nonsense Mabel, this is the twentyfirst century not 'Upstairs,

Downstairs' and in any case Mrs. Lockey will be there and I'm sure young Nicholas will come though I'm not so sure about his father, you'll find plenty to talk about and one thing is for sure I would fihd it very uncomfortable to say the least if you and Thomas were shut out in the kitchen on your own, so would you do it just for me?'

'If you say so Miss Tina I. ..'

'And not so much of the Miss Tina please' Tina interrupted. ' In my business we are used to using first names and I would like it to be no different here, sorry I'm beginning to sound like some school marm.' , She put her hand on Mabel's arm. ' We girls must stick together in this man's world', It was Mabel's turn to smile. They were putting up decorations when Thomas brought in the tree and set it down in the comer of the hall. 'Very nice,' Tina said, 'and I'm glad you didn't bring it in before, 'I like the old tradition of not decorating until Christmas Eve. In London they start Christmas in November, sometimes before, so that by the time it arrives all the excitement has gone. I think the kids miss out don't you?'

'I wouldn't know not having ever lived in a town but I know we used to look foreword to it even though there was always work to be done, The animals don't know it's Christmas and all expect to be fed or milked as usual though we did used to take it in turns so I always worked Christmas Day so I could go hunting on Boxing Day. You know the hounds always meet at the Fox and Hounds on Boxing Day.'

Tina nodded. ' Yes Gloria told me, in fact I'm planning to take our visitors to the meet, which reminds me, there are some groceries and two geese to pick up and some stuff from the pub, do you think you could manage it this morning?

Thomas nodded.' I reckon so as soon as I've finished around here and then checked the ducks'.

'How.are they? Did you manage to get them moved'.

'Yep, though 'twasn't easy, we got stuck in a boggy bit and young Nick had to come and pull us out'.

'Oh, I'm sorry it turned out to be so difficult, but well done, they should be safe there'.

Tina hesitated. 'Did he say anything about tomorrow?'

'Not at the time but I'm pretty sure he'll come.'

'And his father?'

'No telling but I doubt it.'

'Oh.'

Thomas smiled. 'On the other hand he just might'.

'I expect you are right but we'll lay a place for him just in case'.

She picked some mistletoe out of the box of decorations and concentrated on the problem of hanging it over the front door while Thomas struggled into his long waterproof coat and made for the back door.

The Land Rover edged slowly down the hill and over the bridge into Blackaford, headlamps full on and the windscreen wipers barely keeping pace with the rain. The groceries and geese were picked up before it drew into the car park of the Fox and Hounds. Gloria was expecting them. 'Come in and warm yourself by the fire in here.' She poured a generous measure of whiskey which Thomas drank neat.

'Watch you don't get breathalysed on your way home.'

He grinned. 'Tom Bloxham isn't going to be about this weather and if he is he's dafter than I thought. Pity he didn't spend more of his time tracking down them as stole our stock.'

'You know it's not up to him anymore it's all done from Bodmin now and I don't suppose they have a clue what goes on up here, in any case it's a needle in a haystack job although most of us could point a finger.'

'Bloody Slogger Dixon a pound to a penny.'

'You're probably right, I suspect it will be a 'low priority' job for the local fuzz just like policing the anti hunting law.'

Thomas smiled. ' Well we don't mind about the last bit do we, but rustling is a different matter, I know it's cost us more than the boss cares to admit and I bet we have'nt seen the end of it, there will be more I reckon in the Spring when lambs begin to fatten, particularly now prices are picking up. Anyway I'd better get on so where's the stuff to go to Greystone?'

Gloria indicated towards a large cardboard box which clinked merrily as Thomas lifted it from the top of the bar.

'That sounds about right', he grinned. 'There'll be some sore heads come Boxing Day.'

'I hear you are bringing them all to the meet, whose idea was that?'

'I suppose it must have been Miss P's, she seems quite happy with the idea now that we have to hunt an artificial trail. He grinned. ' Unless of course there is an accident and 'Charlie' jumps up in the middle of 'em and we have to try and stop the pack.'

'And by all accounts you don't always succeed, I hear on the grape vine they had one of those 'accidents' a few weeks ago on Greystone land.'

Thomas sighed and shook his head. ' I don't know what the world is coming to Gloria and that's a fact.'

'Never mind old friend, I'm expecting the usual good turn out for pasties and a port stirrup cup.'

'I don't know how you do it every year Gloria, must cost you a bomb.'

'Ah well, it's only once a year and it is good for trade in the long run. I suppose John and young Nick will be coming

Thomas nodded. ' I think Nick is aiming to qualify the roan mare for the Point to Point, always supposing he gets the OK from the owner'.

Gloria smiled. 'I expect he'll get a chance to sort that out tomorrow. Will John go o you think?'

'I doubt it unless you can persuade him'.

She shook her head. 'I don't kid myself he would take any notice of what 1 said, in fact I'm probably the last person to ask'. She paused before adding, 'unfortunately'.

Thomas gave her a knowing look. 'Well I'd better get on my way before this box pulls my arms out, see you tomorrow'. He slammed the door behind him just as a squall threw a torrent of rain against the front of the pub. 'Marvellous', he muttered. ' That's all 1 need another bloody wet shirt'.

The narrow road back to Greystone ran with the dark peaty water which ran out of the neighbouring fields. The Land Rover threw up the puddles in a spray which flew over the bonnet and onto the windscreen so that the wipers could barely keep pace. Thomas hoped the ewes had been brought up to the high ground, and then remembered sadly that it was no longer his concern, he was a gardener - handyman. He drew up outside his and Mabel's cottage which was built onto the end of the main house. There was a connecting door into the house so he could change into dry clothes and deliver the goods without engendering the wrath of his spouse.

By the time he entered the hall the decorations were up and Tina and Mabel were discussing the culinary arrangements for the next day and more urgently the problem of where the guests would be sleeping.

'We can put Marion in the single room along the corridor and Hugh in the room next to mine,' Tina said, and noting Mabel's raised eyebrows added with a grin, 'Don't worry, there's no connecting door but we must do something about our one and only bathroom and loo. Did Thomas fix the bolt on the door?'

Mabel nodded. ' And left mud all over the carpet into the bargain'.

Tina smiled. 'Don't worry. We shall be getting rid of it in the New Year along with a whole lot of stuff.'

Another grunt from Mabel.

'Oh, come on Mabel you'll enjoy the changes, nice carpets, new furniture and lots of interesting guests. I hope'.

The housekeeper was not convinced. ' Tis all very well for you young folk but to be honest I 'm not so sure I could cope'.

'Oh, we'll get you extra help and you'll be able to tell others what to do for a change'.

Mabel shrugged. ' If you say so Miss'.

Tina frowned. ' There you go again, as I said before it's Tina'.

'I'll try, but it don't come natural'.

'But you call John Tregarth John'.

'He was always Master John when he were a little boy but when he was older it seemed natural to drop the 'Master'.'

Thomas came in as Tina went to answer the telephone.

'Where do I put this lot?'

'Tina said to leave them in the kitchen'.

'Oh, it's Tina now is it'.

'That's right , we live in the twenty-first century and there's no more 'Upstairs Downstairs' so she says'.

'Well I never did think much of that programme on the tele but if you say so..'

'No' our boss says so'. Mabel said emphatically

At that point Tina returned with the news that the guests were partaking of liquid refreshment at the Fox and Hounds. I advised Hugh to call in to get final directions, I've no doubt they've had a complete rundown of everything that's happened at Greystone Barton since I arrived, thanks to dear Gloria and I've no doubt they've put two and two together to make five.'

It was mid afternoon when the blue Mercedes pulled up and Hugh and Marion made a quick dash to the front door to be met with open arms.

'Lovely to see you'. Tina gave them the both cheeks treatment and a hug for Hugh.

She showed them into the spacious entrance hall where a log fire blazed in the big stone fireplace giving a welcoming feel to the otherwise dimly lit room.

'Come and dry yourselves by the fire, we'll help you with your bags and things when you've warmed up a bit and you can have a look round while I look for some help.

When she had gone Hugh was the first to speak. ' Good Lord who would have thought our Tina would end up in a place like this'. His eyes took in the well worn rugs which covered the stone floor and the fact that there seemed to be very little furniture, ' I hope we're not going to be sleeping on camp beds with ex-army blankets.'

Marion giggled. ' I bet she's put us in separate rooms so it won't matter anyway.'

Hugh grunted. ' I still don't know why she invited us'.

'Oh, I do. She wants to impress us with her new life style, and I've no doubt that there is a man in the offing, what about this farmer chap? That would be one in the eye for you dear'.

He shook his head. ' No, that's not like her, there's more to it than that, we shall find out all in good time I've no doubt'.

'Right, first things first'. Tina said as she returned accompanied by Thomas.

'This is Thomas the outside member of our team'. Introductions were made and Thomas shook hands not without some embarrassment. 'Thomas' wife Mabel is responsible for inside and eventually will supervise the cleaning staff etc. when we start taking in our holiday guests'.

'So it is true then', Hugh said. 'You are going to turn this place into a Guest House.'

That's right, but let's get you settled and we'll talk about it later. One of the reasons I asked you to come was to tell you what I hope to do here and with the business. I'll show you to your rooms'.

Marion pulled a face and whispered ' There I told you so rooms not room,' as they followed up the broad staircase. Hugh looked more serious, he was beginning to wonder what was going to happen to the fashion business of which he was still a partner. True Tina had kept her side going with the help of the internet but it had not been easy these past few months.

Cases unloaded and the car parked Hugh was able to relax and enjoy the tea with scones, jam and clotted cream laid out in the small sitting room. 'To hell with the waistline', he thought. ' Might as well go the whole hog while I'm here'. He looked at Marion who had obviously got the same idea as she licked the jam from her thumb and forefinger. They were joined by Tina who turned up the electric fire and settled into an arm chair. 'Sorry about the décor', she said. ' I know it is a bit tatty but it's what was here when I bought the place and here just hasn't been time to do much about it.'

They ate in silence until Hugh blurted out ' I'm sorry to bring this up Tina but we have a business to run back in Wimbledon remember? This is all very well,' he waived a hand imperiously 'but where does it fit in with your plans, with our plans for the future?'

Tina smiled. ' Calm down Hugh. It's quite simple I'm ready to bow out of direct involvement in the boutique, you have coped perfectly well up to now so you run the show and I'll take a back seat, sort of adviser if you like and we'll adjust remuneration accordingly. What do you think?'

Hugh settled back in his chair and thought it over. ' Alright but I'll need to appoint a new female director, after all we are selling women's clothing.'

'And I'm sure you will have someone in mind'. Tina grinned and glanced at Marion'.

Hugh coughed and said sheepishly ' Well, Marion and I have come to an ..er.. arrangement since you left'.

'Your decision, Hugh'. Tina chuckled, ' I'm sure you can make it work if anybody can, so let's leave it that and work out the details later shall we. Now what about a tour round the Barton, a freshen up and then a gin and tonic before dinner'.

The meal was simple, cold meat, salad and potatoes followed by fruit and ice cream eaten in the large dining room rather than the kitchen which left Mabel free to continue preparations for the next day. Talk centred round life on Bodmin Moor and Greystone Barton in particular.

'Don't you feel, well, isolated up here miles from any where?' Marion asked glancing out of the window at the mist and rain.

Tina smiled. ' You would be surprised how soon you get used to it and anyway I feel I belong. Don't forget my family used to live here, perhaps it's something in my DNA and of course I'm not alone, there's Thomas and Mabel and John Tregarth and his son Nicholas next door'.

At that Marion gave Hugh a look which said ' I told you so'.

He grinned ' So, with all your farming friends how do you cope with being a vegetarian?'

Tina shrugged. ' I suppose the simple answer is I don't. Up here they all eat meat, it would cause complete chaos if I insisted in eating a vegetarian diet but if you are still keen on it Hugh I'm sure we can arrange something'.

'No that's fine I was never that struck with the vege bit, did it more for you really so just carry on as normal as far as I'm concerned but there is still your thing about animal rights, anti hunting and all that'.

'So far it doesn't seem to matter too much as long as you don't try and force your your opinions onto anyone else.' She paused . 'Anything else you would like to know about the set up here?'

Marion was about to say something but thought better of it. Hugh shifted uneasily in his seat. ' Do they ..er.. know about how it used to be between us. I mean….?'

'Yes I know what you mean Hugh and the answer is no.'

'That's good, don't want any awkward situations to arise concerning any of your other guests tomorrow. I believe the landlady of the pub is coming and your neighbour'. He gave a knowing look to Marion who grinned back.

Tina frowned. 'You don't have to worry on that score. John Tregarth has no interest in me I can assure you, quite the opposite so let's put an end to any speculation on that front. I invited him and his son for two reasons, firstly they are on their own and I don't think that it's right at Christmas and secondly his son Nick is looking after my horse for me and I don't get much chance to chat to him away from the stables, and by the way he is a very quiet young man so don't be surprised if he doesn't say much'.

'You haven't told us much about this horse.' Hugh said.

'Didn't think you would be interested. It belonged to my father.' She replied and told them as much as she knew about the events surrounding the mare. 'She's called Mystery, Greystone Mystery to be precise, you'll see her on Boxing Day when we go to the hunt Meet. Nick will be riding her.' The last piece of information raised eyebrows.

'Don't tell me you're into blood sports Tina, after all you've said in the past.'

'No it's not like that now. They have to follow an artificial scent so there is no killing involved. I haven't been to a Meet since I was a little girl, you'll find it quite exciting, you'll see. But that's enough about here. Fill me in about the goings on in Wimbledon. No matter what they say, emails are no substitute for a good old chat.'

~

CHAPTER 22

It was still pitch dark at seven o'clock as Thomas made his way to the stable yard on Christmas morning. The rain had stopped and there were glimpses of a crescent moon between scudding clouds. All was still in darkness which pleased him, he always liked to be first on the job. A horse whickered as he opened the gate and he knew it was Titan.

'Morning old feller,' he called as he switched on the yard lights before heading for the meal house.

'Merry Christmas Thomas'. John was walking across rubbing his hands. 'Bit nippy but at least it's stopped raining'.

The groom was measuring crushed oats and a proprietary mix of horse feed into a number of feed skips laid out on the floor.

'Not too many oats for the roan mare Thomas, you know she can be as jumpy as a box of frogs and we don't want Nick ending up in a ditch tomorrow'.

Thomas nodded. ' Will you be riding Titan?'

'Not on a Boxing Day, too many Pony Club kids milling about, it would test the old boy's patience too far and I don't want to risk him getting hurt by some out of control little Herbert, no I'll take the chestnut. What are your plans for tomorrow, would you like to take old Prefect for a spin?'

'The bay gelding was a favourite of the ex-stud groom but he shook his head sadly. ' Thanks but I'm ferrying folks to the meet, that'll be the sum total of my hunting tomorrow and for the foreseeable future as far as I can see'.

'You surprise me, I didn't think they would be interested. Whose idea was that?'

'It was Tina's'.

'Oh it's Tina now is it', John smiled. 'What happened to Miss Pendogget the Lady of the Manor?'

'That's not fair John Tregarth, just because you've never taken the trouble to get to know her, okay, she seems to enjoy living at Greystone but you can't blame her for doing that. We've known each other a long time John and I'm old enough to be your father so I hope you won't take it wrong when I say what I think and I think you're just peeved because she's got Greystone and you haven't. You've got to face up it John, you know well it was either that or losing the farm, and I'll tell you something else, that girl has got her head screwed on and you would do well to remember that'.

'Alright, alright you've made your point, now let's get on. If you make a start with the horses I'll go and feed the cattle, I don't suppose young Nick will be about yet, he was watching television until late last night'.

At that moment the person in question appeared looking very sheepish . 'Sorry I'm late, I overslept, the alarm didn't go off'.

'Yes it did', his father grunted. 'You just didn't hear it'. Then as an after thought added ' I know it's not the sort of Christmas morning most sixteen year olds would expect, I'm sorry but the work has to be done and there's only us to do it. Look, when you've both finished we'll have a Christmas drink and something warm before you Thomas slope off next door. Nick and I can plan our day then and let you get on with whatever Miss P wants you to do'.

'Will you be coming over for Christmas dinner this evening then?' Thomas asked.

John shrugged. ' I'm not sure that I would be all that welcome. She doesn't seem to like me very much , spends most of her time talking to Nick when she does come to the yard. Isn't that right Nick?'

'I suppose so', the boy looked pensive and hesitated before adding ' I'm going dad whether you come or not'.

His father nodded. ' You're old enough to make your own decisions boy, it's no big deal for me to spend Christmas in my own company. So let's get finished and then we'll have that festive drink.'

It was still barely light when the three met up in the tiny kitchen of the converted farm building that was home to the Tregarths. Three mugs of tea were poured and John added generous tots of rum to two of them handing one to Thomas and keeping one for himself, then as an afterthought poured a small drop into Nicholas' mug . ' There you are boy that'll help keep out the cold,' he grinned. 'That's more than I ever got at your age, your grandfather was a stickler when it came to the booze. Isn't that right Thomas.'

'Ar, he was as far as you were concerned, mind, he wasn't averse to a drop himself, particularly after a good day's hunting and of course at Christmas. Which reminds me.' He paused to rummage in his inside pocket to bring out an envelope and then from his jacket he pulled out a bottle of single malt. 'Here, I've been lugging this about all morning , Mabel said I had to bring it now as you weren't likely to be coming tonight, so merry Christmas John, and for you young Nick there will be something for you to pick up tonight.'

'That's very good of you Thomas, thank you on behalf of both of us.' John said ,at the same time reaching behind his chair for a gift wrapped parcel. 'For you and Mabel with many thanks, and this,' he paused to open a table draw and bring out two envelopes.

'This is particularly for you old friend,' he said handing one to Thomas. 'And this one is for you Nick, these past months would have been very difficult without you, it's not as much as I would have liked but I hope you'll find it useful, think of it as a bonus for improved attitude and diligence.' He grinned, 'and I really mean that.'

Thomas felt the plumpness of his envelope and without opening it shook his head and said ' I don't need to take your money John. I help you for the love of it and for old times sake , you know that.'

'I do Thomas but I also know that life doesn't get any easier as you get older so take it please, as you say just for old times sake.'

Nick had opened his envelope and was busy counting the notes. He looked up in mild surprise 'Cor, thanks dad.' He said with enthusiasm. 'And I've got something for you two, hang on I'll fetch them.' He disappeared into his bedroom and returned carrying two pictures, gave one to Thomas and the other to his father. Both men studied them intently and it was the older man who spoke first. 'Tis just like him.' He held the water colour portrait of Prefect at arms length. 'Just like him,' he repeated. 'You've got a gift boy and no mistake, I shall treasure this, so thank you very much.'

Nick looked over to his father , waiting for him to say something. After a long pause John cleared his throat and said quietly 'I never knew you could do anything as good as this Nick. You've captured everything that makes Titan special, that makes a stallion different from other horses. I never thought I would say this but perhaps you could take this up seriously, I'm damned sure it would pay better than farming. How did you do all this without me knowing?'

'Oh, Tina let me use her office, you know, what used to be the old gun room, well I used to go in there whenever you were not about. She helped me a lot, she knows people in London with galleries and she……'

'Okay, I get the picture if you'll excuse the pun, but there are a few hurdles to jump before you can think about that.'

'Thanks dad, she said you would come round eventually.'

'Oh she did , did she, well we'll have to see about that. In the mean time we've got work to do and it's your turn to cook breakfast.'

'And I'll have to be on my way too,' Thomas said as he pulled on his waterproofs.

'Hang on a minute, I'll come with you.' John said as he did the same.

When they got outside he continued, 'we don't get many opportunities to have a chat Thomas so if you could spare a minute or two I would value your advice.' He led the way over to where Mystery was contentedly pulling at her hay net. 'I think Nick is angling to ride the mare in the members race at the point to point. ' What do you think?'

Thomas thought for a moment. 'Well, he rides well and he's old enough.'

'But only just,'John interjected turning to face him. 'It's a rough old game as you well know and I don't want the boy to risk his neck just to prove a point; I don't think I could cope if anything serious happened to him, not after what happened to Beth.'

'That was different John, Elizabeth was upset and not thinking straight for whatever reason, otherwise she wouldn't have galloped off as she did and in that sort of weather. Nick is not like that, he knows his limits and he would never risk injuring the mare. In that respect at least, he takes after you.

'I'm glad you think so. I suppose I ought to be glad he's taking an interest at last. There was a time when I really wondered what we were going to do with him.' There was a long pause. 'He took his mother's death pretty hard as you know and I sometimes think he feels that I am somehow to blame.'

'That's nonsense John.'

John shook his head. 'I hope so Thomas, I just hope so.'

They parted as Nick called out that breakfast was ready. The scrambled eggs were eaten in silence, father and son keeping their thoughts to themselves

'Your turn to wash up, I cooked.' Nick said as he stood up and reached for his coat.

His father nodded. 'We'll jog the horses out for an hour at about eleven, we should have finished the chores by then and don't forget there's all our tack to clean ready for tomorrow.'

It was getting dark before the last bridle was reassembled and hung in the tack room. Then it was the evening feeds, water buckets to fill, silage for the cattle and a large round bale to be taken out to the stock wintering out, so that it was nearly six o'clock before the pair got back to the kitchen for tea. Half an hour later Nick had washed and changed and was ready to go across to Greystone. His father looked him over. 'You should put a tie on if you are invited out to dinner.'

'That's old fashioned dad, nobody wears a tie these days.'

'I do,' his father grunted.

'That says it all,' Nick muttered as he pulled on his waterproof coat and went out of the door.

John sat for a few minutes in deep thought. He poured himself a large Scotch added a little water and settled back into the one and only arm chair and with something akin a groan began to mull over the events of the past few months, the missing stock, falling prices and above all the loss of the Barton. Here he was, forty-two years old with nothing much to look forward to other than more hard work with little to show for it. There was Nick of course and it was no small consolation that the boy was at last taking an interest in the farm, well not exactly the farm but at least the horses or anyway one horse, Pendogget's mare and of course, her owner Miss P. Why did he always think of her as Miss P? She wasn't unattractive but perhaps a bit too cocky, too sure of herself, too unlike Beth. Poor Beth, in the ten years they were married she had never been able to come to terms with the remoteness, the isolation and the weather of the high moor. If only he had realised it sooner perhaps he could have prevented her depression, sought professional help, taken her away somewhere for a few weeks, but there was the farm and the stud, Greystone always came first, there were always plenty of excuses not to leave it for any length of time, always more important things to do. Well at least Nick seemed to be coming out of his shell at last thanks to the roan mare and Miss P. - he poured another whiskey – Miss P the successful business woman, Miss P the mistress of Greysone, Miss P Byron Pendogget's daughter.

There was a faint smile as his eyes closed and Talisman came up to nuzzle his hand.

*

The hall at Greystone was bright with Christmas tree lights and coloured lanterns. The log fire blazed as the guests assembled and Tina was pleased to see that Hugh was making an effort to talk to Nick while Marion was busying herself helping Mabel put the finishing touches to the dining table.

'How many places should we lay?' She asked.

'Eight'. Tina replied quickly.

'But there are only sev....'

'Eight'. She repeated and added under her breath 'Just in case'.

At that moment there was a tap on the front door and Tina hurried across to open it, giving a slightly disappointed 'Oh' as Gloria stepped in shaking her umbrella.

'It's raining cats and dogs again', she paused 'and you might at least sound glad to see me,' she added with a grin.

'Sorry I thought it was......'

'Well it wasn't.' Gloria said tartly. 'So where can I help?'

Would you mind giving Mabel a hand in the kitchen when she's finished laying the table? Sorry, it's a bit of a busman's holiday for you I know but she's not used to catering for so many and a bit of advice from you would help her no end.'

Thomas came through the kitchen door carrying a large trug full of logs which he set next to the fire before carefully brushing the odd bits of bark from the front of his best tweed suit. ' That door to the back lobby is rattling like mad in this wind, do you think I should bolt it?'

'No.' Tina said quickly. 'Leave it, there's nothing in there that will come to any harm even if it blows open.'

Thomas looked puzzled but said nothing as he put another large log on the fire.

'When would you like to eat?' Mabel called from the kitchen. 'The birds are about done and the potatoes are browning nicely.'

Tina glanced at the front door. 'No, we'll wait a few minutes, have a sherry and then start.'

'Wait for who.' Mabel muttered under her breath. 'He's not coming. What do you think Gloria?' The landlady smiled but kept her thoughts to herself.

*

Ten minutes later the smoked salmon was placed on the table and Tina agreed, somewhat reluctantly, that they should go into the dining room and take their places at the table.

She had arranged the seating so that Nick sat next to her with Hugh on the other side then Marion next to him then Thomas, with Gloria and Mabel having the vacant chair between them. Crackers were pulled and paper hats donned: Christmas dinner was under way.

Nick and Tina were discussing the future of Mystery when Mabel suddenly looked up and said 'Listen, I can hear scratching noises coming from the back door, Thomas you had better go and see what it is.'

Tina pushed back her chair. 'No, I'll go, you finish your salmon.' She went into the kitchen, turned the door knob and Talisman burst into the room shaking the rain from is coat, his ears flapping as he shook his great head. There was a bang as the lobby door slammed shut and the tall figure stood in the doorway the long riding coat dripping, the flat cap crammed on his head, just as the first time they had met but without the boots and spurs. He pulled the cap off, and cleared his throat. 'I'm terribly sorry, he just slipped round me and was gone like a bat out of hell,' he paused, 'I suppose he thought he was going home, look.' The old hound had curled himself up in front of the hall fire. 'That was always his bit of space even in summer.'

He took off his coat to reveal the familiar pin-striped suit. 'I'm late aren't I', he said lamely.

Tina smiled. ' No not really, and you're very welcome M.....John.' She suddenly realised that it was the first time she had used his first name in all the time she had been at Greystone. She led the way into the dining room and as she made the necessary introductions could not help noticing that Marion's eyes widened slightly as he sat down opposite her.

Mabel hurried off with a wide grin on her face as she went to fetch his smoked salmon while Nick exchanged a knowing glance with Tina as she resumed her place at the table.

As soon as the first plates were cleared Tina and Mabel prepared to serve the main course.

'It's goose,' Tina announced as they retreated to the kitchen while Hugh fetched the Chardonnay from the fridge, then the uncorked bottles of claret from the sideboard. 'Who is for red and who is for white? he asked cheerily.

'Red for me please,' Nick said as his turn came.

'A very small one,' his father chipped in.

Hugh gave Nick a wink and poured a full glass. 'It must be quite a busy time for you,' he said turning to John. ' How big is your farm?'

'We've got just over three hundred acres altogether which is a fair size for this part of the world. It used to be three farms in my father's time but we gradually brought them into one unit. There are also some moorland rights which allow us to graze cattle and sheep on the open moor in the summer giving us a bit more space when we need to make silage and hay.

'And you have a lot of horses so I'm told.'

'That's right. It's only a small stud, just one stallion and we take anything up to twenty mares staying with us for varying lengths of time plus our own horses so we get pretty busy from February onwards and I'm not sure how we shall cope this year without Thomas.' John glanced at Tina but she pretended not to hear. ' Things will ease a bit when we get the new buildings put up but even then Nick and I won't be able to do it all even with casual help and contractors. Horses need special care and there are not many people prepared to put in the hours. Isn't that so Thomas.'

The old man nodded but said nothing.

Hugh continued: ' I understand Tina has a horse with you.'

'That's right, a thoroughbred mare she inherited from her father.'

'And we're going to race her at the point to point .' Nick said hesitantly looking at his father. 'And your father has agreed you can ride her,' Thomas butted in.

'Is that alright dad, will it be okay, I mean, you don't mind?' Nick continued excitedly.

His father shrugged. ' It looks as though I've been out voted on this one,' he said looking at his former groom. 'But in any case we will have to discus that with the owner. Isn't that right Miss P.' He gave her a mischievous glance which caused a smile as she served the goose.

'Yes, Miss P will be pleased to discuss the matter with Mr T,' she replied with a mocking laugh. ' And indeed, with anyone else that's interested. In the mean time I suggest you all help yourselves to vegetables.'

There followed a long pause in the conversation during which the company settled down to do justice to Tina's and Mabel's hard work. Mutters of approval pleased the hosts (Tina considered Mabel an equal in this). The Christmas pudding was brought in soaked in brandy and spectacularly ablaze after which they all adjourned to the sitting room for coffee.

For Tina it was all she could have wished for, a successful meal, the right atmosphere and above all John Tregarth had seemed relaxed and was obviously enjoying himself. She was glad he had come, it was her good deed for Christmas, making sure no one would spend the festive season alone. That is what she told herself.

Marion broke her reverie. ' What are you going to do with that large room at the back of the house, the one full of junk that faces the garden?'

'I don't know yet, guests dining room or perhaps a lounge.'

'It was my mother's work room,' Nick said quietly. 'I remember there used to be a grand piano in there,' he paused 'and lots of paintings and stuff.' He stopped abruptly to gaze into his coffee cup.' There was a moment of silence during which he looked up at his father who, with closed eyes, gave a sympathetic nod.

It was Gloria who made the effort to change the subject. 'Have you hung that picture yet?' She asked brightly.

Tina shook her head. ' Sorry, I haven't really had time to look at it properly, it's still in the hall, I'll go and get it.' She went out and returned, holding it up to show the others It was an enlarged photograph of a hunt scene, a meet outside the Fox and Hounds with the huntsman and hounds in the foreground and a group of twenty or so riders clustered behind together with a large number of foot followers. Thomas stood up to get a closer look, at the same time feeling in his pocket for his reading glasses. When he had adjusted them he leant forward, his finger pointing to two young riders. 'Well I'll be damned,' he said under his breath. Then turning to John ' I reckon the lad on the bay horse is your father.' He paused to study the photograph more closely. 'And the one on the grey,' he looked up at Tina, 'is your father. Tell me Gloria, where did you find it?'

'It was in the old brewhouse with some junk left by my predecessors,' she said with a grin. Old Charlie Hawkins was right, he said you would be interested in it but didn't say why at the time, but now we know. Quite a nice coincidence don't you think?' she asked tartly looking at John but he was too preoccupied with his own thoughts to reply.

'So this could be described as a family reunion.' Hugh said grandly, standing rather unsteadily and waiving his glass in the air.

Tina looked embarrassed. 'Don't be so silly Hugh, it's just an old photograph, interesting I agree but nothing more.' She turned to Gloria. 'I'm not sure where it should go yet but I'm sure I'll find the right place for it once we've got the house properly sorted.

It was kind of you to think of bringing it, although I'm not sure it shouldn't hang in the Tregarth household. What do you think John?' He smiled and merely shook his head.

Gloria chuckled ' Never mind' she said ' I have a feeling that problem will   sort itself out eventually. In the mean time put it somewhere safe, after all we don't want to lose it again.'

'That's right.' Thomas agreed. ' It must have been taken just after the war about the time things were getting back to normal.'

'Talking about things getting back to normal,' Gloria said, settling back in her chair, ' I hear Slogger Dixon has been "done" again for illegally coursing a hare with his lurchers, naturally he swears it was a rabbit and knowing Slogger he'll probably get away with it.'

Hugh looked puzzled. ' I don't understand ' he said. ' What difference does that make, I mean, aren't they both wild animals?'

'That's right,' Nick replied ' I know it sounds daft but hunting a hare is illegal while hunting a rabbit isn't.'

Hugh snorted. 'Not much logic in that'

'Oh, it's to do with cloth caps and miner's whippets.' John said wearily, 'It's something we've learned to live with I suppose, and talking of hunting,' he looked at his watch, ' I'm afraid it's time we made a move, we have to make an early start tomorrow.' Nick is already half asleep, Eh Nick?'

'And I suppose you will also be making an early start.' Tina said to Thomas with a grin. ' Oh, don't worry I've seen you sloping off at crack of dawn, you are not the only early riser you know.'

The old man shifted uneasily in his chair, grunted and stood up. 'Well you see.' he began, but Tina simply waived her hand in a good natured gesture. 'Good night Thomas, thank you for your help and don't forget we want to be at the meet by ten thirty tomorrow.'

John was standing in the hall where Talisman reluctantly got up and moved away from the warm hearth to join him at the front door. The old hound's nose twitched as Tina immerged with a tasty morsel in her fingers. 'He's been very good,' she said patting the upturned head as the dog licked his chops.

John held out his hand. ' Thank you on behalf of all three of us for a most enjoyable evening. It has been a long time since we have had a proper Christmas and you have made it just that.'

Tina suddenly felt self conscious. ' Glad you could come' she said as she grasped his hand. It felt rough just like her father's, she thought of her mother's likening them to peasants hands. Well not in this case that was for sure. She turned to Nick. ' Hope you enjoyed it and don't forget what we talked about, do give it some thought.'

'What was that all about?' John asked when they got outside.

*

'It will be pretty crowded.' Thomas said as the Land Rover bumped down the long Greystone drive, while Hugh and Marion in the uncomfortable back seats gritted their teeth and longed for the smooth tarmac of the Blackaford road.

'At least the weather has cleared up.' Tina commented as they neared the Fox and Hounds.

'No room in the car park, I'm afraid it will be chocker block by now,' Thomas said. 'We had best park on the grass verge and walk the rest.'

They pulled up behind a line of vehicles, mostly four wheel drives but also several muddy pick-up trucks and a number of cars that had obviously seen better days. Hugh glanced at them as they walked by. 'I don't see many Rolls Royces,' he commented. 'I always thought these occasions were reserved for the "upper crust".'

Thomas chuckled. 'Oh, don't worry there'll a few posh cars in the car park, we get a lot of folks from the towns at a Boxing Day meet, I suppose they come to see a bit of old England, a live Christmas card as it were.'

They reached the forecourt of the pub just as the huntsman and hounds came trotting round the corner followed by a number of riders.

'What a lot of dogs,' Marion whispered.

'Sixteen and a half couple I reckon.' Thomas said knowingly. 'We count them in twos you see,' he continued, craning foreword to count. 'Yes that's right: thirty three.'

'How did you manage to count them so quickly?' Marion asked. 'To me they are just a blur of backs and tails.'

'Oh, I used to be in hunt service when I was a young man and you soon learn,' he replied smugly. 'You see the other chap in a red coat, the young lad on the chestnut horse, well I used to do his job; whipping in they call it and one of his jobs is to make sure all the hounds are present and up together, if not he'll call them by name and when he's sure they are all there he calls out "All on" to the huntsman.'

'They all have names then?

'Of course, mind, it takes a while to get to know them especially when so many look alike and we used to have upwards of forty couple in kennels in my day.'

By this time the number in the crowd had risen to well over a hundred Tina reckoned and she began to look for John and Nick among the riders still arriving. Eventually she saw them in their black hunting coats trotting down the road among a group of young riders, some dressed in traditional black but many in waterproof jackets of varying colours.

'I expected to see more red coats.' Hugh sounded disappointed. 'I can only see three: the chaps with the hounds and the old boy over there.' He pointed to a red faced man whose grey hair protruded beneath his black hunting cap. 'That's the Master,' Thomas told him with a grin. ' Toby West, farms over by Blisland, looks smart enough in his red coat but you should see him in the morning when he's milking his cows, you wouldn't recognise it was the same man.'

At that moment Gloria and her staff plus several helpers emerged carrying trays of glasses filled with hot punch which were offered to the riders together with warm fruit juice for the pony club. Then there were sandwiches and small hot pasties brought out, some of which found there way into the hands of the foot followers and several into the mouths of opportunistic hounds.

When the last glass had been emptied and the last pasty swallowed, the master rode his to the front of the crowd and raised his hat, the white of his bald head contrasting with the bright red of his face. He stood up in his stirrups. 'Ladies and gentlemen,' he began. 'First of all we have to thank Mrs. Lockey and her staff for the first class meet. The Fox and Hounds has hosted the Boxing Day meet since well before the last war and it has become a something of a tradition for which we are most grateful(clapping and cheers). It's good to see so many turn out, there seems to be more every year(more cheers). Today we will be hunting trails laid by Andrew,' he indicated towards a young man on a quad bike who was waiving what looked like an old sock on the end of a piece of rope to more cheers and some laughter. 'And David,' he pointed to a youth on a piebald cob who waived a similar article.

'I hope you all had a merry Christmas and we look forward to seeing you in the New Year.'

With that he slumped back into the saddle giving a nod to the huntsman who promptly gave a single blast on his horn and led his hounds out towards the moor followed by the riders and a large number of cars.

'Do we follow on?' Tina asked

Thomas shook his head. 'I don't suppose we would see much once they get over the top, we might as well join the regulars inside.'

The bar was crowded, mostly with locals many of whom Tina recognised including Charlie Hawkins who nodded to Thomas and sidled over to the newcomers. 'Morning Thomas,' he said with a toothless grin. 'I see you'm keeping good company at last.' He turned towards Tina and raised his battered trilby. ' I 'ope your settling in nicely up there.'

He jerked his head in the direction of the moor.'

Yes thank you Mr. Hawkins, kind of you to ask..er.. Can I buy you a drink?'

'Mission accomplished' Charlie thought as he expressed his thanks.

'You not following then, Charlie?' Thomas asked.

'No, not much point these days, 'tidn't what it used to be, they jist fiddle and fart arse about, beg pardon Miss, till they find one of them trails, 'ounds don't like it 'untsman don't like an' I don't like it - a pint of bitter please miss - mind you, if an ol' fox jumps up in front of 'em, there's a fair old ruckus and a lot of yellin' and hollerin' to try to stop 'em but 'tis nigh impossible an' sometimes I don't think they tries too hard, like that time at Greystone when John Tregarth let 'em go on. 'Twas a good thing there were no antis about - your good health, miss.' He took a gulp of his beer, nodded appreciatively and sat down at the far end of the bar.

Hugh bought their drinks: white wine for Marion, orange juice for Tina and beer for himself and Thomas. 'So how long will this trail hunting last?' He asked Thomas.

'Oh, until it gets dark.'

'No I mean will it last or will they get fed up with it like the old boy there and eventually pack it in for good?'

Thomas shook his head. 'Well you've seen it today, what do you think?'

'I'll tell you what I think,' Tina said with a grin. 'I think we should drink up and move out and since I only had orange juice I'll drive.' She held out her hand for the Land Rover keys. Thomas shrugged and handed them over before finishing his pint and leading them out to walk back to their vehicle.

Mabel produced a meal of cold ham, hot potatoes and salad after which Tina, Marion and Hugh retired to the sitting room while Thomas remained in the kitchen to help his wife.

'So what did you think of this morning's jaunt then Hugh? I guess it was a first time for both of you.'

There was a moments silence before Hugh said 'It's a different world Tina and one that I never thought you could be part of.'

She smiled. 'I didn't think so either and I must admit it has taken a bit of getting used to. I suppose it has happened gradually - inheriting the farm, buying Greystone, riding again and then of course actually owning a horse and a race horse at that, well……'

Marion raised her eyebrows. 'And don't forget your neighbours dear' she said with a grin. 'Especially the "hunk", and I thought you said he would be difficult.'

'Did I?'

'Yes you did,' Marion paused. 'He's a pussycat.'

Tina grunted. 'I'm glad you think so but don't be fooled, you have never driven into the back of his horse – I have!'

Hugh stretched his legs, leant back with his hands behind his head and closed his eyes.

'You know, I really don't think I want to go back to the smoke tomorrow; must be something in the air down here and if it wasn't for the fact that I have to earn a crust…..'

'You wouldn't last a week,' Marion interrupted 'You are just too fond of the high life.'

'You and me both luvvy.' Hugh suppressed a yawn. 'So it's back to the real world tomorrow, but I have to say that I for one have some thoughts to take back with me.'

∼

CHAPTER 23

God! I hate these dark January mornings.' Thomas exclaimed as he met John in the stable yard.

'The feeling is mutual.' John shivered and turned up his coat collar. 'It's always a let down after Christmas; nothing to look forward to except a soaked shirt and a wet arse when you ride out at exercise!'

'What you need is someone to dry your shirt and underpants in front of a roaring fire as soon as you get back instead of keeping 'em on until they dry. One day you'll catch your death of cold and with no one to take care of you then what?'

'Then I'll take care of myself thank you. I don't know what you're getting at but whatever it is you can forget it; we've got more important things to think about. I would like you to take a look at the roan mare, she hasn't cleared up her feed this morning.

They both walked across the yard to look over the loose-box door where Mystery was standing dejectedly in a corner. They watched as she occasionally stamped a hind foot and turned her head towards her flank with low grunt. The two men looked at each other and almost simultaneously said one word: 'Colic!'

'I'm afraid it looks like it.' Thomas said frowning. 'Of course it might be just a bit of belly ache if she ate her grub a bit quick but I'll keep an eye on her just in case.'

Half an hour later he called over to Nick who was filling water buckets. 'Better fetch your dad, I think we're in for trouble.'

'Why, what's up?' he asked anxiously as he came over to look over the stable door.

208

'Colic I reckon, look'.

The mare had broken out in a sweat on her neck and flanks and as the watched she lay down and attempted to roll.

'That won't do'. Thomas said, quickly shooting the bolts and going in. 'I'll try and keep her on her feet while you fetch dad'.

John was breathless when he arrived. He looked over the door at the mare then at Thomas. 'Oh shit', he said between his teeth. 'That's the last thing we need, I had better ring Tom Beresford - no point in taking chances. In the mean time put her head collar on and try and keep her on her feet , we don't want her rolling about too much and risk a twisted gut'.

Nick looked alarmed; he had heard of that condition and knew it was both painful and often fatal. 'Will Mr. Beresford be able to do anything for her?' he asked Thomas anxiously as his father hurried away.

The old man smiled reassuringly. 'Vets. can do a lot these days, not like in my day when we had to rely on jollop made with turpentine and stuff, getting that down 'em was no joke'.

He tried to sound confident. 'Now, get her head collar and walk her round the box while I get some more straw to put down in case she goes down again; then I had better go and tell the owner', he looked at his watch. 'She should be up and about by now'. What he did not say was that he would have to warn her that she might have to make a difficult decision if things went wrong.

'Tom Beresford is out at a difficult calving; he'll be here as soon as he can,' John announced breathlessly on his return. 'Let's hope he gets here in time'.

Five minutes later Thomas came through the yard gate followed closely by a distraught Tina, her coat flapping in the wind as she struggled with the buttons. She looked anxiously over the stable door. 'What's the matter with her, is it serious?'

John looked grim. 'Colic I'm afraid and pretty severe at that', he paused. 'You should know that it could be fatal if the intestines get into a tangle'.

Tina gasped. 'How does that happen?'

'Well, something - we don't quite know what - has caused some sort of a blockage and the danger is that the intestine may loop on itself in a sort of knot we call 'Twisted Gut'. If that happens it is excruciatingly painful and……' he paused again. 'If it can't be cleared we may have to put her down. I'm sorry'.

'Oh my God! You mean shoot her?' Tina gasped in disbelief . 'You can't, you can't'. She covered her eyes with both hands as the tears came.

Without knowing quite how it happened John found his arm round her shoulders gently pulling her to him. 'It's alright Miss P, it hasn't come to that yet,' he said gently.

'The vet is on his way and there is a good chance we have caught it in time'. He felt her body relax as she sniffed and cleared her throat.

'The poor thing, she doesn't deserve this after all she has been through,' she murmured.

John removed his arm self-consciously. 'We just have to wait for the vet now,' he said. He turned to Thomas. 'Do you think it's worth trying one of those drenches we've had in the medicine chest since the year dot?'

The old man shrugged. 'It'll be better than standing round waiting. I'll get one'.

It took several minutes for him to return with the long necked bottle of dark looking liquid. In the mean time Nick had managed to keep Mystery on her feet so that John had to fetch a bale of straw to stand on in order to reach her mouth as he raised her head and poured the contents of the bottle down her throat. 'Bit old fashioned that,' he said wiping his arm with a wisp of straw. 'They used to swear by the stuff in the old days and as you said Thomas it's better than just standing doing nothing'.

It was a long half an hour before Tom Beresford's battered estate wagon -the victim of many difficult gateways - pulled into the yard. Now in his late fifties, grey haired and balding, his matter-of-fact attitude engendered complete confidence in his ability to work miracles. He purposefully walked to the loose-box door and studied the mare for several seconds before going in to take temperature and pulse. He said nothing until he had sounded her flanks and examined what dung there was on the floor; it was all completed just seconds before she collapsed and attempted to roll again. 'I'm afraid you are right John,' he said as he went out to his vehicle to rummage in various boxes in the back, eventually returning with bottles and syringes.

'What will he do?' Tina whispered to John

'Oh, something to ease the pain and calm the system I expect'.

'Then what?'

'Then we wait and pray'.

The injections completed Beresford turned to John. 'You and Thomas know the score. Is she yours? If not you had better inform the owner, just in case'.

'She's standing behind you Tom'.

Introductions made, the vet promised Tina he would return in about an hour but if it got much worse before then to give him a ring at the surgery. 'They will know where I am,' he reassured her.

They watched in silence as he backed round and left the yard. Eventually John said 'I suggest a hot drink, so you three take a break while I stay to keep an eye on her just to make sure she doesn't get cast'.

Ten minutes later Tina made her way across the yard carrying two steaming mugs of coffee. She peered over the door to see John kneeling beside the recumbent mare cradling her head on his knee. He was making quiet soothing noises as he gently stroked one ear. Tina coughed; he looked up suddenly. 'I was just trying to keep her calm,' he said as he stood up. She smiled and handed him the mug and together they watched as Mystery groaned and staggered to her feet to walk round the box then lie down and begin to roll again. John shook his head. 'The pain killers should have kicked in by now,' he murmured.

'Will you call the vet again?'

John thought for a moment. 'No, not yet, we have to give the drugs time to work and as I said before, it's a case of wait and see. We'll give it half an hour'.

They sat down on the bale of straw John had pulled into a corner. 'Do you think she will pull through?' Tina asked cupping he hands round the hot mug.

'There's every chance', he replied trying to sound confident.

They sat in silence as the mare paced round and round, occasionally kicking her stomach with a hind foot; then her legs folded and she rolled again. John looked at his watch as the minutes ticked by; then with a sigh said 'That's enough, I'm going to see if I can get hold of Tom. Thomas and Nick will come across if you want to stay'.

She nodded glumly.

When he returned she was still sitting in the same position staring vacantly into space. 'They are going to try and get a message to him but you know what it's like getting a mobile signal up on the moor so he may be some time. Let's hope he calls the surgery'.

Nick and Thomas arrived back together. 'How is she?' Nick asked anxiously.

His father put a hand on his shoulder. 'Not so good I'm afraid but there's nothing you two can do at the moment so you had better catch up with the chores if you can'.

Thomas glanced at Tina. She tried to smile. 'That's alright Thomas , you are more use here than back at Greystone'.

The old man nodded as he and Nick disappeared into the feed barn.

'Are you warm enough? John asked.

She nodded. 'I'll be alright, it's just been a bit of a shock, that's all'.

'Look, you go and get yourself warm; put some more clothes on'.

Tina grinned. ' The last time we were in this sort of situation you told me to take them off John Tregarth'.

'Only because you were wet through Miss P then I……'.' He stopped as Mystery gave a shudder and stretched out flat.

'I think I should stay', Tina said.

'No, it would be better if you left us for a while. I'll let you know if anything happens'.

She stood up stiffly, touched his arm and murmured some thanks before walking out and back across the yard towards the house.

John knelt down to feel Mystery's pulse and began to gently stroke her neck. 'Nice lady'. He whispered to the mare; one ear flicked at the sound of his voice. 'No more grief please, so come on'. He closed his eyes and began to wonder how he would break the news if worse came to the worse and she had to be put out of her misery. Suddenly she groaned and heaved herself into a normal lying position with her nose touching the floor.

Tina heard the car come up the drive. Hurriedly she pulled on her coat, rammed a woolly hat on and ran out to the yard. She arrived just as the vet was getting out of his car; he was carrying a small leather case as he opened the loose-box door. Tina looked in to see that Mystery was standing quietly, neck outstretched, nuzzling John's open hand. 'I don't think you will be needing that Tom', he said, indicating to the leather case.

'Was that more than just a glisten in his eyes' Tina wondered as he wiped his nose on the back of his hand. She watched as he took off Mystery's head collar and encouraged her to walk round the box.

Nick had heard the vet arrive, so too had Thomas. The latter gave an audible sigh of relief as Mystery lifted her tail to deposit a heap of steaming dung onto the straw.

'There's your answer', Tom Beresford said with a smile. 'A warm bran mash I should think John and I don't need to tell you go easy with the grub for the next few days'.

Nick went in to join his father. 'Don't worry Mr. Beresford', he said patting the mare's neck. 'I shall be looking after her. I know what to do'.

'I'm sure you do young man'. The vet smiled and winked at Thomas who gave an imperceptible nod. Then he turned to speak to Tina. 'A nice mare', he said noting her anxious look. 'Don't worry, with a bit of 'Tender Loving Care' she'll be as right as rain, and she'll get plenty of that here'. He got into his car, lowered the window and called out 'If I remember you call her Mystery. Is that right John? After what she's been through since she came here I would think Miracle might be a more appropriate name'. He gave a cheery waive as he drove out of the yard.

*

'Just pop her over the small brush fence.' Thomas called as Nickrode Mystery round the exercise paddock. It was over a month since the mare had recovered from the bout of colic and schooling had gone well. There was no doubt she was quick and gave the impression that she enjoyed jumping; there was general agreement that in a few weeks she would be ready to face the full size practice fences laid out on the improvised gallops they had constructed round the farm.

Horse and rider pulled up beside Thomas having negotiated the fence in good style. 'Proper job,' he said patting Mystery's neck. 'Take her over a couple more times then take your stirrup leathers up a hole and jump it once more. You've got to get used to riding short so I suggest you take 'um up a hole each week until I think it's enough; that way you will gradually strengthen your legs and get yourself fit. Remember races are lost by unfit jockeys as much as unfit horses'

John watched from his office window. He smiled with satisfaction: things seemed to be going well at last: the weather had improved, the grass was beginning to grow and with it the prospect of turning out the cattle early. Applications for Titan's services were trickling in, albeit not as fast as he would have liked and to cap it all planning permission had been granted for the new farm buildings. He went into the kitchen, made a cup of tea and sat down in the arm chair to listen to a Vaughn Williams CD.

He had almost nodded off when he became aware of a tap on the door and a female voice saying: 'That sounds very appropriate.' He jerked awake to see Tina standing in the doorway. He stood up clumsily. 'Sorry?'

'I said it sounded very appropriate - The Lark Ascending - very rural. I didn't know you were into classical music.'

John shrugged. 'Ten years married to a classical musician something is bound to rub off'.

'I'm sorry, I……….'

'You needn't be'. He smiled and indicated towards a chair. 'And to what do I owe the honour of a visit from the Lady of the Manor?' He settled back into his chair and reached out to switch off the CD player'.

Tina frowned; the Lady of the Manor joke was wearing a bit thin as far as she was concerned. She hesitated for a moment . 'I hope you don't mind my asking but I was wondering what Nick is going to do with himself in the future? I know it's none of my business but, well…..he's a bright lad and it seems a pity….'

'A pity to let him waste his time messing about on the farm. Is that it?' John's voice had an edge to it.

Tina stood up. 'I'm sorry I shouldn't poke my nose into other people's business'.

She turned to go.

John closed his eyes and said quietly 'Sit down please. I don't mean to sound negative but when it comes to Nick I suppose like many parents I'm a bit out of my depth when it comes to teenagers and he hasn't been exactly easy since…..well he had to go to boarding school when Beth……he was too young I suppose but I had no other option. I don't think he was very happy there so it was no surprise when he dropped out at sixteen as soon as he could and nothing I could say could persuade him to go back; and to answer your question I don't know what the boy intends to do except he has some vague idea about being an artist and he'll never make a living at that'.

'How do you know?'

John shrugged. 'It's too 'airy fairy'; all right for a hobby but to make a living? I don't think so. Do you?'

Tina smiled. 'You forget, I'm in the fashion business so I'm biased'

'Sorry, I had forgotten but just the same it might be a suitable career for a girl but not for a red blooded lad like Nick'.

'I don't know about that, some of the best designers are men and they are not all gay. Hugh Valcourt is one of the best and he is far from gay I can tell you'.

John grunted but said nothing.

'So wouldn't it be a good idea to have a chat with Nick about it?'

'Which I suspect you have already done'. He gave her a sidelong glance.

'That's right and he asked me to have a word with you. He said you wouldn't listen to him but you might listen to me'.

'Now I wonder what made him think that? And don't tell me, you discussed all this over Christmas Dinner'.

'Yes, didn't he tell you?

'He never tells me anything: I'm his father remember'

Tina chuckled. 'He said you would 'do your nut'. He will have to go back to school or college of course'.

John sat in silence, then slowly got out of his chair to turn and face her. 'You are a very persuasive lady MissP. I'll think about what you say, so now could I offer you a cup of coffee or tea if you prefer?'

She stood up to go. 'No thanks, some of us have work to do' she paused 'Oh but there is one more thing. Thomas mentioned something about the stud fees for Mystery not being paid six years ago; well, with interest that should come to a tidy sum so I'm offering a half share in her'.

John looked surprised. 'That's very generous of you, thank you very much'.

She turned and said with a grin 'Not to you, to Nicholas'.

He leant on the door post and watched the slim figure walk purposefully across the yard in her tight jeans. 'Now that' he told himself 'Is one feisty lady and with a backside to match'

Nick took his role of part-owner and jockey seriously. He jogged round the farm instead of walking; shopped in the village on an old bicycle and did press-ups in his room. Mystery was worked equally assiduously so that by the time the point to point loomed Thomas declared them both fit and ready. 'She's fast and jumps well' he confided to John. 'And the boy is getting better every day. I reckon they could be in with a chance'.

'I just want him to get round in one piece' John confessed. 'They are both novices; there's bound to be a risk'.

Thomas shrugged. 'Tell that to Nick; he's as keen as mustard just like you were before your first race'.

'That was different: for one thing I was older and for another I was riding father's experienced hunter'.

The old man smiled. 'Don't worry he'll be fine'.

*

The evening before the race Nick tried on his new kit in front of the long mirror in his bedroom, The lightweight boots felt strange after the stiff hunting boots he was used to: more like long black slippers, while the body protector made him look like a miniature American footballer. Tina had chosen pale blue with gold chevrons as their colours; he felt a thrill and at the same time apprehension as he put them on and studied his reflection. He had always admired and envied the young (and not so young) men and women who, stony faced, paraded out of the weighing tent to walk purposefully towards their waiting mounts: now he would be one of them. He tapped his whip against his boot as he had noticed jockeys often do when waiting for a 'leg up' into the saddle. Yes, tomorrow he would really be one of them. He had little sleep that night.

The morning dawned dull but dry. There had been rain in the night: 'Going should be good' Thomas had predicted as he swung Nick's hold - all containing his kit into the cab of the horse-box, while Nick checked his tack with his father before leading Mystery - swathed in rugs and leg protectors

– up the ramp, her head up and ears pricked. Thomas grinned. 'She thinks she's going hunting' he said as he fastened the ramp behind her. John looked at his watch. 'Right, your race is one thirty so we'll aim to be there in good time for you to walk the course and settle your nerves'. He gave Nick an understanding smile. 'Thomas will keep your mare happy until it's time to saddle up'. Nick liked the sound of the 'your'.

Father and son climbed into the cab and they set off slowly down the drive trying to avoid the many pot holes in order to give their passenger as smooth a ride as possible.

Thomas followed in the Land Rover with Tina and Mabel who had put together a substantial picnic lunch. It took less than an hour to arrive at the course where cars were already streaming in guided by numerous luminous coated stewards; and the lorry park was beginning to fill with horseboxes and trailers, some smart and new others, like the Tregarth's , showing years of use and abuse.

The horsebox safely parked the Land Rover drew up alongside and Thomas immediately jumped out to make sure that Mystery had not sweated or suffered any knocks during the journey. Satisfied he turned his attention to checking the tack and weight - cloth, making sure there was sufficient lead.

Nick was a ten stone lightweight and so would need some to make up the eleven stone seven pounds required. 'We're going to walk the course', he announced as he and John pulled on their Wellingtons. Tina declared she would come to and did likewise.

The start was some half a mile from the main area and Nick felt a tightening in the pit of his stomach as they neared the flags which marked the place where they would line up. His father was doling out advice as they went along: 'Don't try and get away first, let them give you a lead over the first fence so that she knows what she is in for; and watch the open ditch, you will need to kick on for that. Remember you've got eighteen fences to jump so keep something back, tuck yourself behind first time round; listen to what the mare tells you: if she's blown pull up but if she's pulling 'two hands' second time round then you can go for it'. He paused as they neared the last fence and turned to Nick to put a hand on his shoulder. 'Don't do anything stupid Nick, remember what I said and don't risk your neck or the mare's; it isn't worth it , believe me I know'. The youth nodded as the knot in his stomach tightened further.

Tina had listened intently to John's words. The fences had seemed huge to her and she said so. He smiled. 'They don't look so big from the back of a horse although at less than sixteen hands your mare is not as tall as most but she has the right conformation - you know what they say: 'A good horse should be like an attractive woman - a pretty head and a good round backside, and she has both'. Tina did not smile but it needed an effort.

Nick strode into the jockey's changing tent trying to look as though he had done so many times before. He dumped his bag on a bench and sat down to wait for his father to bring his saddle and weight-cloth. John placed them beside him and went out to declare Mystery as a runner with the race steward, at the same time calling back to remind Nick to hand in his jockey's Medical Record Book.

Nick looked round; there was only one other rider beginning to change in the far corner. He was much older than Nick had expected, in fact he guessed he was at least as old as his father: tall and lean 'As thin as a stick' Thomas would have said, he had a narrow lined face under a thatch of lank fair hair. The face cracked into a broad smile as he nodded to Nick. 'Member's race?' he asked pulling on his breeches over a pair of ladies tights.

'Yes' Nick replied as he watched with interest.

'Oh, the tights'. The man grinned. 'Keep you warm without adding extra weight which is important in my case; excellent as long as you remember to make a hole in the strategic place'. He pulled on his boots and walked over offering his hand. 'Will Stevens', he said as Nick stood up to shake it.

'Nick Tregarth'.

'Ah, you'll be John's boy?

'That's right'.

'Thought I saw him bring your saddle in. We often rode against each other when we weren't much older than you, but then he got too heavy and had to give up'. He paused, 'This your first time?'

Nick nodded. 'I'm on Greystone Mystery, it's her first time as well'.

'Hmm. Well the Members isn't a bad race for a first run; there won't be too many runners and you will be spared the crush of inexperienced horses in a typical Maiden race'. He sat down beside Nick. 'You'll find this is a pretty straightforward course but watch out for the second to last - that will be the seventh first time round - it's trickier than it looks so don't rush it, take a pull, let her see the fence then kick on and go for it'. He grinned. 'But I expect your dad has already given you enough advice'.

'You can say that again'.

Will Stevens stood up stiffly rubbing one knee. 'Anyway, good luck and remember you are supposed to enjoy it! As far as I can see there are only seven runners: five blokes and two females, look out for the older one she's a hard case, I should know I used to be married to her'. He winked as he picked up his saddle and went out.

The three other male riders came in together acknowledging Nick with a cursory nod before getting changed. He did the same and quietly finished putting on his kit then picking up his saddle, weight-cloth and whip he went out to pick up his number five number-cloth. Meanwhile his father was chatting to the Clerk of the Scales, an elderly man in a brown trilby, who smiled as Nick settled into the chair of the scales, placing his helmet and whip on the bench beside him.

'I shall need another two pounds please' the man said peering at the figures.

John produced two slabs of lead and slid them into the pockets of the weight cloth.

Another look at the figures 'Thank you, that will do it. Good luck.'

John took the saddle, weight cloth and number cloth to where Thomas was waiting to saddle up Mystery. A rug was thrown over and John led her down to the paddock where Tina stood watching the other horses. He walked up to her and to her surprise handed her the reins. 'All yours' he said with a grin giving her the number five arm band.

'What do I have to do?' She sounded alarmed.

'Just lead her round behind the others, that's what owners are supposed to do.'

Tina nodded and fell in behind a big grey horse led by a stocky man in a flat cap.

They made half a dozen circuits of the small fenced off enclosure and she began to feel a sense of pride as the bell rang for the jockeys to mount. Nick stood in the centre with the other riders nervously tapping his whip against his boot as the butterflies in his stomach reached a crescendo. He watched the other jockeys, particularly the pretty girl who looked not much older than himself and the older female, tall and formidable. He was pleased to see that neither the crowd nor the other horses seemed to worry Mystery, probably due to the days spent at crowded hunt meets he thought. He walked over to where Tina stood patting the mare's neck. She smiled nervously as Nick waited for Thomas to give him a 'leg up' into the saddle. He felt for his stirrups, took hold of the reins and as he felt Mystery walk on, suddenly the butterflies disappeared: just the familiar feel of the animal underneath him and the adrenalin rush of anticipation as they trotted out of the paddock behind the scarlet coated mounted steward.

The canter to the start made him gasp for breath as Mystery took hold of the bit and did her best to overtake the grey ridden by the ex Mrs. Stevens. It took all of his strength to pull up at the start line where the other riders were already busy tightening girths and adjusting stirrup leathers with the help of the stewards. The call to line up and a cry of 'Not yet please sir' from the young girl who was having trouble getting her big chestnut horse to the flags. It gave Nick a final chance to check his girth while the chestnut calmed down: and then the starter took his position, flag raised. 'Ready now please Jockeys'. His arm came down and they were away.

Mindful of his father's words Nick held Mystery back and steadied her to give a clear view of the fence. She pricked her ears and responded by taking two massive strides and they were over and going on to the next. They quickly overtook the chestnut and over the next two fences experienced the true exhilaration of race riding as Mystery settled into her stride with four horses in front of her, and before he knew it they were coming up to the big open ditch. 'Take a pull, let her see it then kick on and go for it' the words came back as he manoeuvred to the outside, steadied the mare, nudged her with his heels and she took off a yard from the fence and landed well clear. Then the turn downhill; he knew that jumping fences downhill was always tricky so again he steadied to make sure she did not put in a potentially fatal extra stride and again the mare measured it well to take them safely over.

Nick suddenly realised they had almost completed the first circuit as the big fence number seven loomed in front of them: 'Take a pull, let her see what she's in for then kick on.'

'Nothing to it,' he muttered as they landed on the other side. One more and they were on the second circuit.

By now Nick's arms were aching as he realised excitedly that the mare was still pulling the 'two handfuls'. He crouched lower, gritted his teeth and muttered 'G'orn my beauty' as they passed another horse before the open ditch, then before he realised it the big fence was there. Mystery took off a stride too soon and brushed through the top, landing almost on her knees with her nose on the ground. Nick automatically leant back, let the reins slip through his hands then quickly gathered them again to lift the mare's head. She stumbled but picked herself up and within seconds they were on there way again. He swallowed hard as two horses went past but this seemed to spur Mystery into renewed effort as she quickened her stride to recover her place over the next two fences so that as they rounded the final bend Nick realised he was on the tail of the leading horse, and then he was in front coming to the last but one. His heart beat furiously as he began to ride hard and the possibility of winning entered his mind. As Mystery took off two horses came up fast, one on either side. The grey was close and almost touched his boot; Mystery seemed to waiver in mid air, brushing through the birch to land awkwardly, both knees folding underneath her. Nick felt himself sliding forward out of the saddle and as his shoulder hit the ground he knew his race was over. He rolled in a ball as he glimpsed Mystery galloping away then, when he was sure the last horse had gone by he sat up, head in hands and groaned. 'Oh shit, shit shit shit'

'Are you alright?' a female voice asked

Nick found himself looking into the face of a young St. Johns Ambulance girl.

'Yes I think so'. He rubbed his shoulder gingerly. 'Just a bruise, I'll be okay thanks'. He got up stiffly and saw his father and Tina running towards him.

'Are you okay?' John asked anxiously.

'Yea'. Nick picked up his whip and unfastened his helmet chin strap. 'Sorry dad, I've made a real cock-up of that, haven't I'.

His father smiled. 'Not a bit of it son, you rode a good race, sensible and the way you picked her up at the ditch that was really professional. Okay, so you came a cropper but I'm not sure that was all your fault. I think the ex Mrs. Stevens has a lot to answer for, riding at you as tight as she did. Nothing illegal but not exactly sporting.'

Nick looked again at the fence. 'How is Mystery, is she alright?'

Tina nodded. ' She went on and jumped the last fence like a stag and the last I saw the mounted steward was bringing her back. Thomas is there'.

They began to walk back towards the marquees, Nick limping slightly. 'You will have to see the doc'. John told him.

'I'm okay, I told you, it's not necessary'.

'Necessary or not it's the rules so off you go and we'll see you when you have changed'.

After a cursory check by the doctor Nick returned to the changing tent and sat dejectedly on the bench as the jockeys came in. There was a buzz of conversation and some laughter as other riders prepared for the next race. Will Stevens, flushed and mud spattered, dumped his saddle and helmet next to him and sat down. 'Whew, that was a a good race' he said flexing his right knee several times.

'Did you win?' Nick asked.

'Yep'.

'Congratulations. I'm afraid I made a bloody awful mess of it'.

Stevens turned to look at him. 'Naar, course you didn't. Don't be so daft lad, you must have ridden a good race to come up so well at the end'.

'I mucked up the last but one good and proper'.

Stevens smiled. 'You just went at it a bit too fast; it happens to us all from time to time '.

'I know, I didn't take a pull and all that'.

'You'll know better next time and with that little mare I guarantee you'll be in the places before long'.

'Thanks'. Nick began to pull off his boots.

'And I'll have a word with that ex-missus of mine' Will Stevens added. 'She could have left you a bit more space over that fence, but you know what women are'. He grinned and gave Nick a hearty slap on the back.

Nick shrugged, finished his changing, packed his kit and went out. His father was waiting for him at the entrance. 'We'll go and have a bite to eat' he said taking the holdall , 'It's been a long time since breakfast and I'm famished'. They began the walk to the lorry park when a voice behind called 'John, John Tregarth Hang on a minute!' They both turned round to see a stout red-faced man in a bowler hat hurrying after them. 'Glad I caught you' he said breathlessly. Nick recognised the Master of the hunt.

'Hello Toby'. John held out his hand. 'I see they have got you doing your usual stint'.

'That's right, Chief Steward as ever'. He turned to Nick 'And this is your boy Nicholas isn't it? Pity about that fall young man otherwise I'm sure your horse would have won, which is what I want to talk to you about. I see from the programme it's by your stallion The Titan'.

'That's right, she's only a five year old out of old Byron Pendogget's mare'.

'Well, if he gets that sort of quality I would like to send a couple of my mares to him; or is he fully booked up?'

John grinned. 'No, I think we could take one or two more this season'.

'Good, I'll be in touch'. He smiled at Nick. 'And are you going to be a regular point to point rider young man?'

Nick was about to answer when his father butted in: 'No Toby, he'll be off to sixth form college and then hopefully university'. He grinned at Nick who stood with his mouth open.

'And what will he study there?'

John put his hand on Nick's shoulder. 'It appears we have a budding artist on our hands'.

The Master raised his eyebrows. 'An artist eh? Well I suppose it takes all sorts', he muttered as he turned to make his way back to the main area.

'I don't think Toby West thinks much of art as a career' John chuckled.

'Well you didn't, so what change your mind?'

'Let's just say I came up against a very persuasive person'.

Nick grinned. 'You mean Tina'.

'I mean Miss P. Let's go and eat'

The first thing Nick did on his return to the horsebox was to check Mystery. Thomas assured him that the mare was unharmed and, apart from a slight graze on one knee, was as good as new. Satisfied, he relaxed and perched on the cab step to wait for Mabel to unwrap their lunch; which she did amidst laughter confessing she had won more than twenty pounds with Will Stevens' win. 'Well, I knew him when he was all little 'un' she said, 'And I reckoned it would have been unlucky to bet on young Nicholas'.

'Didn't make much difference though did it'. The youth said gloomily. 'I still didn't win'.

Mabel handed him a slice of pork pie. 'It isn't the winning but the taking part that is important. Isn't that right?'

'No'. Nick took a mouthful and wiped his mouth with the back of his hand.

When the meal was finished Tina said she would like to put a bet on the next race but didn't know how and would like someone to show her. She was looking at John who crammed the last piece of ham sandwich into his mouth and stood up, still chewing. 'Oh, right.' He said with a cough. 'We've got time to stay for a couple more races and a look round the trade stands, then we'll have to make tracks for home; so Nick, if you could stay and keep an eye on the mare it will give Thomas a chance to enjoy himself for once, then I'll swap with you and you can go'.

'No'. Tina said firmly. 'I'll swap with you Nick. I'm perfectly capable of looking after our horse.'

John grinned. 'I'm sure you are' he said.

*

On the journey home the drone of the engine combined with the heat in the cab meant Nick dozed on and off. The tension of the morning had given way to a feeling of well being and in spite of his sore shoulder and bruised backside he felt good, in fact better than he had felt for a very long time. It was not just the fact that he had ridden his first race, that his horse - yes, his horse - had performed well,and that it was probable that he could do what he wanted with his life. All it needed was something to get dad settled, or perhaps somebody. He became aware that his father was quietly humming to himself.

'Dad'

'Yes'

'Do you like Tina'

'Miss P? Yes, of course. Why do you ask?'

'Then why don't you ask her out sometime?'

'Oh, I don't think she would want to get involved with me, I'm not in her league.'

'Why not dad?'

John glanced sideways at his son. 'Well, for one thing she is a smart sophisticated young woman and for another I'm afraid I was very rude to her the first few times we met so I've probably gone down in her book as an ill mannered peasant. Asking her on a date would be the equivalent of you jumping that big fence; I would probably come a cropper'.

Nick smiled. 'You know what they say dad: take a pull, let her see what she's in for then kick on and go for it'.

There was a long silence before his father replied 'Maybe you're right Nick, maybe you're right'.

In the back of the horsebox, Mystery whickered contentedly and pulled on her hay net.